THE NEW WORLD ORDER

Also available by Ben Jeapes:

THE XENOCIDE MISSION

THE
NEW WORLD
ORDER

Ben Jeapes

David Fickling Books

OXFORD · NEW YORK

THE NEW WORLD ORDER
A DAVID FICKLING BOOK: 0 385 606869

Published in Great Britain by David Fickling Books,
an imprint of Random House Children's Books

This edition published 2004

1 3 5 7 9 10 8 6 4 2

Copyright © Ben Jeapes, 2004

Papers used by Random House Children's Books are natural, recyclable products
made from wood grown in sustainable forests. The manufacturing processes
conform to the environmental regulations of the country of origin.

Set in 12/15pt New Baskerville

DAVID FICKLING BOOKS
31 Beaumont Street, Oxford, OX1 2NP, UK
A division of RANDOM HOUSE CHILDREN'S BOOKS
61–63 Uxbridge Road, London W5 5SA
A division of The Random House Group Ltd

RANDOM HOUSE AUSTRALIA (PTY) LTD
20 Alfred Street, Milsons Point, Sydney,
New South Wales 2061, Australia

RANDOM HOUSE NEW ZEALAND LTD
18 Poland Road, Glenfield, Auckland 10, New Zealand

RANDOM HOUSE (PTY) LTD
Endulini, 5A Jubilee Road, Parktown 2193, South Africa

THE RANDOM HOUSE GROUP Limited Reg. No. 954009
www.kidsatrandomhouse.co.uk

A CIP catalogue record for this book is available from the British Library.

Printed and bound in Great Britain by
Clays Ltd, St Ives plc

For Charles, George and Oliver,
whose stories are even more interesting

Part I: 1645

Part II: 1651

PART I
1645

One

Breaking the Siege

The castle stood alone and aloof at the top of a hill, surrounded by a hostile army. Four stark, grey walls with a fortified gatehouse at one end, it had once dominated the crossing of two roads – the road that came from the west and ran east to London, and the road from the south that led up to the Midlands and beyond. Now the hill had been sculpted, carved away to make sheer fortifications that bristled with pikes and small cannon and musketeers.

The entire area around the base of the hill was cleared of trees and cover, and this was where the besiegers waited; a ring of tents and sentries, a few artillery pieces poised on their two-wheeled carriages, men dug into earthworks and fortifications of their own. Some of the men paraded with muskets almost as long as their own bodies, but their hearts didn't seem to be in it. Others just sat in circles around the fires, eating and drinking.

It was a typical scene on a warm May afternoon. This was no sudden insurrection and neither side was in any hurry to engage the other. The king had been at Donnington briefly, but had escaped, and the place had been under siege by Parliament ever since. The men waiting outside the castle walls were quite content to starve out the men on the inside. Why waste lives throwing yourselves against fortifications when the laws of nature would eventually do the job for you?

Into this indolent scene marched a train of soldiers like a stick inserted into an anthill.

They were not the first distraction on that lazy day. A few minutes earlier a proudly beaming sentry had hurried into the captain's tent.

'Caught a spy, sir!'

The captain sighed, reached for his hat and followed the sentry out with less than full enthusiasm.

The alleged spy was waiting in the custody of a pair of men armed with muskets. He was stocky and seemed powerfully built beneath his battered, nondescript travelling clothes. He looked middle-aged, with neatly cropped red hair. His gaze wandered around with detached interest, only a small step removed from boredom.

The captain sighed again. 'And why is this man a spy?'

'He's foreign, sir!'

'Are you, sir?' The captain addressed the red-haired man directly. Guileless, bright blue eyes looked back at him from beneath a deep brow.

'I am not English,' the man admitted. His accent was guttural and he spoke slowly, as if searching for every word before saying it. 'I was on my way to Branheath. That is—'

'I know where Branheath is,' said the captain. It was a small village lying further up the river valley from Newbury, about a mile away. 'Do you have a name?'

'I was christened John Donder.'

The captain studied him a moment longer. He was familiar with his men's enthusiasm for capturing spies – it passed the time, if nothing else – and this John Donder almost certainly was not one. Certainly the king had allied with foreigners against his own people, but surely there were enough native Englishmen to spy for him without recruiting someone so obvious? He would have the man searched, just in case, and let him go.

'Well, Master Donder . . .' he said, and that was when the soldiers arrived.

They came in a column, boots tramping and scuffing the dry earth of the track. The sight of these polished, grim-looking marchers stirred the besiegers into at least trying to look smart and capable. There was a rough kind of uniformity to them: jackets of a ruddy brown-red and thick leather overcoats. Each man had an identical firearm slung over his shoulder and what looked like strips of cloth strung across his chest from shoulder to belt. The strips seemed to be weighted with small brass tubes. At the head of the column was an officer mounted on a horse.

'Wait here,' said the captain, and he walked to meet the new arrivals.

'Good day, sir,' said the man on the horse. He had the round, florid face of a country squire; he looked more accustomed to worrying about the state of the fields than being mounted on a charger and backed up by a small army. 'Kindly have your men stand to, ready to attack.'

The captain was unimpressed. 'And who are you, sir?'

The officer held up a scroll and slapped it into the captain's hand. 'Sir Edwin Willoughby,' he said, 'here by order of General Fairfax in Newbury. The Lord General thinks it is time to bring the siege of Donnington to a close and he has entrusted me with the task.'

The captain looked more respectfully impressed as he scanned the scroll, but it was grudging. 'The Lord General should be aware that fortified locations such as this do not just tumble, sir. It is hardly a high priority in the course of this war.'

'No criticism is intended of you, sir,' said Sir Edwin, 'and the affair will prove a valuable exercise for us all. Observe. Sergeant! Have the men fall in!' He turned back to the captain. 'We'll open the proceedings with a small demonstration, and then everyone can join in.'

An amused John Donder sat on an ammunition crate, still under armed guard, and watched the men with approval. The soldiers fell into two parallel lines and a drum began to beat. They marched forward and stopped with the castle on their left.

Well disciplined, he thought. He hadn't realized the English ran to a professional army nowadays. It was something he would have to bear in mind.

At a shouted command the men turned to face the castle, one line in front of the other. They were safely outside musket range – the lines were two hundred yards away – and the castle's defenders stood on the fortifications and watched with interest.

'Load your weapons!'

There was a rattle of metallic snaps and clicks down the lines. The defenders cheered and waved. They could see these soldiers were new to the siege. Perhaps they thought a fresh commander had taken over and was trying to prove a point.

'Take aim!'

The front line of soldiers kneeled. The men in the second line stood sideways on to the enemy, one foot forward, and raised their rifles to their shoulders. On the ramparts, one of the defenders turned around and bared his buttocks.

'Fire!'

It was not the soft *boom* of gunpowder and there were no billowing clouds of smoke. The rifles fired with a definite *crack,* an explosive burst of bullets snapping through the air faster than the speed of sound. The volley echoed around the valley and the row of defenders, standing on the first line of the earthworks, collapsed.

An astonished John Donder leaped to his feet.

There was a stunned silence, broken only by: 'Reload!'

Another series of those metallic clicks. John Donder realized there was none of the usual business of reloading a musket: power poured down the barrel, ball dropped after it, wadding rammed home. Instead each man just worked a small lever beneath the stock of his gun and raised it to fire again. He stood up, took a step forward, stared as closely as he could at the weapons the men were carrying as if seeing them for the first time.

Oh my, he thought.

And then the fortifications erupted in popping clouds of smokes as the defenders returned fire. It was a futile gesture, unless they were hoping that their own weapons had magically increased in range and accuracy, as Parliament's apparently had.

'Fire!'

More defenders collapsed. Some scrambled for the small cannon that were mounted facing the besiegers. They never reached them. Rifle fire cut them down.

The soldiers fired again, and again. The captain and Sir Edwin stood and watched, and John Donder pricked up his ears.

'That's a remarkable range,' said the captain. 'Not the usual gunpowder?'

'Coal dust, believe it or not,' said Sir Edwin. 'Crushed to a fine grain, treated with some mysterious essence, and many times more powerful than gunpowder. Look.' He dug into his belt and produced a small brass tube, the length of a man's longest finger. One end was pointed and a different colour, the dull grey of lead. 'We have many hundreds of these. Each one is primed with coal dust, in place of the usual powder, and this –' he tapped the pointed end – 'which is a separate ball.'

'I should like to inspect one of those rifles, if I may.'

So would I, John Donder thought. He stood up and began to walk forward, ignoring the sentry's objections.

'Certainly. Sergeant! Your firearm!'

The sergeant handed his rifle over to Sir Edwin, who worked the small lever beneath the breech. A metal slot opened in the side of the stock. 'The cases are inserted in here. Each rifle carries a magazine of five, with a sixth in the breech if necessary.' He fed the case he had been holding into the slot. 'After a shot is discharged, the soldier moves the lever, which expels the old case and inserts a new one, ready for firing.' He snapped the lever back, and it jammed halfway.

'Ingenious, sir.'

'Indeed . . .' Sir Edwin was distracted by the gun's misbehaviour. He waggled the lever back and forth. John Donder saw what was going to happen and started to run.

'Devil take it. They have a tendency to jam and—'

The rifle discharged suddenly, blasting a small crater in the turf next to the captain's foot. The captain leaped back and Sir Edwin had the grace to look abashed.

'Blast it— Hey!'

John Donder snatched the rifle from his hands.

His face was livid as he stuck his little finger into the slot and worked out the case that had jammed there. Then he snapped the lever shut.

'They only jam if they are badly treated,' he said curtly. He was twisting the rifle about in his hands, looking at it from all directions, squinting along the barrel. Finally he flicked a small catch next to the trigger guard. 'And you should always have this to the left when you are not using them. It stops them from going off.'

Sir Edwin's eyes blazed. 'And who the devil are you, sir?'

John Donder handed the rifle back. 'I am a man who knows more about these things than you.'

'His name is—' the captain began. Sir Edwin waved him to silence and looked at John Donder more thoughtfully.

'You'll be Hollykor too, I'll be bound?'

John Donder blinked in surprise. 'Holl . . . Holekhor, yes. How did you know?'

Sir Edwin ignored the question. 'The Lord General's Hollykor allies supplied these weapons, so I will forgive your incivility.' He glanced at the castle. 'You may wait here. We may have need of you. Captain, I think we've softened 'em up enough. Pass the word to prepare to attack.'

John Donder was back on his ammunition crate as the battle began.

'Forward march!'

The drumbeat began again and the twin rows of

riflemen marched forward, firing from the shoulder.

The first of them suddenly crumpled and fell. They had come within range of the muskets at last. Another joined him. The survivors halted but continued to fire at will, choosing targets carefully. Three or four more collapsed together as the ground at their feet exploded. Someone on the other side of the ramparts had made it to a cannon. But the riflemen held their line. Admiration for their courage fought a losing battle in John Donder's mind with disbelief at their stupidity.

He hadn't meant to be caught up in this at all. He had important business elsewhere and he had given himself a day to get to Branheath and back. He could be spared for that length of time. But as he had walked along the river towards the village he had left nearly thirteen years ago, his nostrils had alerted him to the siege. His sense of smell had always been so much better than that of his English friends. There had been at least a couple of hundred men (and they *were* men; the scent was distinctly male), who obviously had the English wariness of baths that he remembered so well. There was stale sweat, straw, woodsmoke from numerous small fires, and the pungent odour of those animals . . . what did they call them . . . *horses*. Sheer sense of curiosity had led him to investigate further, and be hauled up by an over-enthusiastic amateur soldier, accused of spying.

Defenders were running out of the castle now, down towards the front line. They had seen the way the fight was going. The only way to respond to these strange new weapons, that could fire so accurately and so far and so continuously, was with a sheer mass of single-shot musketry.

Another line of riflemen ran forward to give aid to their fellows. The battle had opened with a single volley but now the rattle of shots was continuous: up and down the valley, through the trees, slapping flatly back from the castle's stone walls. The smell reached John Donder: acrid, burnt and gritty. It stung the nose and dried up the mouth.

The besieging cannons opened fire, shooting over the heads of the attackers and pounding the lines between the fortifications and the castle. They gave another round, and then all the attackers, the veterans of the siege and the newly arrived riflemen, charged with a mighty yell, Sir Edwin at their head. The smoke from the musket-fire partially obscured the scene but every now and then John Donder caught glimpses: hand-to-hand fighting poised perilously on the lip of the ramparts; a rifleman using the bayonet on the end of his weapon to impale a defender; another rifleman tumbling as someone slashed at his hamstrings with a sword, to be set upon by two others as he lay squirming and screaming on the ground.

'At last,' John Donder muttered. *This* was a proper battle. It had defied all reason to see riflemen just standing there, out in the open, no cover, and soaking up fire. You couldn't take a well-defended position like this with just a handful of superior weapons. You also needed a superior strategy. Enough defenders could hold this place with bows and arrows, slings and stones even, against riflemen who just *stood there*. But now the battle had reached the stage where orders were too slow: every man had to look after himself, an essential instinct in most people.

Those rifles had been a surprise when they opened fire, but he had supposed the English weren't stupid and sooner or later someone had to invent the things. The bigger surprise had come when he had taken the gun from Sir Edwin and actually seen it close up. It wasn't just that English rifles were designed like the ones he knew back home. They were almost identical. The one he had held wasn't military issue, but it was as good as. The steel of the barrel was dull and slightly scored; the wooden stock and grip showed signs of chipping. It wasn't factory made, but it was as if someone had reconstructed a standard calibre infantryman's rifle from memory, using only native English tools.

He hadn't needed Sir Edwin's remark about the Hollykor allies to tell him who. Thirteen years ago he had been the only Holekhor his English friends had ever met. Now, it seemed, a whole group of them were the friends of one of the sides in this war. It could make his life much more difficult.

But John Donder was wasting his time here. He had no need and no desire to get involved in this war. He glanced about. Everyone's attention was on the fighting, even that of his guards. They stood with their backs to him, fingering their muskets while they stared at the battle, obviously itching to join in. And he wasn't entirely defenceless: if his captors had actually got round to searching him, they would have been in for a surprise. So if he could slip away . . .

Something massive plummeted out of the smoke, and it resolved into Sir Edwin astride his charger. They reared to a halt before him. Sir Edwin had acquired a rifle of his own from somewhere.

'You! Get that crate open.'

John Donder was under no obligation at all to obey, but now was not the time to argue. Besides, if he helped Sir Edwin go off to war, perhaps the man would be killed and the problem of his detention here would vanish. So he helped tear the lid off the crate. It was packed with the brass cartridges that Sir Edwin had shown the captain, rows and rows of them, tucked into long cloth strips and imbued with a pleasant oily tang.

'Help me load up,' said Sir Edwin. There was no way to carry the box on the horse, so he helped Sir Edwin hang a strip of ammunition around his neck, then another. By the third, Sir Edwin was wilting under the weight and he looked at John Donder with a speculative gleam in his eye. 'You look strong,' he said. 'You could manage a few yourself.'

'It's not my war,' said John Donder. Sir Edwin's eyes narrowed and he hooked a thumb around the strap of his rifle for a moment. But then his face seemed to clear.

'You are right, sir,' he said. 'Englishmen fight Englishmen's wars. But I have need of a porter.'

John Donder took only a moment to think it through. Sir Edwin was not – yet – his enemy and he needed to find out more about the English at war. Perhaps they were not all quite so suicidal as the riflemen.

'Very well,' he said. A moment later he was seated behind Sir Edwin on the horse and galloping into the fray.

John Donder clung on for dear life as the horse carried them around the battlefield in a wide circle. To their right the once simple strategy of taking the castle by rifle-fire had deteriorated into a free-for-all, still coyly shrouded in smoke that only occasionally parted to give the odd glimpse of the carnage. The impressions filled John Donder's mind: the dark shapes of men locked in mortal combat; the stink of gunpowder and rifle smoke that now contaminated every breath to the point where you had to think to notice it; the continuous sound of gunfire that had merged into a constant background crackle.

He could see that the battle had become bogged down. It had not proved so straightforward as Sir Edwin had hoped, perhaps due to the defenders' perfidious idea of fighting back. The attackers were up on the earth ramparts, but that was as far as they could get. The defence beyond them was just too strong, and close up, there wasn't the room to bring a rifle to bear before someone came at you with a sword.

Something buzzed past his ear like a maddened insect. It took half a second to work out that it must have been a musket ball. *They* were within range now.

But Sir Edwin steered his horse into the trees,

away from the battle and out of sight of the castle. They ran through the trees parallel to the battlefield and pulled up. The two men jumped down.

'This way,' said Sir Edwin, and he jumped down into a small ditch. It was a stream, barely a trickle, and by following it upstream they would be back on the battlefield. They crouched below the banks and splashed through the water, the sound of the fighting hiding the noise as they approached the castle. Finally the banks widened out into a small hollow packed with riflemen.

'Got the ammunition,' Sir Edwin said. He pulled the belts off his and John Donder's shoulders, and his men got busy feeding the brass cases into their rifles. 'Now, look.' He poked his head cautiously above the level of the ground and pointed with his rifle.

The fortifications ahead made a jagged line around the castle hill. They drew a strange shape with many straight lines and many points, the idea being that every wall could be defended from at least two sides. Sir Edwin's small group lay on the ground near one of those points. They were well around the field from the main battle and the spot was barely defended.

'We can take those men from here,' said Sir Edwin. 'We'll run forward, get up the walls and take the point before they can rally. When we raise the standard, the others will see and come to join us. It's a way in, you see? It's narrow and can easily be held.'

John Donder stared at the fortifications. He could see four . . . no, five defenders beyond the ramparts.

They should have been guarding their position but their attention was clearly on the main battle at the front of the castle. They hadn't seen the riflemen assembling close by. Sir Edwin was showing some tactical sense at last. It was the kind of assessment John Donder would have expected of a junior officer in his first taste of combat, but it was better than marching your men towards entrenched positions.

Sir Edwin and some of the men wormed their way forward on their stomachs, each aiming at a defender.

'Fire,' said Sir Edwin, and the shots cracked out. The men in the fortifications fell back and the way ahead was clear.

'Up and at 'em!' Sir Edwin bellowed, and he sprang to his feet and charged the rampart, with his men close behind.

The ramparts erupted with defenders. The guards they had seen had been only a small part of the much larger group waiting below the rim. They seemed to burst out of the ground, wielding muskets, and Sir Edwin's small group was caught right in the open. The defenders rained down musket-fire on their attackers. Sir Edwin was the first to fold, clutching his stomach. He collapsed and tried to push himself to his feet again, but another shot got him and he lay still. His men crumpled around him.

John Donder crouched down in the hollow by the stream and bit his lip. He had seen brave men die before; it never got easier. One of the fallen lay a few yards away, screaming. It was the mortal, nerve-grating sound of real pain. Not fear, *pain*. A gut wound, perhaps. Or a bullet lodged in the spine. There was another shot from the fortifications, and the screaming abruptly stopped.

And John Donder realized he was alone in the middle of a battlefield, and the attention of the castle's defenders had been caught. If he broke cover now, they would certainly see him, and even though a musket was an old-fashioned and inaccurate weapon, he could never outrun a ball from one. He and Sir Edwin's men hadn't been seen coming up the stream because attention had been elsewhere. If he tried to go back the same way, he almost certainly would be seen and shot at.

'*Forzh,*' he muttered. He crept forward very slowly on his front to where a clump of grass might just hide his head, and peered up. The defenders were still up on the fortifications, poised, muskets at the ready. He counted . . . six . . . seven of them. *Forzh* again. One of them looked directly at him and he froze, until the man looked away once more.

John Donder glanced over his shoulder at the trees that lined the battlefield. They were perhaps two hundred yards away. If he could get from *here* to *there* without being seen . . .

But he couldn't. It wasn't possible. The only alternative was to go the other way: to *be* seen, deliberately. He drew a breath, waggled his head from side to side until he heard his neck click, flexed his shoulders. Then he stood up.

'Hey!' he shouted, and waved. Muskets swung round to face him, and even as they moved he was dropping back down to the ground and rolling so that he wouldn't lie where it looked like he had fallen. He curled up into the tightest ball he could as they fired and musket balls whipped through the air around him. Had there been seven shots? Or only six? He couldn't wait to find out. He leaped to his feet, out of the ditch, and before the defenders could reload he was sprinting away from the battle as fast as his legs could carry him, zigging and zagging as he went. He had never run away from a battle before in his life and it was a curious experience. By the time they had reloaded, he was well out of range and into the trees, on the way to his unfinished business in Branheath.

Two

Return to the Natives

Approaching Branheath from this direction, you came first of all to the church. John Donder's footsteps faltered and brought him to a halt without his thinking about it, because there by the hedge, just outside the churchyard, was the headstone.

They hadn't let him carve the words on it that he would have liked to put. Pagan, they had said. UnChristian. He couldn't argue with that – he himself had affirmed that his seven dead companions had never been baptized, never even heard of Jesus Christ. No Holekhor had. He did however debate the logic of putting them outside the churchyard. If this Jesus Christ was who they said he was, was he really going to mind where someone was buried?

He reached out and traced the words on the stone. *Seven unknown travellers, buried here on the 4th day of April in the year of Our Lord 1629.* He had never learned to read English but he knew what the words said. It had been sixteen years since his friends had been killed and John Donder had wandered into Branheath like a deranged loon, unable to speak the language and not knowing what language it was he did speak.

He walked past the church and caught his breath as he came upon Branheath proper. The cluster of buildings around the central duck pond hadn't changed. He might have left just a few days ago.

But when he had left, it had been a proper village – a busy, bustling and happy little community. Now it appeared deserted. His eyes lighted on the inn. He walked around the pond, put out an arm and pushed the inn-door open.

The smell hit him like a slap in the face – smoke from the fire and the reek of tallow candles. Strong drink, insipid food and unwashed people. He breathed in and savoured it, remembering. It took a moment for his eyes to adjust to the gloom. The room was empty but for two men, one young and one old, sat at a table. They paused for a moment, glanced up at him. Neither spoke. It wasn't quite the warmth he remembered.

'Hello,' he said. 'I am looking for Anne Matthews.'

A pause. A long pause. Perhaps his accent had got the better of him – all those accursed extra vowels the English had. He took a breath to try it for a second time and the youth spoke. He looked to be about twenty.

'She ain't here.' He followed this up with a snigger.

John Donder held back a rush of anger. It had been a long time since people had been quite so dismissive when they spoke to him.

'Can you tell me where she is?' he said, slowly, both to calm the anger and to get the vowels right.

The brat just sniggered again. John Donder sighed, grabbed the front of the boy's shirt in one powerful fist and heaved him up. The youth's eyes bulged with fear, and then his face crumpled and his mouth opened in a thin, drawn-out wail. 'I asked you a very simple question,' John Donder said mildly.

The old man didn't move, but he did speak. It was a quiet, cultured voice that could stop a man in his tracks. 'I never thought you were a bully, John Donder.'

John Donder looked down at the old man. 'Francis?' he exclaimed. He lowered the terrified boy back into his seat.

'The same.' The old man pushed back his chair. John Donder was shorter than many Englishmen but Francis Wetherby was shorter still. He had surprisingly shaggy white hair, a long, lined face and dark, intense eyes that could see into a man's soul. Francis knelt next to the wailing boy and put his arms around him. 'Rob hasn't been the same since he came back from battle. His mind has gone. There, Rob, there. John Donder isn't a bad man. He's simply an oaf who doesn't know not to pick on cripples half his age who can't fight back.'

Cripples? John Donder looked more closely at the young man, and finally saw that the left leg ended just above the knee. He groaned and shut his eyes. Francis rocked Rob gently and made soothing noises, while John Donder leaned back against the wall and felt about an inch tall.

Finally, Rob quietened down.

'What happened to him?' asked John Donder. 'What battle was this?'

'He took a ball at Edgehill,' said Francis. He ruffled the young man's hair fondly. 'You remember Rob Smith.'

John Donder remembered a very small child. 'Of course I do!' he said. 'Rob, of course. How's your father?'

The empty, hollow look in the young man's eyes told him the answer to that question.

Francis plucked gently at his sleeve.

'Come for a walk, John,' he said.

'You've kept your English well.' This was the only acknowledgement Francis made that John Donder had been away for a considerable time, some thirteen years, and not just for a day or two.

'I pray in it every night and I've kept the holy days as best I could remember,' John Donder said as they walked past the pond towards the church. Already he was speaking with more confidence and a better accent. 'Francis, what is happening? Where is every-one? Are they all at war?'

'They were at war,' Francis said. 'Now they are at peace.'

'What do you mean?'

'Do you remember Sir Miles at the manor?' John

Donder remembered the man; he didn't think they had ever met. 'He belonged to the king and he took most of our men off with him to battle. The lucky ones like young Rob and Da—' Francis stopped suddenly, and John Donder wondered whom he had been about to name, and why he had chosen not to. 'Like young Rob came back,' Francis said.

John Donder shook his head in confusion. 'Who is this war against?'

'Everyone and no one,' Francis said, and for just a moment there was a trace of bitterness in his mild tones. 'Englishman against Englishman. You are the king's man, or you are Parliament's.'

'And what are you?'

'I am the Lord's man, though that is not considered an acceptable answer in many circles. When I was made to leave my position I dedicated myself to caring—'

'You're no longer the priest?' John Donder said, incredulous.

Francis smiled slightly, indicated his clothes. They verged on the ragged; they were serviceable but certainly not priestly. 'Do I look it?'

'You once told me that priests were appointed by God.'

'And so they are. In the eyes of the Almighty I will always be his priest. But to the people of Parliament, who control this area, I am just an ordinary man.' He gave a small, bitter laugh. 'I am not even a Catholic, yet neither it seems am I sufficiently Protestant to satisfy them.' John Donder had no idea what a

Catholic was. 'And so, John, you see me in my new calling, as innkeeper.'

'It's not a calling I would have expected.'

'Oh, my family has some money,' Francis said. 'I bought the place. I'm too old to fight and there are people like Rob who are too frail to care for themselves. It is a new ministry. Christ requires us to care for widows and orphans, and the war is a good source of both.'

'So, what is this war about?'

'Oh, John.' Francis had reached the churchyard gate, and he smiled a very sad smile. 'Heaven only knows, for I don't. Now, you asked about Anne.'

'Yes! Where . . .' John Donder saw the smile leaving Francis's face, and it suddenly struck him. Francis was apparently no longer in charge of the church here, yet he was leading him to the churchyard. 'Oh,' he whispered.

He had said farewell nearly thirteen years ago, though it had been like tearing a piece from his own body. The scar had healed, slowly, because he had meant to return. When he had learned for sure that he *was* returning, hope had begun to grow. He had kept it under the constant supervision of his more pragmatic nature. She *might* still be alive and she *might* still want him back. But the point was academic now.

Suddenly Francis was scowling at him. He had a mobile face. When he smiled, it was as if you were the sole object of all his affection. When he scowled, it was like a physical blow. He could go from one to the

33

other with no sense of transition. 'I know you're a good man with a good heart, John Donder, and I baptized you myself, but all men must face their sins.'

'Sins?'

'I taught you the scriptures. I taught you right and wrong. And yet you committed fornication. This way.'

'I . . .' John Donder said as Francis led him around the church. He was trying hard to remember what fornication *was*, so he would know if he really had committed it or not.

'Do you deny it?'

'No. I suppose not.' He remembered the word now. It came to him with the memory of a sunny day, a warm, curving body, a smile that was only for him, and some surprisingly scratchy hay. If he had offended his adopted God then he was truly sorry. But at the time . . .

Anne had been the one to nurse him to health here in Branheath. She had been a widow recovering from her loss, working as Francis's housekeeper – even back then, Francis had been taking in waifs and strays. They had been good for each other, and had reached out to each other; slowly and tentatively, then with more and more certainty as they realized it was meant to be. As far as he was concerned their love had been for life. Wouldn't God recognize that too?

'How did you know?' he said.

'How did I—?' Francis stopped, choked in amazement. 'Look!' He pointed. They were at the grave, now. John Donder stared at the small grassy mound and its smooth, grey headstone. Francis kept talking

34

but John Donder barely heard him. Anne, he thought, oh, Anne . . .

Francis nudged him to get his attention. 'I *said*, she died nine months after you left.' He spoke with slow deliberation. 'In childbirth.' And while the ground was opening beneath John Donder, he added, 'But I admit my suspicions had been aroused earlier. Around the third month, when it began to show.'

Every structure, every support in the world of John Donder fell away. He hung suspended in space. 'No!' he said.

'You're not the first, you won't be the last,' Francis said with a shrug.

'No!' John Donder insisted, more loudly. 'It can't have been.'

'I assure you it was. A very pleasant young man named Daniel. I christened him myself. John –' he took John Donder's hand in both of his and the former priest's dark, intense gaze pinned John Donder to the spot – 'did you leave because she was with child? Tell me that.'

'Did . . . I . . .' John Donder stuttered. 'You know me better! Of course not! I . . . I didn't know. If I'd known . . .'

'You'd have stayed?'

'Of course!'

'And what about your precious Hollykor Lord? The one whom you were sworn to serve and that no one else had ever heard of?'

The question hurt. Back then John Donder had genuinely forgotten his Lord, and in that state of innocence he had learned English, received the Christian God, been baptized, made a new life for himself . . . and fallen in love. Then he had remembered, his memory coming back under the beneficent influence of Anne's love and attention, and he had known where his duty lay. He was at war and he had to return home to fight.

'I don't know,' he said. He wanted to scream – *but it couldn't have been mine!* The child *could not* have been his! But an even more impossible explanation was that Anne had lain with someone else while he was here. He would not believe that of her. In which case . . .

Finally he began to register Francis's exact words. *A very pleasant young man.* That was hardly how you spoke about babies.

'Dan'el . . .' he said.

'Daniel.'

'Dan-*i*-el. He's alive?'

'He was this morning.'

'Where?'

'He lives with me.' *Of course,* John Donder thought. 'But he works in the gardens at the manor.' Francis sighed. 'I once had hopes he might make an altar boy, possibly even take up the priesthood himself, until Parliament came.'

John Donder frowned. 'You said Sir Miles—'

'Was killed at Edgehill, yes. We have a new Parliamentary master at the manor now, Sir Miles's nephew, but he likes his gardens kept.'

'And that is where Daniel will be now?'

Francis squinted up at the sky. 'He'll be on his way home soon. Do you remember . . . ?'

'I remember the way,' John Donder said shortly. He was already striding towards the gate.

Three

Just Deserters

'**M**aster Foreman!' It was as resonant and commanding a voice as a twelve-year-old throat could produce.

'*Yes, sir?*' It was the same voice in a higher, lighter, more servile tone.

'Master Foreman, the leaves in the north field are showing signs of blight. I want each one of them inspected for fungus.'

'*Why, sir, I don't know how you does it! Me and the boys'll get right on it.*'

And the foreman would hurry off, shaking his head in wonder. That Master Matthews, he would think: arrived here with scarcely a penny in his pocket barely a year ago, and already one of the greatest tobacco planters in the colonies.

The river was narrow and lazy, trickling along a shallow valley whose sides curved up very gently on either side. Daniel Matthews walked along the track that ran parallel to the north bank, back towards Branheath and supper, playing the scene out in his head. Daniel had heard of tobacco and Virginia, and they filled his dreams. He wasn't entirely sure what the one was or where the other lay, but he knew one was a plant that people grew for a lot of money and the other was far across the sea. If his father could come to England from somewhere so remote no one had ever heard of it, then surely he, Daniel, could get as far as one of England's colonies whose location was presumably known to most sailors. And as for growing plants – he knew he could do *that*. So, he would work at the manor to save up enough to get to London and buy passage to the New World. And then . . .

The breeze carried the scent of the manor gardens, though by now they were a good half mile behind him. He breathed in deeply. He could make out the pure scent of the roses, the slightly more cloying honeysuckle, the sharp relish of the recently scythed grass, the slightest fruity waft from the orchard. Daniel had realized a long time ago that no one could sense smells quite like him. With practice he could even tell from a distance when a fruit was in danger of over-ripening, when a flower was wormstruck. It was one of the things that made him so useful at the manor. That, and a strong body and stamina which meant that at the age of twelve he could outwork grown men twice his size and age, for a boy's pay.

'*Psst!*'

Daniel stopped. He didn't need to look about him for the source of the noise. Now that half his mind had stopped thinking of the gardens and the other half of Virginia, he had his full attention to spare on the fact that he could smell two men behind the bushes.

Then the foliage rustled and a man's head poked out. He glanced from left to right then beckoned a finger at Daniel.

'C'mere, sonny.'

Daniel stayed exactly where he was. He could see that the man wore the red tunic of Parliament's new army. Sir Edwin at the manor wasn't exactly *bad* – indeed, a point in his favour was that unlike his uncle he *hadn't* led the men of Branheath off to their deaths – but the fact was, he was the enemy. If Sir Miles had led Branheath's men to fight for their king at Edgehill, it had been Parliament's army that killed them there. It had been Parliament's men who declared that Francis was no longer the vicar of Branheath, and who had sacked the church and burned the prayer books. Daniel owed his hearth and home to Francis, and as for those books, Francis had used them to teach him his letters. That was two more reasons to hate the enemy.

So Daniel stood his ground. The man pulled a face, but looked from side to side again, then emerged. A moment passed and then he was joined by his companion, who came out with similar caution. Both of them had long, thin weapons slung over their shoulders, which Daniel assumed were muskets.

And Daniel realized that even standing his ground had been a mistake. There were only two of them but the track wasn't wide. One could stand in front of him and one behind, and he was hemmed in.

The man in front grinned down at him.

'Who are you, sonny?'

'Daniel Matthews, sir,' Daniel said. *If in doubt,* Francis had once said, *make yourself look small and your eyes look big.* That was what Daniel tried to do now.

'From?'

'From Branheath Manor, sir.' Daniel pointed back the way he had come.

'That's Willoughby's,' the other man said.

'That right, sonny? Sir Edwin Willoughby?' said the first man.

'Yes, sir.'

'Ah, ha.' The man put a thoughtful hand to his unshaved chin. 'Well, sonny, it's like this. We've had a disagreement with Sir Edwin regarding our continued employment in his army. You might have heard we had a little set-to with the Royalists today.'

Daniel nodded, eager to please. The battle must have been heard for miles around.

'Now, we say, live and let live. Where's the harm in that? But that Sir Edwin, he had us marching to the castle and trying to take it, and we weren't having any of it. But if Sir Edwin found out, why, he'd have us shot – as if there's anything wrong in grown men exercising their freedom of choice, which is why we're fighting this war at all. So if his manor's *that* way . . . What's down this road, boy?'

'Branheath, sir.'

The men roared with laughter.

'As in the famous Branheath Regiment? Who

stood up to us for, oh, all of five seconds at Edgehill before we wiped 'em out?' The good mood vanished. 'Well, it do sound like Branheath is a haven of Royalist shits, but Royalist shits is what we're after at the moment. So, son, I think we'll avail ourselves of the hospitality of Branheath for a day or two. You don't mind, do you? Just until they stop looking for us.'

Daniel finally put two and two together. 'You're deserting . . .' he began. Their expressions told him that silence would have been a better answer.

The front man winked at Daniel with very little humour. 'You've got a careless tongue, boy.'

'He's a kid, Jack. Let him be,' the other said.

'He's a kid who don't know when to keep quiet.' Jack took a step closer.

Daniel lived in an inn. He let Jack take one step more, then brought his knee hard up between the man's legs. Jack howled and curled up, and by the time he hit the ground Daniel was already running for his life.

'*Come back here!*' Daniel ignored the furious bellow and kept running. Then there was a noise, like a loud whipcrack in the air all around him, and something whizzed past his ear. He swerved away from it before he had even thought what it was. The swerve took him off the track and into the trees, and only then did the message finally reach his brain that *someone had shot at him.*

He howled, and ran even faster. Small branches whipped at his face. He heard another shot behind him, and another. They tore through the leaves and the woods around him, cruel, vicious little streaks of death. And then the ground vanished from beneath his feet and Daniel fell forward with a yell. He ploughed face first into some water, sending up a mighty wave that dislodged a pair of angry ducks.

Daniel propped himself up on his elbows, looking up through the dirty water that streamed down his face. He lay still for a moment, sides heaving with every breath. A shallow brook wound its way through the woods, down to the river, and he was lying in it. He scrambled to his feet, and they slipped from under him. He fell flat into the water again. And then he heard the footsteps behind him draw up, and slow down, and stop.

Daniel twisted round on to his back and stared up in breathless terror. Jack and his friend stood over him, and Jack had a gun at his shoulder and it was aimed straight down at him.

'Royalist shit,' Jack said again.

A gun fired, but it wasn't Jack's. Both men jerked their heads up at something behind Daniel.

'Put your weapons down,' said a man's voice. It was harsh and guttural, full of cold anger. It was a voice of command.

Jack just grinned. 'You fired once and you ain't reloaded,' he said. He raised the rifle again.

Another shot, and Jack dropped the rifle and staggered back, clutching his arm. Bright red blood flowered from under his hand. Jack stared at the wound in horror, then back at the man.

The light was blocked out above Daniel as the new-comer came into view. He stood over the boy, giving Daniel a strangely foreshortened view of his protector. The only detail Daniel could see for sure was the weapon in his hand; a pistol, like a flintlock, but smaller and made of ugly, dull grey steel. It was aimed squarely at the two men.

'Now you,' said the newcomer to Jack's friend. The man hesitated, and the newcomer fired three more shots from his gun, *bang bang bang*, no pause, which even Daniel knew was an impossible rate of fire. Earth and twigs at the man's feet flew up into the air and his hesitation vanished. He pulled his rifle off his back and dropped it to the ground.

'Now, run,' said the newcomer, and the men fled, sped on their way by a final shot over their heads.

Daniel and the man looked at each other. The man tucked his pistol into a holster at his belt, con-cealed beneath the hem of his coat, and held out his hand. The outstretched arm was broad and muscular. Daniel's gaze wandered along it and up to the face. It seemed wider than it was high, but not unpleasant to look at. The skin around deep-set eyes was wrinkled as if he smiled a lot, and he was smiling now.

'You must be Daniel,' he said. 'I'm a friend of Francis.'

'And he's got this gun too,' Daniel said, washed and changed, 'and it's got all these bullets in it and it's faster than a rifle, and he shot them, and . . .'

They were back in the inn, and John Donder let Daniel prattle while Francis listened with an amused smile. John Donder took the opportunity to study his son.

Their eyes had met when Daniel was lying in that ditch, and for the second time that day the found-ations had seemed to crumble beneath John Donder's world. The first time it had been the impossibility that Anne should have been pregnant. This time it was see-ing the results of that pregnancy. There was no doubt about it. The stocky build, the heavily boned sockets of the eyes and most especially the hair – not a pale imitation of a redhead like some Englishmen he had seen, but a thick mat of the deep, rich red that he saw in his own mirror and on so many of his countrymen. It was a round thatch, obviously cut around the rim of a bowl placed over the boy's head (and some time ago, at that), and in the westering light of the sun it had almost glowed. The eyes were brown, not blue, which was unusual among the Holekhor but not unknown.

Let no one deny it, this boy had Holekhor in his blood. This boy was his son. And that meant that one or two tried and trusted theories were going to have to be thrown out of the window.

Even Daniel had to draw breath eventually, and Francis took the opportunity. 'Eat your food, Daniel,' he said. 'Eat your food.'

Later, when an exhausted and replete Daniel had gone upstairs to his room, Francis and John Donder sat in front of the fire. The yellow flicker cast deep, dark shadows in the lines and ridges of Francis's face.

'Thank you for saving him,' said Francis.

John Donder just shrugged. What else could he have done? It had been a near thing. After the first shots, he had heard Daniel's blundering progress through the trees and homed in on that. He was doubly grateful for the revolver that he had packed for this little trip. Up till that point he had seen no need to acquaint the English with the many other weapons the Holekhor had at their disposal. With the deserters sent on their way, he had thrown the two rifles into the river, then escorted Daniel back home.

'Did you introduce yourself?' Francis asked.

John Donder shook his head.

'First I want to know how interested he is,' he said. 'He's lasted twelve years without me. He can last a little longer.'

Though, truth to tell, he had been aware of piercing sideways glances all the way back home from his sodden companion. Every time he glanced back, Daniel had managed to be looking at something else.

'I think he will want to know,' Francis said, 'but I understand your caution.'

'How much does he know?'

'He knows his father's name. Do you intend to take him away with you?'

'If he wants to come with me, I will certainly consider it.'

'Would you like him to?'

'I would love him to,' John Donder said, and he saw the pain in Francis's eyes. Francis loved the boy. 'If

I do, it won't be far,' he said. 'I'm here in England to stay.'

Francis sucked in his cheeks and shook his head. 'You have no idea, John, no idea. Royals and nobles can sire little bastards and they do it all the time, but for a good woman like Anne, a respectable widow . . . it's *shame*, John. It's shame, and the people take it out on the bastard. Young Daniel went through torment when he was little and it was only after I'd beaten the daylights out of his worst tormentors that it started to improve.'

John Donder looked at the old man's shrunken frame and tried to imagine him beating anyone. It was surprisingly easy.

'If you English persecute your . . . what was the word . . . bastards then that is a flaw with you English,' he said. 'But thank you for beating those daylights.'

Francis absorbed the slight against his people with good grace. 'I didn't need to for long. Daniel is a strong young man with a good pair of arms. But he has always stood apart from the others in this village. He dreams, you know. He wants to go to the New World— What is it?'

John Donder had coughed and now he smothered a smile with his hand. 'Nothing.'

'He wants to go to the *New World* . . .' Francis paused, looked at John Donder suspiciously. 'To Virginia to grow tobacco.'

John Donder didn't know where Virginia was or what tobacco might be, but he recognized the theme of a young boy's dream. He changed the subject. 'What can you tell me about General Ferfekh?' That was the name he had heard mentioned back at the castle.

'About whom?' Francis said, nonplussed.

'Fayer-feks.' Still no comprehension. 'Faks.'

Francis slapped his knee. 'Fairfax!'

'That's what I said.'

'Sir Thomas Fairfax is the head of Parliament's new army. Why?'

'The very head?'

'None but Parliament above him.'

'And he's in Newbury. Then he is just the man I want to see.'

'You came to Branheath to meet the leaders of the land?'

'No, I came to Branheath to find Anne, but if the leaders of the land are nearby then I should take the opportunity. Your Parliament –'

'Not *my* Parliament, John.'

'– has weapons it should not have. I want to find out more, and that is why I need to see this Fairfax.'

He did not mention his other reason. He wanted to see Fairfax's army at close range. If he was to lead an invasion of England then he should scout out the opposition.

John Donder went to bed soon after that. Francis had given him one of the inn's many empty rooms. He took a candle to light his way and went up the stairs to his door. Then he paused, breathed through his nose, and slowly followed a scent he was coming to recognize, down the landing to the door at the end. He opened it a crack and peered in.

It wasn't much of a room – a cubbyhole barely large enough for a bed and a chair. Daniel would spend little time here when he wasn't sleeping, but John Donder was glad the boy still had somewhere of his own, however small.

Daniel lay in bed on his front, fast asleep, his face tucked into the crook of his elbow. He had kicked the bedclothes down to his waist. John Donder held the candle up to study him more clearly. The boy was his *son*. He should have features that John Donder could pick out of a crowd at fifty paces without even trying. He shouldn't look like a stranger.

Daniel mumbled something as the light fell on his closed eyes and his profile danced with the flame of the candle. John Donder leaned forward. Was that a bit of Anne in the line of the jaw? In the nose? The cheekbones were more pronounced than was usual for the Holekhor – was that her?

He took a step forward and had to make himself stop, with an effort that surprised him. He wanted to pick the boy up, hold him, nuzzle him, stroke his hair, give him the love and attention all at once that he should have had over the last twelve years.

'*Eo khemt,*' he murmured to himself in the One Tongue. *I have a son.*

He allowed himself one indulgence and leaned down to run his hand gently through Daniel's hair.

Then he chuckled to himself, pulled the bedclothes up over Daniel's shoulders and let himself out.

You're growing soft, General, he thought as he closed the door.

Four

Mistress Connolly

The pre-dawn light saw John Donder walking down the valley on his way to Newbury.

He took the town in as he crossed the rickety wooden bridge over the river. Newbury was on a slight rise, and its walls had been supplemented with added ditches and earthworks. Soldiers drilled on the plain between the walls and the river, and small formations of horseback troops practised their moves. He stood to one side to let a platoon of soldiers march past him. Like their comrades at the castle, each man had a repeating rifle slung over his shoulder.

The previous evening, his nostrils had told him about the siege of the castle. Now, they told him there was a much larger army here, with a not insubstantial element of horse. They might not be so easy to over-awe as two errant deserters. It might not be easy to get an interview with the mighty Fairfax. But the Holekhor were apparently in with the high command: he would trade on that if he had to.

So he marched up to the sentries at the gate of the town.

'I must see General *Fairfax*!' he said. He had practised the name over and again to get it right, and he practically shouted it. The two men drew themselves up and he began to rehearse arguments to back up his initial claim.

'Right you are, sir,' said one. 'Mistress Connolly is expecting you.'

The woman called Mistress Connolly crouched down by the small metal ring in the corner of her room. She struck a match, quickly dropped the matchbox and used her free hand to turn a little metal knob. A faint hissing filled the air. She lowered the match towards the portable stove and a circle of clear blue flame blossomed around the ring. She smiled, satisfied, and flicked her wrist to extinguish the flame. Then she put the small pot of water on top of the fire and stood to wait.

She could have called someone from the innkeeper's staff for boiling water to make her tea, but she valued these moments to herself. The army was about to march out again and they would be under canvas for the next few days. She had never especially enjoyed that, but sometimes there were advantages to not sleeping in a bed. She glanced at the straw pallet where she had slept the previous night, and wrinkled her nose. She had used up almost all her flea powder on the verminous heap, and in England this was considered quality hospitality.

Someone knocked on the door. 'Mistress Connolly!'

It still amused her. Women in England were in an absurd position, both inferior to men yet highly valued as bearers of children and keepers of homes, somehow both at the same time. No respectable English woman would or could provide the service she did to her present employers, yet the need of these English was so desperate that they were willing to over-look her strange foreign customs. They called her 'Mistress' as much for their own reassurance as for hers.

'What is it?' she called.

'Your man is here.'

At last! 'Tell him I'm coming,' she said. She grabbed her coat and swung it on, thrust her arms down the sleeves. It was a further concession to the customs of the English. She knew that her employers would far rather she wore a skirt that reached all the way to the ground, and the less ostentatious the better, but even they could see how impractical that would be in her position. So she wore a baggy shirt and leggings, and the coat hung down past her knees. The stitching and embroidery of the coat were not as flamboyant as they would have been back home, but the pastel shades of the patchwork were sufficiently restrained for the natives. It was a style twenty years out of date, but the English could convince themselves she was a respectable woman.

Dressed appropriately, Khonol Le stooped to turn off the gas ring, then rose and stepped from her room to meet the newcomer.

She hurried down the stairs and the scent of a

Holekhor male tickled her nostrils. It was only when she reached the front room that she realized, and her eyes told her, it was not the male she had been expecting. She stood in the doorway and studied the stranger.

'*Vev'ovso-ko Se're Dokh!*' she said. You're not Se're Dokh!

'*Prozh,*' he admitted cheerfully. No. 'Should I be?'

He was middle-aged, a touch shorter than her, and he held himself with a ramrod posture that she immediately recognized. That accent – he was Golekhi, or she was a native Englishwoman. And that stance – he was clearly a soldier of the Might, the army of Golekh that had conquered her country of Toskhes and driven her and her family and friends here, to the New World. The natives could not have known: they had simply assumed he was the man she was waiting for.

'I suppose not,' she said. Normally, in a polite conversation, she would now be holding out her hands, crossed at the wrists, for him to take. A friendly, civilized greeting. She did not feel like being friendly or civilized. 'What are you doing here?'

'Curiosity, nothing else.' The man had his head at a slight tilt. His nostrils dilated slightly. He was scenting something about her and she was abruptly, annoyingly aware that she had not washed as much as she would have liked recently. 'Gun oil!' he said. 'My curiosity is satisfied. You must be the one supplying guns to the natives. Nice work. Though as the Wise would never let weapons through Okh'Shenev, how you managed to smuggle them through I have no idea.'

Khonol Le held his gaze a moment longer, then slowly smiled. There was a distinct rural burr to his voice as well. Southern Alps, if she wasn't mistaken. He had probably been farming stock before joining the Might; in fact, he had probably been conscripted. The Toskhes Campaign could scarcely be his fault. And her own accent must have been just as obvious to him, yet he was ready to be friendly.

'Khonol Le,' she said, 'and I smuggle nothing.' *Now* she held out her hands in greeting. This was the New World, a place where old enmities had no place. 'Every weapon you've seen was made here in the New World. Se're Dokh is meant to be delivering a consignment.'

He snatched his hands away. 'You're showing them how to make modern guns?' he demanded.

'Of course not!' The fragile goodwill evaporated. Who did he think he was, coming in here and pre-suming to judge? Back home Khonol Le would have been a member of a subdued, submissive nation, if she knew what was good for her; here, fond as she was of the English, she had every intention of remaining in charge. Did this idiot think any sane woman or man would do otherwise? 'We operate the strictest controls,' she said. Not that she needed to justify any-thing, but she felt the urge to explain. Maybe it was because he was a Holekhor who didn't already know the operation. She could boast to him and he would appreciate it. 'The natives run errands, procure some of the materials . . . nothing special. Certainly nothing to show them how to do it themselves. All my colleagues, anyone who actually operates the presses and lathes, are Holekhor.'

'Toskheshi?'

'As it happens, yes.' She deliberately put little humour into her smile. 'We're all equal in the New World, Mr Golekhi. We have no conquerors here.'

He just blinked innocently at the word *conquerors*. 'Have you been here long? Where are you based?'

'Oh, we arrived here from Okh'Shenev a couple of years back and set up a foundry in the Tower.'

'What tower?'

She paused. Was he joking? No, it seemed he really didn't know.

'The Tower of London,' she said. 'If you came through London you'd have seen it – the big fortress on the river . . . ?'

'Ah. I didn't come through London,' he said dismissively.

'Mistress Connolly!' said a gruff voice in English behind them. Khonol Le turned quickly and bowed.

'Good morning, General,' she said in the same language.

Two Englishmen had come into the room. The older man was stocky, though still more slender than a Holekhor, with wiry, unattractive hair, a lumpy face, and arresting eyes – eyes that burned. The first time she met him, Khonol Le had picked up a sharp tang that spoke of deep conviction, certainty and ruthlessness. She had always treated him with the utmost respect.

But it was the younger one that spoke. 'Is this the associate you were expecting?' He had a thin, narrow face and curly hair that fell to his shoulders.

'No, sir,' Khonol Le said. She glanced at the stranger: she had never got round to asking his name. 'This is someone I haven't met before.'

'We need those guns, Mistress Connolly,' said the older man.

'I know, General. They will be here any moment.'

The younger man wasn't listening to assurances. He was looking at the stranger. 'So if you are not Mistress Connolly's associate, sir, who are you?'

The stranger bowed. 'My name is John Donder, sir, at your service.'

'That is hardly a Hollykor name,' said the older one.

Another bow. 'I was born and raised Holekhor, sir, but I was baptized into the Christian faith on the ninth day of June in the year sixteen thirty-two and given the Christian name of John.'

He couldn't have known it was exactly the right thing to say. Khonol Le looked at him as if he had just grown another head and thought bitterly of her own long, hard, trial-and-error process of finding out how to get on the right side of the New Model Army's lieutenant-general. Meanwhile the same general bore down on this John Donder with a huge smile on his ugly face.

'You are a convert?' he said.

'I suppose I am.'

'Sir!' He seized John Donder's right hand and pumped it up and down. 'To meet . . . to meet you . . . I cannot say! Sir, the Scriptures order us to make disciples of all nations, and of course it is a sacred duty to bring people to Our Lord and I have many times seen men who were baptized in ignorance as children repent of their sins and turn truly to Him but you . . . you! A man who was born in darkness, raised in darkness, taught nothing but the foulest pagan untruths, who never even knew the faintest whisper of Truth, as even the Catholics do . . . and you believed! "The people that walked in darkness have seen a great light: they that dwelt in the land of the shadow of death, upon them hath the light shined"! Sir, you have . . . you have doubled my faith. To see you, to meet you is a tonic, a privilege . . . I am beyond words.'

'I'm delighted to meet you too, General Fairfax,' John Donder said, a little taken aback by the sheer warmth of the reception. Khonol Le gave an abrupt laugh, which she turned into a cough, and the general dropped John's hand abruptly.

'Oliver Cromwell,' he said. 'At your service.'

The younger man stepped forward. '*I* am General Fairfax,' he said mildly, and though John Donder hid it well on his face, Khonol Le scented his surprise.

Lord General Sir Thomas Fairfax *was* surprisingly young to be leading an army – he was only in his early thirties. But there was an assurance about him, a confidence; this was the kind of man who, like the man Khonol Le had once heard of in the English

Scriptures, just had to speak to get his way. He would say come, and people would come; go, and they would go. And they would feel thankful for the privilege. Fairfax was a man you instinctively warmed to: a general, a leader, but with lines in his face that showed he could smile. He could laugh. If he delivered a rebuke then he could be cold and hard, but it was put on. It was the tone that was *required* for delivering rebukes. Soldiers understood such things.

Cromwell, on the other hand . . . Cromwell could smile. Cromwell could laugh. His sense of humour sometimes verged on the puerile. But he was different.

Khonol Le decided to help John Donder out and she murmured in the One Tongue: 'General Khromell is second in command.'

'Well, it is an honour to meet you both, sirs,' John Donder said.

'So what does bring you here, Master Donder?' said Fairfax. The three of them looked at the stranger and Khonol Le caught the distinct impression that he was trying very hard to think of something.

He was saved by the loud clanging of a bell outside. Suddenly Newbury was in an uproar. Men were running in the streets and one phrase stood out in the hubbub. 'Royalist bastards!'

Newbury was under attack.

Five

Marksmanship

John Donder and Khonol Le crouched on top of the town wall and peered out at the Royalist attackers. They had come up from the south, along the London road. There was a front line of foot soldiers, a row of wagons behind them and, at the back on a small mound, a cluster of finely dressed officers, magnificently be-plumed hats and garish clothes shining in the sun.

An English soldier stood next to Khonol Le and John Donder, hands on hips, gazing at the enemy. Then he smirked down at them.

'You can come out,' he said. 'They couldn't hit you at this distance.'

They glanced at each other.

'Old habits,' Khonol Le muttered. They both stood, feeling slightly foolish. Instinct made them both expect a rifle bullet, though they knew only one side had weapons like that and it wasn't the one grouping a few hundred yards away.

As they proceeded to prove. The front line of Royalist soldiers raised muskets to their shoulders and then disappeared behind a cloud of gunsmoke. The ragged, crackling pop of musketry reached the defenders of Newbury a moment later.

'This is absurd,' Khonol Le muttered. 'They know they're just wasting ammunition.'

'Yes.' John Donder looked askance at the attackers. It was a strange echo of the battle yesterday and it made him uneasy. Yet he could see that they only had muskets.

In the street behind them a troop of Roundhead cavalry was massing. John Donder studied them with interest. He came from a land without horses: he was used to the idea of riding into battle, but not on top of something so agile, and his mad gallop with Sir Edwin the day before had only been a taster. The animals pressed together in the narrow street, rubbing shoulders, stepping back and forth as they were jostled by their neighbours. The riders controlled their mounts with their knees and thighs, holding their rifles in their hands, cocking and checking them with a thoroughly professional air. It matched John's impression, albeit brief, of this General Khromell. Khonol Le had told him the general specialized in cavalry. He was the kind of man who would drill and train rigorously, and John didn't doubt that each of the men below would be a crack shot, even on the rocking, jolting back of a speeding horse. And he knew what would happen now. They would wait for those suicidal Royalists to discharge another volley, then ride out of Newbury, rifles raised, and dispatch them all before they could reload.

The Royalists let off another round of shots and the Roundhead commander shouted an order to the gatekeepers. They pulled back the massive wooden doors and the cavalry charged.

It was a glorious sight; thirty mounted soldiers at full gallop. Several tons of combined assault hurtling towards the enemy, the commander with his sabre pointed forwards, the colours streaming behind him. John wasn't used to warfare with horses but he could see how a cavalry charge could break an infantry line without having to fire a shot. The horses spread out into a solid line abreast and the riders raised their guns.

The front line of Royalists was already breaking, the men fleeing to left and right, leaving the way clear for the wagons.

Khonol Le was suddenly on her feet. 'Pull them back!' she shouted. The soldier who had advised them about safety just laughed.

'That's the spirit, ma'am.'

She had spoken in the One Tongue and the man had thought she was yelling support. 'Pull them back,' she said in English, 'it's a trap!'

'How can you tell?' John said.

'Those wagons,' Khonol Le said. 'They're mine. It's the party I was expecting. Those bastards have captured my guns!' She groaned. 'Se're Dokh was delivering them. They must have caught him.'

The covers of the wagons were cleared away. Each held three crouching men surrounding an evil-looking collection of grey metal tubes that were bound together in a cylinder and trained on the Roundheads. Two of the men twisted the tubes around on their mounting towards the horses, while the third slowly turned a handle at the back of the assembly. The cavalry line dissolved, horses dropping like stones to the ground, some riders struggling to their feet and then dropping themselves.

The wicked chattering of machine gun fire reached John's ears a moment later.

'*Charge!*'

Another cavalry troop was streaming out of Newbury towards the enemy. They didn't realize, John thought in horror. Perhaps they thought the first lot had fallen into a hidden ditch, or met some unseen obstacle. They had no conception of what they were facing.

Then bullets ricocheted off the stonework around him and he threw himself flat on the parapet. He pulled the soldier down with him.

'Send word to General Fairfax,' he said. 'Tell him the enemy have a weapon that can fire a hundred times more quickly than your weapons. You cannot go against it with cavalry. You—'

'Relax, Donder, or whatever your name is,' Khonol Le said in the One Tongue. She had found a rifle and was peering cautiously out through the ramparts. She thumbed the sights up and slowly, surely, aimed. 'The Royalists haven't quite got the hang of this new technology either. Gunner, left-hand wagon.'

She squeezed the trigger and the man on the left-hand wagon turning the handle crumpled over his weapon.

'For Se're Dokh.' She grunted with satisfaction and worked the lever, ejecting the old cartridge and feeding in a new one from the magazine. 'I can't tell you how many Golekhi I saw off this way after the Campaign,' she added, with a satisfaction that was clearly meant to offend.

The surviving two members of the gun crew were hurriedly pushing their dead colleague off the wagon while another man scrambled up to replace him. Another shot, and he too fell flat on his face. His fellows leaped off and fled, and Khonol Le turned her attention to the second wagon.

'Pass me some bullets, Donder,' she said. 'These things take five rounds.'

He knew exactly how many rounds each rifle could take, but he passed on the request in English and the soldier scrabbled to comply. John Donder assessed the situation as Khonol Le reloaded.

So, these were the guns she had been delivering to Parliament's army. The Royalists had captured the train and now it looked like they had ventured all on this one gamble: lure the Roundheads out of Newbury and mow them down. Donder saw what Khonol Le had meant about getting the hang of the technology. Like the riflemen at the castle, they had the new weapons but no idea of how to incorporate them into a decent strategy. Sandbags, an entrenchment, some kind of protection for the gun crews would have been a start, but they were as exposed as the typical musketman. The whole idea of laying siege with machine guns, just because they could shoot so much faster than rifles, was absurd, but that was what the Royalists were doing.

'The officers!' hissed the soldier. 'Can you get them?'

Khonol Le smiled grimly. 'Anything to help.'

She fired, and a moment later the horsemen jumped. She hadn't hit any of them – the range was just a bit too great for that – but they would have heard the whiz of the bullet as it skimmed between them. They would know what it was.

A dimly heard, tinny bugle call, and the Royalists began to withdraw.

'Oh no you don't,' Khonol Le said. With a series of rapid, efficient shots she killed the horses that drew the wagons. They fell dead in their traces and the Royalists couldn't hitch up replacements without exposing themselves to deadly fire. Other Roundheads had finally got the message and were following Khonol Le's lead, peppering the Royalists with rifle-fire of their own.

The skirmishing party finally fled, abandoning their precious guns where they lay. The Roundheads threw caution to the winds, stood on the walls of Newbury and cheered.

'Deadly,' said Fairfax thoughtfully. He walked a slow circle around one of the weapons. The wagons had been towed into the courtyard of the inn and the guns unloaded. The principle was very simple: eight barrels, each fed by a common magazine as they rotated beneath it, giving a rate of fire many times faster than even a rifle in the hands of an expert.

'Deadly indeed,' said Cromwell approvingly. 'Powerful weapons for the Lord's work.'

'You had best make sure the Royalists don't capture any more, sir,' said John Donder. 'They are an old design but they saw off your cavalry.'

Cromwell, Fairfax and Khonol Le all looked sharply at him.

'An old design?' Fairfax said.

'They are brand new, manufactured this very month in London,' Khonol Le said, more brusque than usual with her best customer. She had only wounded one of the gunners, and interrogation had revealed that Se're Dokh was indeed dead. He wasn't family but he was an old friend. And she had no intention of letting Mr Christian John Perfect Golekhi Donder slight her handiwork. 'It is true that back home we have more advanced weapons. One barrel, fed by a belt of ammunition—'

'And you choose to give us your cast-off designs?' Cromwell said coldly.

Khonol Le flushed. 'The more advanced designs require more advanced machinery, sir. We cannot match it, but we can adapt our rifle presses to make guns like this. Yes, sir, the design is old but these guns are better than anything the king has and they are made for you by master craftsmen.'

'Hmmph.' Cromwell did not look convinced.

'They serve their purpose, Oliver, and today's demonstration has convinced me,' Fairfax said. He slapped his hands together decisively. 'Taunton needs me. I will make my report to Parliament and proceed, taking these guns with me. Oliver, continue your mission, track the king's movements – but take care.'

'Thomas.' Cromwell spoke in a low, urgent tone. 'The king is in Oxford. We know this. Let me take these guns, and they may help us keep him there. We have Mistress Connolly to show us their operation.'

Fairfax looked doubtful. 'I would have to clear the matter with Parliament.'

'*Hang* Parliament, Thomas!'

John Donder quietly took his leave.

'This Parliament!' he said as Khonol Le escorted him to the gate. They wended their way around the puddles and the horse droppings. 'How can you run a kingdom by committee?'

'Very badly,' Khonol Le said, 'but it doesn't stop them trying. It works for the Pantheon, why not men?'

'These people don't believe in the Pantheon,' John said. 'Just the one god.'

'A god who has three different aspects,' Khonol Le agreed. 'Don't tell me there isn't a degree of consensus in their theology. Was that line about adopting their god real, by the way?'

'Yes.'

'How extraordinary. I didn't think the Pantheon would let a native god in, but I suppose . . . You're not a Catholic, are you?'

He stopped, looked frustrated. 'I keep hearing that word. What *is* a Catholic?'

She laughed. 'If you were one, you'd know. They

worship the same god, as far as I can see, but they believe his sole representative down here is a man called the Pope, who is some kind of prince in another country. Khromell takes issue with his theology, and the fact that believers in one country must obey the prince of another.'

'I can see his point.'

Khonol Le was far more interested in another topic. 'You were here in sixteen thirty-two? In their calendar that was ... thirteen years ago? You must have been one of the very first Holekhor to get this far from Okh'Shenev.'

'I was. I arrived sixteen years ago, stayed here for four.'

'You must have an interesting story to tell.'

'Perhaps one day. How did *you* get here, Khonol Le? I don't mean up the river. How did you come to be here in England at all, making guns for the natives?'

She looked appraisingly at him, as if weighing something up. 'You want to know? Back home, we made farm implements. We had a small ironworks. At Nhottep.'

'Near the battlefield?' he said.

'*On* the battlefield.'

'Oh.'

She looked at some far-off horizon. 'My great-grandparents founded the business. My father had died, my mother owned the business; I was the foundry mistress. My mother was getting old. She was bed-ridden.' A pause. 'I'm assuming you know how the battle got started?'

'I do,' he said. 'I wasn't there.' The Golekhi forces had bypassed the main roads, gone across country to strike at the Toskheshi capital. Nhottep had had the misfortune to be where the two armies met.

'My mother wouldn't move from the house,' she said. 'Your people set up their artillery line practically in our vegetable garden. Some of our soldiers took over the house and started sniping at the guns.'

'I know the story. They returned fire,' he said.

'Naturally.' Her eyes were cold and distant. 'With artillery.'

John didn't need to be told the rest. There had been no buildings left standing on the battlefield. In a few short minutes, Khonol Le had lost her mother, her livelihood and her home, all to the Might of Golekh.

'What did you do next?' John asked.

'We fought back, of course. Myself, my brother, some of the staff. It wasn't difficult, learning to make weapons instead.'

'The war was over very soon after that.'

'It was, so we went underground. We hid in the mountains for a while.'

'How did you come to be here?'

'Your general, the Conqueror . . .'

'Overlord of Toskhes, I think his title was.'

'The Conqueror,' she said firmly, 'declared an amnesty. The old bastard realized he couldn't beat us.'

'Or it was the easiest way of drawing the sting of the Resistance,' John said mildly. 'Get them out of the country, no more lives lost, make things easier for everyone.'

Khonol Le snorted. 'Believe me, considerations like that would never have occurred to that cold-hearted scum. He knew he couldn't beat us.' She sighed. 'Unfortunately, we realized we couldn't beat him either. So, we came here.'

'As a result of the amnesty,' he said thoughtfully.

'And here we're going to stay,' she said.

He nodded. 'Yes, I can see you are. Had you heard that the – ah – Conqueror has been called to another post? He's no longer the Overlord back home.'

She shook her head. 'Really? I hadn't heard that. But one Golekhi ruler is as bad as any other. I *had* heard that the Domon'el has made some kind of arrangement with the Order of the Wise. That can only be bad news. I think I'll stay here.'

'Well, yes,' he agreed. The deal that the Lord of Golekh had made with the Wise was very bad news indeed, and she would find out exactly how bad in due course. He changed the subject. 'Out of interest, why did you side with Parliament?'

'We arrived by ship in London, London belongs to Parliament. And as a Toskheshi, I've had my fill of despots.'

'You're a puzzling woman, Mistress Connolly. You share my thoughts about committees, yet you serve this Parliament.'

Khonol Le shook her head. 'There's no conflict. Khromell believes a single, strong ruler is best for a state. Believe it or not, he has said more than once that he is willing for that ruler to be their king – if the king will only obey the law that binds them all. It's a sentiment I can follow.'

'You tread a very thin line,' John said. 'Sentiments like that could get you into trouble.'

'Not here. Not in the New World.' Khonol Le looked hard at him. 'Get this into your head. We came to get away from our old lives. A new start for everyone. Look. You're an old soldier, aren't you?'

'How can you tell?' John said with an amused smile.

'If you were a serving soldier, you'd be in uniform,' Khonol Le said logically. 'You walk like a soldier, you hold yourself like one . . . and your ears.' Donder obligingly inclined his head so that Khonol Le could look at his left ear lobe. 'Three holes. A sergeant? A captain? Whatever it was, it shows. I'm guessing you're looking for re-employment yourself. You could do worse than join up with Khromell.'

'You're a very perceptive Toskheshi.'

'Don't hold that against me,' Khonol Le said with impatience. 'I don't hold your race against you. You were conscripted, weren't you? I'm guessing you used to be a farmer?'

'Can you smell the cow pats?' he said wryly. Khonol Le laughed, and the tension was broken.

'The point is, Donder, here in the New World we can be friends. We can start again.'

'I'll bear it in mind.' They had reached the gate and John Donder held out his hands to say goodbye. 'One last question, Khonol Le. Where exactly is Oxford?'

* * *

'Oxford?' said Francis, back in the inn. He pouted. 'To the north, some twenty miles. Just follow the Oxford road.'

John Donder smiled. He wasn't going to get precise directions from a man whose sole means of transport were his own two feet. Khonol Le had had similar problems and had no idea where Oxford was at all. To get even as far as Newbury she had just tagged along with the army and left the navigation up to the natives. 'That may not be enough. I need signs, directions, landmarks.'

Francis rolled his eyes. 'Landmarks? John Donder, when you reach Oxford, you've reached Oxford.'

'You studied there! Describe it.'

A sigh. 'It's a walled city. Built on the land between two rivers. There are hills on either side, to the east and west. It has a castle built around a large mound. Oh, and spires. A lot of spires.' Francis's face became shrewder. 'Why?'

'And another question,' John Donder said, ignoring Francis's own. 'There's a hunting bird whose name is on the tip of my tongue . . . you often see them . . . what is the word . . . ?' He held his hands up at his shoulders and flapped them. 'Hovering, over the bushes. What is that bird?'

'It sounds like a hawk.'

'Hawk! Of course. *Hawk*,' John Donder repeated with satisfaction. It was a good word for a Holekhor to say. You could put good, throat-clearing aspirants into it. 'Well, Francis, thank you for all your help.' He stood.

Francis blinked in surprise. 'You're leaving?'

'I need to go to Oxford.'

'But you can leave in the morning, it will soon be dark.'

'I'll leave now.' He smiled at the barely stifled yelp of protest from behind the door. Francis's ears were old and weren't Holekhor and they heard nothing. 'I won't say goodbye to Daniel. This time I promise I will be back.'

The glider was where he had left it, on the edge of a field by a spinney twenty minutes walk from Branheath. It was a standard one-man infiltration job with an open cockpit and a landing skid. He had removed its wings and stowed them flat alongside the fuselage, then covered the whole thing up with branches.

John Donder opened the compartment behind the cockpit to get at the transmitter. He pulled the antenna up to its fullest extent and spun the wheel to generate a charge. Then he tapped out his recognition signal and the signal for 'immediate recall'.

After a few seconds, the set crackled a confirmation at him. John Donder nodded and pulled a small wooden disc from his pocket. It had a hole in the middle and a copper plate set into the surface. He fixed the disc to a spindle on the transmitter and twisted a key next to it until it would go no further. He released the key and the wheel started to revolve. Every time the copper plate passed over a contact, which was about once a second, the circuit was completed and the transmitter buzzed.

John Donder straightened up and called out.

'Do you want to come too, Daniel?'

A pause, and then the bushes rustled and Daniel shuffled out, managing to look both sheepish and sullen.

'I know who you are, sir,' he said. John Donder was amused at the *sir*. Daniel probably didn't even realize he had said it. He had simply been well brought up.

'Did Francis tell you?'

A sharp, angry shake of the head. 'I'm not stupid. I know who my pa was.' Daniel walked up to John Donder, heroically ignoring the glider though his curiosity must have been killing him, and stared fiercely up into his face. 'Are you going away again? Because it . . . it doesn't matter, we don't need you here but . . .' He blinked. 'I want to know, sir.'

John Donder gently put his hands on the boy's shoulders. 'I'm going away for a very short while. I have business to attend to.'

'You'll go away again for another twelve years,' Daniel said. 'Francis told me you went to fight in a war that no one had ever heard of. People said . . .' He blinked again, furiously, but John Donder was proud to see no sign of actual tears. 'People said you were a liar and my mother was a whore.'

'She was no whore!' John Donder snapped, and Daniel actually took a step back in alarm. John Donder wanted so badly to pull the boy into a huge hug, but he was a virtual stranger and he knew it would be resented. Daniel had the instinct for affection but no actual grounds for such as yet. John

Donder knew there was a hole in this boy's life that he could fill, but first Daniel had to let him in.

John Donder knelt down to put their eyes more on a level. 'You were conceived in love, boy,' he said. 'Your mother was too good for me. She healed me and helped me remember who I was. We . . .' He stopped. Did this boy really need to know the circumstances of his conception? Well, perhaps, under the circumstances, yes. 'When I told her I had to leave, she understood . . . no, no, she *didn't* understand, but she trusted me, and we lay together to seal our love, as a promise of my return. It was sooner than Francis would have liked and if we offended against God then I am truly sorry, because that was not my intention. In our hearts, and I thought in God's eyes, we were husband and wife. And if your mother had lived she would have loved you more than you can possibly imagine. You would have been the luckiest boy alive, as I was the luckiest man.'

Daniel's eyes filled. 'But she didn't live and you didn't come back!'

'No,' John Donder said. 'The war became more complicated than I had thought. We did win it, eventually.' He had gone back expecting to finish his term as a conscript. He hadn't known the term would be extended indefinitely.

'And what about me?'

'Until yesterday, I could never have thought . . . I could not have known about you. If I had, I would have stayed and your mother and I would have walked through the arch together.'

Daniel looked at the ground and wiped his nose on his sleeve. Then he looked up.

'What arch?'

'The . . .' John Donder didn't have time to explain the customs of Holekhor marriage – the man and woman, escorted by their parents and friends from separate directions, meeting in front of a ceremonial arch which they would then step through together, entering the world of matrimony. 'I meant that we would have married.'

Daniel still looked unconvinced and John Donder clenched his fists in frustration. What more could he say? That there had been other women before Anne, but none after? It was true, but he had already stretched the limits of what Daniel could tastefully be told.

'Do I *smell* as if I'm lying?' he said. Daniel paused, then breathed slowly in through his nose, and a look of wonder spread over his face. For the first time in his life Daniel could actually talk in terms of his Holekhor senses to someone else who understood them.

'No, sir,' Daniel said.

'There you are, then.' John Donder couldn't resist it. He ruffled Daniel's hair and Daniel made only a token effort to knock his hand away. 'Besides, if I did go for another twelve years, by the time I came back, you'd be in Virginia.'

Daniel scowled, as if asking how John Donder dared know about his little fantasy. It was probably meant to be a *private* daydream. 'I'm going to come back and buy the manor!'

'Of course you are. And you'll marry a nice Berkshire lass and have children of your own. Then you'll grow old and die at Branheath and be buried in the churchyard. In the meantime, I'll drop in from time to time to see how you are.'

Daniel looked baffled – he hadn't exactly thought that far ahead. John Donder took a breath to speak, then paused. What he was about to say would change everything. If he had any sense, he would leave the boy here, attend to his business and then come back. But now he had raised Daniel's hopes so high . . . He couldn't do it.

'On the other hand,' he said, 'if you come with me . . . I can't say what will happen, I honestly can't, but I do know your life will be very different. You'll be Holekhor for as long as you're with me and Virginia might well not happen at all.' He squeezed Daniel's shoulders. 'But I know I'd be honoured to have you with me, as my son.'

'I don't know, sir!' Daniel wailed. He stepped back from John Donder, paced around. 'I mean, I've heard about Virginia but I don't know anything about you. I don't know anything about being Hollykor.'

'*Holekhor*. Well, if you decide you don't enjoy life with me – why, I'll bring you back to Branheath. Or take you to Virginia myself.'

'Do you promise, sir?'

'I promise.'

Daniel was wavering. To change the subject and as if by accident, the boy's gaze finally fell on the glider. 'What's that?'

John Donder stepped in front of him. 'If you come then you will have to learn about a lot of new things, and this is just one of them.'

'It's . . . *buzzing.*'

'It's meant to. It's guiding my friends to me.'

Daniel scratched his head. 'They've got good hearing. When do I have to decide, sir?'

'Well, I want you to go back to Branheath now –' Daniel looked bitterly disappointed – 'and you can decide on the way.' The boy relaxed. 'If you want to come with me, then you must tell Francis, because he is a good man and he loves you. Then come straight back, but assure him I will look after you and bring you back to him. And you will have to run because my friends are on their way now.'

One corner of Daniel's mouth moved up into a reluctant smile, then the smile spread, and then a huge grin split his face. Without another word he turned and pelted down the lane, back to the village.

Six

The Conqueror

Like it or not, Khonol Le had had to learn to ride a horse. Her most important client had made his name and reputation by fighting wars on horseback so, literally and figuratively, it was the only way to keep up. Now, surrounded by a large part of the New Model Army and led by a jocular Oliver Cromwell, her mount trudged along the road to Oxford.

Two days after leaving Newbury, Khonol Le was gaining an element of control over the brute, which was something. She could at least make it start, and head in the right direction, and occasionally stop, though when it came to making it keep going, she had yet to meet a tasty looking patch of green grass that couldn't defeat her. She *hadn't* learned to sit comfortably, to move her body with the rhythm of the creature's gait. Eventually she might grow crippling calluses on her thighs and buttocks, to compensate for the endless rubbing and chafing, but they hadn't developed yet.

Someone had suggested that she try sidesaddle. She hadn't. At least this way, riding like a man, she could hang on.

She thanked the Pantheon that the end was at least near. They had reached a town called Abingdon, which was apparently downstream from Oxford, but Cromwell had chosen not to approach Oxford from the south, up the Thames valley. The general was aware that the enemy might have artillery on the high ground on either side of the valley, so rather than take the low road through a place called Radley they had followed the main road through Abingdon to head for that same high ground themselves. Now Oxford lay just over the ridge.

Cromwell called a halt and sent scouts out ahead. The hill was wooded, the enemy must have known they were coming and it was quite possible that traps lay ahead. Cromwell knew how to use his infantry.

And here came the scouts now, hurrying back through the undergrowth. Cromwell took their report and sat up suddenly in his saddle, like a hound scenting prey. He twisted to look round at Khonol Le.

'Come with me, Mistress,' he said, and spurred his horse forward. Khonol Le reluctantly flicked her reins and kicked her own creature's ribs, and it ambled condescendingly after the general's charger.

Oxford was a dirty brown smudge lying across the valley between two rivers to the east and the west. The core of the old city was protected by a good-sized wall, now surrounded by further defences. Embankments zigzagged their way around the city, surrounded by an equally jagged line of ditches dug into the earth. The flood plain was almost an archipelago, with several river channels stitching their way through it before merging into one that angled off towards the south-east. The defences were integrated with the channels and the city was well poised to repel attack. A faint morning mist hung low over the flood plain in front of the city, gently blurring the lines of the added fortifications.

'Look,' Cromwell said, and he thrust a pair of binoculars into her hand. They actually belonged to her anyway, brought from the Old World, but Cromwell found them so useful he tended to forget the matter of their precise ownership. Khonol Le dutifully raised them to her eyes and saw what Cromwell was getting at. She drew in a sharp breath.

The lines were manned, not by Royalist foot soldiers, but by Holekhor. And it was the last Holekhor she wanted to see. It was impossible to see any faces clearly, but the Ensign of the High Families flew over the town and the mustard uniforms of the Might of Golekh were unmistakable. The parapets around Oxford were lined with sandbags, punctuated by rifle-toting infantrymen every few paces, and she picked up several different levels of machine gun nests, with overlapping fields of fire. Belt-fed guns, many times faster and deadlier than the ones she had supplied Fairfax. The entire New Model Army on a sunny day and with the wind at its back would never stand a chance against these defences.

She snatched the binoculars away from her eye and looked at the blotch of Oxford lying in the distance. Then she put them back, as if the whole thing had been an aberration. Surely they were broken. Shake them and they would work, show a different picture.

'Who are they, Mistress Connolly?' Cromwell said quietly. 'New allies for the king?'

'I have no idea,' Khonol Le said frankly. It was too much to take in. She had left the Might behind, in a different country, in a different world. She had led resistance against them, been as much a thorn in their collective shoe as she could, yet it was too absurd that they had come all this way just for her. Yet, there they were.

She saw something else, and pointed it out. 'They might be able to help.'

Cromwell followed her finger. The road into Oxford led up a causeway and over a bridge to cross a large pool in the Thames. A small green tent was pitched half a mile south of the bridge. Small figures moved around it and two flagpoles had been erected outside, one on either side. A white flag hung limply from one, a red from the other.

'The red flag is our flag of truce,' Khonol Le said.

'And white is ours,' Cromwell said. 'A signal in two languages.' He closed his eyes and intoned, ' "The Lord said, verily I will strengthen thee for good; verily I will cause the enemy to make supplication unto thee in time of evil." ' He came to a decision and spurred his horse. 'Colonel, Captain ... and most especially you, Mistress Connolly, come with me.'

The small party moved down the side of the valley.

* * *

The tent was standard military issue but the Holekhor officers in it had pushed the boat out to be formal. There were five of them, clad in jackets and leggings of bright snowy white and rich blood red; sweeping, fur-lined cloaks; knee-length boots gleaming black, and silver-plated helmets that crested over their faces and swept down to the napes of their necks.

As her party approached, Khonol Le glanced up towards the city. A curious feature was a row of short-range artillery guns, mounted on a mound between the external defences and the city, but aimed back at Oxford. She turned her attention back to the tent. The officers sat around a table, apparently enjoying a hearty breakfast. As the riders came near, four of the Holekhor pushed their chairs back and stood respectfully. Warily, Khonol Le took them in. Three had yellow sashes around their waists: they would be the infantry. One had a blue sash: Skymight, Golekh's army of the air. One of the infantrymen had an ornate silver bracelet around his upper arm, which denoted a noble, a scion of a High Family. He looked the youngest, so while he was the social superior here he had to do as he was told by his military elders and betters.

She was surprised that they had eschewed the traditional face paint – and a little disappointed. She knew Cromwell's opinion of men with painted faces. This whole thing was obviously designed to impress him, and the impression could have been ruined by one small Golekhi military tradition. But they were ahead of her.

The men held their hands up to their chests, right hand palm outwards and facing towards the new arrivals, left hand clenched.

'They are saluting you, General,' Khonol Le murmured.

'Indeed? And why doesn't *he* salute?' Cromwell indicated the fifth Holekhor, the man who still sat at the end of the table, even more resplendent than the others. Large, heavy epaulets weighed down each shoulder and his helmet was gold-plated, with an inlaid silver hawk over the brow. That was when Khonol Le finally began really to despair. The Might's Hawk Battalion had a reputation all of its own.

'Because he is the general in charge of this army,' Khonol Le said. She thought of adding, 'Your equal', but chose not to.

Cromwell absorbed the information without comment and rode a few more paces, to come to a halt twenty feet from the tent. He returned the salute abruptly, touching his hand to his helmet but nothing more.

'General Khromell!' The Holekhor general finally rose from his chair and came round the table. He bowed and spoke in English. 'It's a pleasure to see you again. And Khonol Le, I trust I find you in good health. Will you join me for breakfast?'

Khonol Le nearly fell out of her saddle. There was no mistaking that not-quite-buried rural burr; and, she just plain recognized him – the face, the scent. It was the same man, the ex-soldier, the inexplicably Christian John Donder – though not, apparently, as much of an ex-soldier as Khonol Le had been led to believe.

No, she contradicted himself: as she had *let herself* believe. She resolved there and then never to trust anything about this Golekhi creature that she couldn't personally verify, ever again.

'Who are you, sir, and why do you block our way into Oxford?' Cromwell demanded.

'The way into Oxford is open, General. You can pass at any time. As for who I am . . .' Though he still looked at Cromwell, Khonol Le knew it was she who was being addressed. 'Although I previously introduced myself by my Christian name of John Donder, among the Holekhor I am General Dhon Do –' Khonol Le sucked in through her teeth – 'with the privilege of serving My Lord the Domon'el of Golekh.' He indicated the two older men with the yellow sashes. 'May I present the Colonel Khre Deb, commander of the Hawk Battalion, and the Centurion En Sel.' The blue sash: 'Centurion Ror D'le . . .' And finally the young noble. 'And my aide, the Decurion Por De.'

Cromwell nodded abruptly. From the innocently blank gazes and the way the men only straightened up at the sound of their names, Khonol Le guessed that none of the others spoke English.

'You are a general, sir?' Cromwell said. 'You command this army?'

'This?' Dhon Do looked around him. 'Oh, this is just a fraction. I have two hundred men here in Oxford, another five thousand at my camp near

Uffington . . . and that is still the smallest, tiniest splinter of what is to come to this island.' The smile faded. 'I am sorry to take these extreme steps, General, but I need you to take me seriously.'

Cromwell looked at him without blinking. Khonol Le knew him well enough to know that wheels within wheels within wheels were turning in his mind.

'You will excuse me,' Cromwell said, and turned to huddle with his officers. Khonol Le was drawn by default into the conversation.

'Where is Uffington?' Cromwell hissed.

One of the men protested. 'It's impossible, General! He couldn't have five thousand men there without our noticing!'

'I asked where it is, Captain. I did not ask your opinion.'

The captain flushed. 'It's . . . oh, twenty, perhaps thirty miles from here, sir. Past Wantage. But it's on no major road, it's—'

'Doesn't it have a white horse?' the colonel said.

'Yes, sir. A white horse carved into the hill, and a deserted hill fort . . . and that's Uffington. But General, it has no military value, no strategic worth and it's surrounded by our armies! We would have *noticed* the arrival of five thousand men.'

'Thank you, gentlemen.' Cromwell turned back to Dhon Do. 'I thank you for your kind invitation to breakfast, General, but I must decline. We are here to arrest the king; after that, we will certainly discuss the situation you have described.'

'Ah. The king is no longer here.'

Khonol Le braced herself for a furious bellow but Cromwell was surprisingly tranquil, perhaps having already prepared himself for the news.

'I see,' he said. His voice was calm and level as he touched his helmet again. 'Then you have declared yourself for the king, General ... whoever you are. That is your choice. We have nothing more to say to each other, except that if you are here to invade this country you will not find the army and the people of England unprepared. Good day.'

'I did not say where the king is.' Dhon Do raised his voice for the first time, interrupting Cromwell in mid-turnabout. Cromwell glanced back over his shoulder.

'If you have arrested him for me, I am for ever grateful. If you have helped him escape, you are my enemy. Which is it, sir?'

'King Charles and his sons are at my camp,' Dhon Do said.

'I have no quarrel with his sons. Are you holding him for me there or are your five thousand soldiers protecting him?'

'They are doing neither. I came here to receive his surrender. He could hardly do that without first assessing my strength, and I therefore invited him to my camp under flag of truce. And now, General Khromell, I extend the same invitation to you. Unless you would like to surrender now?'

'Surrender?' Cromwell wheeled his horse back round to face Dhon Do, and for the first time ever Khonol Le actually saw him speechless. His mouth moved, but no sound came out. Eventually he was able to say: 'Su- . . . su- . . . *surrender?*' His voice trembled, caught somewhere between laughter, anger and sheer amazement. 'I concede you seem to have taken Oxford in a remarkably short time, but I assure you, sir, it will take much more than an army of five thousand men in smart uniforms to defeat an army of God's own people!'

' "Blessed are the peacemakers," ' said Dhon Do, ' "for they shall be called sons of God." '

' "Think not that I came to send peace on the earth," ' Cromwell replied. ' "I came not to send peace, but a sword." I warn you, sir, do not try to bandy sacred quotes with me and do not meddle in matters you don't understand.'

Dhon Do shook his head, slowly, sadly. 'And I warn you, sir, do not ignore matters that *you* do not understand. Let me give you the same lesson that I gave to the king.'

He turned to the young decurion, Por De, and said one word: '*Vev'emos.*' *Go.*

Por De stood to attention, saluted, then turned and ran back towards Oxford. He hurried through the defence lines and up to the mound whereon the row of artillery was ranged. He filled his lungs and bellowed orders in the One Tongue.

'What did he say?' Cromwell said to Khonol Le.

'He told the gun crews to man their weapons,' she said.

Cromwell frowned at the sudden activity around the guns. They were still aimed at Oxford and their muzzles were sinking lower and lower until they pointed almost directly ahead. It suddenly dawned on Khonol Le that none of the lines directly between the guns and Oxford were actually manned.

'When he says "*khes*",' Khonol Le said urgently, 'cover your ears.'

'What does that mean?' said Cromwell.

'Give fire.'

'*Khes!*'

The guns roared, a ripple of eardrum-pounding thunder that echoed round and round the Thames valley. And the south wall of Oxford erupted. It simply disappeared behind a cloud of shattered stone and dust.

The soldiers' horses were battle-hardened and barely flinched. Khonol Le's nag screamed and reared, and with a feeling of inevitable horror she felt herself slithering off the infernal beast's back. She landed on her rump and ducked aside as the animal fled. She pulled herself to her feet in time to hear the order to fire repeated.

She saw Cromwell's consuming gaze fix upon the gunners. With modern guns there was none of the time-wasting business of swabbing the muzzle, loading and tamping. They simply pulled a lever, the spent cartridge fell out, and a new one was slotted in. The same principle as the rifles, only faster, deadlier . . .

Cromwell wanted them for himself.

The guns fired again and this time Oxford's wall was brought down almost to the ground. One last time and there was no longer a southern wall. The dust cleared and Khonol Le could see all the way into the centre of the city. It had taken less then a minute to do what a conventional barrage would have taken hours to accomplish.

The last echo died away, leaving only a faint drone in Khonol Le's ears. She shook her head to stop the ringing.

'You could have managed the same effect with a few charges,' she said in the One Tongue.

'True, but this way got their attention. You should have seen the king's face after I did this to the north wall.' Dhon Do turned to Cromwell and changed to English. 'General, please listen to me. I am not here by my own choice but by the orders of My Lord the Domon'el, ruler of Golekh. The Domon'el has chosen this land for his own people, and I have been charged with taking it. My Lord doesn't know about you or your king and he doesn't care. He has told his people they can come, and come they will. They will come, and keep coming, and you will never stop them. They have weapons like the ones you have seen; you have your muskets and your gunpowder and your cannon. And they will keep coming and keep coming and keep coming, and then they will keep coming and keep coming and come some more, until the people of this island are extinct or driven into the sea.'

The only sign of Cromwell's anger was that his eyes narrowed, but to Khonol Le, who had had some experience of his temper, he was clearly livid. What was important was that he was taking Dhon Do seriously, and even Dhon Do could see it. 'You are talking about war,' he said.

Dhon Do shook his head angrily. 'No! A war must be joined. It must be declared. My Lord doesn't care enough about you to do that. But if you surrender now, your losses will be fewer than if you resist us.'

'We have Mistress Connolly's guns . . .' Cromwell sounded a fraction less certain than before.

'The Tower of London is already mine. It fell to me the day before yesterday.'

Khonol Le drew in her breath with a hiss. She had been the one to tell Dhon Do where the Tower was. Had her family, her friends, already been slaughtered by Golekhi soldiers? No, no, it couldn't be.

'The Tower fell to you . . . ?' Cromwell gave a shout of incredulous laughter. 'You are truly mad, sir! Even if you could get an army to London, unopposed and unnoticed . . . you obviously don't know that the Tower is a solid, well-defended fortress. You would have to get your artillery within its range to destroy it, General, and it would cost you dear.'

Dhon Do gave a very sad smile. 'What are its air defences?'

'Its . . . air defences?' Cromwell looked as if he must have misheard.

'They don't exist.' Khonol Le answered the question for him, her voice level, only trembling slightly, but her gaze boring into Dhon Do. 'General Cromwell, this man could reduce the Tower to rubble in minutes. Perhaps he already has.'

Dhon Do shook his head again. 'They were ordered to surrender and they saw sense,' he said. 'As a gesture of good will, General, I then returned control of the Tower to your Parliament. The Holekhor foundry, and its staff, I kept for myself – intact.'

'Reduce it to rubble?' Cromwell demanded. 'How? Mistress Connolly, how?'

She pricked up her ears. The drone was louder now and suddenly she knew what it was. It was not the after effects of an artillery barrage at all. She turned and pointed south, down the valley. And up. 'Like that,' she said.

There were shouts of amazement from Cromwell's two colleagues. The general himself turned his horse round, cupped his hands over his eyes and gazed up into the clear blue sky.

Eight hundred feet long, one hundred feet wide, the airship coasted towards the city. The golden hawk insignia on its prow gleamed back at them and it made the inexorable, deadly progress of a shark. Khonol Le had a sudden vision of the Golekhi advance into England. It would be like this.

The noise of the engines deepened into a rib-trembling rumble as the airship slid through the sky above them. It took a long time to pass over completely. Six engine nacelles jutted out of the hull at bow, midpoint and stern. It had two gondolas, one at the prow and one at midships, and they were connected by a gallery. Khonol Le could clearly see the faces of some of the Skymight crew peering down. One of them waved.

Then the airship was past, coming in to land in the meadows to the east of Oxford.

'Dear God,' Cromwell whispered. His face was completely pale, drained of colour.

'My ship, the *Golden Hawk*,' Dhon Do said.

'General,' said Khonol Le. 'Those things can carry bombs, and guns, and troops. That is how he reached London.' She glared bitterly at Dhon Do. 'You should know that this man led the army that overran my own country, and his Hawk Battalion . . . they were yours, weren't they, Dhon Do? Everyone knows the Conqueror founded them.'

'Indeed,' Dhon Do said. 'I trained Colonel Khre Deb myself.'

'The Hawks were at the forefront of every assault,' Khonol Le said, her voice suddenly flat and lifeless. 'I beg you, General, listen to this man. What he says is the truth.'

'I . . .' It was the first time Khonol Le had known Cromwell falter. 'I have no authority to negotiate, sir. Can you give me written details that I can show to Parliament? Not terms but . . . a description of the situation.'

'If you can lend me a scribe I will be happy to oblige,' Dhon Do said. 'I will also be happy to send a ship to London to pick up whichever representatives Parliament cares to send. If you like, General, I will take you to my camp first, to view the situation with your own eyes. I give you my word you will be accorded the due courtesies to a man in your position and you will be free to come and go as you please.'

Cromwell nodded curtly, then pulled his horse around. 'For the time being I will rejoin my men, and then, with your permission, we will take Oxford. After that, I will consider your offer. Mistress Connolly, are you still with us?'

Khonol Le gazed with loathing at Dhon Do. He returned the look with a regretful smile. 'I wouldn't join this man to save my life, General.'

'Very well. Wait here; we'll pick you up on the way back.' Cromwell and his colleagues rode off without a backwards glance.

Dhon Do and Khonol Le gazed after them. Then Khonol Le turned to Dhon Do.

'So, how did you get here? You pointed out yourself that the Wise would never let weapons through Okh'Shenev.'

'And you pointed out yourself that the Domon'el and the Wise have made a deal.'

Finally, she began to catch on. 'Oh, no,' she whispered.

'There's a new gate from the Old World,' he confirmed, 'and it belongs entirely to the Domon'el. Perhaps you should reconsider your decision to stay here.'

She bridled. 'Never! Look, Dhon Do, it's not over.' She jerked a thumb after Cromwell. 'That man is dangerous. He's not just an excellent soldier. Unlike Fairfax, he's also a politician. He's a Member of Parliament. He follows Parliament's orders but he can also shape those orders, and he has a religious conviction that you would not believe. He will oppose you, every step of the way.'

'I've faced worse.'

'Yes, I suppose you have,' she said bitterly. She studied him more carefully. This close, she could see the three gold rings in his left ear lobe that designated his rank. 'I thought a captain or a sergeant,' she said. 'A general never crossed my mind.'

'That was my intention.'

'So, you're the Conqueror. You said you weren't at Nhottep.'

She was satisfied, and slightly surprised to see him bridle at the implication he had lied. 'I wasn't,' he said. 'When the Campaign began, I was a junior staff officer with the job of reflecting glory onto my superiors. I was *trying* to get someone in authority to agree to the need for airborne infantry, but I wasn't being successful.'

She had paid little attention to the early military career of the Conqueror, but now she came to think of it, yes, his name had only become famous with the first airborne attacks – and that had been after the Campaign began. It was coming back to her. She had heard vaguely that Dhon Do's plan had the dual attractions of making military sense and annoying the High Command, with whom the Domon'el was at loggerheads. Either way, the Domon'el had championed Dhon Do, raising him to general over the heads of his former superiors and putting him in charge of the Campaign. No wonder Dhon Do was his Lord's man.

'How did a junior staff officer have any glory

to reflect?' she said, curious despite herself.

Dhon Do just smiled. 'That was my return from my first venture into the New World. Look, you said I must have an interesting story. Why not have breakfast with us, and I'll tell it to you.'

Seven

Daniel's Daze

*H*e was back at Edgehill and it was just as he remembered it.

There was Daniel, and there was Daniel inside Daniel's head. One of them was a nine-year-old drummer boy, an eager village lad following the menfolk of Branheath as they in turn followed Sir Miles to their king's side. Sir Miles had heard the king was heading for London and had set out to meet him on his march from Shrewsbury. Parliament's army under the Earl of Essex had set out from Worcester with a similar intention, and Edgehill was where they all met up. It was a glorious adventure for Daniel and he had no idea of what was coming.

The Daniel inside Daniel's head was three years older and knew exactly what lay ahead.

The armies moved into position before first light, the king on the steep slope and Essex on the plain below. The excitement was almost unbearable. The king and his two sons rode around their brigades, encouraging them and giving them cheer. For a moment Daniel caught the king's gaze and almost swooned with pride.

Daniel inside Daniel's head shouted warnings, but the royal party rode blithely by.

The king's cavalry commenced the attack in the afternoon, and Parliament's foot soldiers scattered before them. Surely victory was theirs! From his position on the high ground, Daniel could see the square of foot soldiers that was the men of Branheath. The young Daniel cheered while the older could scarcely bear to watch. He knew what was to happen. The king's cavalry kept charging; they vanished into the distance, and suddenly the king's foot soldiers were on their own, facing the massed horse that Essex had at his command. They charged in their turn, and in the next few minutes the male population of Branheath simply evaporated before Daniel's horrified gaze.

Then a shadow fell over the whole battlefield, Royalists and rebels alike. Both Daniels looked up at the fleet of airships, so vast they blocked out the sun . . .

Daniel awoke from the dream with a gasp. He lay in his bed on his back and stared at the roof of the tent. Gradually his eyes made sense of where he was. The tent. His father's tent. In the middle of a vast camp of men from another world.

He sat suddenly upright. 'Bloody hell, they're invading us!'

He frowned, surprised at his own reaction. He had known all this for days. Why was he suddenly reacting to it like this?

Because, he realized, the daze had lifted. He could finally take it all in.

Daniel first saw the Holekhor camp that was to become his new home from the air, shortly before his mind stopped working.

He had returned to the glider, panting from the run back from the village and wondering what the strange rumble from the sky was. His father had turned him to face in that direction, and just before the ship appeared he had clasped his arms loosely around his son's waist. It was friendly and affectionate, perhaps a bit more familiar than Daniel would have liked, but if his father was prepared to make the gesture then so was he. So he had leaned back happily into the embrace, and then the monstrous machine had hove into view and he would have fled if he hadn't had two strong arms wrapped around him. Which, he later realized, was the main purpose of the hug (though he chose to believe that friendship and affection came into it too). It was impossible. It was terrifying. The sight of that massive bulk defying the pull of the earth, or at the very least politely declining it, just flew in the face of everything Daniel had thought he knew.

But the urge to flee passed with surprising speed, replaced by an equally powerful sense of curiosity. Once the shock wore off, Daniel could see that it was a machine. A machine that flew, but for all that, a machine. From what little he understood of his father's explanation, most of the great hull was taken up with bags full of something like air that helped it float. Daniel could not quite articulate his understanding, but comprehension flickered at the corners of his mind. This ship was just like the inflated bladders the boys of the village liked to kick around. Bigger and vastly more complicated, but the principle was very similar.

Daniel's father kept a strong arm around him as the ship came in to land, but it was unnecessary.

A metal hut hung from the belly of the monster. It had windows in it, and a door, and when the ship touched down on the ground, this was where Daniel and his father boarded. The walls of the hut were lined with levers and wheels, and it was full of noise and Holekhor men. They wore clothes of a uniform dull yellow, with blue cloth on their shoulders. They made a strangely formal gesture with their hands, which Daniel's father returned. They all looked surprised to see Daniel. His father spoke with some of them in a language that wasn't English or Latin, then looked down at his son.

'They have to take the glider in before we leave,' he said. 'Daniel . . .' He paused, looked away, looked back. 'I have to tell you some things here and now. It's not too late for you to go back home, but I want you to know.'

Daniel nodded, nervous and expectant.

'My *Christian* name is John Donder,' his father said. 'To these people my name is Dhon Do. Francis christened me with the nearest name he could find to my own. And . . .' He sucked in his cheeks as though he were going to say something that really hurt. 'And, I am their general. I command this army. I command ships like this, and thousands of men.'

Daniel took in this new knowledge. On its own, it would have seemed strange. But as he had just boarded a flying machine larger than Branheath, which had settled down on the ground with the lightness of a feather, it was almost unremarkable.

'Who does your army fight for, sir?' he said. 'The king? Or Parliament?'

Dhon Do looked distinctly embarrassed. He sucked his cheeks in again. 'Neither,' he said. 'We are invading England.'

The ship chose that moment to take off, so it seemed as if God let go of the world beneath him in more ways than one.

Half an hour later, the camp lay below them. Dhon Do called it Povse'okh. It stood on the edge of a sharp ridge that reminded Daniel of the slope behind the battle at Edgehill. Yet, that had been lined with trees. This was crowned with a different kind of forest – a small city of tents of different shapes and sizes. Square, boxlike structures of dark green canvas, laid out in neat rows. The invaders were already making themselves at home. He saw them carving terraces into the steep side of the hill, building positions for guns, digging trenches.

Daniel watched the flat-topped hill appear through the windows of the airship's command gondola. He pressed his face against the glass, the better to see the invaders spread out before him, and immediately his attention was caught by something else.

'What's that?' he said. He didn't point, but there could only be one *that*.

It was a huge circle of *differentness*, a hollow ring towering above the camp, its edge bounded by a shimmer like a hot summer's day. It stood two hundred feet or more in the air and through it was a scene that was *somewhere else*. The sky was different – a different shade of blue, with different cloud patterns to the sky on this side. There was a town in the distance, through the circle, but not elsewhere on the hilltop. Not in Berkshire. Not in England.

'That is how we came here,' Dhon Do said. 'There's another world through that gate.'

That was when Daniel's mind stopped working.

He had lived twelve simple years in Branheath. Within the space of a day he had met his father, flown away with him in a mighty flying ship, and learned that he was the son of a general who had come to conquer England. Now his mind finally realized it was crammed too full of novelty. Presented with the knowledge that the Holekhor did not even come from this world, it decided enough was enough and tucked the information away for future reference. It took the knowledge in, but would not let Daniel react to it. Eventually, it promised Daniel, it would take that knowledge out again and he could examine it. For now, he was so far out of his depth that the safest thing was to stay with his father and trust him.

So, Daniel's reaction to the news was no more than a faint whimper.

The ship landed and Daniel was swamped by a deluge of new sights, sounds, scents and impressions.

The moment his feet touched the ground, he felt *power*. There was something beneath him, something in the ground that had never been there in Branheath. He didn't know what it was but he knew instinctively that it was a mighty force, if only the right person could tap it. Later, he would learn of the Wise – the people who *could* tap it, for better or for worse. They were how, and why, the Holekhor had arrived at this particular spot.

The Holekhor! Hundreds of them, surrounding him on every side; a riot of uniforms, yellow and red and blue and black. And they all seemed to know his father, or his father knew them. Most had reddish hair and blue eyes, and they were all stocky and muscular in comparison with a typical Englishman, but within those bounds there was as much variety of size and shape and height as in any crowd. There was a scent in the air that Daniel had never known before. It was the scent of hundreds of people *like him.* His eyes and his ears told him he was somewhere he had never been, but his nose made it more homely than Branheath.

He had his first sight of a nenokh – an animal the size of a cottage that strolled past him, dwarfing the Holekhor man controlling it yet humbly obeying his commands. It had four massive legs, a coat of thick brown hair, giant tusks that curled, and a long, snaking nose that Daniel assumed just dangled until he saw the creature using it to pick something up. The Holekhor used it and others like it as pack animals.

When they did not use nenokhs – which he was to learn were usually docile, but temperamental in the mating season – they used steam wagons. Massive metal contraptions, iron frameworks mounted on spoked wheels that chugged past, giving out wafts of steam and a scent of hot oil. Even an Englishman with no Holekhor blood within him could have smelled them a mile off.

It all went the same way as the gate – to somewhere safely at the back of his mind. If he looked too closely at any of this newness, his mind warned (and he entirely agreed), then all his certainties might be swept away. His name, his identity. Everything. He had to remain Daniel Matthews, a boy from Branheath, who was on his travels. This was surely no stranger than Virginia would have been.

'This is our tent,' Dhon Do said, drawing back a canvas flap. It was large, almost as big as the front room of the inn in Branheath. Inside was a desk, some chairs, and a bed in one corner. And it was lit by a strange kind of lamp that hung from the centre pole. It seemed as if the glass itself was on fire.

'And this is Ro Dhen,' said his father. Another Holekhor man stood there, his hands behind his back. He wore the yellow uniform and looked to be a few years older than Dhon Do. He and Dhon Do exchanged words, and then he smiled at Daniel.

'There are things I have to do which will take a couple of hours,' said Dhon Do, 'and in the morning I have to leave, perhaps for some days, and I can't take you with me. For now, Ro Dhen will look after you; just do as he says. I will be back later on, and I promise we will spend the rest of the evening together without interruption. I'm sure there are questions you would like to ask.'

Then he left. Daniel's daze continued, which was

as well because otherwise he would never have submitted so meekly to the bath.

The tent flap drew back and a beaming Ro Dhen looked in. Daniel had discovered that Ro Dhen beamed very easily. '*Eh! Ve'khev! Khovev'fokhopos?*' he said, which Daniel guessed with complete accuracy meant 'Ah! You're up! Breakfast?'

But Daniel simply shook his head and swung his legs out of bed. Ro Dhen moved to help him get dressed, but Daniel's rediscovery of independent thought meant he had no intention of being helped at something so simple. He shooed Ro Dhen out and turned to his clothes. He hadn't seen his old workaday togs since his arrival (he suspected Ro Dhen had burned them) and had been provided with leather shoes, leggings of a light sand colour, a sky-blue tunic and a thick, red jacket with a hood to wear against the wind. He was particularly grateful for the latter: not only was the hilltop windy, but Ro Dhen had inflicted a haircut on him that had removed a lot of his head's natural insulation.

He pulled them on, and was doing up the jacket when Ro Dhen returned with a bowl of hot water. This time there was no shooing him – Ro Dhen wouldn't move until Daniel had at least washed his face. But eventually he was allowed out into the hustle and bustle of the camp.

'*Khen-end-zon!*' Ro Dhen called cheerfully after him. It was something he had been saying a lot over the last couple of days, and Daniel still had no idea what it meant. It was one more thing to find out.

* * *

Daniel wandered through the camp of Povse'okh. It had come to make a kind of sense to him. Even during his daze, he had been learning. He could go almost anywhere, and if he was challenged he could wave a piece of paper his father had given him. It usually worked to let him through.

He had seen most of what there was to see during the daze, but now he was seeing it differently. Now that his mind was letting him take it in, he could finally think through the implications. He, Daniel Matthews, was at the centre of an invasion of England. He was not entirely sure this was a good thing.

By now he was getting to be recognized, and many of his father's soldiers greeted him as he passed them by. They would give a friendly wave or a cheerful greeting, and he would return it with just a silent stare.

He walked past the nenokh enclosure. They had come to know him there. Yesterday one of the drivers had given him a long stick and let him tickle a beast behind its ears. It had shut its eyes and curled its trunk, and its mouth had yawned wide open with a rib-shaking rumble of bliss. Now he could see the same man smiling and holding out the stick again in invitation, but he turned away.

His wandering course brought him to the gate. The gate had that effect. You had to make the conscious choice to stay away from it. It was as if the whole camp sloped towards it, though you could see with your eyes that it didn't. The air buzzed with power, so taut you felt you could twang it. Anyone used to thunderstorms would glance around anxiously, expecting one almighty peal from above. But the sky was clear. It was just the space around the gate that was charged.

This was one place not even the bit of paper could get him near. There was some kind of rampart in the middle of the camp, an old hill fort that predated the invasion by centuries, and the gate stood in the middle of that. Daniel was permitted to go as far as the rampart, but no further.

He gazed up at the gate. This morning, it was just a black circle. He had learned that it came and went. Sometimes you could see through it, in which case, people and objects could pass from the other world into this one. Sometimes it was as it was now, in which case people could pass from this world into the other.

He turned away, and a few minutes later found himself at the edge of the camp, two hundred feet above the mean level of Berkshire. At his feet a white horse was carved into the turf, a series of arched, elegant shapes. Immediately beyond it the ground fell away in a graceful curve, dizzying and precipitous, as if scooped out by a giant; and beyond that was the farm-land, divided by the dark lines of its hedges into patches of green, yellow and brown. To Daniel, land was land and had never been anything else. It was what you worked on to live. But now he suddenly saw it differently. He saw how an outside force like the Holekhor could covet that land. He blinked. Was he turning into one of them?

He was struck by the similarity to the ridge at

Edgehill. Perhaps this was why he had had that dream. He looked thoughtfully at the land below him. Could it be that England no longer *deserved* to rule itself? Had both sides betrayed God's trust, and so He was withdrawing his favour altogether? He remembered Francis's lessons on the many, many sins of the people of Israel and their wicked kings. Eventually, they had simply lost the right to rule their land and had been taken into captivity. To their surprise, God had shown himself quite capable of using pagan kings to teach his own people a lesson.

He shut his eyes and remembered again those few seconds in which Branheath had lost its men. Seconds, nothing more. He would have missed it if he had blinked. And that was what was going on in a hundred other places, all over England.

Daniel's father could put an end to this war. No more villages would lose all their menfolk in one fell swoop. No one else's life would be torn apart with the loss of a father or a brother or a husband. And if the price of that was an invasion . . . Daniel finally decided he would approve.

It was then that he heard a voice speaking in English.

Eight

Boy-Troll

'I say, bro. It's a little boy-troll.'

Daniel looked away from the view. Further up the slope stood two boys.

One was about his own age and size, skinny and with a long, sad face. The other was a bit older than him and several inches taller. His face was swarthier and rounder than the younger boy's, and a very thin, fine dark line that might one day turn into a moustache ran across his upper lip. As the words Daniel had heard had the wavery rasp of a recently broken voice, not yet settled into its adult tones, Daniel guessed the bigger boy was the speaker. They were both dressed in clothes of a quality and finery far above Daniel's usual Branheath attire, and comparing favourably with what he wore now.

Daniel was glancing around to see what the boy was talking about when the insight struck him. There only one other boy present and that was himself. He was dressed like a Holekhor and his red pudding-bowl hair had been trimmed to a more precise, Holekhor-like cut. *He* was the boy-troll.

The older boy was smirking; the younger one still looked sad. Perhaps the older boy had been trying to cheer up his brother, pointing out Daniel in the same way mothers would point out cows to squalling babies. Instincts that had been embedded since birth took over. He could tell from the tone that these boys were noble, superior to him in every way. He could think of several responses, but gave voice to none of them. It wasn't his place to talk back at them. He started to walk away.

'I wonder what his mother charges?' the older boy added.

Daniel stopped in his tracks, as an even stronger instinct took over. Boys back at Branheath who had teased him about his mother had soon learned not to.

'My mother's dead,' Daniel said. 'What does yours charge?'

The bigger boy gave Daniel the full benefit of the languid gaze from his dark, hooded eyes. 'The boy-troll speaks! And we will thank him not to speak of our mother in that way.'

'I'll thank you not to speak of mine at all,' said Daniel. The traditional subservience reasserted itself and he started to trudge up the hill. If he could just put distance between them then he would find some equilibrium between the instinct to be a good yeoman to his superiors and the instinct to cause the older boy injury.

The older boy moved to intercept him, blocking his way. The slope of the hill gave his natural height an even greater advantage.

'We will talk about your mother in any way that we please, boy-troll.'

'Charles . . .' pleaded the younger boy. Charles waved him to silence.

'Enough, bro. We've been brought here against our will and I'm sick of seeing Father do obeisance to these precious Hollykor. They're too high and fancy for any decent Englishman to stomach.'

The word *father* was what tipped the scales. Daniel remembered that yes, he might be the bastard son of a ruined widow back home . . . but here, he was the son of someone much higher up than either of these two. For the first time in his life, he had some rank.

'It's *Holekhor*,' he said. He didn't even add 'sir'.

'I do apologize. Ho-*lekh* . . . or!' Charles managed to turn the word into the sound of someone emptying his lungs of phlegm. A speck of spit fell on Daniel's cheek.

'A-and our mother is French,' the younger boy said helpfully. Charles rolled his eyes.

'Better half French than whole troll.' He reached out an elegant hand and flicked the tip of Daniel's nose. 'What do you say, boy-troll?'

Daniel smiled sweetly. Branheath had seemed a lifetime away; now he remembered it was only a few days, and the memories of defending his dead mother's honour against the jibes of the village boys were all too fresh. 'I'm only half a troll,' he said, and plunged a fist into Charles's stomach. It was more chance than good sportsmanship that made the blow land above the belt. Charles folded double and dropped to the ground with a whoop.

'Charles!' The younger boy cried out and ran to his brother's side, and Daniel kept walking.

Then a mighty weight crashed into his kidneys and he staggered forward. His waist had exploded in pain. Another blow got him between the shoulder blades.

'Turn and face me, boy-troll!'

Daniel lashed out through watering eyes at the pale area towards the top of the vague shape that was Charles, and felt his knuckles split against the older boy's teeth. Charles staggered back with blood gushing from his mouth.

'You're dead, troll,' he gasped, and he flung himself at Daniel, locking arms around his waist and dragging him to the ground. The breath was knocked out of Daniel and Charles scrabbled to sit astride him, no doubt intending to end the fight with a barrage of blows.

With only a slight exertion, Daniel twisted and heaved. Charles slid off his adversary with a look of comic surprise and Daniel rolled on top of him. Charles's original plan for ending the fight recommenced with an unexpected redistribution of the players, and all Charles could do was hold his arms over his face as protection against Daniel's pounding fists.

'Stop it, stop it, stop it!' There was a weight on Daniel's back. Charles's younger brother had wrapped puny arms around him and was trying to pull him off, sobbing all the while. 'Stop it, leave him alone, stop it!'

There was something inside Daniel that couldn't ignore the pleas of a crying child, even one not much younger than himself. He put all his strength into one last punch to Charles's ribs just to make his point – Charles howled – and stood up in disgust. The younger boy was immediately at Charles's side, helping him to his feet. Charles gently slid his arms round his brother and the younger boy buried his face in Charles's shirt and bawled.

'There, bro, there . . . It's over . . . It's over . . .' Charles stroked his brother's hair until the bawls had turned into sobs, and glared at Daniel over his brother's head with a face like battered thunder. 'I hope you're satisfied, boy-troll. Do you enjoy making small boys cry?'

Daniel stood agape at the injustice.

'Satisfied? I never laid a finger on him!'

'*Gentlemen*, boy-troll, never lay a finger on anyone. They *challenge* one another with swords or pistols. They do not resort to crude fisticuffs unless, of course, attacked first in such a way. But . . .' An elaborate, theatrical sigh. 'I shouldn't expect a boy-troll to know civilized manners.'

It was only the shield of the younger boy that stopped Daniel launching a second attack. 'Do *gentlemen* insult the memories of dead mothers?' he said.

Charles, very slightly, smiled. 'Tell me, how is it you're the only troll here apart from the chief who talks like a Christian?'

Daniel wondered if this was the prelude to negotiations for peace or the search for another insult. He decided to take it at face value. Francis would have approved.

'My mother was English, my father's the—' he began, but Charles wasn't listening. The older boy had suddenly perked up, holding his head high like a faithful dog at the first scent of his returning master. His eyes were fixed on something above and beyond Daniel's head. 'Look! Look, bro!' He grabbed his brother's shoulders and spun the smaller boy around. 'They're coming back!'

Daniel turned. The bulbous, grey shape of an airship was emerging from the haze to the northeast. A double thrill ran through him: the sight of the *Golden Hawk* for its own sake, and the fact that his father was returning.

'Come on, bro. Let's see it land.' Charles was already herding his brother towards the tall metal pylon where the airship would dock. Daniel followed, eager to see Dhon Do again but not nearly as eager to get anywhere near Charles.

The airship passed lazily overhead, its engines protesting as it slowed, and lines fell from its nose and its side. Holekhor on the ground ran forward to take them and guide it towards the pylon. The nose of the *Golden Hawk* docked with a *clang*. The engines put-putted to a sudden silence and other Holekhor ran forward with pegs and hammers, to assist their comrades holding the landing lines. The sound of metallic hammering echoed off the curving bulk of the ship.

It wasn't loud enough to drown a brash voice

nearby, explaining how the airship moved. Charles was pointing at the rotating blades and talking about how they were angled to push against the air *so*. His unfortunate brother was treated to a demonstration of the principle with a hand between his shoulders. Charles pulled him up again and continued with the exposition, moving on to how the fins worked. From the references to the chief troll, who had apparently explained it all to Charles, Daniel guessed the boys had met his father. He still had no idea how.

Daniel ignored the rest of the discourse because the chief troll himself had appeared in the hatch. Daniel was still not used to seeing his father in uniform. Two Holekhor ran forward with a wooden set of steps carried between them, and put it up against the ship's side so that Dhon Do could step down.

But Dhon Do held back and gave deference to a man Daniel hadn't seen before. He had hair down to his shoulders and a lumpy, ugly face, but what immediately damned him in Daniel's eyes was that he wore the uniform of Parliament.

The man descended to the ground, looking around him, his gaze darting hither and thither with mingled awe and suspicion. He was followed by a couple of other men dressed similarly. Then Dhon Do finally stepped down to the ground, followed by a Holekhor woman.

'Daniel!' Dhon Do saw him and raised a hand. He said something quickly to Lumpy Ugly and walked briskly over to his son. He beamed and rubbed Daniel's arms. 'It's good to see you again. Daniel, we're making progress. I've brought with me—' He stopped and looked with horror at something behind Daniel. 'Prince Charles, what happened to you?'

Daniel felt the ground open under him and the words echoed around in his head. It was as if a stranger took control of his body and made him turn to face the confirmation of what he suddenly knew.

Charles, Prince of Wales, and his brother, whom Daniel now assumed to be Prince James, stood behind him. Charles's mouth was still crusted with blood, and some fascinating bruises were swelling up on his face.

'This young man and I had a misunderstanding, General,' Charles said, with a tone that was affable and a glance at Daniel that was not.

'Who with . . . what . . . *Daniel*?'

'He said things about my mother, sir,' Daniel muttered in a very small voice.

'About . . . Honestly! I gave the king assurances that none of his family would be mistreated and now you . . . you . . .'

'B-b-but . . .' Daniel wailed. 'How was I to know, sir?'

'How were you to know? I brought them back from Oxford two days ago! You were asleep but I told Ro Dhen to tell you the king and his sons were here! I taught him the words! Didn't he say anything?'

Khen-end-zon! Daniel seemed to hear the voice faintly, mocking him. *King and sons.* And who else could the boys, with the accents of the gentry and the older one called Charles, have been?

Dhon Do clenched his fists and waved them

pointlessly in the air. 'Oh . . . *Daniel*!' He gave Daniel one final glare and turned back to his guests. 'General, will you come this way, please?'

Daniel's face burned and he stared at the ground. He looked up when he realized Lumpy Ugly had stopped in front of him. The man gazed down at him, stern and disapproving, and then his face was un-expectedly split by a grin. He gave Daniel a gentle, friendly punch to the shoulder.

'The House of Stuart does have that effect on one,' he said, in a pitch that was just meant for the two of them, and then he followed after Daniel's father.

Nine

Intersections

Oliver Cromwell stood on the outer rampart of the old hill fort and looked at the thing that had brought the Holekhor to his country. Dhon Do recognized the signs of a man brooding and didn't interrupt. The wind tugged at Cromwell's cloak but it couldn't budge his gaze from the gate.

Dhon Do wondered if even an Englishman could feel the landpower in this place. He certainly could. The air and ground seemed to hum with it. The gate was a hole between worlds, and the substance of this world wanted to pour into it. If you let your mind go into neutral you could find you had taken a couple of steps towards it.

The tide had just changed. It was on the in-tide now, which meant that things could come from the Old to the New World, but not at the moment go the other way. One of the things to come through was light, so Cromwell could get a clear view of the Old World on the other side. The wind blew out of the gate and it was much colder than England in May.

'Explain it to me again,' Cromwell said. Dhon Do sighed.

'I'm not a technical man, General. I do know that buried in the ground, in the earth, there are lines of . . . um . . . power. It is the same in our world. They cover the country. Where those lines cross each other at the same place in both worlds, it's possible to form a gate like this.'

'I know the legends of power in the earth,' Cromwell said brusquely. 'I have no belief in those pagan superstitions.'

'Well –' Dhon Do waved a hand at the gate – 'if you have an alternative explanation, I know people who would be happy to hear it.'

'Indeed.' Cromwell spoke as though he had just swallowed a draught of vinegar. 'It should be impossible and yet I see all too well that you are here. And this . . .' He looked back at the gate. 'Yes. I see.'

Dhon Do didn't need the mind of a general to see what his opposite number was thinking. The Holekhor were invading England through just one point. It was high on a hill and surrounded by a superior army, but it was just one point. If Cromwell had any ideas about resisting the Holekhor invasion, this was where he would have to come. Dhon Do intended to encourage that way of thinking as much as lay within his power.

Cromwell turned away and walked down the grassy bank. Khonol Le and his officers had been waiting a short distance away: he gestured for them to join him. 'Thank you, General. I've seen enough that I can write an informed missive to Parliament.'

Dhon Do bowed. 'Come to my tent and I'll provide you with the materials you need.'

It may have been a general's tent but the inside smelled as much of must and sweat as any soldier's. The side away from the wind was open to let in the daylight. Dhon Do showed Cromwell the desk, some paper and his pen.

'Khonol Le will explain its operation if needed,' he said. 'I will give you some privacy. Good day.'

Cromwell watched them go, then turned to the desk and dropped into the chair. 'I need a great number of explanations, Mistress Connolly, but I hardly think I need to be told how to write with . . .' He picked up Dhon Do's fountain pen, twiddled it in his fingers and looked at it helplessly. Then he held it out to Khonol Le. She took it, unscrewed the cap and handed it back.

'You'll find it's full of ink,' she said. 'No need for dipping it.'

'Ingenious.' Cromwell turned it in his hand, studying the nib closely. Then he lowered the pen and started to write. For half a minute there was no sound but the scratching of nib on paper.

'Gentlemen,' Cromwell said casually, without looking up. 'I would be grateful if you could spread yourselves around the tent outside. I'm prepared to trust General Donder's word that we will not be overheard but I trust you even more. Stay, please, Mistress Connolly.'

The officers glanced at each other, then filed out.

Khonol Le waited for another half minute while Cromwell kept writing, and she jumped when Cromwell spoke again.

'We've known each other for some time,' he said. He still wasn't looking up. 'You have told me, and I have learned, a great deal, but somehow the subject of your coming from another world has never arisen.' Now he did stop writing: he laid the pen down, sat up straight and speared her with his gaze.

Amazing, Khonol Le thought. He is sitting in another man's chair at another man's desk in another man's tent, and yet he's commanding this scene.

'Does it matter where we come from?' she said. 'We're here.'

'That is an admirably pragmatic attitude, but pray indulge me.'

Khonol Le sighed. 'We come . . .' she said. 'I mean, previously we have always come through a gate like this in a land called Latvia. We call it Okh'Shenev.'

'I've heard the name mentioned,' Cromwell said. 'I always assumed it to be some kind of port.'

'It means "Gate of the Gods". And it is a port: it's on the edge of the, um, Baltic Sea. There's a strong Holekhor community there, but we wanted a change. We took a boat going west and we ended in London.'

'Donder calls this place Povsyok. What does that mean?'

'Povse'okh. "Our gate".' Khonol Le paused to assemble the parts of the explanation into the right order in her mind before letting them out of her mouth. Cromwell's unblinking gaze was still fixed squarely on her and she knew it was worth getting everything right first time. 'Okh'Shenev, in our world, lies in our most holy territory. It has always been ruled by priests. They say it is where the first Holekhor were raised up by our gods. The gate was first discovered by a group of . . .' She steeled herself. She could only think of one word in English that matched what the Wise did, and she knew Cromwell would not like it. 'A group of witches, who have always controlled access to the New Wo— to this place. They have made it equally available to all the Holekhor nations.' She took a breath.

'Go on.'

'The Domon'el, the ruler of Golekh—'

'Donder's Lord.'

'Indeed. Him. He wanted his own access.' This was what Dhon Do had explained to her over breakfast at Oxford, while Cromwell assembled his army to occupy the city that the Holekhor had already kindly, and bloodlessly, captured for him. 'He made an arrangement with the, um, witches and they opened this gate for him. No one controls it but him.'

And that was why the Domon'el had invaded Toskhes, whose border was far too close to the gate for his liking. But Cromwell had not asked about that, so Khonol Le did not tell him.

'I see,' he said. 'Does this mean we can expect others of these gates to open? At perhaps any place in the country? Or the world?'

Khonol Le shook her head. 'The gates will only open where the lines of power cross, and opening them is not easy. It will not be something that is easily repeated. The witches tried once; they failed and they died. It took years for them to try again, simply because they had to raise up a sufficient quantity of new ones.'

Cromwell looked hopeful. 'Were the old ones executed for their failure?'

'It was accidental. They tried to open a gate and they got it wrong. A small party went through, but they all died when the gate collapsed, except their commander. On the other side I understand it was terrible. Hundreds died. This was several years ago, and the commander who survived on this side was a young officer of infantry named Dhon Do.'

'Ah . . .' Cromwell said, in the trailing-off tone of final understanding. 'I had wondered how he came to speak English so well, and to have a nearly-grown son called Daniel. He was stranded?'

'He recovered with the mind of a baby, barely any memory of anything. He was taken in by some locals and nursed back to health.'

'A long way for one man to walk with the mind of a baby – from this place to Newbury.'

'I gather the gate on this side was . . .' *Unstable.* Another word she didn't know in English. 'Badly fixed. It moved about, brought him close to his new home. That is one reason it collapsed. Anyway, when his memory returned he made his way back home through Okh'Shenev. It made him famous.'

'All . . . very . . . interesting.' Cromwell steepled his fingers and tilted his head back. 'One lesson I learn from all this is that both this Domon'el and Donder are persistent men.'

'Very persistent,' Khonol Le agreed. 'You should also know that Dhon Do rose to his rank through sheer ability. Our armies were bogged down in stalemate. He had the idea of flying over our lines and attacking from the rear. It's a simple idea, but no one else had thought of it.'

She could see a grudging respect in Cromwell's eyes. Cromwell, too, had risen to his rank through talent. He had educated himself by reading accounts of the great battles of history, and had reinvented the entire concept of the cavalry for the modern age. If he had been in Dhon Do's place with airships at his disposal, he might have done exactly the same.

'At some point you must tell me more. How far will you go, Mistress Connolly, to thwart Donder's plans?'

Khonol Le felt a sudden thrill run through her. 'As far as is needed,' she said.

Cromwell sat up suddenly. If possible, his gaze was even more intense. 'Donder and his Lord think of us in the same way as we think of the heathen savages in the Americas,' he said. 'I am beginning to see that this view is not confined to just a few Hollykor. What do you think, Mistress Connolly? Where do your loyalties lie?'

Khonol Le had never expected to be called to account quite so bluntly. She also knew that the decision she made now would bind her forever in Cromwell's eyes.

'I came to this country owing loyalty to no one,' she said. 'And yes, I too had been taught that the people of this world were inferior to the Holekhor. It was just chance that I sided with Parliament. If the king had occupied London when we arrived, I would have joined his side instead. But you have been good to me, you have been a steady customer and you have always paid me by and large on time. I'm loyal to you, General.'

'Until someone pays you more?' Cromwell asked mildly. Khonol Le snorted.

'Haven't I made it clear? I wouldn't accept a fortune from Dhon Do.'

'I was thinking of our more earthly enemies,' Cromwell said. 'The French. The Spanish.'

Khonol Le looked him in the eyes. 'I honestly can't say. I can say that in the matter of England versus Golekh, I side with England.'

Cromwell pursed his lips and tapped the tips of his fingers together. 'That is probably the best we can hope for at present.' He sat forward abruptly and scribbled his name at the bottom of the letter. He picked it up and waved it to dry the ink. 'Please go outside, fetch Captain Hawkins and ask him to fetch Donder.'

'*London?*' Daniel exclaimed. It wasn't quite what he had expected to hear. 'Me, sir?'

He had been lying as low as he could, fearing punishment for his treatment of a prince of the royal blood and his father's honoured guest. When Dhon

Do had finally tracked him down behind the canteen tent, it had been for a quite different purpose: to suggest that Daniel should fly to London with Cromwell.

'You're the only one I know and trust who speaks English, Daniel,' Dhon Do said.

'There's Francis, sir.'

'He's not here. Cromwell and Khonol Le can only converse in English and if they want to plot, it will be more difficult if they know you can overhear every word.'

'They might just throw me over the side,' Daniel muttered.

'No. The crew will keep a close eye on you, and I've no doubts about their loyalty but, of course, they *don't* speak English.'

So Daniel agreed reluctantly – perhaps, he had to admit to himself at the prospect of another airship ride, not so reluctantly – to fly to London.

'Why's Conn . . . *Khonol* Le going to London anyway?' he said as they walked towards the landing field. Dhon Do had his arm around Daniel's shoulders again. Daniel was coming to realize just how much he enjoyed the feeling of security it gave him.

'She has friends at the Tower and she's worried about them. I can understand that.' Dhon Do gazed ahead. Khonol Le, Cromwell and his party waited at the foot of the steps in the shadow of the looming *Golden Hawk*. Then he noticed another group making their way towards the ship. 'Oh dear,' he said. They speeded up so as to reach the *Golden Hawk* at the same time as the others.

Cromwell had also seen the people approaching. His expression became carefully neutral as they came near.

'General C-Cromwell,' said the leading newcomer. 'It seems we have both been k-kidnapped by our hosts.'

Charles Stuart, first of that name, by grace of God King of England, Scotland, Ireland and (though the French would have contested the title) France, was a slender and graceful man with a mournful visage, and a drooping moustache and beard. His entourage stayed strictly in the background and let their master speak.

'I was invited here to survey the situation,' Cromwell said. 'I have done so and am sending a communication to Parliament.'

'Address my father properly!' A puffy-faced Prince Charles pushed his way to the front and his adolescent voice cracked with anger. 'You call him Your Majesty!'

Cromwell raised an eyebrow. 'Has the prince per-haps missed the point of the last three years?' He looked at Dhon Do. 'Have nothing to do with this man, sir. Do you think we wanted to go to war against our fellow countrymen? Time and again Parliament invited, requested, asked, *pleaded* reason from the king. Time and again he ignored us. Or lied to us. Or treated with foreign nations – heretics – against his own people whom God had given him as a sacred trust to govern and rule wisely. He raised taxes against the will of God and Parliament. He ransomed and extorted his own country, and befriended its enemies. You will have no joy trying to deal with this man.'

Prince Charles looked ready to fling himself at Cromwell.

'That will do, Charles,' said the king. He was a mild man but there was steel in his voice; he was used to obedience, in his household if not elsewhere in his country. He ignored Cromwell as if the man had never spoken and turned to Dhon Do. 'General, our son has expressed a wish to travel again in your sh-ship of the air. For some reason that entirely escapes us he found the first experience too b-brief.'

'That would hardly be appropriate,' Cromwell said.

'It would be very appropriate,' Dhon Do said. 'Your people have a lot to learn about our ways and where better to start than with the next generation? It's a simple trip to London and back. It will take a few hours, no more.' He was aware of Daniel tugging very gently on his coat but ignored it. 'Would that satisfy your curiosity, Prince Charles?'

'I think it would,' Charles said eagerly. 'Can—'

'London is in the hands of our enemies,' the king said. 'We are not sure we can approve of such a trip.' He gazed levelly at Cromwell. 'Let alone with such a fellow passenger.'

Dhon Do bowed. 'He would stay on the ship at all times and have the protection of my own men.'

The king continued to look doubtful.

'Father,' Charles said, 'if he was going to hand me over to Parliament he would already have done so!'

The king finally ceded the point with a slight nod. 'Travel in that infernal machine if you must, Charles.'

'Thank you, Father!'

The prince's enthusiasm was only slightly diminished when he learned that Daniel was coming too. Indeed, when the airship took off twenty minutes later none of the passengers could be said to be over-joyed with the arrangements.

Ten

The Tower

The throb of the engines vibrated in Daniel's body. He stood at the head of the ladder and gazed down the interior of the airship in awe.

He wondered if this was what Jonah had seen. It was like being inside a vast fish with massive ribs of metal. The hull, the body of the *Golden Hawk*, stretched away forever, lined by colossal, bulging bags the size of houses. He wondered what was in them. The engines' deep beat filled the space like the angry heartbeat of the whale.

There were Holekhor crewmen here, clustered in small groups around strange machines and presumably doing things that kept the ship flying. Daniel studied the activity in such wonder that for a moment he forgot his task. He had been told how the engines worked – something about smashing up coal until it was in tiny, tiny lumps, then burning it, which made bits of metal move. He hadn't understood it, and the men didn't look like they were smashing up anything. But he was sure what they were doing was very important.

He had pursued the object of his mission up the ladder and taken a step or two after her before being enthralled by the new sights and sounds. Now she was looking back at him with a scowl on her face.

'Are you following me?' Khonol Le said.

Daniel considered the range of possible answers for the one that would cause the least suspicion.

'No,' he said.

'So if I climb back down that ladder, you will stay up here?' she said.

Daniel considered again. Should he tell her that his father had specifically instructed him to make sure she didn't talk to Cromwell without his being present? He wasn't spying, he was just making sure they couldn't converse in English, their only common language.

'I might,' he said.

He heard a faint growl at the back of her throat. 'If you are not following me, why are you up here?' she said.

'I'm . . . exploring.'

'I thought you had been on this ship before?'

'We only flew from Oxford,' Daniel said, glad of the chance to tell the truth at last. 'I stayed down there.' He pointed down the ladder to the command gondola. Then a thought struck him. 'Why are *you* up here?'

'Why am I?' Khonol Le said with a half smile. 'Well, Young Master Explorer, I have something to show you. Come here.'

She walked off down the catwalk, then stopped

and turned round. 'Come on!' Suspiciously, Daniel followed her.

They came to an empty space as wide as the hull. A metal gantry hung from the ceiling, and fastened to it were rows of streamlined shapes that he recognized. Their wings were folded back for stowage. Beneath them he could see that the floor was a pair of double doors that could swing open.

'Do you know what those are?' Khonol Le said.

'They fly,' Daniel said. He held his arms out by way of illustration.

'These gliders are the secret of your father's success,' Khonol Le said. 'These are how he and his army invaded my country.'

Daniel frowned up at them. He already had the gist of his father's history. The war against Toskhes had become bogged down in a mass of trenches and machine guns and barbed wire, and a hideous loss of life. Dhon Do came from a mountainous region far to the south where gliding was a way of life, and on his first visit to the front lines he had seen the obvious answer. Go over, and attack from behind. The Hawk Battalion had been the result.

Daniel's attempts to get an explanation for how gliders actually worked had not been entirely success-ful, so . . .

'How do they work?' he said.

'How?' Khonol Le snorted. 'They float, boy, just like this ship.' Daniel had the feeling he was perhaps being fobbed off with the kind of simplistic answer that adults like to give children. On the other hand, for all he knew, they *did* just float. Khonol Le looked into the distance. 'I can remember the sky being black with these things.'

Somewhere a bell rang, and the pitch of the engines changed slightly. Daniel clutched at a support as the floor below him tilted. From up above him came the bellow of a mighty rushing wind, as if the whale were drawing breath. He looked up and could distinctly see a giant bag inflating like a bladder, its leathery folds filling out and straightening amongst the girders.

'They're taking in air. We'll be landing soon,' Khonol Le said. She didn't seem happy about it; her memories of the war back at home still had a hold on her. Daniel thought he should probably say something.

'I'm, um, sorry about your country,' he said respectfully. Khonol Le gaped.

'Sorry? *Sorry?* Little boy, you . . . you can't . . . you can't even begin to . . . *ah!*' She flapped a hand at him in vague dismissal, turned and walked away.

It took Daniel a moment or two to remember his mission and follow her.

Sorry! The brat was *sorry!*

Khonol Le stalked down the catwalk towards the midship gondola. *Well, what was he supposed to say?* a small part of her queried.

Oh, shut up, she snarled back. She clenched her fist and slammed it into the side of a gasbag. Gods, why couldn't this entire mass of light, highly inflammable gas explode and suddenly without any kind of transition she had the plan, firm and fixed in her mind.

She had to find Khromell, and quickly, before they landed. And she could hear the brat following her. She slid quickly down the ladder into the midship gondola, pausing only for a moment in the brief gap between hull and cabin roof. She peered out at the horizon and saw thick, dark clouds billowing. A typical early summer storm, still some way off but it would help. Perhaps Khromell's God was going to lend a hand in this. That would be an interesting irony.

Khromell and his officers were where she had left them, in the officers' wardroom, talking quietly amongst themselves. A polite distance from them, the young prince stood at a window, gazing down at the English landscape. Daniel would be ten, maybe twenty seconds behind her.

'General,' she said without apology as she entered without knocking, 'I need to talk to you privately and the boy must not hear us.'

Khromell frowned and glanced at the prince, who had perked up with interest.

'The other boy,' Khonol Le said impatiently, pointing up. 'We . . .' She had to think, and quickly. Khromell and the prince were enemies of each other; Dhon Do was an enemy of them both. Yes, the prince should be involved. 'We can stop Dhon Do's invasion, but first we have to take this ship and we don't have much time.'

Khromell thought for just a beat, then turned to

the prince. 'Your Highness,' he said, as casually as if they were old friends, 'perhaps you could talk to Master Daniel and distract him?'

The prince wore a look of cunning quite in advance of his years. 'And give you the advantage over our enemies, Master Cromwell?'

Khromell scowled. 'You will share in whatever advantages we may gain . . . sir.'

'Your word, sir?'

'My word,' Khromell agreed.

Charles grinned with no humour. 'Your word as a leader of the rebels against my royal father?'

Khromell clenched his teeth. 'My word as a Christian, sir.'

The prince's grin grew wider and nastier. 'Do you see how easy negotiation can be? Well, then, where is the little boy-troll?'

Daniel hurried down the ladder and stepped into the cabin, and Prince Charles pounced on him.

'Boy-troll! Is this not a splendid adventure? We're approaching London. We'll be there in five minutes. Come, let us watch it together.'

Daniel didn't even get the chance to break step. The prince had a friendly arm round his shoulders and was propelling him out of the cabin and on to the observation gallery before he could draw breath or protest. 'But . . .'

The gallery was a metal gangway connecting the command and midship gondolas, with waist-high railings on either side and a safety net that stretched the rest of the way up to the hull. It was quite secure, impossible to fall out of, but the gangway was patterned with hundreds of little holes and Daniel was horribly aware that he could see the ground through it.

'Do you see?' The prince was pointing ahead and down. 'I'll wager you've never set eyes on so large a place.'

Daniel probably could have broken Charles's grip around his shoulders. He knew he was the stronger boy. He also cringingly remembered the occasion on which he had proven that strength, and exactly how pleased his father had been about it. He consoled himself that Cromwell and Khonol Le could hardly plan anything in, what, five minutes? And if the prince was prepared to be reconciled . . .

'Yes,' he said weakly.

The Thames was a shining silver ribbon that snaked across the flat land below, and London was a dirty grey blot around it. Daniel saw the city's massive walls and within them a labyrinth of streets and thoroughfares, packed with moving people and horses and carts. No, he had never indeed seen so large a place. You could fit a hundred Branheaths into it.

'That's the abbey at Westminster,' Charles said, pointing at a very big church passing slowly below them. 'And the palaces of Westminster . . . Whitehall . . . do you see over there? St Paul's . . .'

The *Golden Hawk* was flying low and slow now, and ahead of them was a bridge across the river that was like a small town in itself, lined with buildings and with only a row of tiny arches to let the water through. A large pool of brown water was backed up before it and Daniel wrinkled his nose as the accumulated odours wafted upward. Perhaps a city could be *too* big, he thought. All those people, all those *horses* . . . Ugh.

Charles breathed deeply. 'Ah, the heady airs of the city,' he said. 'Look, there's the Tower. And your father's friends,' he added more thoughtfully.

When Daniel thought of the Tower, he imagined a vast edifice, a soaring structure that loomed over the city below it. In disappointing fact, the square, four-pointed building ahead was dwarfed by the tower of St Paul's that Charles had pointed out, half a mile away. However, it sat at the heart of a much larger complex of turret-studded walls and bastions beside the river, and that satisfied his vague ideas of what a decent fortress should look like. Just uphill from the Tower the land was clear, and parked there was another airship. The area was roped off and guarded by Holekhor soldiers against the gawking locals. Some of them ran when they saw the new ship approaching, others clustered closer and had to be pressed back.

Lines dropped from the *Golden Hawk* and were caught by Holekhor on the ground. The engines stopped and went into reverse, making the whole structure of the ship shake, and then they were at rest on terra firma, next to the other ship.

A door opened in the side of the cabin to the front of them and a ladder dropped down. Cromwell clambered down to the ground, followed by Khonol Le and Cromwell's officers.

Charles was frowning. 'Did you not have *business* to attend to, Master Cromwell?' he called. Cromwell looked up.

'I did, sir, and I still intend to. First I need to communicate with the garrison of the Tower and send a message to Parliament. I will be seeing you again.'

'We sincerely hope you will, General,' Charles said. He kept his eye on Khonol Le and Cromwell as they met with a group of Holekhor and Parliamentary soldiers who came running up to them. Cromwell spoke a few words, and then they all turned and walked down to the fortress. It looked much more forbidding from ground level: solid, towering walls within walls and a deep, foetid moat fed by the river. Yet, Daniel was struck suddenly with how redundant the whole place was, now that attackers could fly.

Cromwell's party walked down to a gatehouse on the near side of the moat, and then across a bridge. Another minute and they had passed into the fortress itself.

'Do you know, boy-troll, I might get off myself,' Charles mused. 'I could do with stretching my legs.'

Daniel considered asking him not to use that name. His elementary grasp of the nature of older boys told him he would probably not be successful. Instead a residual sense of duty to his king, and by unfortunate extension to his king's son, prompted him to say something else.

'You shouldn't,' he said.

Charles raised a very lazy eyebrow but his voice was cold. 'Do you tell a prince what he should not do?'

'My father's soldiers gave the Tower back to Parliament,' Daniel said through gritted teeth. 'The crew can protect you while you're on board but not down there. Down there they are your enemies.'

Charles pondered for a moment.

'You are very ugly but not stupid,' he said. 'Very well, we shall remain here.' He crossed his legs, stretched his hands out along the rail, and surveyed the world about him with a benevolent air, as if congratulating it on its good fortune of being observed by him.

A short, round man in civilian dress was approaching up the hill, followed by a pair of armed guards. He paused a safe distance away, just beyond the ring of Holekhor guards, and swept his hat off in a bow.

'Your Highness,' he called. 'I thought it was you. I am pleased to see you well and safe, though you are wise to remain on board.'

'We are pleased to be well and safe,' Charles called back. 'To whom are we giving the honour of being addressed?'

The man bowed again.

'George Monk, Your Highness. I had the honour of fighting in your royal father's service before my capture.'

'Of course we remember you, Master Monk,' Charles said, who clearly did not. 'You were taken at, ah . . .'

'It was my misfortune to be taken at Nantwich,' Monk agreed, 'and I have been held here ever since. I am not a wealthy man, sir, and the king was good enough to send me a most generous gift of money so that I could continue to live like a gentleman in my captivity. Naturally I wrote to thank him, but perhaps I could prevail upon you to pass on my thanks personally.'

'We shall most certainly do so,' Charles said affably.

Monk bowed a third time. 'Then I shall ask your permission to retire, sir, and hope that we meet again in happier circumstances.'

'As you say, Master Monk.'

Khonol Le hurried up through the inner bailey of the fortress. The colossal stonework, the rough cobbles beneath her feet, the atmosphere and the scents of the place were like coming home, but with every step she expected to see evidence of some atrocity. Bullet holes in the walls, a small line of graves topped by her clan's banner . . . Yet the place seemed strangely untouched. The natives went about their business as usual and the only sign of anything out of the ordinary was the number of Golekhi soldiers who patrolled along the ramparts. You could tell them from their English counterparts at a glance; poised against the backdrop of the sky in their capes and curved helmets, their forms stockier than the English, their rifles grasped continually at the ready.

Two Golekhi solders stood as sentries at the entrance to the armoury building. They blocked her way.

'And where are you going?' said the one on the left.

'Let me through,' Khonol Le said. 'I work here.'

'Then you'll have a pass, won't you?' said the other.

'I came here with General Khromell,' Khonol Le said impatiently.

'Never heard of him.'

'Look, can you at least—'

'Don't bother, sister,' said a voice behind her. 'They've appropriated the works. We're confined to quarters.'

Khonol Le turned even as the familiar scent of her dear brother flooded into her nostrils. 'De Fel! Thank the Gods!' She folded her arms around him in a massive hug and held him tight. They breathed in deep through their noses, each drawing in the scent of the other. He was a hand's breadth taller but she still thought of him as her little brother. 'When I heard Dhon Do had taken this place . . .'

'That was Dhon Do?' De Fel exclaimed.

'Didn't you know?' Khonol Le glared at the sentries, who simply smirked into the distance.

'This lot weren't telling us anything,' De Fel said angrily. 'I could see it was some general in charge, but . . .' His gaze fell on the hawk emblems on the sentries' helmets. 'Oh Gods, of course. The Hawks were his, weren't they?'

'It's not just the Hawks. England is getting the full treatment. The Domon'el is invading and he's sent the Conqueror and an entire army in to do his business. De Fel, was anyone . . . ?'

De Fel lowered his voice and she heard emotion

tremble behind the words. 'A couple tried to be heroes. H'ol Fo got a flesh wound in the arm; Se Oh lost her leg.'

'Oh, De Fel, I am sorry!' Se Oh was his wife.

'I keep . . . I keep telling myself it could be worse. But come back to quarters, sister, and we'll all tell our stories.'

'I know you all fought bravely,' Khonol Le said. She looked around the room – twenty men and women, most of them victims of the *last* Golekhi invasion. A pale Se Oh lay on a couch, De Fel holding her hand. Khonol Le was trying not to look at the stump. 'But we must proceed carefully now. This isn't like last time, when it didn't matter how many of us died because more would always rise up to take our places.'

'They didn't, though,' H'ol Fo muttered. His arm was in a sling and he rubbed it sullenly with his good hand.

'It's not our fault our leaders surrendered,' Khonol Le said. 'This time, we are the leaders and we will not surrender.'

'The English will,' De Fel snapped. A murmur of agreement ran around the room. He had already described the attack: soldiers dropping out of the sky, the airships circling overhead, the panicked English swarming all over the place and thwarting the attempts of her friends to put up even a half decent resistance. 'You're right, sister. If this has taught us one thing, it's that we're on our own. But why is that so bad? It's how we thought it would be when we set out. We thought we would have to conquer, set out our stakes, claim our land . . . True, we learned different. We learned there were a lot more natives than we had thought, and we needed customers, a market for our goods, so we made friends with them. Allies, even. But then, at the slightest setback, they fold!'

The murmur was louder now. No doubt about it, her friends were of one mind when it came to the reliability of their customers.

'They had never seen gliders or airships before,' Khonol Le said. 'Now they have, and they are swift learners. General Khromell is no happier with this than you are and he is *not* the kind of man to give up. Trust me on that. Furthermore, he is backed by a damn good, professional army. The soldiers out there –' she waved an arm at the window – 'are just time servers. Khromell is a man who can adapt and learn. And, he is going to help us capture one of the airships.'

She had to smile at the dumbstruck expressions around her.

'And what are we going to do with an airship?' Se Oh said. 'Just one, with no resupplies, against the Hawks' fleet?'

Instead of answering – she had to admit to herself that she enjoyed the attention – she turned her head slowly to look at each one of them and her gaze settled on Me Tor, her nephew, a quiet young man keeping his own counsel in the corner of the room.

'Dhon Do is the only Holekhor I know outside this room who speaks English,' she said. 'How do the Hawks communicate with the locals?'

De Fel answered; Me Tor was looking surprised that the question was directed at him.

'They do it through us,' he said.

'Good,' Khonol Le said. It was exactly what she wanted to hear. And she still hadn't looked away from Me Tor. 'Me Tor,' she said warmly. 'I'm pleased you survived.'

The young man looked suspiciously back at her. 'And I'm not complaining, aunt,' he said.

'How many Golekhi did you get with that rifle of yours during the invasion?'

Me Tor grinned. He didn't know where the conversation was going but he liked its drift already.

'Seventeen,' he said. And they all knew what lay behind the boast. It hadn't been seventeen conveniently motionless, high visibility targets, silhouetted against the skyline. Rain, fog, wind, sometimes no more than a dark patch against a dark sky . . . but still this farm boy from the midland plains had got seventeen of them. One for every year of his life. 'But I don't have my rifle with me. The soldiers impounded it.'

'If we got you one of the ones we make for the natives . . . do you think you could manage a couple more?' Khonol Le said.

Eleven

A Shot in the Back

Out in the fresh air of the bailey, an argument was going on. It was being conducted in two completely different languages and neither participant had a hope of understanding the other.

'Mistress Connolly!' Khromell called as she emerged with De Fel close behind. 'Perhaps you could translate for me. I am trying to explain to this man how grievously I have been insulted.'

They had worked out the act in the few minutes before landing. Just in case Dhon Do had secretly trained his men to speak English – and she wouldn't put it past him – they would play straight.

The man with whom the English general was arguing was a Golekhi centurion. He looked warily at her.

'Who are you?'

'Armsmistress Khonol Le,' she said. 'This is General Khromell, the second-in-command of the natives' army.'

'Is he?' The centurion didn't look impressed. 'As far as I can tell, he was ordering the cannon on the ramparts to be loaded and I can't permit that, general or not.' They both knew what a red-hot cannon ball could do to an airship. It seemed odd that the lifting gas, a component of water, could burn so nicely.

'He was saying to me as we flew in that he had been badly snubbed,' Khonol Le said.

'How so?' the centurion said suspiciously.

'A general of his rank should be given an armed salute, naturally. I did explain to him that his people weren't to know he was on board, but now that they do know . . . and surely Dhon Do told you to keep in with the locals?'

'Ah . . .' The centurion looked as if comprehension had dawned suddenly. 'Still, I don't know . . .'

'Should I also mention that the general has spent time as a personal guest of Dhon Do, and when we return to him later he won't be happy to hear that his guest was insulted?'

'Tell him he can have his salute,' the centurion said quickly. 'But tell him the loading of the guns will be closely supervized by my men to see that they are blanks, and they will be discharged over the river.'

Khonol Le passed this information on verbatim and Khromell gave his reply.

'The general is satisfied,' she said.

'I'll see the ship is informed,' the centurion promised.

'I've sent the message,' Khromell said as they walked back up the hill with his officers. 'Everything we want will be waiting for us if we can just get the ship there.'

'We will,' Khonol Le said. They reached the ladder and she paused to give Khromell and his men a chance to climb up first. Then she looked up at the sky. The storm she had spotted earlier was much closer, a solid mass of black cloud hanging over London.

She also saw that the two boys were still in the gallery. She wasn't sure what to do with them. The taller one, the prince, it would be best to keep out of danger. The smaller one . . .

Yes, the smaller one too. He was half Golekhi, and the son of her enemy, but that wasn't his fault. This wasn't his war and he might be useful as a hostage.

'You?' said the airship captain as she pulled herself into the gondola. 'I thought you were staying.'

'I work for General Khromell,' she said. 'He needs an interpreter.'

The captain looked hard at her for a moment, then nodded. 'I can see he would. I understand he's getting a salute?'

'He's a stickler for protocol.'

'Fair enough.' The captain turned to the task of getting the *Golden Hawk* into the air and Khonol Le retired quietly to the back of the cabin with the natives. 'Fire engines. Planes ten degrees up.'

'Ten degrees up, sir,' said the planesman as the engines rumbled into life. Khonol Le's gaze drilled into the back of his head. He wasn't much more than a boy, Me Tor's age, and to look at him with cultivated hate was the only way to hold back the pangs that came at the thought of a young death. But younger had died in Toskhes.

The boy turned a wheel and a dial fixed to the wall moved, to show the position of the ship's airfoils.

She looked around the gondola. The captain, the planesman, the helmsman and three others. Which meant eighteen other crew elsewhere on the ship.

'Have you noticed the thunderstorm?' Khonol Le said innocently. The captain's look was patronizing.

'Of course I've noticed,' he said. 'Don't worry, we can get up over it and never feel a thing. Rudder to midships.'

'Rudder to midships, sir,' said the helmsman. He was even younger. His voice had barely broken.

'Stand by to release lines . . . Release. Forward engines ten degrees down. Vent air bladders to fifty per cent. All engines to three-quarter thrust.'

The commands were all passed on by telegraph. The second in command would pull on a handle and another dial would turn to show 'ten degrees' or 'three quarters ahead', as a bell rang up in the envelope. As Khonol Le had suspected, there was no need for anyone not in the gondola to know who had given the orders.

The *Golden Hawk* was moving forward and tilted upwards. The Tower slid slowly down and out of sight and Khonol Le suddenly saw how the plan might go wrong.

'Now,' she murmured to herself. '*Now!*'

The salute needed to start. Those cannon needed to boom out from the Tower walls, because how else could the sniping shots from Me Tor – who even now should be drawing a bead on that frighteningly young helmsman – go unheard?

A cannon roared out its salute ahead of them and a cloud of white smoke billowed up from the ramparts. Then another, and another.

But it was too late. The Tower was below the sills of the windows and her nephew would no longer have a clean shot.

At the third salute there was a small tinkle of glass and a hole appeared in the front window. The helmsman yelped and jumped back, wringing his hand. A spoke had vanished from the wheel. He turned to the captain, his mouth opening.

Khonol Le punched him, hard, on the jaw. 'Now, General!' she shouted. One of the crew was already jumping forward to grab her, and she twisted down under him.

'Stop!' Cromwell shouted. The command in English didn't get their attention but the shout at least made them look his way. He and his entourage had produced pistols from under their cloaks and they had the crew covered. The guns were native flintlocks, not Holekhor revolvers, but the effect was the same. The crew froze.

Khonol Le jumped to take the steering wheel and was surprised by the force it exerted in her hands. The ship badly wanted to go in some other direction, presumably away from the wind. It was a novel experience but she could handle it. 'All of you, along the wall there.' She looked down at the helmsman, who lay completely still, but was breathing. 'Drag him over there with you.'

The captain was pale. 'Do ... do your friends

know what would happen if one of those things they're waving about set off the gas?'

'Yes,' Khonol Le said, which was an outright lie. Khromell had no idea at all about the properties of lifting gas and she was going to keep it that way. An airshipman's natural fear of all things flammable had been why she had told Khromell to arm himself with native weapons rather than Holekhor ones. A flintlock sprayed sparks and flames in all directions when it was fired.

She looked down at the Tower. The salute continued and, as far as she could see, no one had noticed anything. The occupation garrison would radio to Dhon Do that the ship had taken off as planned. She turned the wheel to take them over London, westwards. It would have been expected on the ground and it was where she wanted to go anyway.

She felt a strange vibration through the wheel and through the soles of her feet. Somehow she sensed that it wasn't right, the ship was fighting back.

'Signal forward engines to straight ahead,' the captain said. 'They're still trying to push us up.'

Khonol Le paused just a beat, then reached for the telegraph and pushed the lever forward. A bell rang, the pitch of the engines changed and the vibration went.

'What's the point of stealing this ship?' the captain said. 'You don't know how to fly it and there's no fuel, or weapons, except back at Povse'okh.'

'Let us worry about that,' she said. 'Captain, I'm

handing back to you. We still need to get above that storm. The slightest sign of—'

'There won't be,' the captain said. He stepped forward and took the wheel himself. 'You, take the planes. You, signal engines . . .'

Within moments the *Golden Hawk* was back in professional hands and flying smoothly, but under Khonol Le's control. She smiled. It was a pleasant feeling to remember, after years of fighting the Golekhi, that bloodless victories were possible after all. She spoke in English. 'General, you had better open up the arms locker. There is the rest of the crew to attend to. I'll promise them their lives if they surrender.'

'That is acceptable,' Khromell agreed.

A flicker of lightning flashed in the massing clouds outside.

Prince Charles was pacing up and down the gallery. London was far below and the wind was making his hair stream. 'If they were going to do anything they should have done it,' he muttered.

'What should they have done?' Daniel said. Charles glared at him.

'Don't concern yourself with the affairs of princes, boy-troll.'

Daniel bridled, prince or no prince. 'I'm getting tired of you calling me—'

The door to the command gondola opened. Cromwell stood there.

'We have taken the ship,' he said. 'Thank you for your help, Your Highness.'

Charles rubbed his hands together and turned a gleeful face to Daniel. 'Thank *you*, Master Cromwell. Now what do we do? Are we flying to attack Dhon Do?'

Daniel stared at Cromwell. Surely Cromwell hadn't just said those words? Surely this airship, flying so magically above the ground, this pride of the mighty Holekhor – surely it couldn't have tumbled just like that? He looked from prince to Cromwell to prince again, the one handsome and beaming, the other stern and ugly.

'We are flying to Windsor, sir,' Cromwell said.

'Windsor?' The smile vanished from Charles's face. 'What is at Windsor?'

'A secure castle garrisoned by Parliament,' said Cromwell, 'where you and Master Daniel will be kept until the outcome of this affair is known.'

'You said I would share the benefits!' Charles shouted.

'An England free of the Hollykor is to everyone's benefit,' Cromwell said. Two of his officers had appeared behind him, each with faces as grim as the pistols in their hands. The pistols weren't quite aimed at the two boys, but their presence was felt. 'I mean neither of you any harm. My quarrel is with your respective fathers, not with yourselves, but I intend to see England free of the menace that both men represent. Now, please, walk ahead of these two to the cabin.'

Charles paused a beat, then spun with a face like thunder and marched back to the midship gondola. 'Apparently we are on the same side after all, boy-troll,' he muttered.

In the cabin Daniel nervously took a seat, his gaze never leaving the two men, or rather, the guns they carried. Charles paced up and down in front of them.

'You would do better to sit down, prince,' one of them said. Charles glared at him.

'We choose to stand.' He looked back at Daniel. '*We* choose to stand,' he said more clearly. Daniel got the hint and chose to ignore it. He crossed his arms and snuggled down more firmly in his seat.

'I see. I see.' Charles turned away. 'Traitors everywhere I look. On the one hand oath-breaking so-called gentlemen who call themselves Christians, and on the other . . . *boy-trolls*. Well, until I can find a way of flying away from this infernal machine on my own I have no choice but to bide my time.' He settled down in a chair in the corner of the cabin and looked moodily out at the sky.

Daniel looked at him, then back at the guards. He glanced up at the ceiling, then down at the guards again. There was a rushing in his ears and he seemed to see himself from far off. It was a completely different red-haired boy who stood up and walked slowly over to the guards.

'I . . . I need to go,' he said timidly. It was not so far from the truth.

'Oh, Christ help us,' Charles muttered.

One of the men laughed. 'So go in the corner.'

'The *other* corner,' said Charles behind him.

'But,' Daniel said, and clenched his hands, 'I need . . .' And with all his strength he sank his balled fists into the midriffs of the two men. They doubled over and Daniel grabbed each by the hair, then brought their heads together with a loud crack. They collapsed and lay groaning.

Daniel stepped slowly away and stared down at them. Charles was looking at him as if he had just grown wings. Neither boy could quite believe what Daniel had just done.

'That one's still moving,' the prince said quietly. Daniel looked down at the twitching form, but suddenly he didn't have the heart to commit any more violence. He had always known he was strong. He had never before used that strength unprovoked, and *never* against a fully grown man.

'We can fly away from here, like you said,' he said. 'There are things up there.' He jerked a thumb up the ladder. 'Khonol Le told me about them.'

'Can you make them work? We are rather a long way up.'

Daniel shrugged. 'She said they float. We can work it out.'

Charles grinned and rubbed his hands again. 'When I am King, I will dub you Sir Boy-Troll. I hadn't expected this loyalty. Well, come on!' He set foot on the ladder and began to climb.

'I've always supported the king,' Daniel said as he began to follow. 'I was at Edgehill—'

'Bastards!' wheezed a voice behind them. Daniel glanced back over his shoulder and the world seemed to slow down. The man had his gun out and the dark hole of its barrel filled Daniel's vision. He thought he should shout a warning to Charles. He began to draw a breath, put out a hand to push Charles out of danger. And then there was a flash and a deafening roar filled the cabin, a roar that seemed to linger for ever as time slowed down and something colossal punched into his body. He felt his fingers loosen their grip on the ladder. He felt himself falling slowly away, falling and falling, until he was sure he must have hit the floor by now, but all he could see was a horrified Charles, so far above him and receding by waves into the darkness.

He didn't feel the crack his head made against the deck.

Khonol Le threw the door open and barged into the cabin, followed closely by Khromell. 'What happened?' And then her gaze followed everyone else's down to the floor and the still form lying there in a pool of blood. The prince crouched over him, almost in tears.

'Who shot him?' Khromell demanded. One of his men, pale faced, opened his mouth and the general struck him. 'We do not fight children!' he bellowed.

'Apparently you do,' Khonol Le said. She crouched down and touched a finger to Daniel's neck. The pulse was irregular but not faint. He was un-conscious, his face white and his breathing ragged. Blood leaked out from beneath him in two small pools. He had hit his head when he fell, but that wasn't the wound that worried her. She pulled back gingerly on his tunic. He had been shot in the back and there was no exit wound.

'He knocked us out, sir,' the man protested, before realizing this was probably not the wisest admission to make. Contempt shone out of Khromell's eyes.

'He knocked you out? A small boy knocked out two grown men?'

'Sir, he was escaping!'

'*Escaping?*' Khromell shouted. 'To where could he possibly escape?'

'I heard him say there were flying machines on board.'

'The gliders?' Khonol Le exclaimed. She had a sudden memory of this same boy, the one lying and possibly dying in front of her, marvelling as only a boy could at the technological marvels of Dhon Do's invasion machines. She shook her head and muttered in the One Tongue. 'You idiot child, you have no idea . . .'

'The boy's dead,' Khromell said in a matter-of-fact tone.

'He is not!' Charles knelt by Daniel, supporting his head in his hands. His eyes pleaded with Khonol Le. 'He's still breathing!'

'We are a long way from a surgeon,' Khromell said. 'There will be shock and infection. He isn't long for this world.'

Khonol Le was still examining him. The ball had caught him in the left shoulder but as far as she could see, it hadn't hit a bone or, to judge from his breathing, a lung. All the damage had been caused by the shock of the shot. She probed his skin gently with her fingers and thought she could feel the ball inside him, just beneath his collarbone.

'He has a Holekhor's body,' she said. 'He's strong. I need a knife.'

One of the men handed her a dagger. It had obviously been used to cut up his last meal and still had traces of food on the blade. If the ball didn't kill the boy, this would.

'There must be a galley on board,' she said. 'Fetch boiling water.'

'He doesn't need a drink!' Charles said. She ignored him.

'First he needs to stop bleeding. Pass me that box, there.' She gestured at the first aid box that hung on a wall. It wasn't exactly a surgery but she wasn't entirely clueless when it came to treating bullet wounds. This one wound would soon empty the box of its bandages and disinfectants but it was a start.

Khromell nodded for one of his men, the one who had fired, to help her.

'Did you see how the crew reacted when they heard the shot?' he said as she began to cut away Daniel's tunic. 'These aren't soldiers, they're old women. One loud bang and they cower as if the world were ending.'

Khonol Le shuddered and turned to her task.

Twelve

Golden Hawk Down

Dhon Do filled his lungs and bellowed, '*Halt!*'

It was his best parade-ground voice and it worked. The small convoy drew to a halt and the wagon at its head shuddered and clanked, giving off a gout of steam in a loud hiss.

The procession had been making its way down a row between tents. The soldiers who were walking behind the wagon looked suitably sheepish, but Dhon Do wasn't concentrating on them. He glared up at the two civilians in the cab but his tone was mild.

'Do you know these people, Por De?'

'No, sir,' said Por De. The decurion's voice trembled with suppressed rage. Por De stood behind Dhon Do and helped glare.

The two civilian men in the cab, sat behind the driver, seemed singularly unimpressed. They were much the same age as Por De, in their early or mid twenties, and they wore fine civilian dress in what was no doubt the latest style from the capital. Their boots were polished and shiny, with silver tassels hanging from the back. Their cloaks were lined with fur and cut in a graceful curve so that they flowed behind when the men walked. And most important of all – the reason why they were here, wasting Dhon Do's time – was the shining silver bracelet that each wore on his arm.

Por De wore a similar bracelet. He and these two fools came from High Families. If Por De's family had outranked theirs – if his was older, if his line was better established – then he could have just told them to turn round and leave. As it was, by the esoteric arcana of the aristocracy that was a closed book to Dhon Do, they outranked him. All Por De could do was call on the camp's highest authority – Dhon Do.

'You must be the Conqueror,' said the older noble. He swung down from the cab and held out his hands. His tone was bored and it was scarcely a cordial greeting. Dhon Do got the feeling he was meant to be honoured at being greeted. Conqueror or not, he didn't have a bracelet. He wasn't High.

What he *did* have was a warrant from the Domon'el commanding him to take and hold all lands surrounding Povse'okh in the New World and any territories that adjoined to them, and that outranked everyone. So Dhon Do ignored the hands and let his gaze rove slowly back along the convoy.

'And where do you think you're going?' he said.

'This?' The man waved an indolent hand. 'My brother and I thought we'd spend a couple of days hunting, here in the New World that you have so kindly annexed for us.'

'*Hunting!*' Por De exploded. Dhon Do waved him down without turning round.

'That explains what *you* are doing here,' he said. 'You haven't explained the presence of –' he did a quick, rough count – 'about twenty of my men and a steam transporter belonging to the Might.'

The man looked wary and a hint of belligerence entered his tone. 'I don't believe I have to explain anything,' he said, and the way he stood angled the silver bracelet slightly forward. Dhon Do had wondered how long it would be before he hid behind his nobility. 'Quite clearly, my brother and I alone can't carry our guns, our tents, our supplies . . .'

'It is customary to ask,' Dhon Do said.

The man ostentatiously yawned, patting his mouth twice, then patted his bracelet.

'All the authorization we could possibly need. The commoners do as they're told, Dhon Do. Don't you remember?'

Dhon Do could sense Por De tensing to deliver a furious rebuke.

'Of course,' he said. 'We all exist to serve the Domon'el.'

'Well, naturally . . .'

Dhon Do walked up to the nearest soldier. 'What were you doing before these gentlemen commandeered your services?'

The man swallowed. 'Perimeter duties, sir.'

'I see.' Dhon Do nodded and walked up to the next. 'And you?'

'Same, sir.'

There were a lot of men on perimeter duties. Now the natives knew he was here, Dhon Do had ordered the guard doubled and minefields laid around the whole camp.

'And didn't you point out that you had more important duties?' he said.

'Well, yes, sir, but . . .' The man's tongue seemed to seize. He didn't want to disobey his general, but the instinct to do as the nobility told him was even stronger. Dhon Do turned slowly back to the two nobles.

'This camp is on full alert, and you stroll in and set about compromising our defences by taking away my men?'

For the first time the man looked vaguely contrite. 'Well, if we'd known . . .'

'I don't recall your asking,' Dhon Do said. 'This camp is part of the Realm. You have compromised the security of the Realm.'

Now the younger noble looked alarmed.

'Oh, come on.' The older one looked scornful. 'That's a fine argument for lawyers, no more. Now, I don't mean to be brusque—'

Dhon Do let his anger finally begin to show. 'Brusqueness I can forgive,' he said in sharp, clipped tones. 'Even rudeness, coming from people who were clearly not brought up to show manners and obligations that come with rank. But what I cannot forgive, gentlemen, is your purloining my soldiers to carry your guns. Your tents. Your . . . *picnic hampers*. My men are veterans of Toskhes and they have much better things to do than carry your packed lunches.'

'Well, of *course* they're veterans,' said the older

one, as though speaking to a child. 'That's why we trust them to carry our weapons. We have some expensive hardware with us and we don't want just anyone handling it. Credit us with some intelligence, Dhon Do.'

He could see he wasn't getting through. Bored, spoiled sons of the High Families; it just wouldn't occur to these creatures that there were places and things they could not do. To them, the annexation of this island in the New World was a given fact; therefore, there was absolutely no reason why they couldn't go hunting here if they so fancied. And they were High, which gave them every right to conscript commoners to carry their luggage. Even battle-hardened veterans of the Toskhes Campaign; even men who had fought for their country and risked their lives under the fire of Toskheshi machine guns. So they had turned up through the gate, without warning, and simply set about commandeering men left, right and centre to act as their porters. Every eye in the camp had been on their little caravan as they sauntered out into the New World, but it had taken Por De to do something about it.

Dhon Do was pleased with his aide, very pleased indeed. Por De might well have been putting his own High rank on the line for this.

'Your weapons,' Dhon Do said thoughtfully. 'Of course.' He walked over to the wagon's trailer and picked up a hunting rifle. It was very well made, with ornate silver inlay down the walnut grip, aromatic with gun oil and polish. He worked the bolt, squinted down the barrel. 'Nice workmanship. Exquisite.' He hefted the gun in one hand. 'Finely balanced. An excellent piece.'

'It cost me one hundred pledges,' said the older one. 'Do take care of it, there's a good chap.'

'What do you think, Decurion?' said Dhon Do. 'How do they compare to military issue?'

Por De took his cue and picked up another of the rifles. The nobles rolled their eyes, letting the commoners play their little game. They were secure in the protection of their bracelets.

'A bit lightweight, sir,' Por De said. 'It wouldn't last five minutes in the trenches. One tiny bit of grit and the whole mechanism would seize.'

'Which is precisely why it's going nowhere near the trenches, and not even the tiniest bit of grit will get into the mechanism,' said the gun's owner.

'But worth a bit,' Dhon Do said thoughtfully, 'as our guest has just pointed out.'

'Must be a thousand pledges worth here, sir,' Por De agreed. 'In total.'

'Hmm-hm.' Dhon Do again scanned the convoy slowly. The eyes of every man were on him. 'Bearing in mind the average wage of a soldier nowadays, and the time that has been wasted . . . I would say our friends here have cost the Might somewhere in the region of . . . say, a round one thousand pledges.'

'I would entirely concur, sir,' said Por De. 'What a fortunate coincidence.'

Dhon Do beamed. 'Excellent!' He threw his rifle to the nearest soldier, who had to drop the package he was holding to catch it. There was a tinkle of fine china breaking. 'Have this lot taken to the armoury – strip them of all that useless fancy finishing, it will just get in the way – and we'll say no more about it.'

'Now see here!' The older noble stepped forward, and three of Dhon Do's men immediately moved into his way. They would be ordered around, but they would not let anyone physically assault their general.

'Stand down,' Dhon Do said gently, and reluctantly they moved aside. 'Decurion, you have your orders. This camp is under military law and you may take whatever measures are deemed necessary with any civilians who interfere with its operation, up to and including shooting them if necessary. Detail some men to take these guns to the armoury. As for yourself, confine these gentlemen, under armed guard but with all courtesies due to their rank, and escort them back to the gate on the next out-tide. They are hereby barred from re-entry to the New World. That's all.'

He checked his pocket watch. 'When you're done, meet me back at my tent at third quarter and we'll catch up on the paperwork. In the meantime, I need to see our new chaplain.'

'General!' The chaplain rose to greet Dhon Do as he pushed his way past the tent flap. 'This is an honour. Please, come in. My name is Re Nokh.'

'It's a pleasure.' They crossed hands, and Dhon Do sat in the chair that Re Nokh indicated. He glanced casually around the tent, where green canvas

and the bright burning yellow of the light bulb combined into a sickly, fuggy miasma. Icons of the deities
whom the chaplain was licensed to serve were hung on
the walls and a small altar stood to one side, flanked by
dark, heavy copies of *Confirmed Divinities* and the
Sacred Tellings on their lecterns. It had occurred to
him, and often been pointed out, that as a successful
general and conqueror, he could reasonably expect
his own name one day to appear posthumously in the
former volume. But he remembered Francis's
admonition that the Lord God was a jealous God, not
to mention the priest's gleefully favourite story of the
fate of King Herod Agrippa when that Biblical
monarch claimed divinity. It involved, so he recalled,
maggots.

'I'm flattered that you asked to see me, sir,' Re
Nokh said as he sat down behind his desk. He had a
long, jowly face, but also a pair of keen, grey eyes. 'To
tell the truth, my superiors have asked that I gain an
interview with you anyway.'

'Really?' Dhon Do had wondered when this would
come. 'For what reason?'

'Well.' Re Nokh cleared his throat. 'Perhaps we
should concentrate on your reason for seeing me.'

'No, I insist,' Dhon Do said. He wanted to get it
over with. Re Nokh looked unhappy.

'Very well, sir. They question your, ahem, lack of
activity.'

'I also question this, ahem, lack of activity, as I am
not aware of it,' Dhon Do said. 'I have in this camp the
king of one of the native factions, and a senior general

of the other faction is now communicating with his superiors in the native capital. I am confident of a swift surrender to the force of the Might, with nary a shot fired. So perhaps you would explain this alleged lack of activity?'

The chaplain looked *very* unhappy. 'I am sorry. My superiors have said that, ahem, it seems you are sitting here on a hilltop and doing very little.'

'A misconception that I am sure you will now be more than willing to clarify to them.'

'You have explained your actions with regard to the politics of this land – not that you need to explain anything to me at all, of course – but there is more. They want this land claimed for the Congregation. There is little work being made in that direction.'

'Oh, send in the missionaries by all means,' Dhon Do said casually. 'Let 'em walk into the middle of the natives' Civil War and be slaughtered. It might be more useful, however, if they wait until I have established peace. As I am sure you will point out to them.'

This conversation, he decided, had gone on long enough. He was the general; he was the Conqueror. This was his camp, and here he was justifying his actions to a junior clergyman. It was time to change that. He sat back and crossed one leg over the other. 'And now, my reason for seeing you,' he said. 'Simply an administrative matter.'

Re Nokh looked surprised at having his part of the conversation dismissed so abruptly, but he put on a smile. 'How can I help?'

'You register the births of soldiers' children when you conduct Giftings, do you not?'

'It's one of my more pleasant duties, yes.'

'Could you register a child without Gifting?'

'They are two separate legal processes, so yes, certainly.'

'Then I would like to register my son as my legal heir,' Dhon Do said.

'But you do not want him Gifted?' Re Nokh said with a frown. It was an item of faith that children were born without souls. The soul was gifted to them by the Pantheon through the medium of a priest. Thereafter the Pantheon kept a permanent lien on that soul, and come the Great Sorting, they might or might not choose to receive that soul into Paradise.

'No need,' Dhon Do said. 'The native god gifts souls without being asked.'

'How quaint,' Re Nokh murmured.

'Now, he's already been named and registered according to the law of the natives, but I want him registered according to Holekhor law and custom as well.'

The chaplain looked nonplussed. 'How on earth does native law come into this?'

'Because he's a native,' Dhon Do said.

'You have a native son, General?'

'The boy who lives in my tent,' Dhon Do said impatiently. 'Twelve years old, so high, only boy in camp. You must have seen him around.'

'Ah, of course. And he's your . . .'

'Son!' Dhon Do snapped. 'Why else would I keep a boy in my tent?'

The chaplain looked as if he were very aware there was a right and a wrong answer to that question, but it was the right one that emerged from his mouth.

'Why else?' he agreed. 'And you want to adopt him. Well, that's quite in order.' He pulled open a drawer in his desk and rustled some papers around before drawing out a form. 'It's not the first time a soldier has adopted a child from a conquered land so there is certainly precedent, and as you're no doubt aware, the General Meeting of the Congregation in the fifth year of the reign decreed that natives of the New World who showed, and I quote, "a sufficient sense of the Divine" could be adopted as Holekhor . . . so I have to ask, does he in your opinion show a sufficient sense of the Divine?'

'He was raised by a priest and I know he believes in his god.'

Re Nokh beamed. 'Then there seems to be no obstacle. Of course, I need to examine him myself to give a formal certificate of . . .' He trailed off under Dhon Do's glare, then said hurriedly, 'That is, I *should* need to if this were one of the men making the adoption, but the word of a man of your rank is quite sufficient. So.' He took out his pen and positioned it expectantly over the first box on the form. 'The young man's name?'

'Daniel Matthews.'

'Ah.' The chaplain's nib still hovered. 'I can write that phonetically if you say it more slowly, but it might be worth giving the young man a proper Holekhor name as well.'

'His native name is a good one.'

'Have you considered, um, Dhon Do the Younger?'

'Daniel Matthews,' Dhon Do said again, distinctly. The chaplain sighed.

'Very well, General, if you could just repeat that more slowly . . . ?'

Dhon Do said the name for a third time and Re Nokh made as good an imitation of it as he could.

'Now, I will need to know his date of birth . . .'

Dhon Do had already worked that out, and had gone over his calculations several times to make sure he had the calendars of the Old and New Worlds correctly aligned. The sixth of April in the year of our Lord 1633 was . . . 'The fifty-third of Fellen in the tenth year of the reign.'

The chaplain scribbled more confidently. 'Good, good. And of course the names of his gods.' He bit his tongue and glanced up again at Dhon Do. 'God,' he said, enunciating the singular with distaste.

'God.'

The chaplain waited for a polite moment. 'Yes?'

'God,' Dhon Do said again.

'A-ha.' The chaplain laid down his pen and folded his hands in front of him. 'I did *say* "God", General. I need the god's *name*.'

'The name of his god,' Dhon Do said, 'is God.'

'That is not a name,' Re Nokh said, as if speaking to a child.

'It is here,' said Dhon Do, responding in kind.

'But it's like calling a cat Cat!'

'It avoids ambiguity.'

Re Nokh, caught on the dilemma of facing the indignation of the Congregation at some time in the future, or the wrath of his general here and now, bowed to the latter. He scribbled the one name across the boxes allowed for a child's guardian deities, though the stiff set of his back shrieked a formal protest. 'And last of all,' he said, 'the child's parents.'

'I'm the father, of course. His mother was a native woman named . . .' Dhon Do slowed down again so that the chaplain could spell out the syllables. 'Anne . . . Matthews . . . resident in . . . Bran . . . heath . . . who is now deceased.'

'That will suffice,' the chaplain said when he was finished. He carried on talking as he put the day's date and his own signature at the bottom. 'Since you're adopting him we hardly need the name of his native father.'

Dhon Do shook his head. 'He doesn't have a native father,' he said. 'I am his father.'

'Of course you are, General, of course you are,' Re Nokh said. His smile was kind but not a little condescending. 'His native father is an irrelevance, a—'

Dhon Do leaned over the desktop. 'I am the boy's father in every sense of the word,' he said. 'I slept with his mother. She conceived him with me. Would you like me to describe the occasion for you?'

'A-ha,' Re Nokh said once more. Then again,

'A-ha.' His smile was wobbly. 'General, that is just . . . just not possible.'

'I thought so, once, but one look at the boy tells you he's Holekhor.'

'Perhaps . . .' The chaplain looked as if he were about to give wise advice but it had suddenly dried in his mouth.

'Go on,' Dhon Do said, very low, very dangerous.

'I was about to say that . . . um . . .' The chaplain mopped his brow. 'A much more likely and, I think you will find, convincing hypothesis . . .'

'Hmm?'

'Well, clearly the mother . . .' The chaplain swallowed. 'The mother was attracted to you, to a Holekhor male, a man doubtless of great virility in his younger days and . . .'

Dhon Do growled at the back of his throat and the chaplain hurried on.

'Then perhaps she was, um, also . . .'

Dhon Do's gaze was friendly as a firing squad.

'Also,' the chaplain squeaked, 'at the same time attracted to a *native* male who, um, perhaps *resembled* a Holekhor, and, um, *he* in fact is the fa—'

'What kind of slut do you think I would want to marry?' Dhon Do roared.

The tactical impossibility of giving an honest answer to that question finally gave the chaplain courage.

'Look!' he said. It came out shrill: he cleared his throat and tried again. 'Look.' He jumped up and crossed to the *Sacred Tellings*. He hauled the volume open with practised ease. 'Do I have to remind you of the Great Blessing as recounted in the First Telling? "And the holy ones did gather before them on the plain the blessed children and they said unto them, *To you, our dearest beloved, do we give this land; know that* ye *are our offspring; yea,* ye *are* Holekhor, *the blessed children of the gods; to yourselves only shall ye be true—*" '

Dhon Do finished it for him. ' "Only to one another shall ye bear children and thy children shall themselves be called Holekhor."'

Re Nokh slammed the *Sacred Tellings* closed. 'I have to warn the general,' he said, still flustered, 'that he would be best advised not to try and out-quote an ordained member of—'

Dhon Do pushed himself to his feet. 'The last man to warn me not to try and out-quote him was a masterful general and a very dangerous man,' he said. 'You are chaplain to a military camp and I have stated facts that it would be best for you to accept.'

The chaplain backed off slightly as he considered that wisdom. 'General, I am your loyal servant and will obey your orders to the best of my ability, but I have to warn you that more senior members of the Congregation will not. Do not, I beg you, sir, go about announcing that Holekhor can breed successfully with the natives. It is not only impossible but it will lay you open to charges of heresy, and even you would not be immune.'

Dhon Do glared at him for a moment longer. 'I will take your advice in the spirit it is intended,' he said. 'The contention of the boy's paternity aside, is he now my legal heir?'

Re Nokh breathed a small sigh now that they were heading back to more mutual ground. 'Once the paperwork is filed, General, yes.'

'It seems suspiciously easy.'

'Well, yes, if you were adopting the child of two other Holekhor then there would be more to it, but as the boy has never before been registered and you are, um, prepared to be acknowledged as his father . . .' The chaplain glanced cautiously at Dhon Do but his choice of words was sufficiently neutral for the general's taste. '. . . then he is a citizen of Golekh and a loyal subject of the Domon'el. You legally have a son and you can make what provision you like for him in your will.'

'That is satisfactory,' Dhon Do said. He bowed. 'Thank you, sir.'

He stood to leave, and then half-turned back because the chaplain spoke up again. 'General, I have often wondered: why exactly did you adopt the native religion on your earlier stay here?'

Dhon Do paused. There were three particular reasons.

One was that the religion was shared by his closest friend and the woman he had fallen in love with.

The second was that he had gone into the New World full of the assurances of the Congregation that the natives were no more than savages. The kindness and wisdom of Francis, the love of Anne, his friendly adoption by the whole village had plainly taught him that they were not. On the one hand he had dogma from people who had never seen the thing they were talking about, and on the other, fact. Fact won, and thereafter he had always been inclined to doubt the Congregation's assurances on any topic.

However, he knew full well that what he said would be reported back to Re Nokh's superiors. The first reason was subjective and they would not like the second at all. So he gave the third.

'The god of the natives is a commander,' he said. 'He doesn't discuss things in committee. He says, and it is. When he made this world, he just said "Let there be light". He's a military man's god.'

'I see.' The chaplain gave a weak smile. 'I was just curious. But the Pantheon also ordains the affairs of men.'

'Eventually,' Dhon Do said. 'And once they have ordained, they enforce. They smooth over the rough patches, and harmony is imposed upon everyone.'

'Is that such a bad thing?' Re Nokh said mildly. Dhon Do snorted.

'You're talking to the Conqueror of Toskhes, Chaplain. I had to occupy an unfriendly country and bring the people into line. I know that enforcing harmony is at best a staging point on the way to peace. Ultimately you must work within the hearts of men. If there's no peace in there, there will never be lasting peace outside.'

'Are you saying this is what the native god does? I understood the natives were having a civil war over their religion.'

This was a fact for Dhon Do to file away: Re Nokh was remarkably well informed.

'That is one of their causes,' he said. 'No, as a native priest once explained it to me, the god of this land knows full well that men do not live up to his ideals. He wants perfection but he expects otherwise, and he uses what he has to make something better. Now, please excuse me, I have business elsewhere.'

'One last question, sir,' said Re Nokh as Dhon Do turned to go. 'Do you intend to make the boy your heir in everything?'

'Everything,' Dhon Do confirmed.

'Because that will make him . . .'

'Overlord after me. I know,' Dhon Do said, and left.

There was a spring in his step and he rubbed his hands together, overcome with a sudden feeling of well-being. Things were looking good. He had brought his army through into England; he had, he felt, responded to the unexpected fact of the natives' civil war quite well, and set up communication with both sides; and he now legally had a son. Yes, life could be much worse.

Dhon Do returned to his tent to the news that *Golden Hawk* was missing.

Dhon Do yanked aside the flap to the radio tent and bore down on the hapless operator. 'Report!'

The young man stammered and he had to stop himself shaking the idiot. *Tell me where my son is!* 'It was a broken transmission, sir. They reported, um, a thunderstorm, strong southerly winds . . . and then a distress call, and then they went off the air.'

Dhon Do turned to Por De. 'And the Tower?' he said.

'The Tower reports she took off and headed west as planned,' his aide said. 'They confirm there was a thunderstorm brewing.'

'*Forzh.*' Dhon Do strode back outside and glared at the bulk of *Avenging Cloud*, the third and last of the airships he had at his command in the New World. Big as the gate between worlds was, it was not much wider than an airship and getting them through was a fiddly business. He had brought three through in one piece, and the rest of the fleet had followed in parts. Putting them all back together would take too long, much too long.

'Send my compliments to Colonel Khre Deb,' he said. '*Conqueror's Talons* will take off from the Tower immediately and fly along *Golden Hawk*'s intended course. Meanwhile *Avenging Cloud* will take off from here and fly five degrees north of that course.' Southerly winds, they had said. 'I want both ships up within five minutes. Then find the nearest intact ship on the other side and bring it through as quickly as you can to join the search, five degrees north of *Avenging Cloud*. And so on, until we find them.'

'Yes, sir.' Por De saluted. 'Sir, I . . .'

'If you offer the slightest hint of condolences, you're sacked,' Dhon Do growled. Por De saluted again and quickly withdrew.

* * *

'*Quick, mop his brow!*'

'*Sir, I just did.*'

'*Mop his brow, I say!*'

A sigh, a pause, and then a delicious feeling of cool, moist cloth on his face, soaking up the blazing heat in his head. Daniel became aware of other things around him. He was lying on his back, apparently in a bed. His shoulder was throbbing fit to kill and something was bound tight around it. Something else was tight around his head. He breathed in through his nose. It was a stone room, or a room surrounded by stone. There were two people, a . . . man? And . . . yes, definitely a woman. The woman was closer. A small part of his mind mused that it was interesting his Holekhor senses were so much stronger when they were all he was using.

He opened his eyes and at once the information coming to him through his nose vanished. Blurs in the gloom resolved into two faces, a young woman and Prince Charles. Charles stood at the foot of his bed, the woman sat on a stool by his head. Both were peering anxiously into his face. She was dabbing a cloth in a bowl of water and wringing it out.

'He's awake!' Charles exclaimed. 'We were worried about you, boy-troll. You've had a fever, despite everything Mistress Connolly could do for you. But now you're better!' He was beaming with a foolish kind of happiness as though Daniel's health was all his own doing.

Daniel moved his lips.

'What's that? Alice, get him water to drink.' Alice

177

pursed her lips but moved away to obey the command. As she moved past Charles it seemed to Daniel's blurry eyes that he did *something* that made her twitch and take a sharp breath. Perhaps he was imagining it. 'See how well I look after you, boy-troll? I haven't left your side since they brought us here. I've been caring for you all this time.'

Daniel distinctly heard a *huh!* from Alice which Charles clearly chose not to. He tried to speak again.

'What happened?'

It came out as a whisper but this time Charles caught it. 'Don't you remember?'

Daniel tried to shake his head and gasped as agony stabbed into his shoulder.

'One of Cromwell's bastards tried to shoot me and you took it for me, boy-troll. I will certainly have you knighted for this! Listen, you haven't eaten for days. I'll bring you some soup. Some good, strong broth.'

The offer would have been more generous if Charles had then done more than look pointedly at Alice, who was returning with a pitcher of water. She sighed and thrust the pitcher at Charles, who took it out of surprised reflex. Alice turned and left the room, and Charles looked around with an air of helplessness for any other servants that might materialize out of the stonework. Eventually he put the pitcher down on the stool.

Daniel moved his mouth again and all that came out was a breath of air. He tried once more.

'Where is this?'

Charles's naturally sulky features were enhanced

by his scowl. 'We are in the castle at Windsor,' he said, 'guests of Parliament once more.' And bit by bit – for at each stage of the story, Charles seemed to assume Daniel knew what he was talking about and needed prompting for further information – he told of what had happened since Daniel had been shot.

The crew of the airship had cowered under the pistols of Cromwell's party, Charles said, as if afraid the entire ship might explode or something. By some kind of mechanical witchery, Mistress Connolly had sent a message claiming that the ship had been over-taken by a storm and was breaking up. She said they were blowing north, when in fact they had turned south. 'And so my father thinks I'm dead,' Charles said darkly. He paced around the room and kicked a chair. 'How he must be suffering!' Daniel's jaw dropped at the thought of who else must be suffering in that manner and he was so absorbed with the idea that he missed some of what Charles was saying. 'Now the rabble have got us all except James. God knows, I haven't seen Lizzie or Harry in years, Parliament has them somewhere.'

After the ship had been taken they had flown here to Windsor. Cromwell hadn't been seen since they had landed. Mistress Connolly had looked after Daniel for a short while, giving strange instructions such as that his bandages should always be fresh and always be boiled before use ('The woman has an obsession with boiling water, I tell you.'), but other than that she too hadn't been seen much. She was definitely somewhere here in Windsor but Charles didn't know where.

He jerked a thumb towards the window. 'The ship's out there, moored on the ground at the foot of the north terrace. You should see it, boy-troll.' He clenched one fist and covered it with the fingers of his other hand. 'It's nestled right up to the side of the hill like a kitten suckling its mother. It's covered in netting with bushes and bits of trees. I don't know if they intend to hide it indefinitely but they've done a damn good job so far.'

Alice returned with some broth. Daniel finally got the drink of water he had been craving from the pitcher that had been waiting two feet from his head, and then Charles solicitously supervized her helping Daniel sit up in bed for his meal. Charles was Prince of Wales and could demand considerably better fare than the Royalist prisoners of war held elsewhere in the castle. He was able to get hot, strong beef soup with chunks of meat floating in it. Daniel devoured it ravenously and felt much healthier with it inside him, content and sleepy. Alice gave him a warm, friendly smile as he lay back in his pillows. She leaned over him to pull up the bedclothes and this strangely made him feel even better. He gave a weak smile back and she stroked the tufts of his hair that poked over the edge of his head bandage.

'There's colour back in your cheeks, boy-troll,' Charles said. 'That's a good sight to see, after all these days lying like a corpse. Thank you, you can take the broth away now.'

Again Alice had to pass in front of Charles and again that thing happened that made her twitch.

Daniel fancied there was quite a saunter in her step as she left the room. Charles watched her go, then grinned and rubbed his hands together. 'Do you know, boy-troll, now I know you're not going to die on me I might as well make the best of this irksome situation that a man can. You don't mind if I leave you for a while? No, I thought not. I'm a man who always speaks highly of the fairer sex, though –' he pushed his voice up in imitation of Daniel's own unbroken tones – 'perhaps not so highly as you.' He dropped back down to his usual voice, 'And I must attend to a man's needs.' He patted Daniel absently on the shoulder – fortunately the good one – and had just reached the door when the stones of the castle shook to a deep, throaty roar.

'What the—?' Charles exclaimed and crossed the room in two long paces. Daniel used his good hand to push himself up but he had already recognized the noise. Outside the window a long, grey shape pushed into his frame of view; acres of stretched, ribbed canvas blocked out the light and glided slowly past. The airship was taking off.

Thirteen

Gentlemanly Conduct

Flanks heaving and glistening with sweat, hooves pounding on the turf, Cromwell's horse at last topped a small rise on the London road and brought him within sight of the army. It gave him no joy.

The man on the next horse must have had similar feelings. 'When we planned this army in committee,' the officer said, 'when I first saw it on the parade ground . . . it seemed so strong!'

Cromwell grunted.

The sun had shone on a fine day and was approaching the western horizon. Its reddening light glinted off pikeheads and musket barrels and gave a golden hue to the banners and flags. Cromwell's heart swelled with pride and pity. Several thousand men, hundreds of horses; well trained, disciplined, professional. Yes, it was a sight to gladden the eyes. Parliament had entered this war with nothing but rag-tag bunches of volunteers, commanded by men more qualified by birth than by experience. Yet now, just three years later, it had this army of the *new* model. An army of common people qualified by experience and knowledge. An army where pay was fair and equal. An army of free, righteous, Christian men under God, that could go anywhere and accomplish anything. The greatest military heroes of the Bible at the height of their powers – Joshua, Gideon, David – had not had an army like this.

Yet, Cromwell had seen the forces of the Holekhor at work. If his plan worked then this fine military force would be reduced to tatters.

He took heart from the source that never failed to inspire him. '"And the Lord said unto Gideon, by the three hundred men that lapped will I save you, and deliver the Midianites into thine hand,"' he muttered. 'Let us meet with Sir Thomas,' he said out loud, and spurred his horse down the slope.

The two generals rode a short distance ahead of the army. They both knew there were things one kept from those one was meant to lead. A disagreement between gentlemen was at the head of the list.

'A gate between worlds?' said Sir Thomas Fairfax. 'Ships that fly? Oliver, this is … not entirely believable.'

The Lord General looked wearier than when Cromwell had last seen him. He had been marching post-haste to relieve the siege of Taunton when the orders from London had caught up with him, where-upon, with commendable speed, he had turned the army around and marched post-haste back again. His face looked more worn than was usual in a thirty-two-year-old man and his hair hung lank.

It was also clear that the young general wanted an explanation, and he wasn't entirely satisfied with what he had heard.

'Am I in the habit of spinning fanciful tales?' Cromwell said.

'Of course you are not, and it is only because this tale comes from you that I give it the least credence. This man Donder, I hear, the one we met in Newbury, is in fact a general at the head of an army of invasion, and that is the least extravagant of your claims. Another problem, Oliver, is this.' He reached inside his cloak and produced a sheet of paper that Cromwell recognized. 'You know what it is?'

Cromwell nodded. He had written it himself at Windsor, then dispatched it while he was still forced to remain at the castle and attend to details.

'A fast messenger brings me this,' said Fairfax. 'I am exhorted to abandon Taunton to its fate, to turn around, to meet with you on the London road to lend my weight to what you describe as a holy war against demonic forces. Oliver, Donder looked singularly flesh and blood to me and I have never met an enemy that could not be dispatched with a good sword blow or musket ball.'

'You are a Christian gentleman, Thomas,' Cromwell said. 'You know that evil will always walk among us, and in many guises. Yes, Donder is flesh and blood and he too professes a Christian faith, but what Christian could command such forces as may open a gate between worlds? I confess I understood little of his explanation for how the gate was opened –

indeed I suspect his own understanding is more limited than he will gladly confess – but what little I did comprehend said plainly it was no Christian work.'

'And you would have us fight this with . . .?'

This was the crux of Cromwell's argument. 'Thomas,' he said earnestly, 'mighty as this gate is, in military terms it is much less. Imagine that our worlds were separated not by who knows what but by a simple range of mountains, impenetrable save for just one pass between them. Capture the pass, block it, and the invasion is prevented. Likewise this gate. If we can capture that hilltop then we can stop the Hollykor.'

'Oliver . . .' Fairfax cast his gaze up and down the paper one more time, then held it out for Cromwell's inspection. 'I see your signature at the bottom. I see no seal. I see no validation or authorization by Parliament. They do not know about this, do they?'

Cromwell had known it would come to this. 'They do not,' he admitted. 'That collection of talkers and merchants would never know how to act quickly enough. We must strike now, Thomas.' He thumped a gloved fist into his hand. '*Now.*'

Fairfax's eyes stayed cold and Cromwell put all the persuasion and sincerity he could muster into his voice.

'Thomas, Parliament gave us command of this army. Yes, they must dictate our overall campaigns, but do they direct the battles? If you are ambushed by Royalist skirmishers, do you send word back to Westminster to ask their guidance, or do you simply repel the ambush and report the affair back to

Parliament as a *fait accompli*? This is no different; just the scale is bigger. Sir, can you afford to let our land be invaded simply because it has yet to work its way through the third committee hearing?'

Fairfax held up a hand. 'Enough, Oliver, enough. I am persuaded that the presence of an army un-invited on our soil at least warrants investigation, and to that end I am persuaded you were right to call me back without authority. We will ride to this Povsyok and I will meet with Donder. But, Oliver, if I decide he poses no threat, if I decide you exceeded your authority with no just cause . . . Oliver, I will have no choice but to require your resignation.'

Cromwell's heart surged with relief. *My soul doth magnify the Lord*, he thought. 'You shall have it, Thomas,' he said. 'My word upon it. However, we will need to reach Povsyok by the day after tomorrow.'

'Wednesday?' Fairfax said. 'Oliver, you set us a mean pace! For what reason?'

'Because that is when Mistress Connolly will join us,' Cromwell said.

The atmosphere in the court of King Charles, temporarily removed to a tent on a hilltop in Berkshire, was quiet and withdrawn. The king sat at a table opposite his second son, a chessboard between them. In the background, the handful of courtiers that the king had been able to bring with him from Oxford were at a loose end. Their normal existence would have been as invisible presences behind their master, interpreting his wishes before they were uttered, seeing that his needs and wants were fulfilled before he had to wait. Off duty, they would have had chambers to which they could retire, wives or mistresses with whom they could spend time. Even before the terrible news that the heir to the throne was missing, they had felt superfluous, their opportunities for service limited by circumstances. But now . . .

All eyes turned to the courtier, another of their number, as he entered the tent, but his solemn expression told them what they wanted to know. The man bowed deeply to the king, sweeping the floor with his hat.

'The general begs to report that there is no further news, your Majesty,' he said. The king shut his eyes for a moment of inward communion, then opened them again and nodded.

'Very well,' he said, and turned back to the board. 'And what of the—'

Prince James could bear it no longer. '*Father!*' he blurted. The king looked up into his son's tear-filled eyes.

'And what would you have me do instead, James?' he said. 'I would d-dearly love the luxury of reacting as a common man, but the Lord has or-ordained me to the position of King, and so I must wait. Wait, and pray, and spend time with you, my darling boy.' He reached across the board and fondled his son's head. 'The general has lost a son too, James,' he said. 'I am con-confident he is doing all that he can to locate him and Charles.'

'It's gone on too long, Father!' James said. His eyes widened when he realized that he had contradicted the king, and in public. The king made his face cold but his eyes stayed warm.

'Should I send you to join in with the search, James?' he said. 'Should I entrust another son of mine to those p-pagan contraptions? Still, you are correct to say that this has gone on too long.' He looked back at the courtier and finished the original question that James had interrupted. 'And what of the other matter?'

The man shifted on his feet. 'The general regrets that he cannot advise our leaving his camp.'

The king drew himself up. 'We did not request his advice. We sought to leave. We reminded him that we have duties to our people that we are unable to fulfil as his guests.'

It was a given in court that when the king's stammer vanished, he was angry. The man's voice quavered as if on the edge of tears. 'The general cannot spare one of his ships of the air for you, your Majesty,' he said.

'Did you ask for an escort as God intended us to travel, upon the ground?'

The man's mouth worked like a fish. 'No, your Majesty,' he whispered.

'Never mind. It is clear to us that the general has no intention of letting us go. We are far too useful to him.' He sprang to his feet and clapped his hands together. 'Gentlemen, at the first opportunity, we must abscond!'

He beamed a smile around the tent. No one returned it. A couple of glances darted towards James. Someone had to point out the flaws in the plan and the twelve-year-old prince was the best qualified at least to initiate the conversation.

James obliged.

'Father, we have no horses, we are miles from our allies . . .' He looked beseechingly at one of the men. 'Are we not?'

The man gratefully took his cue.

'The prince is quite correct, your Majesty. By now your royal nephew Prince Rupert will be far to the north of Oxford, and Oxford with its garrison of Roundheads and Hollykor lies between us—'

'We are forced to act without our armies, gentlemen. We shall travel lightly. We shall circumvent Oxford. We shall live off the land until we rejoin our royal nephew.'

There was a long, stunned silence.

'Live . . . off the land?' James said faintly. His sole experience at taking sustenance from nature came from riding to hounds in the royal parks.

'Scripture tells us that David and his men evaded their enemies for years, until he was able finally to take his rightful place as King of Israel,' the king said. 'David was the Lord's Anointed, as are we. We are surrounded by heathen who would deny us our crown and take our territory. Can you not see the parallels, gentlemen? Surely the Lord will provide. Come, let us pray about it.'

He folded his hands together, closed his eyes and

dropped to his knees, followed quickly by everyone in the tent. The king, the prince and their courtiers each prayed, in their own ways, for a miracle.

Perched on his saddle ten feet from the ground on the woolly, gently swaying shoulders of a nenokh, and dressed once again in his gleaming white, formal dress uniform, Dhon Do went to meet the oncoming army.

The brief warm spell of early May was over; the year was growing perversely cold again and a cold wind whipped around them. The army was sandwiched between land that was just ripening, its greens and browns frozen as if waiting for the sun to return, and a dull grey sky.

In front of the nenokh, leading it with a stick grasped in its trunk, walked the driver and on either side walked Colonel Khre Deb and Por De.

'Isn't this an excellent chance, sir?' Por De called up to his general.

'How so?' Dhon Do said. He hadn't taken his eyes off the approaching force of Englishmen. How many were there? Ten thousand of them? Twenty? Given the nature of modern warfare at home it was rare to see an entire army all in one place and he wasn't used to having to estimate. But, they had come. He had been gambling that they would. Cromwell, he had been sure, would find a way. England's New Model Army would turn up on his doorstep, and five minutes after the machine guns opened fire, it would be no more. It would be a short, tragic, bloody victory, and it would be so much easier for the Might to invade England this way.

'Well, sir . . .' Por De said. Dhon Do swung his hard gaze down to his aide and the younger man flushed. 'I mean . . . we have the native king in our grasp . . . we can obliterate his enemies, he will be in our debt and—'

'Perhaps that is your idea of soldiering,' Dhon Do said shortly. 'It's not mine.' Yes, he had wanted Parliament's army here, but he didn't relish what was to come. He glanced down the other side of the nenokh and caught a wry smile and shake of the head from Khre Deb.

Dhon Do turned again to the army. Which of the various forms of obliteration at his disposal should he use, he wondered. Lure them within machine-gun range and let the gunners have their fun? Give the artillery some medium-range target practice? Recall the airships and bomb them? The natives didn't stand a chance. A mighty army was marching squarely to its doom. He even considered – for a brief, fantastic moment – ordering his men to throw down their guns and fight with their hand axes only. Madness, yet surely even that would be preferable to his God compared to the slaughter he was going to have to commit if these brave, noble fools did not withdraw.

A small party of horsemen broke away from the front lines and trotted towards him. Dhon Do recognized Fairfax at the head. It must have taken great courage to ride towards the nenokh. The beast was the ceremonial means of transport for a general of his rank, but to them it was a mighty behemoth: several tons of wool and muscle; a sweeping, prehensile nose; and long, curving, fierce tusks. As he recalled, they weren't native to this island.

The smell of the nenokh reached the horses and they suddenly began to buck, their riders barely able to control them. Maybe the men would go up to a nenokh, but horses obviously thought different.

'Halt,' he ordered. 'Leg.' The nenokh obligingly lifted up a foreleg and he swung down on to its knee, then dropped to the ground. 'Wait here.' He walked forward a few paces. Fairfax gratefully dismounted, leaving his horse in the care of one of his men, and came forward on foot to meet him.

'General Fairfax,' Dhon Do said.

'General Donder.' Fairfax bowed, then straightened and looked him in the eye. 'I need to know your intentions, sir. I have heard reports that you intend to invade.'

'I would be willing simply to take your surrender, sir.'

'You jest, sir, but it is not funny. I ask you fair and square. Are you for the king or are you for Parliament?'

'I suppose both, or neither, is out of the question?'

'It is, sir.'

'Then I cannot answer.'

'Then I must treat you as my enemy.'

They looked at each other in a complete impasse. They both knew what had to come, and they both knew what would transpire. It was as if, by standing here, they could delay the evil moment. Fairfax broke the silence.

'What time shall we fix for the battle, sir?'

The question caught Dhon Do by surprise. It was not one he had really expected. He kept forgetting that in fighting the natives, he was going back in time to an age when armies were commanded by gentlemen.

'What time would you like?' he said. Fairfax considered.

'Would nine o'clock in the morning be acceptable? The sun will be safely up by then.'

Dhon Do tried to remember how the local time matched the Holekhor day, with its four hours and sixteen quarters. He had a vague idea of nine o'clock being something like the twice-second quarter.

'We will be ready for you,' he promised. Fairfax's artillery would open up, to be wiped out within seconds by his own far superior guns. The cavalry would charge and be mown down. And then thousands of men would come marching into the jaws of certain death. With a bit of luck, their morale would be so broken by the fate of the first attackers that they would turn and flee.

It was difficult. It felt wrong, just sitting there and waiting for an attack he knew was coming. But it would keep his casualties to a minimum, and in the long run it didn't matter whether Fairfax's army was wiped out now or in the morning.

'Until tomorrow, then, sir,' Fairfax said, with another bow.

'And will General Khromell be joining us?' Dhon Do said.

'General Cromwell's movements are—' Fairfax said, and stopped suddenly. Dhon Do's heart leaped. By admitting any knowledge at all of Cromwell's movements, Fairfax was admitting that he knew Cromwell was alive. Cromwell had not been lost with the airship, therefore the airship had not been lost. And so, neither had Daniel.

'Until tomorrow, sir,' Fairfax said again. He bowed for a third time and returned to his men.

Dhon Do breathed out slowly and turned back to the nenokh. 'Apparently we will fight in the morning,' he said to Khre Deb. 'Double the sentry guard immediately, man the machine-gun posts and black out the camp. Oh, and prepare anti-aircraft defences. I think they have the *Golden Hawk* and they might use it against us.'

Dhon Do groaned silently as the chaplain Re Nokh let himself into the tent.

The sun had gone down and Dhon Do had spent a tiring two quarters double-checking the camp's preparations. There was the barest sliver of a new moon in the sky and the camp was dark – all lights outside extinguished, nothing more powerful than a candle inside the tents, all generators shut down. The gate was on the in-tide and so light shone in from the Old World, but that would change naturally before long.

He was happy. The best soldiers in the world were

on watch, every man was armed and ready, and – it still brought a smile to his face – Daniel was probably alive. He was eating his dinner and he felt he deserved a peaceful meal . . . which clearly he was not going to get.

He opened his mouth to say as much, but then the chaplain held back the flap and let someone else enter, and Dhon Do had just a second's warning as the hair on his head literally started to rise. His mood worsened as the black-robed woman entered and the air seemed to draw tight around her.

Dhon Do could only sense the landpower in the earth around him – any Holekhor could. Wise were sinks for that power. It clustered around them. The air in the tent had become as tense as the atmosphere before a thunderstorm, poised to rip with a blast of energy.

So Dhon Do glared up at the chaplain and his guest, swallowed his mouthful and deliberately did not stand. He nodded at his orderly Ro Dhen, who tactfully withdrew into the gloom beyond the candlelight.

'My respects to the Order of the Wise,' Dhon Do said. 'How can I help you?'

Without waiting for an answer he speared another slice of steak and popped it into his mouth. He used some bread to mop at the gravy.

'General,' Re Nokh said, 'I am sorry to disturb you. Um, may I present the Speaker of the Povse'okh cell . . .?'

Dhon Do inclined his head. He detested the Order of the Wise. You never knew where you stood with them. Standing in front of him now was a middle-aged woman with greying hair and a face that would have been pleasant if it had not looked so impassive. If this woman was here then so were the five or six or seven other Wise of her cell, linked with her mind through the landpower. The Wise were not individual people. They were one mind, an amalgam of several different personalities that just happened to have several bodies. He would be speaking to someone who was mostly elsewhere.

'How can I assist the Order?' he said.

'We have stabilized the gate,' the woman said. 'It is time for us to survey the New World. Five cells should suffice for this island: we therefore require five airships at the soonest opportunity.'

Dhon Do could only believe his ears because he had met this kind of arrogance before. It was the kind that comes not just from lack of knowledge about the real state of affairs but from an inability to care about that lack.

'This camp is on alert,' he said. 'Speaking of which, chaplain, would you close the flap? We wouldn't want a native sharpshooter to use his high-powered Toskheshi-made rifle on . . . oh, say, the first person he saw standing in the light.' Dhon Do took a sip of wine.

Re Nokh paused, then turned and closed the tent flap.

'It is most unlikely that the natives could harm an airship protected by the power of the Order,' the woman said.

'Forgive me, but it is most likely that they could,' Dhon Do said. 'They have gunpowder, they have cannons, and they are being armed by local Holekhor. And even a primitive musket can have the same effect as a rifle in the long run. The fact is, if you went out into the countryside beyond Povse'okh then I could not guarantee your safety.'

'A Wise in contact with the land fears nothing.'

'Oh, please, spare me that convenient story for the gullible,' Dhon Do said. 'I think that what you mean is a Wise in contact with the landpower fears nothing. But, as I said, the natives have cannon, and we all know the landpower isn't everywhere.'

The woman stayed silent, her lips pursed. Re Nokh smiled a thin smile and took over. Dhon Do noticed that the man showed much more courage when backed up by a Wise than he had on his own at their first meeting.

'General, a reasonable man might question why you do not simply take this opportunity to eradicate the native rabble and declare your unquestioned mastery over this land. Why do you let them camp on your doorstep unchallenged? Why put good Holekhor souls at risk?'

'Every man in this army is a volunteer,' Dhon Do said calmly. 'If you yourself are unhappy about being in a battle zone, why, safety lies not half a mile away, the other side of the gate. The tide will turn in, what, a quarter? And none of my men will impede your access.'

'I choose to remain, sir, and to improve my sadly

deficient knowledge of military tactics by observing a master.'

Dhon Do raised his glass. 'Learn from the best, as I always say,' he agreed. 'But be warned, when it comes the battle will be quick and fast. Blink and you may miss it.'

As it happened, the battle began soon after midnight.

Fourteen

The Battle of White Horse Hill

The boom of guns sliced through Dhon Do's sleep and he was out of the tent as he had gone to bed, fully dressed and with his boots on, before the echoes died away. He heard, but did not see, the rush of cannon balls through the air as they struck the ground well in advance of the Holekhor lines.

Not such a gentleman after all, General Fairfax, he thought with a strange degree of approval as he buckled on his helmet.

He reached the command post, a sandbagged shelter with messengers running to and fro while Khre Deb snapped out orders and gazed into the night through night sights. The English guns fired again and this time Dhon Do saw the flashes, the gouts of flame that they spat into the dark.

Then from behind him came the multiple roar of modern guns, sharp cracks that smacked at the eardrums and echoed around the night. Shells flew through the cold dark and landed among the English guns. Brilliant white explosions blew away the darkness in a tangle of wood and metal and human beings.

The stores of native gunpowder erupted in larger explosions, finishing the job that the Holekhor artillery had begun.

There was another brief flash, closer to them, a fountain of flame and earth and then a scream, a shriek of a mortally wounded man that went on and on. And another similar explosion after that. The natives had discovered the minefield.

'That took 'em by surprise,' Khre Deb said, and for just a brief moment, Dhon Do gaped into the darkness. Of *course* it had taken them by surprise! It had simply not occurred to him: Fairfax would have had no idea what mines were. Mines were not just intended to defend. They were intended to deny land to the enemy, forcing him down avenues of your own choosing. Povse'okh was surrounded with them save for clear, mine-free strips of land going into the camp that were nicely covered by machine guns. Fairfax didn't even realize the threat and was going to march into the camp straight through the minefield. He probably thought the explosions beneath the feet of his men were remarkably accurate small cannon fire.

'Permission to send up flares, sir?' Khre Deb said. 'We have to finish this at some point.'

Dhon Do sighed, and nodded. 'Yes. Send up the flares and give them to the machine guns,' he said.

'Very good, sir.'

And Dhon Do suddenly became redundant. Khre Deb could handle a fight like this with his eyes shut; he certainly didn't need a general breathing down his neck. Dhon Do turned and walked away from the command post. He would find a quiet observation tower and see what was happening.

White flares blazed out in the sky above him and he frowned upwards. They shouldn't have been above *him*, they should have been above the *enemy*. A familiar sound tickled his ears. He hadn't heard it through the sound of gunfire, but now . . .

The black shape of an airship passed over the camp. So, the natives had learnt to fly.

More flares dropped down from the belly of the ship, and then a scattered line of explosions broke out in mid-air between the ship and the ground. He saw running Holekhor suddenly fold and crumple. Red-hot rain hissed past him and instinctively he crouched down, curling into a tight ball. The bombs were raining shrapnel on the camp, and everyone who realized what was happening did the same as him. Then the ship was gone.

Rifle and machine-gun fire sounded from the front lines and Dhon Do ran back to the command post. Khre Deb was already on top of the situation.

'I confirm,' he barked into a field telephone, '*Golden Hawk* is in enemy hands. Shoot it down!' He slammed the telephone back into its cradle and looked at Dhon Do. 'They've turned our flagship against us. The gods help any survivors our men get hold of.'

Midnight. You could wax poetic about it. The boundary between one day and the next, the division between old and new. Or you could view it as the time when both the Holekhor and the English clock co-incided, making it the best time to launch a combined assault.

Khonol Le tightened her grip on the spokes of the steering wheel and peered out into the dark. The engines idled at barely more than a *put-put-put*. An English navigator had got them this far; he was more accustomed to guiding ships that floated than flew, but he could read the stars and get them on to the right latitude. After that it was just dead reckoning and the compass.

She had dropped below the clouds and signalled the engines to throttle back to dead slow. The cabin lights were out. Behind her, her borrowed Parliamentary crew peered out of the windows of the command gondola into the darkness.

'On the port bow,' said one suddenly. 'Gunfire.'

'Port?' she said.

'The left, mistress.'

And sure enough, there it was. Tiny flashes of light, billowing smoke and flame. She could see no sign of Dhon Do's camp – he must have called a black-out – but the flashes of the New Model Army's artillery were guiding her in. She smiled grimly. The plan was working.

She thrust the telegraph to 'half ahead', and braced herself as the ship surged forward.

'Open the doors,' she said. 'Drop the flares and the bombs on my command.'

'Yes, mistress,' said a soldier with only a slight reluctance, and he shouted the message up the ladder, to be relayed down the ship. Khonol Le smiled. He couldn't hide his distaste at taking orders from a woman, and that went for all the hurriedly trained Englishmen on board, but Cromwell had been ... *insistent*, in the way that only Cromwell could.

Now the Holekhor guns were returning their fire. She saw the English rows of guns smashed to pieces by the withering barrage, a brave sacrifice of men and materiel.

'Drop the flares,' she said, and the order was passed on.

Moments later the bright white light blossomed out over the camp, and seconds after that the home-made bombs went off in mid-air. They had been an extravagance, but the opportunity to shower the camp with shrapnel had been too good to waste.

She signalled 'full ahead', the engines roared again and she took the ship back up into the gloom of the night. Cromwell could do his work now, guided in by the flares. Then would come the final attack, the one that counted.

In a cluster of trees to the south of the camp, Oliver Cromwell waited with his cavalry, his Ironsides, the fighting force he had built up from nothing. His horse was twitching, sensing its master's mood and ready for the charge, but he held it back. A charge across that ground in the dark would be suicidal. He watched the flashes, the pinpricks of rifle and machine-gun fire, and wondered how many more souls had just been added to the judgement list.

'Listen,' said an officer. Cromwell cocked his head. The rumble of airship engines; Mistress Connolly was spot on time.

The flares dropped out of the ship and he turned his face away. When he felt able, he looked cautiously back. Seconds ago there had been only black, but now the square shapes of the Holekhor tents and the Holekhor invaders were as clear as day. It was as if God himself had cast the world into darkness yet shone a light on this one place, the site of the infection that threatened England. The target for the Ironsides.

'And it came to pass the same night,' he cried, 'that the Lord said unto him, Arise, get thee down into the camp, for I have delivered it into thine hand!' He drew his sabre and held it towards the enemy. '*Charge!*'

The Ironsides pounded across the field.

The first explosion went off only seconds later, to his right. He heard the scream of horses and men. Then another, and another. The ground was exploding beneath them. It was some other devilish trick of the Holekhor. But his horses were fast, their feet were widely spaced, and the chances of any one horse hitting a mine were low. Though he gritted his teeth against the blast, clenched his bowels and hunkered low in his saddle, he made it through, as did most of his men. A Holekhor soldier stood in his path, his rifle raised. The man fired and the shot buzzed past Cromwell's ear. 'He shall give his angels charge over thee!' Cromwell cried and slashed down with his sabre. 'They shall bear thee up in their hands lest thou dash thy foot against a stone!'

Ahead he saw the first of his targets. Khonol Le had described what to expect: smaller guns than the field pieces, surrounded by sandbags and aimed up at the air. Povse'okh's air defences. He gestured one troop of his men towards the nearest, and galloped on with his own troop to the next in line.

More Holekhor were pouring out of a nearby tent and Cromwell turned his mount to face them. 'The Spirit of the Lord is upon me!' he shouted and his men bore down on the invaders.

Prince James was sobbing as the battle raged around them beyond the canvas walls. The king held his son close to him.

'Courage, my d-darling,' he said gently, and raised his voice to the courtier who peered out of the tent flap. 'Well?'

'All the sentries have gone, sire,' the man said.

'Then we shall leave too. Come.' The king put a friendly hand on his son's back and propelled him forward, and they crept cautiously from their camp.

And then the king could scarcely believe his eyes at the shape he saw mounted on a horse, silhouetted against a burning tent. *Roundheads!* How had they got into the camp?

Three or four more charged by. The king didn't know what they were after but it did not seem to be him. 'The Lord has sent our enemies to be our saviours,' he said. 'He will have His little jest.'

'The edge of the camp is this way, sire. We can climb down the ridge and then we will be away.'

'Lead on,' the king said. He kept a gentle hand on his son's shoulders to still the boy's trembles and the small party made its way through the battle. They froze when a group of Holekhor soldiers ran out of the darkness towards them, but apart from a shout in their incomprehensible gibberish from one, and some very definite gestures that they should return from whence they had come, the soldiers ignored them and ran past. The Holekhor had other priorities.

And then they were at the camp's edge. The ground fell away at their feet and beyond was only darkness. The king had seen the Ridgeway in daylight. It was not a vertical drop; it would be uncomfortable for a man to climb all the way down, but not impossible and by no means lethal.

'Gentlemen, we have m-made it, by George!' he exclaimed and took a step forward. There was a distinct metallic *click* beneath his feet, and he just had time to glance down before the ground erupted up to meet him.

The wheel bucked in her hand, the ship protesting at the turn she required of it, and the deck shifted beneath her. Then she slowly let the wheel spin back to midships as the nose of the *Golden Hawk* came round. It was aimed directly at the gate.

'Vent,' she said. The man nearest her nodded and passed the command up the ladder.

The deck plunged beneath her feet as lifting gas spilled out of its bags, and her stomach seemed to leap into her mouth. They were dropping. Too fast?

Impossible to tell. She had never done this before. After its capture she had bought the ship in to land at Windsor good and slow, with advice from the Holekhor crew who were all too happy to preserve their necks. Now she was on her own, and a manoeuvre like this wasn't in the manual.

Khonol Le kept a close eye on the dials. Timing here was crucial.

'Arm the fuses,' she said.

They were coming in low, over the camp. The battle was still raging below them. Khonol Le flinched as bullets smashed through the glass of the gondola. More ricocheted off the floor of the cabin. Cromwell had taken out the anti-aircraft defences but the *Golden Hawk* was still vulnerable to small arms fire. Doubtless the hull was being peppered with rifle shots, not large or hot enough to cause the ship real damage.

And then they were over the last of the tents and coming down on to the clear area, the parade ground, directly in front of the gate. The camp was still bathed in white light but the gate was darker than the night around it. It was on the out-tide, which was excellent. If she flew the ship properly she could get it wedged in the gate before it went off. The damage would be all the greater.

A man jumped down the ladder into the gondola, followed by the rest of the crew. The cabin was getting crowded. 'All armed,' he said.

'Good.' Khonol Le looked out. They could not have been more than twenty feet up, with soft turf below them. 'Start jumping.'

They needed no further bidding. The ship was packed with barrels of gunpowder, and any soldier who knew what that quantity could do had an instinctive desire to put as much space as possible between him and it before it went off.

The ship was ten feet up and the gate was dead ahead. Khonol Le could bring it no closer than this. She abandoned the wheel and was the last out.

She stumbled as she landed and fell, but then was up and running. Behind her she heard the crunch as the gondola ploughed into the turf, then a deathly screeching as the main body of the ship struck and the aluminium ribs began to crumble. Then a loud, violent hiss. She had been almost dead on in aiming for the gate and most of the nose had passed through, but some had not. It stayed in this world, and the effect was for the ship to be sliced cleanly as if by a giant knife, the blade the edge of the gate. Lifting gas was spilling out into the air.

She and the English crew weren't the only ones running from the crash. The Holekhor didn't know about the gunpowder but they knew about the gas. Any moment now a spark of clashing metal would—

A *whoomph* caught her in the small of her back and sent her flying forward. She crashed, dazed, into the ground, then twisted and looked back. Clear, blue flame crackled all along the hull, and it bucked and writhed as if alive. But the fact that she could still see the ship, more or less intact, said that the gunpowder hadn't caught yet. Well, if the fuses didn't spark it then the gas would.

She staggered to her feet and pain lanced sharply up her ankle. She cried out and fell forward again. She tried again to get to her feet but could only manage a rapid hobble away from the crash site.

Something large and black and massive rushed out of the darkness and reared to a halt in front of her.

'Mistress Connolly!' Oliver Cromwell's eyes blazed behind his three-barred visor. He held out a gauntleted hand. 'Climb up!'

She gratefully helped him pull her up on to the horse's back behind him. Around her, she could see the Ironsides rescuing the rest of her crew. She put her arms around his waist and he kicked his spurs against the horse's flank.

Not all the Holekhor were fleeing. The chaplain Re Nokh and the cell of the Wise stood on the edge of the circle of light thrown by the burning ship and watched.

'A futile attack, surely,' said Re Nokh. 'Destroy the gate with an airship? Never!'

'Perhaps not,' said the Speaker. In unison, the Wise shut their eyes and leaned forward slightly, as if studying something closely. 'No,' said the Speaker. 'The ship is packed full of explosive.'

Re Nokh went pale. 'Explosive! We must run!'

'It is of a most inferior grade,' the Speaker said, 'but it could still cause damage to this camp. Now is the time to show General Dhon Do that we are not entirely superfluous. We ask you to stand back.'

Re Nokh took a few steps backwards and the Wise

stood in a circle. They raised their hands up, their fingertips touching, and the air around them crackled. Re Nokh felt his hair crawl with the charge. He took a step back against a metal tent pole, and hissed as a spark flew across the gap.

The Wise began to chant and a vibration began to fill the camp.

This explosion was no *whoomph*. The sound was a solid force, a slap in the back as if nature itself had dealt a single, deadly blow to all around it. The night lit up for miles around with the flash, panicking Cromwell's mount to even greater speed. Yet somehow Khonol Le knew that something had gone wrong. There should have been a gale of burning air. The shock should have knocked them flat. What had happened?

Cromwell gradually slowed the horse down and brought it round in a wide half circle. They gazed back at what they had wrought.

A column of fire blazed up from Povse'okh, in front of the gate. It lanced up from the ground into the heavens, a burning beacon to sear the affair into the eyes and the memories of every man and woman present that night. It was the explosion, but it was channelled impossibly away from the camp, away from the gate. The gate was still there.

Meanwhile the rattle of machine guns and the popping crack of rifle fire said that the battle was still going on, and above it Khonol Le could hear a rumble as of hundreds of voices, humming in a low harmony.

'No!' Khonol Le howled. She thumped her fist hard against Cromwell's back. 'No!'

'You did what you could, Mistress Connolly,' Cromwell said grimly. 'We gave them a bloody nose if nothing else, but alas, even an army of righteous men is no match for witchcraft in this godless age. Bugler! Sound for the Ironsides to regroup and retreat.'

'You're not going back to the battle?' Khonol Le said.

'No,' Cromwell said with a quiet, sure calm and a shake of his head. 'No. Sir Thomas Fairfax will have no choice but to surrender now. If I surrender with him then England will be defenceless. The Lord has chosen another day for our victory, Mistress Connolly. Come.'

Oliver Cromwell and Khonol Le rode away into the night.

Fifteen

The End of the Beginning

'I can't,' Daniel gasped. He staggered against Prince Charles, who caught him. 'I can't.'

'Come on, boy-troll!' the prince urged. 'It's not far.'

But Daniel had had enough. As the prince obviously wasn't going to help him he made his own way for a couple of yards to some stone steps. He sat down gratefully and put his head between his knees.

Charles stood in front of him, hands on his hips. 'Perhaps I pushed you too hard, boy-troll,' he said, 'but it was you who wanted to go for a walk.'

He was right on both counts. Daniel squinted up the near vertical slope he was expected to climb, though in truth it was a very gentle gradient. The castle of Windsor was built on a slight incline, the far end of the south ward lower than the Round Tower in the middle and the north ward beyond it. It hadn't looked too hard and he was getting restless, confined to his bed as he was, and with Charles spending more and more time with Alice in the next room. The walls of the castle were not nearly as proof against sound as

Charles apparently thought they were, which was another reason he wanted to get out.

So he had proposed this walk to test his recuperation, in the hope that Alice would be his escort. How could he have known that Charles would choose this particular day to start being helpful? But, while one arm was still heavily bandaged and in a sling, he still had one good arm and two good legs, and the bandage was off his head, so he had thought he could make it.

It had been a mistake. He had managed the downhill part of the walk without too much difficulty, though he had felt very weak by the end of it. Now, on the way back up again, he was finished. There wasn't enough blood in his body to do everything that was required of it. They had got as far as what was apparently the castle's chapel, though it was bigger and grander than the fully-fledged church back home, and that was as far as he was going. He sat on the steps by the chapel entrance and drew deep, low breaths with his head bowed.

Charles gazed around them, looking for inspiration to make conversation while Daniel recovered his strength. A team of horses clattered through the gate at the castle's south-west corner, pulling a coach behind it. 'Friend or foe, do you think, boy-troll?' he said. 'Some other poor sod who's been brought in to share our durance or . . .' He squinted. Then he stiffened, standing bolt upright like a rabbit that has heard a strange noise. Daniel looked wearily over at the coach. A guard of soldiers was drawn up around it and a small girl, younger than him, had climbed down, followed by a very little boy who clutched her hand and looked about him with large eyes.

'It can't be . . .' Charles said. He took a couple of hesitant steps forward. Surely, Daniel thought, even Charles wouldn't be interested in a girl *that* young.

But Charles broke into an unprincely run, all royal dignity gone. Suddenly he was just a gangly adolescent boy, a tangle of long limbs waving in odd directions about his body as he pelted across the ward.

'Lizzie!' he shouted.

The heads of the girl and the boy turned as one, and both their faces lit up. 'Charles!'

And then Charles was on top of them, pulling them into a loud and joyful three-way hug. He picked the girl up and spun her around, then put her down and grabbed the boy under the arms, throwing him up into the air. From his distance, Daniel couldn't tell if the three were laughing or crying or both, but they were all talking loudly and at once. He sat on his steps and waited.

Eventually Charles came back to him. He was carrying the toddler on one hip and holding the girl's hand. The sheer happiness that radiated from the three of them was so infectious that for a moment Daniel thought he could almost forgive Charles for being . . . Charles.

The goodwill lasted until Charles opened his mouth.

'Lizzie, you must meet Sir Boy-troll. He saved my

life and gained that noble wound of his in the process. Boy-troll, this is the Princess Elizabeth and –' he jiggled the little boy, making the child squeal with pleasure – 'the Prince Henry.'

Daniel found the strength to stand up and meet them. He tried not to smile. Charles was no longer the Prince of Wales, the oldest son of the king, an arrogant fifteen-year-old with his brains in that part of the body for which Daniel knew no polite words. He was simply a proud big brother, and clearly an adored one, and Daniel found he was happy for him.

Elizabeth had a puzzled, polite frown and Daniel saw her mouth the words, 'Boy-troll?' He had no intention of letting another of the Stuarts become accustomed to using that name.

'I'm Daniel Matthews,' he said, and stopped, uncertain of how one addressed a princess. 'Um, miss.'

She smiled, warm and friendly. She couldn't have been more than about ten and she had the piping voice of a child, but she carried herself with an adult assurance. 'I'm delighted to meet you, Master Matthews,' she said and held out her hand to him. Daniel took it and stopped again. What did you do? Shake it?

Charles rolled his eyes and looked up at the sky. 'You kiss it, boy-troll,' he murmured, so Daniel did so with as much aplomb as he could muster. 'And then you let go.'

'I look forward to hearing how you saved my brother's life, Master Matthews,' Elizabeth said. Her smile was still warm. Despite the apparent debt of blood, Daniel always got the feeling that Charles was lowering himself when the prince spoke to him, but with the young princess it seemed much more real. She was a little girl with a kind thought for everyone in her heart.

He gave a bashful smile in return. 'I don't remember much.'

'I can see a fish in the sky!' Henry exclaimed suddenly with a peal of laughter. He was pointing upwards.

'A flying fish, Harry?' Charles said. 'It would have to fly a long way from the sea to get . . . Oh.'

An airship was cruising above them. It did look – almost, perhaps – like a fish; a slender, streamlined form that glided casually through the air like a trout through water. Perhaps Prince Henry's five-year-old eyes didn't have the perception to work out that it was something much larger, and a long way away.

'So, Mistress Connolly is back from her little jaunt,' Charles said shortly. His good humour was gone. 'Can you walk yet, boy-troll? I suggest we all go inside and –' he nuzzled his little brother's neck, eliciting another giggle – 'we can share our adventures!'

'It's not the same ship,' Daniel said. 'Look. Our ship had a bird on the front.'

'I think it was a hawk, boy-troll, but . . . do you know, you're right.'

Elizabeth clutched at her brother and stared up with eyes like saucers. 'What is it?'

'Just one of the many things we've seen in our escapades, Lizzie,' Charles said. 'But, boy-troll, either your father has been damned careless and lost another of his ships to the rabble . . .'

Sudden hope swelled in Daniel's breast. He didn't want to say the words in case for some perverse reason it made them not come true.

'Perhaps we should remain here,' Charles said thoughtfully. 'Interesting things are about to happen.'

The ship put down beside the castle on the north side. There was no question of their leaving to meet it, so they waited beside the chapel. Elizabeth told a few stories about the years she and Henry had spent in the custody of Parliament, being moved hither and thither around the country.

Eventually a party of soldiers marched up through the gate and Daniel's heart leaped. They wore a mixture of uniforms – the reddish-browns of Parliament's army but also the oh-so-welcome sight of dark yellow. Holekhor troops!

And suddenly it was Daniel's turn to run forward. His strength was barely back but he staggered across the ward and fell into the arms of the frail, white-haired figure who stood dwarfed and incongruous among the hulking soldiers.

Francis threw his arms around the boy. 'Daniel!' he said. 'Oh, Daniel.' It was the mild, cultured tone that Daniel loved so much. 'Oh Daniel, I am so relieved.' He kissed the top of Daniel's head and buried his face in Daniel's hair. 'At the last report to reach General Fairfax you were at death's door and he honestly had no idea whether you would live or die.'

'I . . . what . . .' Daniel lifted his head from the priest's shoulder and gazed into his face through streaming eyes. 'What are you doing here?'

'Your father is too occupied with important tasks to come here himself, so he sent me as someone who could identify you. I tell you, it was a surprise when that machine of his landed by the church. Of course, you are a grown man of the world now and such things hold no wonder for you.'

'I've been away a week,' Daniel said with a grin and a snuffle.

'Much can happen in a week,' Francis said, and ruffled his hair. 'Read your scriptures.'

'I take it you have met Sir Thomas Fairfax if you speak so freely of him?' said a familiar voice. The three royal children had reached the pair, Charles in the middle with his siblings holding his hands.

'Indeed I have, young sir,' Francis said with an affable nod at the prince. 'He has surrendered to your father, Daniel.'

Four faces gaped back at him.

'Fairfax has surrendered?' Charles said. '*Fairfax has surrendered*? But he is the rabble's general! He commands its army! And if he has surrendered, then . . .'

'The war is over!' Francis said with a broad smile. 'It only remains for young Daniel's father to fly to London and take the formal surrender of Parliament.'

'Francis,' Daniel said, remembering his manners. 'I have to introduce you. This is Prince Charles—'

The blood drained from Francis's face. 'Charles, Prince of Wales?' he said.

'The same, sir,' Charles said affably, and Francis dropped as quickly as his age would allow to one knee.

'Kneel, Daniel. I am Francis Wetherby, your Majesty, your most humble servant.'

'Francis,' Daniel protested, 'you—'

'Well, boy-troll,' Charles said, with a short, surprised laugh. 'I have to say it is nice to meet someone of your acquaintance who will treat us with a bit of respect for once.'

'But tell your friend he should not call my brother "Majesty",' Elizabeth said gently. 'That title is reserved for the king alone.'

'Daniel, kneel,' Francis said, and tugged hard at Daniel's belt. Daniel had a choice of kneeling or being publicly debagged, and reluctantly dropped down to one knee himself. Francis bowed his head. 'My choice of words was entirely correct, your Majesty.'

'But I tell you, sir,' Charles said, 'that title would only apply to me . . . if . . .'

Elizabeth gasped and her hand flew to her mouth. Charles turned slowly white.

'Oh, no,' he said.

'I am most sorry, sir. There was a battle, Fairfax attacked the camp and . . .' Francis trailed off. 'I am sorry, your Majesty.'

'My father?' Charles said in a flat voice.

'And your royal brother, your Majesty. It was a tragic accident.'

Charles and Elizabeth stood silent.

Prince Henry saw two people kneeling in front of his brother and drew the obvious conclusion. 'Is it a game?' he said. 'Want to play!'

'Certainly, Harry, you may kneel too,' Elizabeth said, her voice trembling. She matched her actions to her words, discreetly lifting up her skirt and dropping down to the cobblestones. 'We all have to kneel to Charles.'

And so the loneliest boy in the world stood, fighting to control his tears, as the first four of his subjects, then as word spread more and more of the garrison at Windsor, came to offer their homage and their duty.

Re Nokh stood in his tent with his hands outstretched, and the Wise knelt in a circle around him.

'And we give thanks,' said Re Nokh, 'to the guardian deities of the faithful in the New World, for the deliverance of the last night.'

Re Nokh felt exalted. This was what he was born to do. The Congregation and the Order of the Wise were traditionally separate, because in the Old World that had proved the best way to keep the peace. But here in the New World, where the natives had no particular awe of either, surely it would be better for them to work together? He felt he was in at the start of something brand new and wonderful, but he could not quite place what it was. The Congregation and the Order together, and a world full of heathen to convert. If only . . .

'We ask their blessing upon we their humble servants . . .' Re Nokh said, just as someone entered the tent. He glanced up in annoyance, and when he saw who it was, the ending of his prayer seemed even more apposite. '. . . that the light of the Pantheon may shine upon this land of darkness,' he said, clearly. 'Hear our prayers.'

'Hear our prayers,' the Wise murmured, as one voice. Then, with the eerie choreography that Re Nokh had long since grown used to, they stood and turned to face Dhon Do. The general steeled himself against their combined gazes, but he was the first to speak.

'I haven't thanked you for your actions last night,' Dhon Do said. 'I'm very grateful.'

The Speaker glanced at Re Nokh for permission to speak: he gave a faint nod. She turned back to Dhon Do. 'We saved your camp and your men from severe damage, certainly. The rebels could not have damaged the gate.'

'Their theory was sound, though?'

'Oh, certainly,' the Speaker said with a dismissive wave. 'They hoped to distort the shape of this hilltop sufficiently to deflect the landpower away from the intersection. The gate would snap shut and we would be stranded. But no, they would have needed much more explosive, and it would never have worked on the surface of the hill. It would have needed to be deep underground.'

'On that subject,' Dhon Do said, 'I intend to fortify this hilltop. I want to turn it into a fully-fledged citadel, our first and greatest point of presence in the New World. It will mean driving tunnels into the mountain for storage and I wondered . . .'

'You are unlikely to distort the landpower yourself, if that is what concerns you,' the Speaker said. 'Still, we will be glad to advise you on the plans for your fortress.'

'Thank you, madam. I would be most obliged.' Dhon Do bowed and withdrew.

Re Nokh scowled after him. 'That man served his country faithfully during the Toskhes Campaign,' he said, 'and will continue to do so here. But the Toskheshi were already children of the Pantheon. The natives of the New World are not, and while he shares their religion, I wonder if they ever will be.'

The Wise turned as one to face Re Nokh. 'That is a serious charge to bring – for an army chaplain,' said the Speaker. Re Nokh flushed.

'Naturally, I mean no disrespect to my senior officers, and I have no great experience of military tactics. Yet I observed a certain . . . reluctance in his engagement of the natives.'

'Had you ever thought,' the Speaker said mildly, 'that you might be in the wrong branch of the Congregation?'

'I am Golekhi,' Re Nokh said coldly. 'I joined the Might to serve the Domon'el, as did Dhon Do. I requested secondment to the invasion force so that I could enjoy the honour of bringing the grace of the Pantheon to those who walk in darkness.'

The Wise all bowed. 'May we never doubt your patriotism or your missionary zeal,' the Speaker said. 'Yet, as you have no doubt come to realize, while you are in the Might you will always be subordinate. To exercise that zeal to the fullest, a move to the Hierarchy . . .'

'I . . .' Re Nokh looked embarrassed. 'I am not high born. I have never considered the Hierarchy as an option.'

'With the right introduction it can be within the grasp of anyone possessed of sufficient enthusiasm and initiative. We would be glad to consider such an introduction.'

Re Nokh looked at her with wide eyes, then allowed himself a bashful smile. 'And I would be honoured to be introduced,' he said.

Khre Deb found Dhon Do standing on the edge of the camp and the Ridgeway, gazing out over the lands he had taken. He was just the right side of the minefield where the king and Prince James had met their ends.

The colonel coughed discreetly and Dhon Do turned. Khre Deb held out his report.

'Your most successful campaign, sir,' he said with a broad smile. 'The fewest casualties ever, for the greatest reward. An entire country.'

Dhon Do twitched one corner of his mouth. 'Thank you.' He took the report and scanned it quickly. Yes indeed, a most successful outcome to the battle if one thought in terms of proportions. Even in the raids that had first made his name, taking his glider squadrons in behind the lines of entrenched Toskheshi machine guns in a devastating series of surprise attacks, he had lost proportionately more men than this.

He should not have lost any.

'I can also report that *Conqueror's Talons* has picked up your son and the new king, sir,' Khre Deb said. 'They are both well and returning here. So, celebrations all round?'

'Get the camp back into shape, then declare a half day festival,' Dhon Do agreed. 'We still have work to do here.'

'Yes, sir,' Khre Deb said, and returned to his duties. Dhon Do could tell that the colonel was puzzled by his general's downcast mood.

It's easy for you, Khre Deb. This is just newly conquered territory to you.

Dhon Do looked back to the horizon.

This land was my home once before. The Domon'el decided to take it and he gave the job to me. I had to accept it, because if I declined then another general would be given the task, and however the English are now to suffer under my rule, it would be as nothing to what they would have suffered otherwise. I want the natives, my friends, my co-religionists, to remain a free people. They cannot. And now, to make sure that I remain as their new master and am not recalled in favour of who knows which tame bastard from back home, I must tread a fine line between treachery to my Lord and doing what is pleasing to my God.

So I might join in with the celebrations, because the men must see that their general is with them, but forgive me, Khre Deb, if I do not celebrate in my heart.

He turned to the southeast to see if there was any sign of *Conqueror's Talons* and its precious cargo yet. Then he looked back over the farmland below him.

He had smashed the army of this country's rebels and he had its boy-king in his control. He would let Charles rule in name, certainly – it was easier that way – but he, Dhon Do, was the real master and ruler of England. It was all his.

He didn't know what he would do with it, but he would think of something.

PART II

1651

Sixteen

Latin and Holy Water

A mass of freezing water exploded against the freighter's iron bows and the ship shuddered. Pellets of shattered sea pounded against the windows of the bridge.

The captain put out a hand to steady himself and turned to the figure at the back of the bridge. His most senior passenger, a Hierarch of the Congregation, stood in the hatchway and the captain could just see two black-clad Wise behind him.

'Sir,' the captain shouted over the wind's howl, 'I beg you, let us turn around. Let us run with the wind at our backs. Maybe we'll end up back in Okh'Shenev but at least we'll be afloat and able to try again.'

The Hierarch had a long face, but his jowls curved out and gave a roundness to his cheeks that made it seem that he smiled very easily. That and his grey eyes gave him a benevolence that did not fool the captain for a moment.

'We will keep going,' the Hierarch said. 'We are close.'

The captain felt the ship rise beneath the next

wave, teeter at the top of the swell and then plummet into the next watery valley. The ship was solid and heavy, a thousand tons, but the gale tossed each of those tons about as casually as a toy.

'Hold steady,' he said automatically, though the helmsman's powerful arms were straining at the wheel. As the stern tilted up he felt the vibrations of the engines through the deckplates die away, then pick up again as the ship surged forward. He had long ago ceased passing down instructions to the engine room from the bridge. The whole process of telegraphing orders was too slow. He had had to leave it to the guts and instincts of the chief engineer to work out when the stern was so high that the screw was out of the water and would tear itself from its shaft unless revolutions were cut. Then, the moment the blades were back underwater, they had to engage the pistons again and go full ahead to have any steerage way at all against this monstrous wind.

'How close, sir?' he demanded, almost begged. 'We must have overshot your intended landing place by now.' They had been heading for a port called Dover.

'Oh, we almost certainly have,' said the Hierarch calmly. 'We are much too far to the west, but my colleagues tell me there is somewhere ahead we can use.'

The captain ground his teeth and pitched over to the exposed starboard wing of the bridge. He peered round the combing. 'Lookout, there! Anything?'

'Black as night, sir,' the man called back. *As night,* the captain thought as he swayed over to the port wing, aware of the Hierarch's gaze. It was barely third second quarter, the middle of the afternoon, and he had been assured the sun rose and set in the New World at just the same times as back home. They should have had another quarter of daylight.

The port lookout was just as unforthcoming and the captain made his way back to his chair in an agony of doubt. The ship was wending its way down a channel of water that simply didn't exist back home and there was no guessing anything useful from the charts he had.

They had started at Okh'Shenev, which was in much the same kind of place in Old and New Worlds, on the coast of an almost inland sea that here was called the Baltic. Then they had wended their way westwards through some narrow straits. But back home, back in civilisation, the top left corner of the continent – which was to say Golekh's northern land frontier and its northern neighbour Toskhes – formed the Toskhes peninsula, which stretched in a north-westerly direction into the upper reaches of the Great Ocean. Here in the New World, apparently, Toskhes and a large chunk of northern Golekh formed an island, Enkhlon. It was separated from the rest of the continent by a stretch of water that ran approximately from the northeast to the southwest. The stretch gave direct access to the Great Ocean without needing to risk the Arctic weather, and they were in that stretch now. Apparently it was quite wide, several miles even at its narrowest, but he had a horrible, claustrophobic feeling of being squeezed in by walls of rock on either side, just the other side of all the spray, just out of sight in the darkness.

A whistle penetrated his thoughts and he snatched at the speaking tube. The ship moved and he pawed ridiculously at thin air, catching the tube on the second attempt.

'We're taking water in the hold, skipper,' a thin voice shouted. 'The hatch has sprung.'

'Get whoever you need on the pumps. Rouse the offwatch crew if necessary.'

'Right-o.'

The captain slammed the tube down, took a breath to steady his resolve, and turned. He would face them. He would tell them it was impossible. Yes, it had been a privilege – an enormous privilege, with far-reaching beneficial consequences for his soul and the souls of his family – to carry a mission from the Congregation to the unevangelized lands of the New World, but . . .

One of the Wise, a woman with grey hair, had stepped on to the bridge and she pointed in the direction of the starboard beam.

'Three miles in that direction,' she said.

The captain hesitated for just a moment, then turned to the helmsman. 'Starboard . . . starboard . . .' He kept one eye on the Wise's outstretched arm, which moved slowly round to the bows as the ship turned beneath him. The ship bucked madly as it presented its broad, flat sides to the wind and the waves, but then the wind was on its quarter and it settled down again.

Immediately the Wise was pointing dead ahead he snapped, 'Hold that course.' Then: 'A harbour, your Reverence?'

'No, open sea,' said the Wise, 'but we will be safe there. Landpower discharges into the ocean and we can use it.' For a moment the calm, measured tones wavered with eagerness. Here on the ship, the Wise were removed from the landpower; the cell had been subsisting on the power it stored within itself, almost like a battery. They looked forward to returning to the source as much as a fish to water or as the captain, at that point, looked forward to returning to dry land.

The captain said, 'You realize we are now pointing straight at the coast of Enkhlon?'

'We will not hit it if you do as we say,' the Wise said. The captain had not been talking to her but the Hierarch. He looked directly at the man.

'And, sir, you realize Enkhlon is the Domon'el's territory?'

'Precisely,' said Hierarch Re Nokh, formerly a chaplain of the Might of Golekh. 'It will be good to be back.'

Too cold for farming, too stormy for fishing, and the people of Brighthelmstone weren't in the least disturbed. It was only to be expected, as their fathers and grandfathers and great-grandfathers had expected it in their turn over the centuries. It was part of the great cycle of Brighthelmstone's existence, and on a tempestuous February day the cycle decreed that the men of the village – and not a few of the women or indeed the children – should congregate in the taverns and alehouses and while away the winter.

The walls were thick, the shutters were down, and the thrumming of the wind and the tearing crackle of the waves on the shingle beach were only background noises above the hubbub and the smell; the sour stink of people, the nose-cloying scent of woodsmoke and the sweet tang of spilled beer. Perhaps that was why no one immediately noticed that the noise outside had stopped.

The realization spread slowly, starting near the door and spreading out into the rest of the room. People heard something, or rather they realized they could *not* hear something, and stopped talking, the better not to hear it. The silence spread with the dawning awareness that the storm was over. Not just passing, *over*. The wind no longer howled. The fire rose straight up the chimney, drawing out the smoke, unimpeded by gusts of cold air coming in the other direction. Even the sound of the swell against the beach, which should have lasted several more hours, had stopped.

The door opened. 'There's a boat off the coast! Hollykor!'

The crowd of drinkers poured out like the tide.

Outside there was a noise after all, but not the noise of a storm. It was like a thousand voices humming, very faintly. The sound was all about them but somehow there was no doubt it came from the ship that was anchored a quarter of a mile away. It was bigger than any Christian ship they had ever seen, black and rusty and ugly. Two puny masts fore and aft, no sign of any kind of sails, and a tall, thin chimney amidships that vented a stream of black smoke.

The ship sat in the middle of a circle of pond-calm water. In a large half circle around it they could see the waters of the English Channel continuing to rage and blow, but the waves broke as if hitting a submerged sea wall. Within the circle, the sea shone blue in the light of the sun from the matching circle in the clouds above. The waters lapped gently at the beach at their feet and the air was as still as a June morning.

'It ain't natural!'

' 'Course it ain't! It's Hollykor witchery!'

Nervous murmurs spread through the crowd at the 'W' word. Brighthelmstone had had very little to do with the red-haired strangers in the six years since the end of the Rebellion. Their experience was limited to the sight of the occasional Hollykor steamer on the horizon, heading to or from Portsmouth further down the coast.

They knew by rumour and gossip about the Leased Territory, but it was nowhere near the South Downs and hence no danger to them. They knew that the chief of the Hollykor had their Christian king in his thrall, but it didn't interfere with the fishing and that was as far as their patriotism extended. And they knew without a shadow of a doubt that the Hollykor were pagans and witches, because everyone knew it anyway and because they were foreign so what else would you expect?

This was different. These Hollykor weren't passing

by on the horizon. They were *here*. The ship had put down a boat and men were climbing down into it.

'Fetch a priest,' someone said. The reluctant minister was duly pushed to the front of the crowd. 'Nah, not that one. *You* know.'

The crowd fell silent. This was serious, but needs must. The people of Brighthelmstone were good Protestants and would damn the Pope as cheerfully as the next man, but you fight fire with fire and they all knew that magic of this magnitude called for Latin and holy water.

So Father Peter, who hadn't worn his vestments or said the Mass publicly in years, was dragged out of his cottage and paraded down to the beach. The Hollykor boat had just reached the shingle.

'Go on, Father!'

'We're right behind you!'

'Give the heathen sons of bitches – excuse my French, Father – what for!'

The people of Brighthelmstone clustered nervously above the high water mark and Father Peter stood, just as nervous but firm, on the shingle before them. He held out his Bible to the figures approaching him, so that the gold cross on it caught the sun and shone.

The man in the lead wore robes not unlike his own, of scarlet and white. A cluster of black-garbed figures followed behind, and on either side were men in red tunics, kilts and silver breastplates and helmets. These, Peter noticed too late, carried rifles.

The scarlet and white one, a jowly man with grey

eyes, was walking without fear or hesitation up to Peter. Peter drew a breath

'Get thee behind me, Satan!' Then it occurred to him that if this Hollykor were indeed to get behind him, he would be standing closer to Brighthelmstone than he now was. 'Behold, I have given you authority to tread upon serpents and scorpions, and over all the power of the enemy, and nothing shall in any wise hurt you!'

The man stopped and looked at him quizzically.

'Thou shalt not suffer a witch to live!' Peter said hopefully. The words were starting to run together in his head and he plucked with increasing desperation at familiar phrases. 'He that sacrificeth unto any god, save unto the Lord only, shall be utterly destroyed.' The man just stood there. 'And . . . and if a man sell his daughter to be a maidservant she shall not go out as the menservants do!'

Peter realized with horror that while he might still be quoting from the right book he was definitely in the wrong chapter. He raised his other hand and used his last resort. He flicked his hastily consecrated holy water at the Hollykor.

The man blinked, bowed his head, then slowly put a finger to his eye and rubbed away the drops. He turned to one of the armed men behind him and said the last thing that Peter was to hear this side of martyrdom.

'*Vev'khetem efeov.*' Shoot this idiot.

And while the man cocked his rifle and raised it, the Hierarch strode on up the beach.

Seventeen

Time and Tide

The February storms had died down but the air battered against the trees around the graveyard, warm and wet and heavy. The moisture in the air was somewhere between rain and mist; damp seeped into everything but the dry voice of the priest. It occurred to Daniel Matthews that if he were facing the wind so that it blew into his face and his eyes, rather than buffeting against his back, then he would be able to explain away the tears that coursed down his face.

Or perhaps no explanation was needed. He hung his head and let the sobs come as the mortal remains of Francis Wetherby were consigned to the soil of Branheath.

The graveyard was packed. Francis had made his mark on many lives. He had never officially been re-instated in the incumbency of the parish following the defeat of Parliament, but few paid attention to such legalities. Besides, Branheath was within the Leased Territory and exempt from the usual rules of the Church of England. Francis had been the spiritual leader and bastion of the village in a time of turmoil and crisis. He had been father and husband to many children and women who would otherwise have been left destitute. Daniel's tears were not the only ones.

Daniel sneaked a sideways look at his own father. Dhon Do's face was grave, solemn, but his eyes were dry. Daniel remembered Dhon Do's only words on the subject: 'He died in his own bed in a time of peace, and that's more than most of my friends ever had.' At the time it had seemed callous. But if you had seen armies wither away under the flickering muzzles of machine guns, Daniel supposed, then the death of an old man who had seen his three score years and ten was put into perspective. Of course you mourned, but in your own way.

Eventually it was over, the last 'Amen' said, the grave filled in. The mourners filed slowly out of the churchyard, some of them nodding to Daniel and Dhon Do, others ignoring them. They had known Daniel all his life and they remembered John Donder, but once the true identity of Daniel's father had become known to them a barrier had come up.

The arrangement, so long ago now, had been that Daniel would come with his father just for a short while and decide if he liked it; if not then he could return to Branheath. Then the airship carrying him had been seized, and he had been shot and got caught up in the succession of the king and the defeat of Parliament and ... somehow he had never made a formal decision to leave Branheath and throw in his lot with his father, yet somehow it had never been in question.

Dhon Do put an arm around his shoulders. 'We should move,' he said quietly. 'The tide will turn soon.' Daniel nodded mutely, and they turned to follow the crowd.

A mournful whistle sounded in the distance, drifting through the trees, and a faint smell of oily steam brushed against their noses. They exchanged glances.

'I told them to keep it quiet,' Dhon Do said. 'Don't they have any respect?'

Daniel managed a very faint smile. Francis would have been amused.

'They're giving us a hint,' he said.

They had followed the crowd as far as the inn, but they had been hanging back and now they were on their own. It said everything there was to say about the gulf that lay between father and son and their former fellow villagers. Six years ago, Dhon Do had politely asked Francis if he would be his chaplain. Francis had just as politely refused, not wanting to spend his days surrounded by unashamed heathen he would never be allowed to evangelize. So, Dhon Do and Daniel had made the trip down to Branheath every Sunday, and in Daniel's case more often than that. Yet always the gap had been growing, and now they didn't even have to say goodbye – there was no one to say it to.

'We should take it,' Dhon Do said. On the other side of the inn door the sounds of the wake were just starting, but he guided Daniel away from it and into the trees that surrounded Branheath.

Daniel stopped suddenly and looked back. He

rubbed his shoulder absently. His wound often ached in damp weather.

'Did you forget something?' Dhon Do said. Daniel shook his head.

'No . . .' His gaze traversed slowly across the village. Inn, cottages, green, pond, church – the cradle of twelve years of his life. 'Now Francis has died . . .' A look of wonder crossed his face. 'I probably won't come back. Ever.'

Another hoot. 'I'm coming, I'm coming,' Daniel said. He turned his back abruptly on the village and kept walking. Dhon Do paused a moment, then followed him.

A minute later they were in the clearing, filled by two railway carriages and the black, gleaming bulk of the locomotive. It was one of the latest steam turbine models from the Old World, and the engine was turning over idly. There was no station as such here – the train had simply stopped at the point of the First Railway closest to Branheath. Two sets of tracks ran through a tunnel in the trees. To the east they now ran all the way to London and beyond, and to the west they ran the short distance to Povse'okh. Golekhi soldiers stood around the clearing in their mustard yellow uniforms and capes, rifles at the ready, and a machine-gun crew perched in its nest on the roof of the rear carriage. Dhon Do was a marked man according to Oliver Cromwell's God's Army of Albion, as by extension were Daniel and anyone else foolish enough to come close to the Overlord of Enkhlon. Security was taken seriously. It had only been by severe force of character that Dhon Do had avoided an armed guard accompanying him to the graveyard.

They climbed up into the Overlord's carriage, Dhon Do pulled on the cord and the train started to move.

His son was silent as the train pulled away. Oblivious of his father's gaze, Daniel sat in a chair by the rain-specked window with his chin resting in his hand. He looked moodily out at the countryside passing by to the rhythm of the engine's beat. To give him privacy with his thoughts, Dhon Do sat at his desk and shuffled through a few papers. They were all reports he had read beforehand. The steward poked his nose in to offer refreshments; Dhon Do waved him away quietly before he had opened his mouth.

Every now and then Daniel would rub his shoulder again. *My boy*, Dhon Do thought with a sudden, bitter burst of pride and sorrow. *Not yet eighteen and he has more war wounds than his father to boast about. What has my son become?*

Well, at first his son had become a teacher. The only two friendly Holekhor to speak English were Dhon Do and Daniel; furthermore, thanks to Francis, Daniel could also read and write in the language. So, much of the last six years had involved Daniel handing on his knowledge in that area. By now the first wave of pupils were sufficiently proficient in the language to teach it themselves, and they were professionals – teachers by vocation rather than chance. Daniel was still employed in checking the quality of their work but he had effectively put himself out of a job.

And he would be eighteen in another month. The young boy that Dhon Do had first met fleeing for his life had grown into a young man to be proud of. Adolescence, exercise and a good diet had given him a physique not unlike a full-blooded Holekhor. He was intelligent, with a lively mind, and he spoke the One Tongue in a pleasant tenor voice almost as well as Dhon Do spoke English.

Yet, where did he go from here? If Dhon Do had never returned and upset his life, if he had stayed in Branheath, by now he would either be married and settled down to a lifetime working in the manor gardens, or following his old dream to Virginia. Dhon Do suspected the latter. Even if he had never got as far as the Americas, he would have left home for somewhere. It was in the blood.

Whatever it was, it would still have been too tame for this Daniel. This Daniel's horizons had been broadened beyond anything that his old life could have provided. But what could he do? All the opportunities for an eighteen-year-old Holekhor male lay back in the Old World, in which Daniel had never shown much interest. By the time Daniel spoke the One Tongue well enough that he could have made his mark back in what Dhon Do considered home, he and Dhon Do had become too used to his being around here.

Daniel was Dhon Do's legal and natural son by the standards of both worlds. The Domon'el had declared Dhon Do Overlord of this island of Enkhlon, and one day Daniel would inherit that title. You couldn't take a young boy who had never been more than ten miles from the village of his birth and make him Overlord of an entire country; you could however take him and groom him so that when the time came, he was up to the task. That was what Dhon Do had been quietly doing for the last six years, and would continue to do, he hoped, for many more. But there is more to life than grooming and Dhon Do wanted it for his son. He hadn't missed the sighs, the gloomy looks, the occasional withdrawn reverie. Daniel needed company. Society. Friends.

Girls! What was he going to do about them? In this, as in everything else, Dhon Do had complicated Daniel's old life out of recognition. The old life was so simple: boy and girl grew up together. Boy and girl found they enjoyed each other's company, and one day boy would find he had managed to put a baby into girl. Boy and girl married and everyone, even Francis, pretended the baby must have been conceived on the wedding night. And they were happy with each other for the rest of their lives, because life was simple and uncomplicated and you could do that kind of thing without outside distractions getting in the way. Perhaps it fell short of the Biblical ideal but it worked, and while God wanted all his followers to be perfect, he knew they weren't, which was why he had sent his Son.

No more. Daniel had been raised by a priest in the Christian belief and he would never accept a Holekhor High Marriage, while the kind of Holekhor girl who married the Overlord's son would expect nothing else, and that was before you even began to consider the differences in religion and outlook. So, if Daniel was to marry, it would be in the Christian tradition and to an English girl.

But which English girl? His prospects and his horizons were social worlds apart. The Overlord's son ought to marry into at least minor aristocracy. Dhon Do had met a few English lords and he couldn't see any of them handing their daughter over to a half-breed bastard commoner, formally uneducated beyond a few basic social graces, conceived in a hayloft and born in the back room of a smoky inn.

It was a conundrum. Daniel was caught between two worlds, and as the man who had got him there, Dhon Do felt more than a father's normal responsibility.

The thrum of the rails changed in pitch and the engine slowed slightly, snapping Daniel out of his pre-occupation. Excess steam boiled out of the valves and billowed past the windows. They were coming into Povse'okh. Daniel glanced glumly over at Dhon Do, who smiled. 'Just time to change,' he said. Life went on, and Francis's funeral had been just a hiccup in this day full of much more important business.

The Overlord of Enkhlon shuffled the papers back into some kind of order and put them away while Daniel held on by the door and waited for the train to come to a halt. Dhon Do had other worries now, problems more immediate than perpetuating his line. Time and tide waited for no one, and a third example of something in this category was coming through the Povse'okh gate in – he checked the watch at his waist – just over a quarter.

Were it not for the gate itself, still towering over the hilltop and dominating the countryside, Povse'okh would have changed beyond recognition in the six years since the arrival of the Holekhor. The gate stood in the middle of a highly fortified citadel. Ramps and ditches and walls had been cut into the hillside and the chalky turf of England. The hill itself was riddled with a network of tunnels, a colossal magazine that held most of the occupying army's munitions. The main store was underground, almost directly beneath the gate. Around the gate, the rings of the old hill fort had been flattened and the entire area where the tented camp had once stood had been cleared, replaced by more permanent structures of brick and wooden buildings half a mile away. The old camp was a flat staging place and normally it was packed full of Enkhlonki goods destined for Golekh back in the Old World: tin from Cornwall, coal from Wales and the Midlands and Northumberland, livestock and crops from all over the island.

Now even that had been swept away. Gusts of rain swept over a staging area packed full of soldiers. Yellow-clad infantrymen stood at ease in squares, rifle butts resting on the ground. Around them, more squares: the blue of Skymight, the black of engineers. Rows of well-groomed nenokhs, hair plaited and tusks polished, loomed at the back of the parade, dwarfing their drivers and the foot soldiers ahead of them. Red-clad artillery crews waited by their pieces, guns loaded and awaiting the order. The faint murmur of an air-ship formation overhead tickled the ears, hidden the other side of the cloud layer.

At the very front, his entire army behind him, stood Dhon Do in his smartest, whitest dress uniform and nenokh-hair cloak. Drops of water formed on the rim of his gold-plated helmet and its silver hawk, which he had personally burnished until they gleamed. His epaulets were heavy on his shoulders. He hadn't turned himself out like this since greeting Oliver Cromwell at the gates of Oxford.

Dhon Do was so close to the gate that he couldn't see its edges without moving his head. The gate was still on the out-tide and it was like gazing into the deepest, darkest night. Nothing could come out of the Old World on the out-tide, even light; but while he couldn't see into the Old World, the Old World could see him. So he kept his face impassive, even though he really was not looking forward to what lay ahead. Any moment now . . .

The dark turned grey; specks of colour and light began to appear; and suddenly a live picture emerged out of the gloom as light and sound from the Old World flooded in on the in-tide. On the other side of the gate was a scene that was almost the mirror image of this one, right down to the solitary man standing at the head of his forces, wrapped in a white cloak; though these massed ranks of military might were there to say goodbye, not hello, and the man was bare headed. There was an easterly wind blowing into the gate in the Old World. The imported breeze blew rain into Dhon Do's face and stirred the feather plume in his helmet.

The solitary man on the other side began to walk. From his point of view he would be walking into the dark, but to Dhon Do it was as if he simply strode across the parade ground. He stopped when he was ten feet away and nodded with a faint smile at Dhon Do. Neither man came any closer to each other.

'*Parade! Atten-shun!*'

The glorious sound of a thousand feet slamming into the ground in perfect unison. Not a single step out of synch.

'*Present the loyal salute! Gun the first – FIRE!*'

The first gun roared its tribute, and while its echoes were dying away the second followed suit, then the third and so on down the line. Finally the last reverberations had faded away.

Dhon Do marched two steps forward and dropped to one knee, head bowed.

'Welcome to the New World, Lord,' he said.

Eighteen

The Ruling

The 134th Domon'el of the Realm of Golekh sat on a dais at the far end of the mess hall. His grim-faced honour guard stood around him in full ceremonial: gold-laced kilts and cloaks; silver, curving helmets. Drawn from the oldest of the Common families and selected for height and stature, they were the only people permitted to carry an unsheathed weapon in their Lord's presence. They held their polished battle-axes at the ready.

And yet, the Domon'el who sat in their midst seemed to dominate them. It went against all reason. Rather than the determined leader of a powerful nation, he looked more like a scholar, or perhaps a bookkeeper to a well-to-do businessman. And indeed, as Khorovo-domon, heir elect to the 133rd Domon'el, his interests had always been more bookish than military. Many had thought his inauguration would usher in a safe period of unambitious peace. Unfortunately, his scholarly interests had lain in quite different directions. His inauguration had taken a scholar with an interest in military history and given him supreme reign over a powerful, military state.

He had close-cut greying hair over the back and sides of his head, and a longer fringe at the front to hide a receding hairline. A smart, short, clipped beard covered the lower half of his face and a quite prominent jaw. Steel-rimmed glasses, round, would sometimes catch the light and conceal his eyes. The angle at which he held his head always suggested a faint air of challenge, as if daring you to contradict him. In contrast to the splendour of the uniforms his clothes were far simpler; shining, knee-length boots, a white kilt and a grey tunic with a light gold chain draped around his shoulders. His elbows rested comfortably on the arms of the chair but the fingers of his right hand were poised slightly above the velvet, as if it would only need a slight nudge to bore him and cause the fingers to start tapping.

Daniel walked slowly through the crowd towards the man who was, technically, his Lord and Master. He had changed out of his funeral clothes into something more Holekhor: a short cloak, a tunic, and he had even been persuaded to wear a kilt for the occasion. Daniel still thought of himself as English, but turning out like a native would only have embarrassed his father and it would not have been helpful.

He could feel the eyes of the court drilling into him, but he had been prepared for this and his child-hood experiences with the boy who was now King of England and Scotland gave him no illusions about the greatness of rulers. He held his head high and kept his step steady.

Dhon Do stood to one side of the dais. His father winked at him, then turned to face the Domon'el.

'Lord, I present my son, Daniel.'

Daniel bowed with a flourish, in the manner he had seen on his occasional visits to the court of King Charles. He wasn't wearing a hat that he could have swept off – the Domon'el's court did not go for head-wear – so he mimed the action.

'Young man,' said the Domon'el. His voice could have been deep and musical but his tone seemed almost flat and uninterested. It added to the implied challenge behind every word the Domon'el spoke. 'Stand up.' Daniel did so. The Domon'el's gaze was appraising but his fingers had finally relaxed. 'We have heard a great deal about you. How old are you?'

'I'm seventeen, sir,' Daniel said. 'I'll be eighteen next month.'

'You speak the One Tongue very well.'

'Thank you, sir. It's a very easy language.' It occurred to Daniel too late that this might not have been the wisest way of putting it. But it *was* an easy language. The hardest part was learning the new words; once you had them in your head, they were all handled in exactly the same way. Latin was harder.

The Domon'el finally smiled, which is to say, he showed his teeth. There was little humour in the expression that reached his eyes.

'Though your native accent is noticeable. It is quaint, but not an obstacle. We shall make a Ruling.' He nodded to an aide who waited at the edge of the dais. The man carried a gold-plated pole and he thumped one end on the wooden boards.

'Attend to the Ruling of the Domon'el!'

There was only a slight pause, a momentary silence as the crowd was taken by surprise – a Ruling had not been on the agenda, so far as anyone knew – but suddenly everyone save the guards and Daniel dropped down on to one knee. Daniel followed half a second later when he saw that even his father had followed suit. The wide-eyed glance he gave Dhon Do was meant to say *What's going on?*

The neutral gaze he got back said quite clearly, *Shut up and pay attention.*

The Domon'el rose to his feet.

'This island of Enkhlon has been a loyal tributary of Golekh for six years. Our devoted general and servant Dhon Do has governed here in an exemplary manner, and while we have seen little of him at our court, we have no doubt his time has been usefully spent. Too many of our territorial rulers use their appointments as excuses for living well, with their responsibilities a mere technicality worthy of as little of their attention as they can spare. Dhon Do, you work hard and well and I intend to make your life even harder here in Enkhlon.'

Daniel breathed again, without realizing that he had stopped. For a moment he had had a horrible feeling that his father was going to be recalled to Golekh.

'But first we must reward you properly for your achievements so far. Enkhlon is no longer a tributary of Golekh. We declare it to be a province. Dhon Do, you are no longer Overlord of this island. You are its Prefect. Commensurate with your new position, you and your family are no longer Common. We declare you High. Welcome, noble Dhon Do, High Man of the Inner Ward.'

The Domon'el paused to let the applause ring out. Everyone was still kneeling, so the assembled crowd thumped their fists on the floor. Daniel looked open-mouthed at his father. He knew Dhon Do well enough to see that the look of polite, pleased surprise on his face was a mask. Dhon Do was waiting to see the catch.

The Domon'el held up his hand, to immediate silence.

'Dhon El son of Dhon Do,' he said. Daniel swung his gaze back to the man on the dais. 'It is no longer appropriate for you to live your life in low-born anonymity. Your father is one of our most trusted servants and you must be treated accordingly. We raise you to the rank of High Man of the Outer Ward and we look forward to seeing much more of you at our court.'

More applause, and Daniel felt a vast, empty space opening up beneath him. He hadn't expected this. He knew Dhon Do hadn't expected it either – if he had, he would have briefed Daniel on how to react.

The Domon'el held his hand up again.

'Enkhlon is a rich island and it makes Golekh rich in turn, but that is no longer enough. Golekh's population has been growing for a generation and we need somewhere to put these people. Before leaving

Golekh we announced our new policy on emigration. Dhon Do, five thousand Common families and a hundred High are poised to enter this land through the gate. Within six months, we intend to see those families settled here. You will see to it. That ends my Ruling.'

The aide thumped the floor again. 'The Domon'el has Ruled!'

'And now,' their Lord said. 'Dhon Do, Dhon El, stand up in front of me.' He stepped down from the dais and clicked his fingers. An aide hurried up to him with two silver bracelets, intricately carved, on a large purple cushion. Only Dhon Do's people had been unprepared for the Ruling; the Domon'el's people had it well in hand. The Domon'el took the first bracelet, snapped it open and fastened it to Dhon Do's left arm above his elbow. 'Congratulations, Dhon Do,' he said. Dhon Do bowed. Then the Domon'el took the other and fastened it to Daniel. 'And you, young man.' He patted Daniel's arm, and his smile was that of someone watching a mouse walk unawares towards a waiting cat. 'Mhor Sen, the Khorovo-domon, is your age and is looking for groom-spouses to join his High Marriage. We cannot dictate whom they should be – it is a matter for young hearts – but now you are High, do not be surprised if you are invited.'

'Five thousand families,' Dhon Do muttered. 'Five *thousand*!'

'Marry his son!' Daniel had his own worries. '*Marry* his *son?*'

There was half a quarter's grace before lunch with the Domon'el. The mess hall was being set for the meal, and the guests had time to reflect and time to change. Daniel and Dhon Do were in their private rooms.

'Five thousand!' Dhon Do stared at a map of Enkhlon that hung on one wall, as if hoping the answer would magically appear. Perhaps an invitingly large empty space, marked 'settlers here'.

'I'm not . . . I'm not a . . .' Daniel paused, unsure as to exactly what he wasn't. He knew a few choice English words but none in the One Tongue.

'I know you're not and neither is Mhor Sen,' Dhon Do snapped. 'Furthermore, he is the Khorovo-domon, our Lord's heir and not his son, and no one is asking you to marry *him*. It's a High Marriage, not Common.'

'But . . .'

'For pity's sake, Daniel, I have more important worries. You're sitting next to Por De at lunch – have him explain it to you. He's heading for a High Marriage himself, one of these days. He's only got out of it this long by being the youngest son.' He turned back to the map and scratched his head. 'Frankly, boy, if I thought Mhor Sen shafting you would solve my problems, I'd hold you down myself.'

The deafening silence behind him finally made him turn around again. Daniel was staring at him in horror.

'I'm sorry.' Dhon Do smiled wryly. 'The Domon'el was right, he can't make decrees in a matter like this, but he can hint strongly to Mhor Sen and I'm sure you will receive an invitation. I'll support you all the way if you refuse. *When* you refuse. You can't be forced. All I ask is that you phrase it politely.'

'But if . . .' Daniel was learning to look ahead, to see his way through future deeds to the other side. 'If it hurts you, I mean, if it offends the Domon'el . . .'

Dhon Do gave a short, barking laugh. 'I won't be hurt. Now.' He put an arm round Daniel and turned his son towards the map. He tapped the Leased Territory with his free hand. It was roughly egg shaped, pointing safely away from London, with Povse'okh near the lowest point of the base. It had been negotiated at the Treaty of Oxford with King Charles II after his coronation and it was the core of Dhon Do's overlordship, a compromise that suited both sides. Charles could say that it was only leased to the Holekhor and that England was in no way occupied by a superior and hostile force. Dhon Do could settle the officers of his army within it, giving them land confiscated from local English landowners who had backed the wrong side in the Rebellion, and project the appearance back home of a conquered territory. Meanwhile, Golekh became the prime market for most of England's goods. Money for them went into the Leased Territory and hence to the rest of England, and everyone was happy.

'Will five thousand families fit into that?' he said.

'No,' Daniel said immediately.

'Will Charles agree to expanding the territory?'

'I doubt it.'

'Exactly.' Dhon Do gave a grim nod. 'The Domon'el is testing me, Daniel. He gave me a free hand in how I chose to govern this country, and he gets the expected financial returns, so he has no grounds for complaining about the Leased Territory, even if he doesn't agree with it. But the only way I can now please him, indeed the only way I can do my job with any degree of competence thanks to his new Ruling, is to seize more land and forcibly remove the English occupants. And you'll note I'm no longer Overlord. A Prefect is technically a step up, but it also binds me. I can no longer impose my own laws – I must impose the laws of Golekh. All of them.'

Daniel gazed at the map as the reality of the situation sunk in.

'Oh,' he said.

'Meanwhile,' Dhon Do said with forced cheer, 'let's see your bracelet.' Daniel held out his arm and they compared ornaments. The designs were very similar. Dhon Do's had an added wreath to show that he was the father of the family line, but otherwise both were an intricate filigree of interwoven strands that surrounded a rifle crossed with a sword, showing Dhon Do's military legacy. These were surmounted by something square and sharp that Daniel couldn't make out. Dhon Do gave an amused 'Hmph'.

'It's a plough,' he said. 'Their delicate way of reminding everyone that you and I come from farming stock. Doesn't matter, we're High now, and so will your children be, and their descendants. And this is your name – looks like you're officially Dhon El from now on – and the date of your investiture.' He tapped Daniel's bracelet. 'Do you know what this entitles you to?'

'Um . . . no,' Daniel admitted.

'Anything and everything. You can only be over-ruled by another noble from a longer pedigree, which at this moment means everyone, or a member of the Domon'el's household. And there won't be a Common girl in the Realm who will turn you down.' Daniel gave an abashed grin – it was not the first time he had had thoughts in that direction but he had never shared them with his father – and Dhon Do laughed. 'Use it wisely,' he said.

Somewhere a bell chimed for lunch.

'Look,' said Por De over the chatter in the mess hall. Three long tables stretched the length of the room in parallel lines, with the high table set across the top. He and Daniel sat at the near end of the first long table. Por De was a Centurion now but still one of the youngest Holekhor that Daniel knew – there was a mere fifteen years between them. Like Daniel, Por De was High; unlike Daniel, he had been born to it. Por De had once confided to Daniel that he found the conversation of Commoners much more intelligent.

Por De took an apple and a nut from the fruit basket in the centre of the table. He put them down on the tablecloth and tapped the nut with one finger. 'Man.' He tapped the apple. 'Woman.' He picked them up and knocked them together. 'In love, go to bed, babies happen.'

'I know that much,' Daniel said mildly.

'And that is where you English and Commoners leave it, as would anyone with sense. We High are much more sophisticated.' Por De took a fistful of nuts out of the basket, laid them down around the apple and tapped them each in turn. 'Man. Man. Man. Man. Man.' He picked up the apple and moved it around the circle. 'This one excellent poet. This one rich. This one, oh so boring conversation but hung like a nenokh and able to go till sun-up.' Daniel couldn't help it; he began to laugh as Por De moved the apple faster and faster around the circle. Por De paused for a sip of wine, then set out another arrangement of a nut surrounded by apples. 'And of course, the same can apply in reverse, several women and one man. All the men and all the women are heirs to land or money or power. In a Common marriage, one man and one woman, two families are united to their mutual advantage. But why just unite two families when you can unite many?' He pushed both circles together into an untidy pile of nuts and apples. 'One good High Marriage and an entire generation of power is made stable. As, my friend with a silver bracelet on his arm, you will find out.'

Daniel was still laughing until Por De delivered that last line. He had heard of High Marriage, of course; perhaps it was because his father had chosen to stay single that he had never pursued the matter further himself. He had heard talk of so-and-so's third wife or fourth husband, but had always assumed that the numbering was in sequence.

'So if Mhor Sen invites me to join . . .?' he said.

'He will choose his primary wife and will invite other men to join as groom-spouses. She will invite other women as wife-spouses. You give your pleasure to whichever of the women you like the most. Trial and error tells you which one that is.'

Daniel looked thoughtfully at the ring of apples. 'Is that before or after I marry them?' he said.

From the high table, Dhon Do noticed Daniel laughing and it made him glad. Laughter made Daniel's face light up and he hadn't seen that for a long time. He felt a sudden pang, even after all these years, because when he laughed Daniel resembled his mother.

'We are looking forward to this tour,' the Domon'el said. He showed his teeth again, with only slightly more humour than when he had smiled at Daniel, which probably meant he was quite pleased. 'We've seen it all on a map but that's not the same. When do we meet the boy king?'

'Tomorrow, Lord,' Dhon Do said. A reception had been booked at Hampton Court. Charles had been very good at finding excuses not to be at Povse'okh for the Domon'el's arrival. It would have been too like a vassal lord come to greet his master.

'And we open this railway . . . ?'

'Also tomorrow, Lord.' The First Railway now reached all the way to Dover. One of the Domon'el's faceless aides had noted that this happened almost at the same time as their Lord was due to visit Enkhlon and made the arrangements for a formal in-auguration. The Domon'el usually went along with these tedious tasks set for him by his subordinates on the grounds that they eased the path of good government.

'You have a lot of work ahead of you, Dhon Do,' the Domon'el said. 'This Army of the Gods . . .'

'God's Army, Lord,' Dhon Do said. 'The English only have one.'

'One too many, Dhon Do, if he goes around raising armies. There isn't room for five thousand families and these terrorists in the same island.'

Dhon Do let the Domon'el keep talking. His Lord wasn't saying anything that he didn't already know. Of course he knew that the elusive Khromell had to be dealt with. The question was, how? The dead-or-alive reward hadn't worked – there had been far too many not-Khromells turning up, and far too many already dead. To prevent time-wasting and casual murder, all such claims now had to be personally verified by Dhon Do, as the only senior Holekhor who had actually met the man for any length of time.

Someone coughed discreetly at his shoulder and handed him a note. Dhon Do excused himself to the Domon'el and took it. His eyebrows shot up.

'A problem?' said the Domon'el. He said it with a mix of offhandedness and threat; it suggested that if there was a problem, it was already dealt with or soon would be, and either way it had best not interfere with his visit.

'An incident on the south coast, Lord.' Dhon Do

took a breath to ask that he be released, and then glanced at the top of the nearby table. Daniel and Por De were still chatting and laughing, and the light glinted on Daniel's silver bracelet. Well, he thought, no reason why Daniel's new rank can't be put to the test. And Por De is experienced enough to look after him.

'An incident,' he said, 'that requires military response and intervention by a senior Holekhor. With my Lord's permission, I would like to send my newly ennobled son. It will be good practice for him.'

The Domon'el nodded. 'Good idea. By all means send the young man. We will observe his progress with interest.' Again there was that suggestion of a problem already solved; Daniel's progress would be interesting, because the Domon'el had said so.

'Then, Lord,' Dhon Do said and pushed back his chair. 'I must ask your permission to withdraw so that I can brief him.'

Nineteen

Daniel and the Prophets of Baal

'There's a Holekhor ship anchored offshore, sir,' said the lookout's voice from the tube. He was up in his eyrie at the very fore of the airship. 'And . . . and yes, there's a town above the beach.'

Daniel and Por De stood side by side at the front of the gondola, and the south of England passed slowly by beneath them. Charts of England were still less than ideal for course-plotting, but Brighthelmstone had not been hard to find. It was on the south coast, a few miles east of Portsmouth, and Portsmouth was the home of one of the radio beacons used for navigation. The small village was nestled in a valley that led down to the shore, which was why the lookout had seen the ship first. It was nothing special – a church and a collection of buildings around it, built on either side of a stream that trickled down to the sea. Black, greasy smoke smouldered from a large fire on the beach.

'Do we land, sir?' Por De said. He was playing the game, for which Daniel was profoundly grateful. Por De was born High and took orders from Dhon Do because Dhon Do was his superior officer. Daniel was just Daniel, raised to the nobility because the Domon'el said so, but Por De was extending him the proper courtesies as his father's representative. So Daniel just nodded and Por De gave the orders to the captain.

All they knew at the moment was that Holekhor of unknown provenance had landed on the south coast at Brighthelmstone and claimed the place for their own. One of the locals had been able to get away and had made it as far as Portsmouth, where he had been arrested for assault on a group of Holekhor that he passed in the street. He had been screaming about murder and witchcraft. The local Holekhor garrison commander had reported the fact by speak-wire to Dhon Do, and this was Dhon Do's response.

The garrison commander and Dhon Do had both drawn the same conclusions – if the Holekhor had arrived by ship then they probably weren't Golekhi and hence were trespassing. Daniel was English enough to consider that even Holekhor who *were* Golekhi were trespassing, but he kept the thought quiet. He peered at the ship through the binoculars.

'The Wise have been here,' Por De said quietly.

'How can you tell?'

'Look at the sea around the ship.'

Daniel looked. Everywhere else, the water was choppy; in a circle around the ship it was flat as a millpond. He felt the first gentle twinges of fore-boding. Over the last six years the Order of the Wise had surveyed the lines of landpower in England, but had otherwise left the place pretty well alone. Why were they suddenly becoming more involved?

He continued to scan ahead with his binoculars and suddenly he gasped. He swung on Por De and his face had gone white.

'You have to obey my orders, don't you?' he said.

'You're your father's deputy,' Por De said. 'Your orders are his orders, if I believe they are what your father would actually want.'

Daniel pointed. 'Then he'd want us to land on the top of the far hill. Where those crosses are.'

There were thirty crosses at the top of the slope that led down to the village, each with a man or a woman or a child nailed to it. The bodies hung limply and their hair and clothes fluttered in the breeze. The airship sucked in heavy air to bring it down to the ground, and made a pass to drop a smoke bomb and gauge the wind direction. A few minutes later it came back to land. Daniel was first out after the ground crew, and as they hammered in the guy ropes to secure the ship he ran to the nearest cross. It held a balding, middle-aged man, and Daniel stared up at him in horror. He had seen dead people before. He had seen men and boys killed in battle. He had seen people who had died naturally and he had seen the displayed heads of executed criminals in London. But he had never seen someone just murdered. He had never seen the result of one man deciding on a whim that he had the arbitrary right over another to decide whether the other lived or died.

Por De and some of the soldiers were following him. 'Cut them down!' he shouted. 'Cut them—'

There was a groan, a rattling cough from above him. He looked up, wide eyed and pale, as the man head's head twitched and lifted slightly. Bloodshot eyes glared down at him and thirst-blackened lips moved.

'Murderin' Hollykor bastard,' the man wheezed, and then the head dropped and the breath left his body in a long, slow sigh. His eyes stayed open and Daniel had to step aside to avoid the accusation in the dead stare. A dark stain spread across the man's trousers as all the muscles in his body relaxed in death.

Daniel barely realized his head was shaking. The monstrous injustice had pierced him to the core. 'No,' he whispered. 'I'm not. No. I'm not. I'm not. I'm not.'

Por De had seen the movement. 'On the double!' he shouted, and suddenly there were soldiers at every cross, lifting the victims down and laying them gently on the ground. Daniel watched it all through a trembling haze. He made himself breathe calmly, in, out, in, out. Medics were called for and they moved from victim to victim. Those who were still alive were covered in blankets and pillows put under their heads. Those for whom it was too late were simply covered up.

Daniel looked up at the cross again. It was empty now but he could still see the man there. And the hate, the accusation in those dying eyes that he thought would stay with him forever.

'The men can take care up here,' Por De said. 'Let's assess the damage below.' They walked down into the valley.

Daniel walked slowly through the ruins of Brighthelmstone. Closer to, among the buildings, he could see the damage. Bullet holes pockmarked the walls. Doors and windows were smashed in. The village was deserted.

'What happened?' he said. 'What the hell happened here?'

Por De just shook his head.

They came at length to the beach. It was a broad, steep shingle slope that swept down to the sea. The waves hissed onto it and dragged themselves back into the sea: a peaceful, sleepy sound.

The fire they had seen from above was much closer now, and Daniel felt far from peaceful and sleepy as he walked up to it. He had already guessed what it might be for, but guessing did little to prepare him. Whoever had made it had smashed up the village's fishing boats and piled the broken hulls up high. Before setting fire to the pile, they had drenched it with oil, probably from the ship. But first they had thrown the bodies on.

The corpses were charred, partly cooked and bald. All the clothes and hair had burnt away. What covered them didn't look like skin: it was rough and leathery and cracked, in some places still bubbling slightly. From the sizes and shapes of the bodies he could see that no one had been spared. Children and women as well as men were here, thrown casually on to the pyre so that they lay in all attitudes, upside down and right way up, on their fronts and on their backs, arms and legs splayed in all directions. The dead of Brighthelmstone stared at him from eye sockets that were dark and empty, their contents boiled away by the flames. They grinned at him, their faces pulled back by the heat but their teeth blackened and begrimed.

'Ahoy!' called a faint voice. Por De nudged him, and then nudged him again to make him turn away. A small boat was rowing over from the ship. Its bow crunched into the pebbles of the beach and the lead figure jumped out.

It was a grizzled man with a typical Holekhor beard that covered only his jaw. He smiled at them cheerfully as he clambered up the shingle.

'Good day, young sirs!' he said. Then he must have seen the silver bracelets that both wore. 'I'm sorry, I should have said my young noble sirs. Any chance of getting a new oil pump off you fine folk?'

'Who did this?' Daniel said. He was surprised at how calm his voice was. Then it suddenly burst out and he jabbed a finger at the fire. '*Who did this?*'

'Congregation, noble sir.' The man indicated the ship that was still anchored offshore. 'See, that's my boat there, and we got a bit knocked about in the storm—'

'The Congregation?' Por De said.

'What were they doing? *Why?*' Daniel demanded. The man looked blank.

'They're here on a mission, and all this . . .' He

waved a hand at the empty buildings. 'Well, heresy, the Hierarch said. Not my place to quibble with 'em, really.'

'*Heresy?*' Daniel shouted.

'Apparently, the local religion says someone nailed to a cross will die and come back to life again. Pretty daft, if you ask me. So the Hierarch thought he'd show how wrong they were . . .'

'Not *any* person!' Daniel shouted again. 'Just one and he was—'

Por De put a hand on his shoulder to calm him. 'The Hierarch might have been misinformed,' he said. 'Where is he now?'

'Whole party went inland, Centurion. Put a curse on the place and set off. Now, about that oil pump . . . only, you see, the Wise were able to calm the sea down for us but they said it'll wear off in another day or so without them around to top it up, so there's not that much time to make our repairs.'

Daniel turned and stormed away, and Por De had no choice but to follow him.

'Where are you going?' he said.

'Up to the ship.' Daniel didn't look round. 'We'll signal my father and tell him what's happened. Then we'll take off, track those murdering shits by air and blow them to—'

'We'll do no such thing, Daniel.' Por De sounded sorry but firm.

'*What?*'

'You can make your report,' Por De said, 'but I know what he'll say.'

'He'll say—'

'That this island is now a province of Golekh, as decreed by the Domon'el.' Por De completed the sentence for him. 'He'll point out that Golekhi law applies, and that means the Congregation can go where they will.'

'Where they will?' Daniel was shouting again. 'Do the laws of Golekh say they can just nail people to crosses if they want to?'

'The Congregation has free reign in matters of heresy, Daniel, and you Christians are heretics. Only one god, all other gods inferior or non-existent . . .' He shook his head. 'I really am sorry.'

Daniel glared at him with hatred. 'We'll make our report,' he said. 'And while we're waiting for a reply, we'll give these people a Christian burial. Unless, of course, that upsets the Congregation.'

'I can't think why it should,' Por De said.

It was gloomy inside the church but light enough for Daniel to see the desecration. It brought back memories of Parliament's troops sweeping through Branheath. They too, by some twisted logic, had been doing their religious duty. They had been sweeping away the detritus of the old, corrupt, Roman-style church and making sure the common folk could worship God in their own way – as long as their own way was the way that Parliament said it should be. The men who had wrecked his childhood and the missionaries of the Congregation really were two sides of the same coin.

Daniel had welcomed the Holekhor invasion because it ended the war. But if this was what it was to lead to . . .

Over the altar, someone had erected a wooden screen of icons of Holekhor deities. Daniel strode up to it, grabbed one side and heaved. It fell down with a crash. He looked around for the cross that had once stood there and found it lying on its side beneath the altar. It hadn't even been stolen, just contemptuously swept aside. He stood it carefully back on the altar.

A figure stood in the door of the church and blocked out the light. It was Por De, and he looked on in horror. 'Daniel, please.'

'Am I a heretic?' Daniel said bitterly. 'Crucify me.'

Por De took a step forward. 'Don't make jokes, Daniel.'

'Are the graves ready?' Daniel said.

'Not yet. There's a problem.'

Daniel glared at him and waited for him to spit it out.

'Some of the men guessed there might be a curse on this town, and that captain confirmed it,' Por De said. 'Even digging graves might upset the Pantheon.'

'The people are dead!' Daniel exclaimed. 'What more can they do to the Congregation?'

'If they're dead, they're past caring what happens to their bodies,' Por De said logically.

'We will bury them,' Daniel said. 'We will bury them because that is what Christians do, and we will bury them because the Congregation have said otherwise.'

Por De's voice became very quiet. 'Daniel, a commander only commands with the respect of his men. Order them to take on the curse of the Congregation and you will not remain a commander for much longer.'

'Assemble the men outside,' Daniel said.

'Daniel . . .'

Blood thundered in Daniel's ears. It was as if Francis stood beside him, and behind him all the saints of sixteen hundred years, and behind them all the heroes of the Old Testament. 'Assemble the men, Centurion! That's all I ask.'

'At once, sir,' Por De said. 'Can I ask what you intend to do with them?'

Daniel had found what he was looking for. Like the altar cross it had been swept to one side and it lay face down in the aisle. He picked the Bible up, dusted it down, smoothed the crumpled pages. He cradled it in his arms.

'Out,' he said.

Five minutes later the men were fallen in by the beach. Daniel stood in front of them and handed the Bible to Por De. 'Hold this,' he said, and turned to face the assembly. 'This book,' he whispered. His throat was dry. He swallowed a couple of times and took a deep breath, filling his chest.

'This book,' he said again, more loudly, 'is the holy book of the god of this land.'

Immediately he could see he had their attention. To the Holekhor, the only definitive scripture was the

Sacred Tellings. Individual gods of the Pantheon might have slim little volumes describing their attributes and giving a brief history of their deeds, but none of them had a book this size. To have all that number of pages devoted to one god had to be good.

Francis had once entertained the hope that an adult Daniel might enter the priesthood. His training had started early. Daniel had learned from his master during uncounted church services as an unofficial altar boy. He opened the Bible at Genesis.

'Let me tell you about the god of this land,' he said.

He described the creation of the world. He could have read it out loud but it would have been a long, slow process, delayed yet further by needing to translate as he went along. He could remember the details and so he just used the text to reinforce his memory. He described how the Lord God took some dust and breathed life into it, and that was the first man.

'The god of this land has been here right from the start,' he said. 'He is no newcomer. He is older than anything or anyone else.'

His ears just caught a few murmurs of interest, which stopped when Por De gave the men a hard glare. But the point had been made. The god of this world did things differently. Few gods of the Pantheon, even, had that kind of antiquity to back them up.

He described how Moses and his brother Aaron had gone to the Pharaoh of Egypt and demanded that the Lord God's people, the Israelites, be set free.

Pharaoh had laughed. To show the Lord God's power, Aaron had thrown down his staff on the floor. It turned into a snake. To show their power, Pharaoh's magicians performed exactly the same trick. Aaron's snake ate their snakes.

Still Pharaoh would not let the people go, so Egypt was inflicted with plague after plague, and his magicians could do nothing against it. The plagues never touched the Israelites. The final plague was the death of every firstborn male, human and animal, in Egypt. Pharaoh's own son was struck down . . . but the Israelites were spared.

Daniel paused to take a breath. The wind and the waves breaking were the only sound. He looked up at the men from under his brows.

'The Lord God, the god of Moses,' he said, 'is the god of this land too.'

He kept talking. He described the Israelites' invasion of the Promised Land, driving out the gods of the people already there. Again, he could see that he was getting through. By the thinking of the Pantheon, a variety of gods who were well established in a territory and worshipped by the inhabitants should have had much more power than the one god of a group of interlopers. But apparently not.

He described Samson, one man who could see off entire armies when the power of the Lord was in him.

He described Elijah, the one remaining servant of the Lord when the entire nation had turned to Baal. Elijah had challenged four hundred and fifty prophets of Baal to a contest. They would meet on a mountaintop, sacrifice a bull to their respective gods, and call on their gods to burn the body. The prophets killed their bull early in the morning and prayed to Baal all day, while Elijah made fun of them. Nothing happened. They started slashing themselves with spears and swords so that the blood ran. (Daniel saw a few faint nods at this point. Blood running – big power.) Still nothing. Finally, that evening, Elijah made his own sacrifice. Not only that, but he drenched the body and the altar with water. Then he prayed to the Lord God, and fire came down from the sky and burned up the soaking wet offering. The people of Israel were suitably convinced: they turned on the prophets and massacred them.

Finally, Daniel moved forward to the New Testament. He described how the message from God, which previously had just been thought to apply to the people of Israel, in fact applied to everyone. Officers from the invading army of Rome had turned from their gods and accepted just the one. The apostle Philip had converted an official of the Queen of Ethiopia. And as Paul and the other apostles commenced their travels throughout the empire of Rome, followers of the local gods had turned to the one true god time and time again. Everywhere the Lord's people went, other gods fell.

'Have I got through yet?' he murmured without looking up.

'You're getting there,' Por De murmured back in kind. 'May I take over? Please?'

Daniel glanced up at him, then nodded.

Por De closed the Bible and turned to his men.

'I don't know what arrangement the god of this land has made with the gods of the Pantheon,' he said in his address-the-men voice, 'but I for one am unwilling to antagonize him. If it is the custom for his followers to be buried in a particular manner, then I think we should do it.' There were quiet murmurs of agreement. Por De handed the Bible back to Daniel. 'With your permission, sir?' he said. Daniel took the Bible and nodded, and Por De started to give orders.

Daniel watched them keenly as they buried the people of Brighthelmstone. Digging Christian graves in the absence of the Congregation was a small, hollow victory – as Por De had pointed out, the inhabitants could no longer have any interest in what happened to their bodies – but it struck him suddenly that it was still significant. It was standing up to the rule of the Holekhor in England. And more important than that, for the first time *he* was standing up. He wondered how much more standing up he would have to do.

The airship had landed at the top of the east side of the valley. Across from it, at the top of the west side, two people lay on their fronts in the grass. A man with an ugly, lumpy face and a woman with a mop of red hair. Each had powerful field binoculars trained on the scene below them. The same incident that had led Daniel to Brighthelmstone had drawn the attention of God's Army of Albion.

'Holekhor nail them up, Holekhor take them

down,' the man said. '"And if Satan casteth out Satan, he is divided against himself; how then shall his kingdom stand?"'

'I don't know about Satan's kingdom, General,' said the woman. 'I do know that cracks are starting to show in the Domon'el's kingdom if the Congregation is here. I've heard whispers about this. The Congregation is unhappy that Dhon Do isn't promoting the Pantheon more vigorously.'

The man nodded slowly. 'It is a false hope, then. Holekhor fight Holekhor . . . but both factions are just as bad.'

'But the whole is weakened.'

'Very true. That is encouraging.' He peered down at Brighthelmstone again. 'The young man in charge looked almost as if he were preaching from the Bible. See where he is going with it.'

Down below, the young man they were watching had vanished into the church, still carrying the book in his arms. He reappeared a moment later without it.

'Yes, I would say, almost certainly a Bible.'

'Do you remember, Dhon Do had a son?' said the woman after a moment.

'I am unlikely to forget. Yes, it could be him.'

'He would be the right age by now,' she said thoughtfully. 'I'm glad he lived. I honestly thought that shot would kill him in the long run.'

'I take no pleasure in a child's death, and so I too am glad he lived. The fact remains that as a boy, he went where he was led and could not be held accountable; as an adult he has thrown in his lot with

pagans and witches. He has become our enemy too.'
The man rolled on to his back so he could put the
binoculars away in their pouch, then got to his feet but
stayed crouched low. 'We have seen what we came to
see. We should not get too close. With the Domon'el
in England, no doubt all Dhon Do's forces will be
especially vigilant.'

The woman stared at him. 'The Domon'el is in
England? The *Domon'el* is in *England*? You never said
that!'

The man paused for only a beat and had the grace
to look almost abashed. 'Did I not?' he said.

Half an hour later, they were still arguing and the man
had finally lost his temper.

'No, Mistress Connolly, I forbid it. No!'

It looked like a tinker's cart wending its way along
a track across the South Downs – unspecified junk in
the back, an old nag of a horse plodding along in
front and a man and a woman driving it. Oliver
Cromwell held the reins and looked fixedly ahead.
Khonol Le was animated, her hands gesticulating.

'But it's the Domon'el! Their leader! The head!
Cut off the head and—'

'Another one grows to replace it,' said Cromwell.
He sounded very tired. 'Every word you say only
convinces me that I was wise not to tell you about his
presence here. Killing him will sate your desire for
vengeance but it will do nothing to free this land of
the Holekhor.'

Khonol Le put her hands on her hips. 'What *will*

free this land, General? We've been trying for six years.'

'We have struck against the targets that the Lord has placed in our path. We have inflicted wounds upon Dhon Do's army. There is not a Holekhor in the land who walks abroad in security and comfort.'

'Don't dream, General! You're always talking about this Gideon of yours. Did he *scare* his enemies away?'

'No,' Cromwell said shortly, 'he did not. He stood and fought them, and one day, so shall we. Our strikes against Dhon Do are pinpricks, designed to anger him and remind him we are here. He cowers in his citadel at Povse'okh, and one day we shall have arms and men enough to beard him there in his den. Until that day we prepare, we gather the men and the weapons we need, and we do not do anything so mad as to kill the Domon'el, because that would bring down upon us a hornet's nest that we could never fight.'

Khonol Le kept her next thought to herself, because it was a treacherous one. Would Cromwell *ever* raise that many men? She doubted it. England was at peace; not a perfect peace, but a peace where fewer people died. She understood little of the causes that had led to its civil war, but they seemed by and large to have been resolved. The king took wise counsel, he listened to his Parliament – not as often as they might like, but more often than his father had ever done. And the Catholic religion, though not suppressed, was barely tolerated. Much of that came from the wise counsel. Whatever Cromwell said about Charles's private life and inner convictions – that he was secretly a Catholic and a whoremonger to boot – Charles had the sense to swallow his pride and present a public face with which no one could find fault.

Charles was king of two kingdoms. His job as King of Scotland seemed to be to turn up from time to time and tell the nobles how well they ran the kingdom for him. King of England was harder – it involved picking a course between different classes and religious convictions and often very touchy vested interests, navigating the minefield in such a way as to set off as few of them as possible. Yet England was healing. It was a slow, hard recovery with frequent relapses. In any healing process there comes a time when medicine and surgery have done all that they can, and one can only stand back and let the body's own mechanisms mend itself. That was what was happening now. To add another metaphor, England was an applecart that no one, but no one, wanted to overturn.

Meanwhile, Dhon Do blatantly courted the good will of England's rulers with gifts and favours, and in this land where the common people had so little power and the rulers had so much, that did much to ensure there would be no further uprising. At the same time, Khonol Le had grudgingly to admit, Dhon Do did what he could to see that the benefits of those gifts and favours did trickle down to the common people. There was little point in holding up a trunk if the base was not sound.

It was exactly what he had done to Toskhes. One reason Khonol Le had left her home country for the

New World was that the Conqueror's tactics had made motivating a decent resistance so difficult. And Dhon Do had followed her. Here, she was determined to draw the line.

So, instead, Khonol Le simply said, 'As the General commands.'

Cromwell shot her a suspicious, sideways look but said nothing further. A rumble came down from the sky and they both looked up. The airship had taken off from Brighthelmstone and was flying above them.

'I must head north,' Cromwell said. 'I need to check our cells in the Midlands and beyond. I am leaving you in charge here, and when I get back, I do not expect to find you have engaged in anything foolish. Do you understand, Mistress Connolly?' He glared into her eyes. 'Do you understand?'

Khonol Le simply repeated: 'As the General commands.'

Twenty

Full Facts and Fillies

The signal in one hand read:
Report full repeat full facts to king. Meet at Hampton tomorrow. DD.

The other was a terse confirmation that the king would grant Daniel an audience upon his arrival at Hampton Court.

Daniel had retired to the commander's cabin. Beneath the airship the South Downs fell away in an escarpment almost as impressive as the Ridgeway beneath Povse'okh, but he ignored the sight and read the first signal again for the tenth time. He had informed his father of all that had happened, with the necessary abbreviation of telegraph code; this had been the answer. Now he was heading for Hampton Court, as instructed.

But what to say when he got there? That Congregation missionaries had landed in Charles's kingdom, crucified some of Charles's subjects, and were still free? That Golekhi law wouldn't let Daniel lift a finger against them?

Yet the orders were clear. *Full repeat full facts.*

Daniel groaned and lay down on the bunk. He closed his eyes, which was a mistake, because inside his lids two dying, bloodshot eyes looked back at him in accusation from a cross.

There were two maps hanging on the wall of the Domon'el's quarters. One showed the island of Enkhlon and northern Europe, the other the Old World's Golekh and the occupied territory of Toskhes. The absolute ruler of the latter stood in front of them. The Domon'el, Dhon Do thought privately as he entered and shut the door behind him, was like a small child with a new toy.

'It's fascinating, Dhon Do, fascinating,' the Domon'el said. The light glanced off his glasses and made his smile yet more brittle. 'So similar and yet so different. Look . . .' He ran his hand up Enkhlon's east coast. 'Up here it's almost identical to Toskhes but down south . . . it seems so odd that Enkhlon should be an island.'

Dhon Do had been the one to report that fact, years ago, on his very first return from the New World. It could hardly be news to the Domon'el. Perhaps actually *being* in the New World had brought it home to him.

'It makes it more secure, Lord,' Dhon Do said.

'Yes. Unfortunately it has the same effect in reverse. I see no reason to stop with Enkhlon, Dhon Do. Consolidate here, of course; bring it fully into line . . . but one day . . .' He slapped the north of France. 'No reason why we can't continue to expand. No reason at all. It will just be a little harder than originally planned.'

Considerably harder, Dhon Do thought. The European nations had seen what had happened to England. Their northern coasts bristled with armaments ready to repel a further Holekhor encroachment.

'Did you know that in the New World the Great Pan is an inland sea?' the Domon'el said.

'The Mediterranean, Lord,' Dhon Do agreed. As it was his airships that had made the discovery, this was no news either.

'Think of it! Direct access to the heartland of the continent, rather than having to tramp across or around all those salt flats. There are opportunities here, Dhon Do. Vast opportunities. But forgive me, you know all this. Will you have tea?'

Dhon Do was awash with tea. The Domon'el didn't believe in drinking alcohol by day and yet no visitor to his quarters was allowed to escape unrefreshed.

'Thank you, Lord,' he said.

The Domon'el made a vague gesture with his right hand and his stewards immediately appeared with a tray. Dhon Do and his Lord sat on either side of a tea table made from native oak.

'So, what news from young Dhon El?'

Dhon Do reported the Brighthelmstone incident as concisely as he could.

'Here already? Well, it had to happen.' The Domon'el took a casual sip and gazed out of the window.

'Lord?' Dhon Do said, and got the full blast of the Domon'el's tooth-baring, humourless smile.

'The Congregation and the Order of the Wise have come to an arrangement, Dhon Do. Accordingly, I have felt it expedient to shift the basis of our relationship.' The Domon'el leaned forward and dropped his voice to a more confidential tone. His eyes were cold behind the steel glasses. 'The Congregation is not happy with the way this island is being proselytized, not happy at all, and you have given the barest co-operation to their missionaries and to the Wise who have been trying to survey the place. Don't argue: I'm too old a politician not to recognize all the blocking tactics. And I can see your point; I even agree, to a certain extent. This is *my* island, after all. But you have been perhaps overdoing it. You've been here six years, Dhon Do. Six years, yet apart from token presences in our various camps I have seen no reports of the Pantheon spreading here. None! The native god is still worshipped in every church, in every temple –' he meant *cathedral,* but the word did not exist in the One Tongue – 'and it must change! Milk? Have a biscuit.'

'Lord,' Dhon Do said carefully, 'I . . .'

'I know you follow the native god, Dhon Do.' The Domon'el nibbled on a piece of shortcake. 'He helped nurse you back to health when you were stranded here and good for him, but he is only a *native* god!' Small crumbs flew out of his mouth with the emphasis. It was rare for the Domon'el to emphasize anything; he must have felt this strongly. 'His name does not appear anywhere in the *Sacred Tellings* and while you can apply for him to be admitted to the *Confirmed Divinities* ... well, you know these things take time. If your boy gives you grandchildren, they might just live long enough to see him added to the Appendix. Now, you know that the Congregation and I have never seen eye to eye, but I can't just ignore them. To put it bluntly, I'm in a situation back home where I need their good will, and the long and the short of it is, I have granted their missionaries free access to Enkhlon. They will proselytize and the Order will provide them with the necessary support.'

Dhon Do almost choked on his tea.

'I respect your faith, Dhon Do, but I can't let your predilections stunt the spiritual growth of my subject peoples. They must be taught the true beliefs, and taught them fast. If that means crucifying a few natives then so be it. You want to protect them and I understand that, but needs must. These missionaries, and the many more that are to come, will not be interfered with. At all. I take it that is clear?'

And Dhon Do could only say, 'Of course, Lord.'

Hampton Court was a labyrinth of buildings, a maze built in red brick lying beside the silver Thames.

The royal palace was accustomed to visiting airships and Hampton Court had its own airfield. The king's own ship, *Ariel*, a gift from Dhon Do, was moored to one side and a mooring tower was always standing by, manned by a Holekhor ground crew. Hence it took Daniel just ten minutes from the first sighting of the palace to walk through the great front gates.

He was met, as he had thought he would be. He walked towards the guardhouse with Por De and a retinue of guards, and just as he got there he was greeted by an Englishman with a plump, round face and dark, arched eyebrows. The man was at the head of a similar retinue.

'Sir George,' Daniel said with a bow.

'Master Matthews,' said Sir George Monk, responding in kind.

When Parliament fell, the then unadorned and plain George Monk had been languishing in the Tower as a Royalist prisoner of war. Once he was officially on the winning side he could have simply walked out of the gates and returned to his military duties, but he had expressed a desire to meet his new king and pay homage. He had been flown to meet the still-grieving Charles at Povse'okh, and found that his new monarch was a heart-broken boy with little idea of what to do to consolidate his newly regained kingdom. Parliament might usually have insisted on a formal Regency, but Parliament was in no position to insist on anything and by the time it was again, Monk's accustomed place was at the king's side.

Daniel knew his father enjoyed dealing with the man. He spoke sense. Every idea Monk had seemed to be in the best interests of everyone. Monk had been the one to broker the Treaty of Oxford, which granted the Leased Territory to the Holekhor and saved face for both sides. Monk's suggestions had made sure the expected wave of retributions against the former rebels had not happened, and that had helped England heal as no one had ever expected it would. Toleration of the many forms of Protestantism was widespread; toleration of Catholicism barely existed. Charles had even expelled the privately hired priests of his mother, whose Catholicism had so inflamed tensions before the Rebellion, from the country. Charles didn't always like Monk's advice but he usually took it and had never regretted doing so.

And now he was Sir George Monk. He held no official title but he was the king's voice and conscience in almost everything.

'It is unusual to see you on your own,' Monk said.

'I've been, um, promoted, sir,' Daniel said with only a slight shyness. 'I'm ordered to speak to the king, then wait here until tomorrow.'

'We'll have a room made up for you,' Monk said. 'Follow me.'

Daniel told Por De to take the airship back to Brighthelmstone, pick up the burial party and return to Povse'okh. Then he went with Monk.

Hampton Court was like a small city, bustling with courtiers and officials. Some Daniel knew by sight, most were complete strangers. Many bowed slightly to Monk as they passed but for Daniel the usual expression was of reserved neutrality. It occurred to him that he was of course still wearing clothes that were pure Holekhor. He had changed out of the kilt but the leggings were baggy, he wore a small cape rather than a coat, his hair was shorter than allowed for by contemporary court fashion and he wore no hat or wig. If he had changed into more native . . . more *English* clothes, then he would probably have been taken for a young friend or relative of Monk's.

Monk led him along a network of panelled passages and as usual Daniel completely lost his bearings. He knew the general direction because Charles's state apartments were at the southeast corner of the palace, as far from the main gate as you could get. Eventually Monk knocked on a door and entered without waiting for an answer.

'Boy-troll! A sight for at least one mildly discomforted eye. How the devil are you?'

King Charles II had reached his full six-foot height since Daniel had first met him, and as a man he had filled out too. He was no longer gangly but graceful, with the poise and balance of a dancer. He came forward with his hand held out and a smile on his face. They were in the receiving room of the king's private apartments, a panelled chamber hung with portraits and drapes. It was warm and comfortable; the sleepy tick of a clock in the background made it almost soporific. Daniel noticed the large brass stargazing telescope, a present from Dhon Do on the king's last birthday. It was mounted on a tripod by the window and showed signs of frequent use. Charles loved science, and while he loathed the Holekhor – Daniel was the only one he was prepared even to try and be civil towards – he was quite happy to make use of their technology and devices.

'Charlie?' said a woman's voice, with the coo of

someone trying hard to be beguiling. Daniel blinked as the voice's owner entered the room. Even among the Holekhor he had never seen hair of such glowing redness. He would have been the first to admit his knowledge of women was not extensive but he would have been very surprised to find it was natural. She looked as if she was in her late twenties, a few years older than the king, but with the make-up it was hard to tell. She wore a dress of many complex layers that would have flounced even without her inside it. It presented a hazard to anything small and breakable on nearby tables. She came across the floor with a seductive saunter that must surely have been much more tiring than walking in a simple straight line.

'Charlie, please introduce me to your handsome young friend,' she said, and flashed Daniel a winsome smile. Charles rubbed his hands together.

'Boy-troll, this is Miss Dolly Witherspoon, the finest product of London's stage. I knew I was making the right choice when I said that women could be actors, and by George, I was proved so. Ain't she marvellous?'

'Hello,' Daniel said faintly.

'Aw'right?'

'And you can stop feasting your eyes on him, you little hussy,' said Charles. 'You ain't used me up yet.' Miss Dolly responded to his chuckle with a piercing cackle.

Daniel glanced in desperation at Monk, who had the look of someone trying as hard as he could not to be there without actually leaving the room.

'Go on, Dolly, show my guest what you can do,'

Charles said. 'Give him your Shakespeare. You'll like this,' he added to Daniel with a wink.

Miss Dolly took a step back, clasped her hands together over her waist, drew herself up and gazed up at a corner of the room.

'Yet, here's a spot.' She spoke in a higher voice than before and every word was followed by slightly too long a pause before the next. She began to rub her hands together, making the same repetitive motion over and over again. 'Out, damned spot, at my breast, that sucks the nurse, asleep! Deny, thy father, and refuse, thy name.'

Charles guffawed and clapped.

'Perfect, perfect! Ain't she the best, boy-troll? You'll see more of her tomorrow. She's to be my hostess at the banquet for your Domino.'

Daniel couldn't help it. '*What?*' he said. Monk looked as if he were in serious pain.

Charles patted Miss Dolly on the rear. 'Dolly, my sweet, I understand the boy-troll has something important to say to me, so take yourself off for the moment.'

'That's not all I'll *take off* for you, Charlie,' she breathed, and exited with much more thigh movement than was strictly necessary for the act of walking.

'She's your hostess?' Daniel murmured. Charles's grin was abruptly evil, very intelligent and not the least clouded by lust.

'What was that *bon mot* that came to me, Monk?'

Monk was studying the ceiling plaster. 'I don't recall, sire.'

'Oh come, surely!'

Monk sighed. '"A trull for the troll", sire.'

'That's it! A trull for the troll! Rather good, eh?'

And Daniel saw exactly what he was doing. Charles had picked the flooziest floozy he could find, he had probably made her dye her hair that colour . . . all to indicate his opinion of the Domon'el in the most concisely diplomatic manner that he could.

Charles threw himself down on a chaise longue and put his hands behind his head.

'Now, boy-troll, what's so damned important that it can't wait until tomorrow?'

There were raised voices on the other side of the door: Charles's a high and furious tenor, Monk's more bass and soothing. Daniel paced in the anteroom, too agitated to sit and wait. He walked to the window and leaned on the sill, looking out at the gardens and the Thames beyond them. If he rested his head against the glass it was pleasantly cool. He shut his eyes.

'Master Matthews?'

Daniel quickly straightened and turned at the voice, with his heart pounding in hope. He wasn't disappointed.

The newcomer was a young woman, and the best contrast that he could imagine to Miss Dolly. Like her brother, Princess Elizabeth had grown and filled out; unlike her brother, she had always been graceful, even as a little girl. She came towards him with a warm and friendly smile that he had no difficulty in returning. Her maids lurked in the background.

'Your Highness,' he said, and stopped abruptly. Suddenly he had never been more aware that while he spoke the One Tongue with the accent of Golekh's officer class, when he opened his mouth to speak English what came out was pure Berkshire.

'I thought it was you but, my, you have grown.'

Daniel smiled. 'So have you, your Highness.' He had seen her on occasion since their first meeting at Windsor, but not recently and never this close. It made the changes in her all the more apparent and pleasing.

Elizabeth nodded at the door. 'I had hoped to speak with the king, but he sounds as if he is occupied.'

'He's had bad news,' Daniel admitted. Her glance at him was no less friendly for being very shrewd.

'Did you bring it?'

'I'm afraid I did.'

'And . . . ?' She waited, then looked displeased when it was obvious he would say no more on the matter. 'You have indeed become a man. Charles will never share disturbing news with me either.'

Daniel didn't have an answer and felt it would be impolite to shrug. But Elizabeth changed the subject, looking at him more closely.

'It *is* bad. I see it in your eyes.'

Eyes. The one word made Daniel see a pair of dying ones, the hate in them indicting him for murder. He tried to look away while she studied his face, but when he finally looked back at her, he found he couldn't look anywhere else.

'I can see you are carrying a heavy weight,' she said softly. 'I hope you find a way to let it go. Will you be staying here tonight?'

'Um . . . yes, I will.'

She smiled. 'Then I will see you at the evening meal.' She held out her hand and he kissed it, and then he watched her leave. The door opened behind him but Monk had to say his name twice to get his attention.

'Sit down, boy-troll.'

Charles gestured at the chair with a short, angry wave of his hand, then paced about the room for a moment before dragging up a chair of his own. His previous bonhomie had evaporated. He sat opposite Daniel and glared.

'Your news,' he said. 'You may be interested to know that rumours had already reached us through the speak-wires. We were interested to see if what you had to tell us had anything to do with them. We thank you for your honesty.'

Daniel breathed out in relief. The *full repeat full* was suddenly explained. Dhon Do had realized that others would hear of what had happened in Brighthelmstone, and reports would reach Charles. Daniel had had to make sure that the first official account of it was a full account, because he could not afford to leave out details that might reach Charles from another source. This way, he had demonstrably told the truth and Charles trusted him.

'To summarize,' said Charles, 'these murdering

turds, these swine, these ... these ... *creatures* are *missionaries*. It's not even as if we were being decently invaded, as your father did to us, so there is no one with whom we can go to war. Because war is what it is, boy-troll, let me tell you. But sending in the army would be like going to war with the Church of England. Bloody ridiculous.'

Daniel had to work his mouth to lubricate his voice with some saliva. 'Th-that's right, sir,' he said.

Charles grunted. 'You also tell us there is nothing under Holekhor law to permit you to throw these scum out of the country. Well, I'm reasonably certain there is nothing under English law to prevent me from grinding them into the dirt and pissing on their remains, and I can probably find a couple of clauses that would lend support to the idea. What have you to say?'

It all appealed to Daniel, but he could see an immediate problem.

'They have Wise with them,' he said.

Charles jutted out his jaw. 'I see.' He had never seen the Order in action – apart from the obvious effect of what they could do, in the form of the gate at Povse'okh – but Daniel's point struck home. 'I thought your Wises only have power on hill tops, like Pox the Ox?'

'They draw their power from the landpower, and Povse'okh is where several lines of landpower meet,' Daniel said. 'Sometimes the lines go up, sometimes they go down. Um ... have you seen Brighthelmstone?'

Charles sighed. 'There are doubtless good reasons

why a king should visit a little fishing village on the south coast, boy-troll, but none of them come to me just now.'

'Well, there's a valley, and my Centurion said the landpower runs straight down the valley into the sea. But it won't be the same elsewhere.'

'Very well. But is there anything to stop us ranging artillery away from a line of power and hammering them?'

'Nothing, sir,' Daniel admitted. 'But pissing on them might not be possible at that range.'

Charles chuckled. 'Thank you for that intelligence, boy-troll. You know, you probably shouldn't have shared it. It will work against the interests of your own people.'

'They're not my people!' Daniel snapped. Charles gave him a calculating look that reminded him of Elizabeth.

'Your problem, boy-troll, is that you don't *have* any people. You really should choose a side and commit to it, as my tailor is always telling me. Monk.'

'Sire?'

'Take *Ariel* down to Portsmouth, call on the garrison there and get artillery taken to this, um . . .'

'Brighthelmstone, sire.'

'To there. Then track those evangelizing filth, wherever they've gone to, and blow them to kingdom come. They deny our Lord: give our Lord the opportunity to point out their error personally.'

Monk beamed. 'At once, sire.' He bowed and withdrew.

*   *   *

Sir George Monk had been a professional soldier for much longer than he had been the king's counsellor. The prospect of action was alluring.

He strode out of the palace and towards the landing field. The sight of the two airships there made him scowl, and think. Monk thought a lot: as he walked, as he talked, often as he slept. It was what had got him to his present position. And now, not for the first time, he was thinking about the Holekhor.

The airships said all that was to be said. The Holekhor had brought with them superb machines, weapons, vehicles; to some, their presence could be nothing but a blessing. To think in that direction was doubtless just what Dhon Do wanted, but it was dangerous, because look at them whatever way you liked, they were invaders. England would never be free while they were here.

Monk had learned to keep thinking when others gave up.

Where exactly did they come from? What exactly were they? He had seen Povse'okh, but to say 'they come from there' was no answer. Charles, he suspected, might be closer to the mark than he imagined with his blanket dismissal of them all as trolls. There was something *different* about them. Monk had seen black men from Africa, brown men from the Arab lands, and once a distinctly yellow-tinged chap from even further east. But the Holekhor, though their skins were fair and their hair red, seemed more different than that.

They could not be *that* different, though. The existence of Master Matthews showed that English and Holekhor could interbreed, and reports from certain quarters of the garrison towns indicated that inter-breeding was frequent. (Holekhor men paid well, they were strong and muscular, and rumours of their physical endowment presented a challenge to many empirically-minded English women.) Yet the fact that the same towns were not crawling with little red-haired bastards showed that *successful* interbreeding was rare. Unusually rare. Given a fixed population of Holekhor, still very much a minority in England, Monk could see that within a couple of generations they would have all but vanished, absorbed into the main body of the English. But if they just kept coming through the gate, and coming and coming, as Dhon Do said they would . . .

He scowled. They had to be stopped.

Ariel's crew had seen him approach and the captain was coming forward to meet him.

'Portsmouth,' Monk said, 'with all speed.'

Daniel, undismissed, stayed seated after Monk had gone. Charles continued to sit across the room and scowl at him. Daniel had no idea how long they sat in silence but it felt longer than it surely was.

Abruptly, Charles stood. 'Ain't your fault, boy-troll,' he muttered. 'You're just the messenger and believe me, I do appreciate what you did there.'

He crossed to the sideboard and poured two glasses of wine, then handed one to Daniel and dropped back into his chair. He crossed his long legs casually.

'No reason we can't be civil for the time being. Tell me about your Dom . . . your dommy . . . damnit, boytroll, why can't he call himself King like any Christian?'

'He's not a king,' Daniel said. *Or a Christian*, he couldn't help thinking, but he knew Charles's definition of the word extended far beyond mere religious belief, to encompass anything remotely civilized. 'He didn't inherit his throne.'

'No?' Charles was intrigued. 'How did he come by it, then?'

'The Domon'el—'

'That's the fella!'

'He always comes from one of the High Families,' Daniel said. 'He chooses his heir but his heir isn't allowed to be related to him within, um, three generations, I think.'

He paused as a sudden thought struck him. The Domon'el wanted Daniel in his heir Mhor Sen's High Marriage . . . which would have rendered Daniel, and indeed Dhon Do, ineligible for the office themselves. It would bring Daniel over to his side as a young man, before he came into any real political power; and it would keep Dhon Do, the experienced and perhaps too-successful general, away from the office. Was that why his father had been so emphatic: 'I won't be hurt'?

He went on. 'And when he's Domon'el, he is absolute ruler of all the High Families, which means he rules the nation.'

'No Parliament?'

'No Parliament.'

'By Gad, I could live in a system like that! I understand the Lord Steward was disturbed that the chap ain't bringing his wife. Upsets the seating arrangements. Is he not married?'

'He's married,' Daniel said, not adding *to several wives and a couple of husbands.* 'He just travels alone.'

Charles breathed a sigh of relief. 'Thank God! I thought he might be tilting a lance at Lizzie. She's the one that every royal family in Europe has their eye on at the moment – well, after myself, of course. But marry her to a troll . . . I'd rather she died.'

Daniel couldn't help a smile at the conceit – the thought of the Domon'el stooping to marry a native princess. Charles flattered himself if he thought he was that important. But Daniel liked Elizabeth and it was disconcerting to hear of her marriage talked about in such blunt terms, though doubtless it was no more than she expected for herself. She would marry whichever European prince or duke Charles and his advisers thought most advantageous to Britain.

Her elder sister Mary had married at the age of ten and thereafter moved to the Netherlands. The Rebellion, and its aftermath, had so far spared Elizabeth a similar fate, but surely it would come. Where Daniel had spent his childhood, you usually married because you had to, but bride and groom would have known each other since the cradle and there was at least an element of fondness in the union.

Fondness seemed quite alien in this world that revolved around politics.

'So, how did he take to you?' Charles asked.

Talk of marriage was still at the fore of Daniel's mind, so the first thing he said was, 'He wants me to marry too.'

'Indeed?' Charles looked politely sympathetic but clearly not that interested. 'Having your spouse chosen for you is the price for consorting with princes. But doubtless you'll have had plenty of practice with the troll-fillies to call upon, though there's few would envy you.'

Charles casually sipped his wine with these last words while Daniel mumbled something and looked away. The silence that followed was so profound it caused even Charles to notice something amiss. He looked at Daniel askance.

'Surely you *have* had practice with the troll-fillies?' A pause. 'Any fillies? At all?'

Daniel's ears blazed scarlet and Charles was aghast. 'Ain't you made like a normal man? What about the headaches?'

Daniel was nonplussed at the strange change of subject. 'What headaches?' he said.

'What headaches? Why, the headaches a man gets if he don't have a woman at least . . .' Charles coughed. 'That is not important. Well, it's not too late to make up for it, though God knows your education is certainly lagging behind mine. I started when . . . well, that too is not important.' He gave a condescending smile. 'Besides, you were too young to understand.'

Daniel had understood. He had been in bed trying to heal from a gunshot wound, the other side of a thin wall. It hadn't aided his recovery.

Suddenly Charles's grin was evil again. 'Not to worry,' he said nonchalantly, raising his wine. 'I'll send up a couple of doxies to your room tonight. They'll see you right.'

Daniel must have looked panicked because Charles hooted with laughter.

'A joke, boy-troll, a joke! But for goodness' sake, get some tuition before you get hitched. Think of the poor tart you have to marry, if nothing else. She'll be just as delighted at the prospect as you, no doubt, so the least you can do is be good at it, for her sake. It's just courtesy.'

It was not, Daniel thought when he was finally able to make a polite exit, the most useful conversation he had ever had.

Twenty-One

Faith, Hope and Charity

Steam hissed impatiently from the locomotive in the bright light of a new day. The hoot of its whistle echoed from the towers and chimneys of Hampton Court. The royal locomotive was poised at the head of the track and the Royal Standard and the High Ensign flew from the cab. Its boiler was fully up to pressure and it was ready to start the rolling journey down to Dover. The crowd milled, restless, waiting for the ceremonials to start.

Nothing was going to happen without the presence of two particular men. The airship of one of them was finally coming in to land at the palace field, and the other had had no intention of appearing to be kept waiting, so had taken an especially long breakfast. But now the Domon'el was here and Daniel followed in the entourage behind Charles as the king strolled casually out to the landing field, at a pace nicely timed to coincide with the airship touching the ground.

Soldiers jumped from the airship first and stood at attention in two rows, rifles held at the ready. The Domon'el's honour guard had stayed behind. They only carried axes, and away from Povse'okh, surrounded by natives, real soldiers with firearms had seemed a better guarantee of the Lord of Golekh's safety. Then the Domon'el stepped down to meet the king. Even from this distance, Daniel could see the tension, the reluctance in Charles, but – after a pause of just a bit too long, and then very abruptly – Charles bowed. The Domon'el inclined his head in return.

'Welcome to Hampton Court, sir,' Charles said in English. 'I trust you had a pleasant journey.'

The interpreter whispered in the Domon'el's ear, took the response and passed it on. The pleasantries continued as Charles led the Domon'el over to be introduced to everyone else. The Queen Mother, Henrietta Maria, was glacial in her royal froideur and her smile was as fixed and humourless as the Domon'el's. Then came Elizabeth and eleven-year-old Prince Henry. Finally Miss Dolly was presented and the Domon'el recoiled slightly, eyes for a moment as round as his glasses. She gave an elaborate curtsey which partially made up for the 'Aw'right, my love?'

The Domon'el's retinue had climbed down from the ship and were following their master, and Daniel's heart leaped when he finally saw his father. Dhon Do smiled grimly as they came up to each other.

'You look terrible,' he said.

'Thank you,' Daniel said. He had not slept at all well. His thoughts had been racing too much, coming back always to a few especial topics – his unwelcome experience of murder, his almost equally unwelcome inexperience of women, and the strange rush he had felt as he preached to the soldiers. It had all blended into a strange melange that had run through his waking thoughts and his dreams so that he had been unsure as to where one theme ended and another began.

They turned and followed after the Domon'el. Dhon Do put a hand on Daniel's shoulder. It was a brief moment of tenderness in a day destined for ceremony and protocol, and it made Daniel feel slightly better.

'You did well yesterday,' Dhon Do said. 'I'm sorry I sent you into that situation.'

Daniel mumbled. He couldn't say, 'It was nothing,' because they both knew it hadn't been.

Dhon Do craned his neck and studied the crowd. 'Where's Monk?'

'Charles sent him down to Portsmouth. He's to take the garrison out to Brighthelmstone.'

Dhon Do paused for just a second. 'Ah,' he said. 'Well, much good may it do him.'

'Pa,' Daniel said. 'Even if he does manage to deal with them, more will come, won't they? Isn't there anything you can do to . . . ?'

'Daniel, our Lord has made a new arrangement with the Congregation, granting them unconditional access to this land of Enkhlon.'

'*What?*'

'Under the circumstances, boy, it doesn't make much difference. Have faith.'

Daniel was outraged. 'What do you mean, it doesn't—'

But then they had reached the locomotive and the royal carriages. Dhon Do gave Daniel's shoulder a final squeeze, put on his best smile and stepped forward.

Sir George Monk sat in the driver's cab at the head of a procession of steam wagons and smiled grimly as they trundled across the South Downs at a steady ten miles per hour.

Ariel had got him to Portsmouth shortly before sunset the previous day, too late to do anything about the Congregation's incursion. The airship was too small and light to carry any artillery, but the Portsmouth garrison was blessed with another fruit of Holekhor science in the form of the wagons. The drivers had been up before dawn, stoking the boilers to their fullest head of steam. They had set off at first light – three wagons towing heavy guns, which he had whimsically named Faith, Hope and Charity, and a fourth towing a trailer full of soldiers with rifles and machine guns. All the weapons, of course, were Holekhor-designed. *Ariel* trailed them, keeping a constant watch from the air. Monk glanced enviously up at it and thought of how he could have used air support in the European campaigns he had fought as a young man.

Five hours later, they were almost there. *Ariel* was signalling that Brighthelmstone, empty and abandoned, lay over the next rise. It added that there was a Holekhor ship off the beach.

The new, smooth surface of the south coast road

306

had given out a few miles east of Portsmouth. After that the clanking and wheezing steel behemoths had to contend with the centuries-old rutted tracks that wound their way along the cliff tops, but their broad, chain-clad wheels dug into the turf with a grip that inexorably hurled the king's vengeance towards the invaders. Monk felt like Hannibal crossing the Alps, a fighting force of such power that it must surely crush all that stood in its way. It was an intoxicating feeling, to be riding to the defence of your country against its enemies. It had been satisfying to defend his king during the Rebellion, right up until the ill-fated encounter at Nantwich which had led to his capture by Parliament, but even then that had been a double-edged sword – the exhilaration of battle against the fact that he was fighting his fellow Englishmen. But these Holekhor weren't English. They were as much the enemy as it was possible to be – of England, of God, of all decent civilisation – and he was to be their vanquisher.

If only, he thought, there was a way to reap the benefits of the Holekhor's knowledge without the Holekhor's actual presence. Charles would have an army greater than any in Europe.

Soon they were over the high ground and Monk could see the situation for himself. It was just as Master Matthews had described. The wagons trundled down into the deserted town and his military eyes took in the damage, recreating the scene as it would have been: armsmen storming the town from the direction of the beach, townsfolk not knowing where to run to and eventually finding themselves herded together to await their grisly fates.

They drew to a halt in front of the church and Monk walked down to the shore. There were rows of graves by the beach, but otherwise the only sign of life was the ship out to sea. He shaded his eyes with his hand and studied it. Crewmen moved about on deck and he could hear the working of the engines. Steam was coming out of the funnel. He presumed they had effected their repairs.

The thing was offensive to his eyes. It was black and ugly, and it was the vessel that had brought the invaders here.

'We will do our duty to our King and country,' he said. It was time to put the advantages of Holekhor ordnance to good use. 'Range the guns along the shoreline and break out the timer fuses. Like all good Christians, we will fight our enemies with Faith, Hope and Charity.'

The first shell landed on the ship's foredeck and penetrated down to the hold before exploding. The deck blew open in a hail of flame and wooden fragments. The next shells struck the superstructure and tore it apart. The wooden cabins burst under the blast. The iron bulkheads held, but a blazing inferno raged behind the shattered windows and torn-off doors.

The merciless shelling continued as the ship began to settle. Cold water rushed into its burning interior with a mighty hiss and the panicked Holekhor crew threw themselves into the sea.

Monk watched it all through his binoculars. The heads of the floating crew bobbed small and dark in the grey waves. They were alone and helpless, swimming for the shore.

'Carry on,' he said, and the view through his lenses exploded in a rush of boiling white water as the shells continued to fall. One body was blown up out of the water and up, up into the air at the head of a fountain of steam and flame. It spun almost gracefully before plunging back into the turmoil below.

'Cease fire,' he said. The ship was gone, just an oily smudge on the surface. Bits and pieces that might be wreckage, might be bodies, might be both, twitched and swayed in the water. But no one was alive, of that he was certain.

'Hitch the guns back up and get the men back on board. The invaders apparently took the road away from town; so shall we.'

'That is the road to Lewes, sir.'

'Then that is the road we shall take.'

The king had fidgeted with visible impatience while the Archbishop of Canterbury beseeched Almighty God's blessings on the newly opened railway. The Domon'el, who was quite happy to placate the native god in the absence of any representatives from the Congregation, had taken it more placidly, looking around while the prelate droned with the abstracted interest of a scientist surrounded by intriguing specimens. But then the Archbishop was finally finished, the Domon'el had declared the railway open, and the royal party boarded the train. The driver engaged the gears to the steam turbine and, wreathed in clouds of billowing white steam, the train had finally set off.

The interior of the royal carriage was far grander than Dhon Do's own train. Enkhlon's Holekhor Prefect had more modest tastes than England's English king, and it had been furnished even more grandly in honour of its special guest. At the rear end sat the Queen Mother – skilfully avoiding the conversational gambits of Miss Dolly – Dhon Do and Daniel, and assorted courtiers of Domon'el and king. Two large, red plush, throne-like chairs had been set up at the front end. The Domon'el sat in one, looking bored. Charles, the rightful occupant of the other, was nowhere to be seen.

Then the door from the locomotive cabin swung open and Charles staggered into the carriage, braced against the swaying of the train and with his eyes gleaming.

'By George, this is marvellous! Sheer bloody marvellous! You know we're doing sixty miles in the hour? *Sixty!* Faster than your airships, ain't it, General?'

'The boy is easily impressed,' the Domon'el murmured in the One Tongue, and his retinue chuckled politely. Charles didn't notice as he headed for the drinks cabinet.

'A glass of wine with you, sir,' he said, 'to the benefits the Holekhor have brought to my land.'

'Easily impressed and easily bought,' the

Domon'el elaborated. 'You really think we have business to do with this oaf, Dhon Do?'

'There is that other matter I mentioned, Lord,' Dhon Do said.

'Of course!' The Domon'el took his glass and Charles slumped down in his chair with a glass of his own. 'Young King, I have heard interesting tales of how this country separated itself from its ruling church under a previous monarch. I wondered if you could elaborate upon that?'

Charles gazed at him blankly while the interpreter passed the message on.

'Eh? Yes. Great-Uncle Henry and all that. All in the past now.'

'Even so, I would value your assessment.'

'Would you, sir?' Charles glanced at his notoriously Catholic mother. He was obviously weighing up in his mind the contrasting advantages of provoking her and provoking the Domon'el. There was great potential for sport either way. He grinned and leaned back in his chair. 'Well,' he said, 'it's an interesting story . . .'

Daniel and Dhon Do sat together at the rear of the carriage and observed the scene of unlikely bonhomie, as Charles tried to sum up the entire Protestant Reformation in a few words.

'But Charles hates us!' Daniel murmured.

'Charles knows full well he's being bribed, Daniel,' Dhon Do said. 'He's not as foolish as he likes to appear, and I doubt the Domon'el is taken in for a second. But our Lord's interest in this particular matter is not feigned. He has no intention of being the Congregation's instrument forever.'

Daniel jumped when a court official tapped him on the shoulder.

'Master Matthews? Her Royal Highness will receive you in the next carriage.'

Daniel looked up at him, at Dhon Do, back at the official.

'I didn't ask to be received!'

Dhon Do smiled. 'I wasn't aware so many attractive young women want to see you that you must make appointments.'

Daniel shot to his feet.

Henry and Elizabeth were of secondary importance in affairs of state, so confined to the second carriage. It was a saloon like the first but quieter. It was further from the locomotive, yet it also seemed more tranquil through the sheer absence of the two rulers. Henry sat at a table and pored over a chessboard; Elizabeth sat in a chair and smiled as she laid aside her petit point. Apart from a couple of servants lurking discreetly at the rear, they and Daniel were the only ones present. The rest of the servants would be in the third carriage and the soldiers, there to guard their Lord, in the final fourth.

'Master Matthews.' She held out her hand for Daniel to kiss. 'I hope I was not presumptuous?'

'Not at all, your Highness,' Daniel said, his heart pounding. All the problems of the last twenty-four hours were suddenly just background irritations. He wondered if anyone had told her about the situation, and whether she would be so friendly towards him if she knew what he represented.

'I know how tedious matters of state can be to those of us not directly involved. I thought I could perhaps relieve your tedium with some tea.'

Daniel smiled. 'Thank you.'

An unseen force picked him up and hurled him back against the wall of the carriage. Elizabeth's scream blended into the ear-piercing screech of the brakes. Elizabeth was thrown face forward on to the floor, Henry flung headfirst against a lampstand. Daniel slid to the floor, dazed and with the breath knocked out of his lungs.

An explosion outside rocked the carriage and the windows shattered. Only the chaise longue lying on its side protected Elizabeth and Henry from lacerations. Machine-gun fire tore through the sides of the carriage.

Dhon Do could tell the end of the carriage was off the rails from the angle of the floor. He cast one final, agonized glance to the rear and the second carriage, then firmly shut that door in his mind and turned to his duty.

The Domon'el was on his hands and knees, shaking his head, still dazed. Dhon Do scrambled forward and hauled him to his feet by the scruff of his neck. '*Into the locomotive! Now!*'

A groan from the floor made him look down. Charles was picking himself up. The king looked back to the second carriage and lunged towards it. 'Lizzie! Harry! *Urk*—'

Dhon Do grabbed his collar with his free hand and lugged him along with the Domon'el.

There were two feet of open air between the carriage and the driver's cab. Two of the soldiers posted to the cab were just about to come back. Their eyes widened when they saw their leader.

'Catch him!' Dhon Do shouted and thrust the Domon'el forward. They caught him and dragged him over the gap. Dhon Do stepped after them, still keeping a firm grip on the struggling Charles.

'I . . .' gasped the Domon'el. Dhon Do pushed him down into the corner of the cab, in the corner between the sideplates and the boiler.

'Stay there!' He looked at the driver. 'Why did we stop?'

'Tree across the line, sir.'

'*Lizzie!*'

Dhon Do hauled Charles down by his belt and turned to a soldier. 'You! Sit on the king. He is not to move until I say so. And give me your rifle.'

More people were making their way out of the carriage and into the cab. The Queen Mother's servants were pushing their mistress over the gap. The cab was going to be crowded soon; the Queen Mother's dress would see to that if nothing else did.

Daniel . . . howled a voice inside him. But Daniel was in the second carriage, and a secondary priority to protecting the Domon'el. As for Elizabeth and Henry . . . well, Charles was still capable of begetting his own heirs. The first thing was to get that tree off the rails.

He stuck his head around the sideplate and began to bawl orders.

Daniel, Elizabeth and Henry lay flat and looked helplessly at each other across ten feet of floor. It seemed a much vaster distance.

There was more shooting, from directly fore and aft. The soldiers in the rear carriage and the driver's cabin were defending their Lord against the attack.

'*Get that thing off the rails! Just do it!*' The voice was barely recognizable as Dhon Do.

'We must get into the front carriage!' Daniel shouted over the din.

'What did you say?'

'We must—'

Another explosion, even more violent. Burning black smoke burst through the door of the carriage, and Daniel heard the crackling of flames over the screams of mauled and scorched human beings. Another explosion, this one almost underfoot, and the whole world shook. The floor seemed to spin, and then he realized with horror that the whole carriage really was moving, but sideways, one side tilting up and the other down, as with a mighty groaning crash it slid down the embankment.

He didn't know if he lay unconscious for a while or if he just stopped noticing the world, the sheer violence of the attack overwhelming his senses. But gradually he came to and found himself strangely glued to the wall of the carriage. Then his senses returned fully and he realized that the carriage was lying on its side. He lay on what had been one of the walls, and daylight shone through the door where previously he should have been able to see into the first carriage.

Part of the chaos of noise around him resolved into a howl from behind. Prince Henry was showing that he, at least, was still alive. Daniel glanced back and his heart leaped to see Elizabeth shakily pushing herself up. She pulled Henry towards her and wiped the blood from his face with her sleeve. Her face was white. 'Who could do this?' she hissed. 'Who?' It was the white, Daniel realized, not of fear but of fury.

'I . . . I'll see,' he said. He shuffled forward and gazed blearily out. He could just see the rear end of the first carriage up the embankment, torn and twisted and with its rear wheels off the tracks. The front wheels were still on. Further along he could see the locomotive, all its wheels securely on the rails, and beyond that the tree that had been felled to stop it. The locomotive was surrounded with Holekhor soldiers, guns raised and blazing away at attackers he couldn't see. Some were wrestling with the tree trunk against a constant barrage of rifle and machine-gun fire. Sometimes one would collapse with red blotches staining his uniform; another would take his place. The locomotive had to get out of this in one direction or another, and a fallen tree was easier to shift than a derailed carriage.

He couldn't see any of the attackers, but the ring of soldiers so valiantly defending the locomotive presumably could. 'It's probably God's Army,' he said.

'The . . . the *traitors*! Attacking their king!'

'Your Highness, you should lie down.'

'Master Matthews, do not tell me what I should do!'

'Lie down!' Daniel snapped, at the same time as a stray shot burst through the carriage. It was accident more than design but the combination made both Elizabeth and Henry throw themselves to the ground. Henry's howls grew louder.

'Oh be quiet, Harry. Master Matthews, can you see what is happening?'

Daniel glanced out again. 'I think the Dom—' But of course, she wouldn't be interested in the Domon'el. 'I think everyone's in the locomotive.' And then he saw the men finally tip the tree from the track and the defenders begin to retreat into the cab. 'We have to get out there,' he said sharply. 'We have to—'

It was too late. The locomotive belched a cloud of white steam and began to pull away. The last of the soldiers ran alongside it and heaved themselves on board. A final shot, a final casualty as a soldier crumpled and fell back to the ground. But then the locomotive was accelerating away from the carnage, away down the track, and they were stranded.

Movement outside, and a pair of men peered cautiously round the door, pistols drawn. They were flintlock pistols of English design, not Holekhor, but just as capable of killing. The men ran their gaze over the prince and princess, and then settled on Daniel, who immediately found himself staring down the barrel of a pistol from a range of three feet. For the first time he truly felt terror.

'Are you a Christian Englishman or a heathen Holekhor?' the gun's owner demanded.

'C-Christian!' he finally managed to say. 'I'm Christian!'

The man frowned; the pistol wavered only slightly. 'What's your name?'

'Daniel Matthews!'

Maybe it was because he answered so promptly; maybe it was because no Holekhor could so easily pronounce such a name with all its extra vowels. The man lowered the pistol. 'If you are a Christian then dress like one. Wearing those heathen clothes can only lead to confusion. I want the three of you outside now.'

They picked their way out into the daylight, Daniel helping Elizabeth, whose skirts were hardly practical for crawling through a horizontal door. He also took the opportunity to remove the silver bracelet on his arm and pocket it – nothing identified him more as a Holekhor than that. Outside, the front carriage was still burning and the stink of the fire mixed with the sharp tang of gunpowder and explosive. Some of the servants were climbing slowly out of the remains of the third carriage, which had rolled with theirs down the slope. A line of Holekhor soldiers knelt with their hands on their heads. An Englishman stood behind the first of the line with a Holekhor-made revolver in his hand. He cocked the hammer, put it to the back of the Holekhor's head and pulled the trigger. The soldier jerked with the bang and fell forward on to his face. The man moved down to the second in line.

Daniel felt sick and looked away.

'Don't say anything, don't do anything,' he murmured to Elizabeth. She hugged Henry to herself and nodded, pale and wide eyed.

But then one of the crowd from the third carriage, a middle-aged woman, flung herself at Elizabeth and burst into tears.

'Oh, your Highness, your Highness, Jesus be praised that you're safe!' she sobbed.

'Highness?' Immediately they were the centre of everyone's attention. Elizabeth glanced down at the clothes she wore, obviously decided there was no point in pretending and drew herself up.

'I am the Princess Elizabeth and this is the Prince Henry,' she said.

Several men laughed. One of them stepped forward, tugging at his belt. 'We've got ourselves a princess, boys! Anyone ever had a royal?'

Elizabeth blanched and without thinking Daniel took a step forward, placing himself between her and the man. 'No,' he said.

The man frowned down at him in surprise, then grinned, bowed, and took a step back. Then in one blurred movement he had his pistol out and the barrel smashed in an explosion of pain against the side of Daniel's head. Daniel staggered and fell. He climbed slowly back to his knees and there was another detonation inside his skull as the man clouted him across the back of the neck. He lay, paralysed and gasping, and his blurred eyes looked up dimly to see the man step forward and grab Elizabeth's wrists.

'No!' she shrieked. 'No! Take your hands off me!' She pulled back in vain, and then little Henry leapt to her rescue, trying to pull the man and his sister apart. The man backhanded him casually and sent him flying.

'Mind the fort for me, fellows,' he said casually. 'This won't take long.'

'*Stop that!*' The furious bellow came from behind them. Another man strode forward and he struck Elizabeth's captor across the face. 'You know the General's orders. We're righteous men. We don't do that.'

The first man trembled, not with fear but anger; but then he made a show of releasing Elizabeth and shrugging casually. He tucked his gun into his belt. 'And since when did you jump to Cromwell's tune, Master Lilburne?'

Lilburne thrust his face at the dissenter. 'We are *righteous* men,' he hissed.

'You speak for yourself, Master Lilburne,' the other muttered, but he stepped away.

Someone kicked Daniel in the ribs and he toppled over. It barely made a difference to the blinding pain in his skull. He lay there, pinned down by a strong foot. 'And who's this? Looks like a Hollykor. Maybe he should join his friends in the ditch.'

Elizabeth held her head high and looked him in

the eye. 'Master Matthews is my brother's valet. He is as Christian as you or I. Is that not so, Harry?'

She had to pinch the sobbing prince, but the boy gave a nod.

'Enough of this hanging around,' said Lilburne. 'They'll be on us like flies as soon as word gets out. Bring these two – leave the servants.'

Men with rifles began to herd Elizabeth and Henry away. Daniel they just left on the ground, and for a moment he felt sheer, blissful relief. They weren't going to kill him; they weren't going to hit him any more; he could just stay quiet and be safe.

But then he locked glances with Elizabeth. Perhaps Cromwell had given orders about the treatment of women, but that didn't mean she would be safe.

'I should stay with the princ—' he said. He had been about to say 'princess' but bit his tongue just in time, remembering that he was meant to work for Henry. The man called Master Lilburne glared at him.

'Please, sir,' Daniel said quietly.

Lilburne glanced at him, at the still blubbing Henry, and back at him. 'If you can shut the brat up, you're welcome,' he said, and stepped aside.

Daniel staggered to his feet, balanced on legs that still felt weak, and hurried to join the other two.

'You could have stayed! You would have been safe!' Elizabeth hissed. But then her features softened slightly. 'Thank you, Master Matthews.'

Daniel just nodded, still clutching the side of his head, not wanting to think too hard about what he had just done. God's Army of Albion showed no mercy to captured Holekhor, that was one of their axioms. But he wasn't in uniform, and as long as he could convince them he was a native Englishman – which of course he was – he should be safe.

'Bring 'em,' said Lilburne, who seemed to be in charge. 'They'll be a pleasant surprise for Mistress Connolly when we meet her.'

Twenty-Two

Lewes Ends

The sobbing woman flung herself at the man's feet.

'Mercy! In Jesus' name, have mercy!'

The two women on the other side of the room had seen such scenes before and they carried on tying the restraints to the wooden backed chair. It was up to the tall, black-clad man to look down at the accused and respond.

'Confess,' he said, 'and Jesus will have mercy.'

'I have done no wrong! I am no witch!'

Matthew Hopkins deliberately put his hands behind his back, to show his uninvolvement with the accused. 'That is what we are here to establish.' He nodded at the guards, and they picked up the now screaming woman and dragged her to the chair. She was forced to sit back to front, her breasts against the back of the chair, and her hands and feet were bound to the frame. One of the other women stuck a knife down the accused's collar and ripped. Her bodice split open and the bare skin beneath was rough and coarse. Hopkins caught a brief glimpse before he turned away, and was pleased to note that the sight caused no especial desire within himself. It was good that so many witches were born ugly; it meant a man could do the Lord's work in a state of purity.

'We shall await the results of the examination outside,' he said to the guards, and – not without regret, he could not help but notice – they turned to follow him out of the room and into the high street of Lewes.

There *was* witchery in the air, here. He could smell it. He had known it as soon as his horse carried him over the Downs and he was looking down on the town. The magic was old and well established. It was part of the fabric of the town, of the air he breathed, of the dust on his feet. He could never say exactly what it was like – a different colour in the background, a different taste in the air, a different timbre in the background noise of the town. But there were places where there was *power* at work, and it was not God's power.

It went back to his childhood in the Fens. As a boy he had known that what he felt was unlike what others felt, and he had lived in terror that he would be found out. He hadn't known what it was but he had known it was different, which probably meant it was wrong. Yet as an adult he had finally divined it. He knew he was a good Christian and had no consort with Satan, so if he could sense a power in the land then it could only mean one thing. His mission in life was to use this sense of his to find the witches. For legal reasons, of course, he had to produce evidence to substantiate his claims; he could never just accuse someone based on his own feeling. The appropriate investigative procedures of pricking, perhaps floating if that wasn't enough, had been worked out over time and he had begun a promising career of witch hunting in Essex and the Fens.

The fall of Parliament meant the end of Puritan approval for his actions; his partner John Stearne had been lynched by an angry mob, outraged at the number of witches he was uprooting in their cosy little community; and finally a weak chest had driven him out of the damp county of his birth. A feeling for the power in the land had led him to the warmer, drier south. Witches were the same, wherever one went.

'The landpower is rich here,' said the Speaker, looking down at the town in the gap in the Downs. The row of carts which they had commandeered from the last town drew to a halt so that everyone could take in the sight.

'Richer than that seaside hamlet?' said Re Nokh. The Wise nodded.

'That was a discharge point. This is an intersection.'

'I have read reports which suggest the natives can sense the landpower, though never so well as a Holekhor,' Re Nokh said. 'And unlike the Holekhor, they have no idea what it is.'

The Wise nodded again and greed shone in her eyes. Re Nokh was amused. This was precisely why the Order of the Wise was at best co-equal with the Congregation. Any mundane Holekhor could sense the landpower; only a few had the talent to use it. A Wise standing on a line was powerful; Wise at an intersection of lines were almost unbeatable. But a Wise off a line had no power at all and was prey to any stronger, better Holekhor with a club. Or a sword. Or a gun. Thousands of years ago, the scriptures said, the struggle had come to a head between those who could use the landpower and those who could not, and the struggle had been won simply by the mundanes building their towns elsewhere.

Here in the New World, guided only by a rough instinct and without the counsel of appropriate scripture, the natives actually sought out the centres of landpower and built their towns and cities on them. It was like moths to a flame. Perhaps there were some sensitives among them, but mostly they would have no idea what they were doing, or why. It was a useful habit, which they would come to regret.

Re Nokh saw two more things that pleased him. This town was on the river; the docks held ships that had clearly come up from the sea. It would be easy to bring reinforcements in. And there was a line of poles across the fields, carrying speaking-wires into and out of town. Unlike the fishing hamlet, this place was in touch with the rest of the world.

'This will be our base,' Re Nokh said. 'We will establish ourselves here, with the blessing of the Domon'el, and the word of the Pantheon shall spread throughout this land. Driver – forward.'

Lewes was a thriving town but its castle was all but derelict. Two mottes, one still crowned with the remains of a stone keep, stood at either end of the old bailey. Once the open space between had been used as a tilting ground by the castle's inhabitants; now it was more commonly used as a bowling green. Matthew Hopkins had thought of holding the execution in the high street, on the site of the Protestant martyrdoms during the reign of Bloody Mary, but the setting was too narrow for the crowd of witnesses he hoped to attract. The bowling green was much more suitable.

And sure enough, there was a crowd gathered there now, but scarcely a sound to be heard. At the back, a baby crying, quickly shushed; otherwise the silence hung heavily over the green, broken only by the soft sobbing of the woman standing at the gallows. Her back was a raw, weeping mass of torn, red flesh. Hopkins had ordered her to be covered after the examination for the sake of propriety, but the blood was seeping through.

'Shame!' cried a voice from the crowd, and there was the faintest murmur of agreement. Hopkins turned and raised the paper in his hand.

'I have authority to investigate this town! Signed by the magistrate in due accordance with the king's law!' He glared at them. 'There is no shame here! No innocent man or woman need be afraid of me! Examination by two good Christian women has conclusively shown Mistress Wetheril to be a witch.'

He glanced towards one particular part of the crowd, where stood a small family of Holekhor. He had made enquiries and found that they ran the local speaking-wire station. Only a fool would take on the Holekhor directly – the king's edict of free passage, which followed the fall of Parliament, had been widely and publicly enforced – but he intended to send them a message they would understand.

'Those who serve Satan let him suckle their blood, as a child suckles its mother's milk,' he said loudly. 'They suckle through an extra teat. This teat has no feeling in it. My assistants have examined Mistress Wetheril and they have found the mark, clear as day.' He held up an awl, its metal spike crusted with dried blood. They had had to stick it into a lot of blemishes on the guilty witch to find the one that had no feeling, but they had eventually succeeded. 'And we have her confession. Let sentence be passed.'

Hopkins nodded to the hangman. He pulled the lever and with a final despairing cry Mistress Wetheril fell through the trapdoor, jerking sharply as the rope caught and held her. The fall did not snap her neck as it sometimes did, so her death was slow and painful. Hopkins just prayed it was long enough for her to turn from her satanic master and accept the true love of Jesus.

Finally, Lewes had one less witch and Hopkins could turn away satisfied.

He walked towards the castle's barbican gatehouse, straight into a bunch of Holekhor. They were led by a man in scarlet and white; behind him was a small cluster clad in black robes, and behind them a larger group of kilted men carrying rifles. Suddenly his witch-sense was screaming inside his head and he knew where it came from. That feel, that texture in the air around Lewes – these people *reeked* of it.

He opened his mouth to speak but no words came out. It was as if his tongue had withered. He tried to move but his legs were gripped by something he could not see.

Lord Jesus! he howled inside his mind. *Help me!*

Re Nokh walked a slow circle around the immobile figure. The native's eyes strained to follow him as far as they could. The man's expression was of sheer terror.

'Who is this man?' the Hierarch said. 'He's terrified of us.'

'He's a native called Khopkhin,' said someone in the One Tongue. A Holekhor man had stepped forward from the throng. 'Welcome to Lewes, sir.'

'How good to hear a civilized language. Who are you?'

'Ohsen Dhe, sir. Wirespeaker.'

'Are you a Son of the Congregation?'

Ohsen Dhe looked surprised. 'Of course, sir! All my family are.'

'Marvellous!' Re Nokh clapped him on the shoulder. 'We're opening a mission here and we could use someone who speaks the language. We ran into communication difficulties at the last place. Now, what is this man doing?' He looked at the swinging body on the gallows. 'I can see that woman was tortured before her execution. I claim this town for the Congregation and we will not tolerate such barbarity here.'

'As I understand it, sir, this woman was accused of, um, being a Wise. It's contrary to their religion.'

Re Nokh's eyes widened. The Wise and several armsmen burst out laughing. Then they laughed some more.

'A Wise would let . . .' Re Nokh finally broke down in laughter himself and wiped his eyes. 'A Wise would let herself be strung up like that? In somewhere as puissant as this? I think not.' The Hierarch gestured to his men. 'We have to show the natives the benefits of the Congregation. Cut the woman down; she is an affront to my eyes. And then we will put some crosses up here on this green. I think we have our first candidate. But first, I need to send a message.'

All was quiet in the Operations Room at Povse'okh. The Domon'el was safely out of the way and had taken the Prefect with him. General Khre Deb was elsewhere, taking the opportunity to catch up on paperwork. The Decurion on duty could afford to feel relaxed. His feet were propped up on the operations desk, a novel was in his hand. A similarly indolent air hung over the whole room. It was silent, but not the tense silence of waiting. It was just that everyone had run out of small talk.

The Decurion dimly heard one of the speaking-wire terminals chatter into life; a moment later, one of the operators stood over him.

'Signal from a Hierarch, sir.' The Decurion swung his feet off the table and took the signal. *Request confirmation that Domon'el's edict of full co-operation with Congregation activities now enforced in island of Enkhlon. Re Nokh, Hierarch.* That was easy – he had entered it into the Active Orders book himself.

'Reply, confirm edict in force, Duty Officer, Povse'okh,' he said. 'Where are they?'

'Place called Khloos, sir. Never heard of it myself.'

The Decurion shrugged and went back to the novel. Another terminal began to clatter.

'Oh, shit!' The shout made everyone in the room jump and the Decurion almost fell off his chair. He staggered to his feet.

'Report properly, soldier!' he snapped. To his astonishment the guilty party waved him to silence with one hand while scribbling furiously with the other over the message pad. The Decurion jumped down to look over his shoulder as the message from Dover came in.

'Oh, *shit*!' he exclaimed. 'Messenger!'

The messengers had already divined they might be needed and hovered at the Decurion's elbow. 'Get to Hanger Division. Two airships and a full complement of troops in each, in the air in ten minutes, destination Dover. *Run!* And you – Prefect's compliments to General Khre Deb, and Povse'okh and all fighting units in Enkhlon are to stand to. Go!'

'I want reprisals, Dhon Do. I want reprisals.' The Domon'el paced to and fro across the floor of the stateroom in the castle at Dover with short, choppy strides and swung on Dhon Do as he entered the room. 'They *dared*! They *dared* to attack *me*! I want them to know the precise magnitude of their error to the finest degree. You will see to it.'

They hadn't had a chance to talk during the locomotive's mad run to Dover. The Domon'el had been
pushed down into one corner of the cab with a pair of
large soldiers on top of him, and this had suited Dhon
Do so well he had made sure it stayed that way, even
when they were apparently out of danger.

'Lord . . .' Dhon Do glanced at Charles, who was
arguing furiously with a group of the castle's English
officers and the Queen Mother. He was just glad
Charles had never shown the slightest interest in
learning the One Tongue. 'The attack was not against
you. It was the same rebels who fought the king's
father. *He* was their target.'

The Domon'el dismissed the argument with a
curt, angry gesture. He rarely raised his voice, and this
was the case now; his words instead grew more
clipped, more precise, more certain that there would
be no contradiction. Every syllable was precisely
enunciated. 'I don't care about the petty squabbles of
the petty natives, Dhon Do. The majesty of Golekh was
on that train and they attacked it! They attacked *me*!'

'Lord . . .' Dhon Do tried again. 'I've sent men
back down the rails to investigate the scene and I've
called for an airship to give them support. They will
search the area, pick up survivors, and investigate.'

In his mind's eye he saw the scene they might find.
The burnt-out wrecks of the carriages; the scene
strewn with bodies; a soldier turning over the corpse
of a young Holekhor male, and Daniel's dead eyes
staring blankly up into the sky. But he could not think
that way. Even as the locomotive had pulled away

Dhon Do had, in his mind, taken the subject of Daniel, folded it neatly, and tucked it away with all his private, unthinkable thoughts. *Forgive me, boy. I must do to you what I've had to do to England for six years. I must give the Domon'el what he wants, but my way; otherwise he will take it his way, and it will be a hundred times worse for everyone.* Daniel had to wait.

'There is nothing to investigate,' the Domon'el said. 'We were attacked, we shall retaliate.' He jabbed Dhon Do in the chest with a rigid finger. 'You will determine the exact location of the ambush, and the nearest town to it. That town will be razed to the ground, and I will witness the attack myself from an airship. I take it you have laid on an air journey back to Povse'okh?'

'Of course, Lord.' Dhon Do tried one last time. 'But Lord . . .' His heart sank. The Domon'el was finally smiling – his teeth were bared – which never meant anything good.

'General Dhon Do. You are known as a man who fights campaigns with the minimum of losses, on either side. That is all to the good. But perhaps you have grown soft in your new position? Would you rather I took you home with me and gave your job to someone else? Because I tell you, *these* are losses that *will* happen. I have *commanded* it. Do you obey?'

Dhon Do clenched his fists, but behind his back, where the Domon'el couldn't see. 'Of course, Lord,' he said.

The Domon'el smiled with slightly more warmth. 'Good. Now, have someone show me to where I can

333

wash and change. The floor of that cabin was dirty.'

Dhon Do watched his Lord leave the room, and had nearly a full second of peace before a hand fell on his shoulder and he was spun round. Charles stood right behind and glared down at him. 'Retaliate?' the king shouted from a distance of six inches. '*Retaliate?* You will do no such thing, sir!'

And Dhon Do saw the Domon'el's interpreter standing behind the king, looking pale and earnestly wishing to be somewhere else. Dhon Do hadn't been the only one in the room to speak both languages. So, denial was out of the question.

'My Lord has commanded,' he said.

'I care not a fig for your Lord, sir! Englishmen fight their own wars!'

'My own son is missing, sir,' Dhon Do said. 'We will find your brother and your sister, and—'

'Forgive me, sir, but I recall similar assurances about the safety of my late father,' Charles sneered. 'No, sir. First, *we* will retrieve the survivors, and by God I hope for your sake that my sister and brother are among them, and then *we* will find who was responsible for this outrage and we will take our own steps but I forbid, I absolutely *forbid* that *Holekhor* will—'

Dhon Do dismissed the interpreter with a jerk of the head, took the king's arm and guided him to a corner of the room.

'Don't be a fool, boy,' he said quietly. 'The Sovereign of Toskhes was taken home in captivity with his eyes put out. Lesser kings do not contradict the Domon'el.'

Charles went almost apoplectic. '*Less*—' It seemed there was not enough breath in his lungs to say the word. 'You call me a *less*—'

'My Lord commands the airship that will flatten this town, wherever it is, which is yet to be determined,' Dhon Do said. 'You have no way of stopping it. That makes you the lesser king. Sir, as soon as I can, I will have you returned to Hampton Court and my Lord to Povse'okh. We will return too close to nightfall to fly any more missions. During the night we will look on a map to find the town that was nearest to the attack, as my Lord has dictated, and I suggest you do likewise. Once *we* have that information, we will arm an airship with bombs, and at first light we will fly down to that place and destroy it from the air. What *you* do with that information, once you have it yourself, is entirely up to you. You will have twelve hours at most in which to do it, but that is what speaking-wires are for.'

He gave the king a pat on the shoulder, hoping against hope that the boy would actually show some military sense and work out what he was saying, and left the room to follow his Lord. Dear God, he thought, I could use Monk right now. *He* would keep the king from doing anything foolish.

The guns were in place. Monk had stationed them in a long line, each by its own wagon. He stood by Faith at one end of the line and looked through his binoculars at Charity at the other. A soldier standing by the gun held up a flag, and kept it above his head until it was acknowledged by Monk's aide with a flag of his own.

Lewes lay in a gap in the Downs below them, where the road met the river. Between the Downs proper and the town, which was built on a small hill that had once been fortified, was a larger hill, rounded like the bowl of a spoon. This was where Monk had put the three guns. Now, with his soldiers, he was ready to enter the town.

Monk only knew Lewes by reputation. He remembered it had a Puritan tradition, and had backed Parliament during the Rebellion. They might not react well to an officer of the king wearing the king's uniform and bearing his commission. Well, he would have to risk that.

He took a flare gun, cracked it open, inserted a charge. 'Pass the word,' he said brusquely, to conceal his own nerves. 'This flare will be the signal. Upon seeing it you will open fire, regardless of where we are. You will cease fire only when you are certain that the intruders have been entirely destroyed.' He tucked the gun into his belt, next to his revolver.

'Sir George . . . ?' His captain didn't want to finish the question. He just glanced eloquently at Lewes, then back at Monk. Monk grunted as he climbed up into the cab.

'I will do what I can to get the people out of the way,' he said, 'but remember that we are being invaded. Casualties are to be expected. Get back to the guns and pass on my orders. Driver, forward.'

The steam wagon lurched into life and trundled

down the hill. A nervous corporal was at the wheel, Monk sat in the cabin next to him and a trailerful of soldiers was towed behind.

The narrow high street was almost empty. Here and there some children or women cowered in the houses, but he knew where most of the people would be. *Ariel*, scouting ahead, had signalled that there was a row of crosses planted on the castle green, surrounded by a large crowd of townsfolk. He remembered Brighthelmstone, and would look there first.

They came to the small lane that led up to the castle's massive barbican. It wouldn't take the wagon. 'Halt,' he said, and they shuddered to a standstill with a clanking and a loud hiss of escaping steam. 'Wait here,' he said to the driver. He checked that his sidearm was fully loaded, double-checked that the flare gun had its charge, and stepped down to the ground. 'Men, dismount. Fall in.'

They reached the crowd a minute later. The inhabitants all had their backs to the newcomers and those on the edges were craning their necks to see what was going on. Monk was not a tall man and could see nothing. He stuck his hands between the first two people in the way and pulled.

'Make way!' he commanded. 'Make way in the name of the king.' They swung round to glare, then saw the uniforms and immediately subsided. They pulled back reluctantly and thus Monk made his way to the centre of the throng, Moses parting a grudging Red Sea, trailed by forty soldiers bearing rifles.

There were the crosses, and Monk's heart

pounded. But they were still empty, and he relaxed. They were propped up halfway between the horizontal and the vertical, ready to receive a victim and to be raised up fully, but for now they were empty.

Or not. His eyes panned along the row and he saw there was one crucified figure at the end, dressed black in an archaic Puritan manner. The man's face was sheet-white, and red blood stained his wrists and his feet where he had been nailed to the wood. His face was a rigid mask of agony, and as Monk drew nearer he could hear the victim murmuring the Lord's Prayer, over and over again.

Robed Holekhor stood in front of the cross, looking up at the victim. Most were clad in black, one was in bright scarlet and white. There was also a Holekhor man whose clothes suggested some kind of tradesman. A band of armed Holekhor in more soldier-like clothes and kilts stood with their backs to their masters, facing the crowd. They too had rifles, and they held them at the ready. The crowd didn't look as if it was going to rush the invaders; in fact, it seemed so complacent that the armsmen were barely necessary.

Blood rushed in Monk's ears and he strode forward. 'In the name of King Charles, take that man down at once!' he shouted. Immediately the armsmen drew themselves up and twenty rifles aimed at him. He walked forward until he was almost staring down the nearest one. At his back he heard the metallic clicking of forty English rifles being cocked and the muffled thump as his men brought their own guns to bear, rifle butts slamming into the leather jackets at their shoulders. The two parties stared at each other through their sights.

Another sound that impinged upon Monk behind him was that of a large crowd trying to disperse without drawing attention to its leaving.

The Holekhor nearest the cross turned slowly round. The tradesman looked nervous; the one in the colourful robes smiled benignly.

'I said, take that man down, in the name of the king.' Monk looked around him; sure enough, the crowd had shrunk to a fraction of its size. 'What is wrong with you?' he shouted. 'You let these heathen nail up a good Christian Englishman without quibble?'

'Witch finder,' said the nearest local, in a tone that suggested no further explanation was needed. Monk sighed.

He knew his royal master had little truck for witches, but less because he regarded them as worshippers of Satan, more because he regarded them all as charlatans or deluded old women. His views on witch finders were scarcely more charitable. Still, it was an aspect of life in his kingdom with which Charles did little to interfere.

'I thought this was a Puritan town?' he said. The man scowled.

'We're good Christians, but he ain't from around here and he falsely accused Mistress Wetheril. We all know she weren't no witch.'

Monk looked back at the Holekhor in charge, the

one in scarlet and white. He guessed the man to be a priest, and spoke slowly and loudly.

'Do you speak English?'

The tradesman spoke nervously. 'I am the translator, sir. My name is—'

'Then tell these ... *gentlemen,* sir, that the king commands they withdraw from this town and from this country at once.' The latter requirement would be difficult as he himself had sunk their ship, but they weren't to know that. 'He also commands that this man be taken down.'

The translator gulped. 'I . . .'

Monk pulled out his revolver and swung his arm up to sight directly between the priest's eyes. The armsmen stiffened, but the priest said something and no trigger was pulled. The priest's tone had been gentle but his grey eyes blazed warning.

Monk added, '*Now.*'

There was a sound, a gentle whisper in his ears, as if someone, somewhere was singing quietly. It was a hum, a gentle vibration. The air grew tense with the promise and threat of an incipient thunderstorm.

The scarlet-and-white man spoke; the translator said, 'Re Nokh suggests you consult with your king. The Congregation have been given permission to come and go as they please in this—'

'*Open fire!*' Monk shouted.

Forty metallic clicks sounded through the charged air. His astonished men looked at their rifles as if they were bewitched. Which, of course, they were. He looked back at the priest, this Re Nokh, raised his revolver again and pulled the trigger. *Click.*

Twenty Holekhor rifles barked and twenty of his men crumpled. Time seemed to slow down. Monk saw the armsmen working their bolts, ejecting the spent cartridges, loading fresh ones, raising their guns again, and he was throwing himself at the nearest one before it had even occurred to him that this was what he should be doing. The only thing he could do, to save his life.

Time returned to its usual speed and his men hurled themselves at the enemy with angry cries. His men had bayonets; the armsmen did not. His Englishmen were slim and light on their feet; the Holekhor were short and stocky but very strong. Monk saw his sergeant impale an armsman in the guts, just as a large, heavy fist slammed into the side of his head and he fell to the ground with coloured lights in his eyes. Then an English soldier was standing over him, lunging with his bayonet at the armsman who had hit him and the Holekhor was parrying the blows with his rifle, trying to find time to cock it again. But then there was another shot and his man fell.

And all the while there was that strange singing in the background. Monk suddenly knew what it was. He had heard accounts from witnesses of the Wise in action, and he could do nothing against it. The air was charged with their power.

'Fall back,' he gasped. He pushed himself to his hands and knees, then wobbled to his feet. 'Fall back.'

Two of his men – two of the seven survivors – crowded in front of him, their bayonets held out, shielding him as they withdrew from the melee. It would have been futile if the Holekhor had opened fire with their unbewitched weapons, but they seemed content to let the fight end with withdrawal.

Monk paused in his flight, and a second later was knocked to his knees by the fleeing people of Lewes. A soldier picked him up and drew him into an alley until the crowd had passed. He pulled out his flare gun, sent a brief prayer to the Almighty that this weapon which the Wise had not yet seen would still be working, aimed it at the sky and pulled the trigger. The flare soared up into the air above the town. Bare seconds later he heard the roar of artillery and the whistle of the approaching shells.

He covered his ears against the explosions but they came far too soon, up in the air and nowhere near the green. He peered gingerly round the corner to look back, and up. The clouds of smoke and fire from the explosions were just dispersing, a hundred feet up in the air. It was as if they had hit an invisible shield above the castle.

The Wise were all staring up at the high ground above the town, where the guns were positioned. Blue sparks flashed along the ground, skittering across the turf towards the black-clad group like snakes eager to return to their home. Light began to coalesce in the air around them, growing in seconds from a faint shimmer to a bright ball, then a burning globe of flame. The fire lunged suddenly up from the ground into the air, high above the town, leaving a green streak across the back of Monk's eyes. It arced down on to Charity and hit the hillside, consuming gun and men and wagon. The gun exploded, and seconds later the sound reached Lewes. A multiple, rippling boom told Monk the explosion had taken all the shells at once.

Sick at heart, Monk saw the process repeated. He could see the crew of Faith scattering as the ball fell on them, but it burst and spread too quickly. There was another wave of explosions.

The crew of Hope were running already, even before the final fireball was launched. The wagon began to move as well; some brave, doomed soul was doing his duty. The ball fell squarely on him and the gun, consuming both in a third and final blast.

Then the air around him began to sing its Wise-music again, and with horror he felt something take hold of his body. The hairs on his head and his arms stood, as phantom hands grasped his feet and his legs and made them move back on to the green. His men were under a similar spell.

'Th'L—' he wheezed. His voice dried up and he swallowed. 'The Lord is my Shepherd, I shall not want . . .'

The psalm came to him naturally and he chanted it as his treacherous limbs walked him back to the certain death of his body and his soul. One of the men broke down in tears and wept, but kept walking. The others took their cues from Monk and prayed out loud.

And there was nothing they could do. Nothing at all. Now Monk wept as he was forced to stand and watch – he could not even close his eyes – as the last men of his command were taken from him, and laid themselves down on the crosses, and screamed as nails were hammered into their arms and legs, and the crosses were raised up, falling into their postholes with sickening thuds.

The invisible bonds relaxed, so suddenly that Monk collapsed into the arms of the translator.

'Re Nokh says: Call down your airship, go to your king and tell him that the Congregation will not be stopped. They are here with the permission and blessing of the Domon'el. They will set up their mission here, they will send word back home and more will come to join them. The natives of Enkhlon will turn to the worship of the Pantheon, or pay the price. Go now.'

The translator glanced from side to side, then leaned forward and whispered: 'I'm sorry.'

Twenty-Three

I Saw Three Ships

'Hurry, hurry!'

Daniel, Elizabeth and Harry were herded away from the scene at the points of a dozen guns. Daniel's head still pounded and his eyes watered from the beating. He staggered against one of the armed men and was shoved off with a rifle muzzle in his chest. He resolved to start feeling better.

'Get back!' Some of Elizabeth's loyal retinue of servants had tried to follow. The man called Lilburne fired a shot over their heads and they hastily retreated.

'Come,' Lilburne said, and they were into the trees.

They were shoved along a track through the woods with ever increasing urgency. A light drizzle began to fall, and its moistness seeped through the canopy of leaves and into the air around them. The track was muddy and rutted. Elizabeth gasped and stumbled into Daniel, and he had to catch her quickly before she fell headlong in the dirt.

'Move along!' Lilburne snapped.

Daniel helped Elizabeth stand straight again.

Much as he would have liked to believe she had fallen just to end up in his strong arms, he could guess the real reason.

'I can't walk like this,' she whispered. She was a princess and a lady, accustomed to walking on polished floorboards, not muddy roads. She wore a many layered, very wide dress. Daniel couldn't see what was on her feet but doubted it was a practical pair of boots.

Sparks flashed in his eyes with another clout across the head. 'I said move along!' Lilburne shouted.

Daniel turned angrily on the God's Army leader. Pain and injustice gave him more courage than he had been feeling a minute before.

'She can't walk on this road!'

'Ah!' Lilburne sneered down at him. 'England's good, honest dirt too coarse for the spoilt princess's feet?'

'Look at what she's wearing,' Daniel said. 'Do you want her to take it off?'

'Master Matthews!' Elizabeth exclaimed. Lilburne and Daniel ignored her, not budging their glares from one another.

'No,' Lilburne said after a moment, and Daniel realized he had actually been considering the suggestion seriously. 'No, that would not be seemly. Jeremiah!' One of the shorter rebels came over, an enquiring look on his face. 'Your feet are small. Give her your boots.'

'Give her my boots?' Jeremiah exclaimed. 'What do I walk in?'

'You've worked barefoot in the fields since you was a littl'un. Do it.'

Jeremiah paused, then reluctantly handed his rifle to Lilburne and bent to undo his buckles. Elizabeth looked aghast at the reeking leather shapes that were finally handed to her.

'I can't . . .'

'Put them on,' Daniel said in a low, determined voice. She glared at him with total dislike.

'I will remember that you suggested I disrobe entirely, Master Matthews. Perhaps your breeding is showing after all.' His jaw dropped at the unfairness. 'And I trust you do not expect me to change my footwear with you and the rest of the world looking on?'

Daniel threw his hands up, but resolutely turned his back on her. After a moment, Lilburne joined him and they stood side by side, shielding the princess from prying eyes. A moment after that they were joined by Harry and the three of them stood together, the unlikeliest of temporary alliances.

'I am ready,' said Elizabeth. She walked between them, her head held high, then stopped and looked back. 'I thought we were hurrying, Master Lilburne?' She didn't even look at Daniel.

Lilburne and Daniel glanced at each other, then followed after her.

'Maidstone, Lord,' said Dhon Do.

Finally, after quarters that had felt much longer, they were back at Povse'okh. They had returned to a report from the squad sent to collect the survivors from the train wreck: no sign of Daniel or Charles's siblings. All the Holekhor who had been left behind seemed to have been massacred on the spot, yet Daniel was not among them.

Now the sun was nearing the horizon; it had been a long day and Dhon Do felt deathly tired in his mind, his body and his heart. And he was hungry. After dropping Charles back at Hampton Court there had been little question of the planned banquet actually happening.

The Domon'el and his retinue stood by a map of southern Enkhlon. Behind his steel glasses the Domon'el's gaze on his realm was greedy, but it was not the greed of someone calculating its worth. It was the greed of expected vengeance.

He didn't look a bit hungry for food, which probably meant that Dhon Do's next meal was still some time away.

'Mhed-ston,' the Domon'el said in his rich, flat voice. 'That is the nearest town to the ambush?'

'Without a doubt, Lord.'

'Then Mhed-ston will be the stage for our reprisal. The natives will learn, Dhon Do.'

'Lord, doubtless the king is planning his own reprisals against his people – he *was* their target.'

'Doubtless he is, Dhon Do, but he does not have an airship capable of delivering it. I have several and I intend to use them.'

Dhon Do nodded. 'Several will not be needed, Lord. Most native buildings are made of wood. A few incendiaries . . .'

'We will use three,' the Domon'el decided. His eyes glittered behind his round glasses. 'That, I believe, is the usual attack wing. I want a crater. I want Mhed-ston removed from the map with no possibility of its ever being rebuilt.' His fist thumped the table. 'I want the natives to *learn*.'

'Three airships, Lord,' Dhon Do agreed with barely a pause, hoping against hope that Charles had taken the very heavy hint he had dropped back at Dover. He turned to Por De. 'Centurion, have an attack wing standing by for first hour.'

First hour by the Holekhor clock was the sixth hour of the English day. The three ships would take off just before daylight. If Charles had taken the hint, and if he worked through the night . . .

'Ready them now,' the Domon'el said. 'I do not want Mhed-ston to see another sunrise.'

Dhon Do's world lurched, but the only external sign of this was a slightly longer pause. 'Lord, it will be dark by the time we get there.'

'The radio beacons are in place?'

'Of course, Lord.' Getting the radio beacons up, giving his airships a secure means of navigating the air above Enkhlon, had been one of Dhon Do's first accomplishments after the Treaty of Oxford.

'Then we can find this nest of traitors with no difficulty.'

Dhon Do made one final, desperate try. 'Lord, you won't see your crater in the dark.'

'No.' The Domon'el's teeth flashed white in his beard and, as usual, his grin was entirely free of humour. 'But the flames will be all the more spectacular.'

It felt like hours; it probably was. Even Daniel's Holekhor legs were beginning to ache.

They had left the track a long time ago and were hurrying through the trees. Elizabeth was still striding determinedly ahead, but her face was set. The hem of her fine dress was ragged and filthy; she had been ready to wear a man's boots but not to lift her dress up. She hadn't spoken to Daniel since changing her footwear. He deliberately hung back behind her, though it irked his longer stride, so he could keep an eye on her progress, ready to offer an arm or a hand if needed. Harry trudged wearily beside him, his face pale. They both ignored the polite fiction that he was the prince's valet.

Daniel didn't have a watch on him and he wondered how long it had been. Dhon Do would have sent soldiers, and they must have reached the train by now. Had they followed? Or had they been wary of heading into another ambush? He had thought he had heard the noise of an airship; Dhon Do had probably called one in to support the men on the ground, but it would not serve much purpose looking for a band of rebels beneath the trees.

'Here,' said Lilburne. They stopped suddenly and Daniel looked around. Still surrounded by trees, bushes, layers of mulching leaves on the ground . . . and one of the rebels grabbed a bush and pulled. Behind it was a square, dark hole.

Daniel had no time to take it in before he was being hustled underground. He was not tall but had still to duck as he hurried down the passage, and Elizabeth in her dress could barely squeeze through at all. But suddenly they were out into a much larger, dimly lit room.

Rather, Daniel realized, after a moment, it was dimly sunlit, the sun shining through the canvas ceiling. It was mostly a natural hollow, here and there further excavated by artificial means, and covered by a wooden framework with canvas stretched above it. On the other side of the canvas Daniel could see the shapes and shadows of bushes, sewn against the material.

The God's Army men were relaxing as if relieved of a load. They laid their guns down against the walls, sat down, laughed and joshed with one another. Two men still stood guard over Daniel and the royal children. They were pushed into a corner and Daniel opened his mouth to ask Elizabeth how she was.

'Quiet,' the guard snapped, and he looked towards a far corner of the partially underground chamber. A figure approached out of the gloom.

Daniel frowned. There was something familiar . . . and the faintest memory of an old scent tickled his nostrils, in a way that would have completely bypassed someone not blessed with a Holekhor's sense of smell. But then the figure was close enough and he remembered.

'Mistress Connolly,' said Lilburne, and Daniel's heart sank. 'You've arrived.'

But Khonol Le just glanced at them. 'Prisoners?' She put her hands on her hips. 'You took prisoners?' She raised her voice. 'The purpose of this raid was to kill the Domon'el! Were you successful?'

Lilburne flushed. 'Perhaps we were at cross-purposes, Mistress Connolly. We understood it to be a raid against Charles Stuart, as well as his pagan allies.'

Khonol Le smiled sweetly. 'And you were no doubt successful? You have Charles Stuart's head to show me?'

'Perhaps my Christian sister should have accompanied us on the raid!' Lilburne shouted. 'She could have made sure we only killed the right people!'

'Ach.' Khonol Le waved hand in disgust. 'It's done. You executed Dhon Do's men?'

'Of course. Just English left.'

'That is something. Why these three? Who are they?'

'A princess, a prince and his servant.' Lilburne spoke the words with distaste and Khonol Le finally looked more closely at the three. She groaned and looked away again.

'Not just prisoners,' she said. '*Royal* prisoners. Master Lilburne, you have surpassed—'

She stopped, looked back. Now she gazed at Daniel and her eyes squinted with curiosity. Her nostrils widened as she breathed through them.

'*Dopevs've*,' she said in the One Tongue. *I know you.* Daniel drew a breath to respond, then bit his tongue and kept silent. He essayed a look that he hoped reflected puzzled incomprehension.

Khonol Le smiled. 'Very well,' she said in English, as if tacitly agreeing to play a game. 'I said, I know you.'

'I don't believe so,' Daniel muttered. Slow enlightenment dawned on her face.

'Take your shirt off,' she said.

'No!' Daniel exclaimed.

'Oh, for—' Khonol Le reached out, grabbed the lapels of his shirt with both hands and pulled. The row of buttons popped and the shirt tore with a loud rip. Lilburne frowned, bewildered.

'Mistress Connolly, this is not seemly for a Christian woman.'

Khonol Le was taken aback at the smooth, unblemished skin of Daniel's bare right shoulder. 'Odd,' she said. 'I must be mistaken.' She turned away again, then back with a grunt of realization. 'It was the *other* shoulder.'

Another rip and Daniel stood bare-chested. He was suddenly intensely aware of Elizabeth's presence, but foremost in his mind was his left shoulder, and the thin white scar across it where Khonol Le had cut it open to remove a pistol ball.

'Well,' Khonol Le murmured. She walked slowly around Daniel but it was just a formality to confirm that the entry wound she remembered was there as well. 'I was proud of that work. What a shame it turns out to have been a waste of time. Do you know who this is, Master Lilburne?'

Lilburne frowned again. 'He's the boy's servant.'

Daniel barely dared breathe. A hundred possible

responses ran through his mind – *I don't know what you mean*; *Yes, that's me,* and many more – but he couldn't make his mouth move to say any of them.

Khonol Le chuckled. 'He said that?' Then there was a certain sadness in her eyes as she looked back at Daniel. 'Do you know what these people do to pagan Holekhor?'

It finally dawned on Daniel that he had now heard the word 'Christian' used in reference to Khonol Le, twice. 'And what are you?' he said. He tried to cover himself up with the remains of his shirt.

'I'm a sister of God's Army. I was baptized into the one true faith five years ago.'

'I was baptized eighteen years ago,' Daniel said. 'I'm no pagan.'

'Mistress Connolly, who is this?' Lilburne said loudly. Khonol Le ignored him.

'That would not be the general's assessment,' she said. 'He has made certain decrees regarding anyone, English or Holekhor, Christian or pagan, who associates with your father's invaders. Master Lilburn –' she looked Daniel in the eyes, and seemed genuinely regretful – 'you know the general's orders. This young man is the son of Dhon Do.'

Lilburne stared at Daniel with a predatory greed. 'A real, live witch?'

'No!' Daniel shouted. He heard Elizabeth behind him gasp as she caught the implications. 'No, didn't you hear me? I'm a Christian!'

'Clearly not Christian enough, if you continue to

consort with the enemy.' Lilburne looked thoughtfully at Daniel, then shook his head and for a wonderful moment Daniel thought he had had some kind of reprieve. 'Too close to town to shoot you. Men! We're hanging a witch!'

Elizabeth screamed, 'No!' Khonol Le restrained her and hands grabbed Daniel. He flung them off as easily as any Holekhor would, and then a rifle butt thudded into the back of his skull and he collapsed. They dragged him to his feet and marched him outside.

'No!' he gasped. 'No! You can't! You—'

One of his captors thumped him hard in the stomach and the breath whooshed out of him. They reached the open air. Another punch and he fell to the dead leaves on the ground. He squirmed, too weak to keep them from binding his arms behind him, and then his tongue dried as he saw the noose slung over a branch. They hauled him to his feet and he felt the noose slipped round his neck, tight and prickly against his skin.

'Put a hood on him,' someone ordered. 'Ladies present.' The last thing he saw as they slipped a sack over his head was a weeping Elizabeth, still held back by Khonol Le.

'You're a murderer,' he choked, and then the noose was hauled upwards. It drew a strangled gasp out of him that caused Elizabeth to scream again, '*No!*' and break into further sobs.

Khonol Le still sounded sorry. 'It's the general's orders,' she said, and another voice spoke.

'How good of you to remember, Mistress Connolly. So few of your actions to date have been driven by a desire to obey me.'

Time stopped. So, thankfully, did the upward pressure of the noose. Daniel held his breath, stood on the tips of his toes and squinted uncertainly into the darkness of the hood. He heard a horse approaching at a casual, rhythmic pace. Its harness jingled and its hooves rustled against the damp leaves.

'What are you doing, Master Lilburne?' said the voice.

'Hanging a witch.' Lilburne sounded surly, like a child who thinks he has outgrown parental rebukes.

'He's no witch!' That was Elizabeth. 'Sir, if you are any kind of Christian then I implore you—'

'Quiet, child.' The double thud of someone dismounting, the sound of his approach on foot. 'Release this prisoner.'

The noose was released and Daniel dropped down to stand properly on his feet. He drew a deep, thankful breath. Then the hood was pulled from his head and he looked goggle-eyed into the lumpy, ugly face of Oliver Cromwell.

They were back in the hideout.

'You were going north,' Khonol Le said.

'I was going north,' Cromwell agreed. The last time Daniel had seen him, Parliament's general had worn the uniform of the New Model Army. Now he wore a dark and dusty riding cloak and carried a wide-brimmed, floppy hat. Even as he shucked the cloak off and passed it and the hat to someone nearby, he still *seemed* to wear his uniform. He had a dignity and a presence that could not be ignored. 'My horse threw a shoe and I had to turn back. Imagine my surprise upon returning to camp when Richard told me Mistress Connolly had gone east. Imagine my further surprise when I learned the nature of the orders she had wirespoken ahead of her, to Master Lilburne's cell. Did you by any chance, Mistress Connolly, fail to understand my instructions concerning the Domon'el?'

Lilburne looked puzzled. 'Do you mean . . . ?'

'I mean, Master Lilburne, that you have doubtless followed your orders to the fullest extent,' Cromwell said. He scowled at Khonol Le. 'Sadly you did not check the provenance of those orders. I am disappointed, Mistress Connolly. Very, very disappointed.'

'The Domon'el is a tyrant!' Khonol Le hissed. 'He invaded Toskhes. He began a war which—'

'Toskhes began the war,' Daniel said.

'You be quiet! You know nothing.'

Cromwell said, more mildly, 'Young man, you are only alive because this entire operation has been so full of irregularities that I wish personally to ensure that no more take place. If I decide your execution is nonetheless appropriate then we shall proceed.'

A wave of lassitude swept over Daniel. He was under sentence of death and it would probably be carried out, and suddenly it scarcely mattered whom he antagonized. 'Povse'okh is thirty miles from the border,' he said wearily. 'Toskhes kept sending raids against it. They provoked the Domon'el.'

Khonol Le's mouth worked for a moment like a fish. 'That is—'

'Certainly a version I have not heard before,' Cromwell said. 'It is also irrelevant.' He gazed coolly at Daniel. 'I know we have met but I confess I have forgotten your name.'

'Daniel Matthews.'

'Of course. I saw you at Brighthelmstone. You took those people down from the crosses and you preached the Word to the heathen.'

'Yes,' Daniel said. 'I did.' There was an impressed grunt from Lilburne and an approving murmur from the crowd of God's Army.

Cromwell nodded. 'Scarcely the typical behaviour of a witch. Yet your continued association with your father cannot be denied.'

'He *is* my father!'

'And he associates with witches and gives them the benefit of his protection. We monitor all the heathen's communications. Your father has given free licence to the Congregation. By your people's laws they are free to preach their false gods and crucify any Christian Englishmen or women who will not recant the true faith.'

There was another murmur from the crowd; this time, much less approving.

'But . . . but . . .' Daniel said helplessly. 'He was ordered!'

'It is not unknown for Christians to be given

orders by tyrants,' Cromwell agreed, 'in which case their higher duty is to God, as was ours when the tyranny of the king's father became too much to bear. Master Matthews, I ask no one to make sacrifices that we have not already made ourselves. During the Rebellion, families were split apart, the country was riven, the weeping and suffering beyond reckoning. I have not seen my wife or daughters in six years, because the king's agents keep careful watch on them. Mistress Connolly has not seen her friends or family since they were deported through Povse'okh by your father. But every choice we have ever made has been because it was the Lord's will.'

Daniel bit his tongue on an innocent question, *Did it work?* As the prospect of his execution receded, however slightly, so life became dearer to him once more. Cromwell would probably – *probably* – not execute him out of irritation but it would serve no purpose to rile him.

Perhaps Cromwell guessed what Daniel had not said. He scowled. 'You are an enigma, Master Matthews. The arguments for letting you live and die seem equally strong.' He came to a decision. 'Master Lilburne, have the boy and the girl fed and refreshed; I have contacts on the other side and we will make arrangements for them to be returned under flag of truce. As for Master Matthews here . . . have him fed, but continue to confine him. He may yet be hanged as a witch, but not without due process that we cannot provide here.' He looked at Khonol Le. 'And as for you, Mistress Connolly; we must have words.'

* * *

Dhon Do had put Daniel away in a locker at the back of his mind. As the three airships detached from their mooring masts at Povse'okh, he took his conscience, his compassion for Maidstone, his regret at what was to come, and put them away with his son. The locker was becoming worryingly full and Dhon Do had no idea of its total capacity. He was testing it in interesting ways.

Thus it was almost in a dream that he saw the Skymight crew, his crew, going about their tasks of making the airship fly and pointing it in the right direction. The Domon'el had no particular interest in this part of the proceedings and had retired to the officers' wardroom. Dhon Do knew there was nothing more distracting to a crew doing their job than a senior officer lurking in the background, but at this particular moment their company was preferable to that of his Lord. So he sat at the back of the command gondola, and gazed at the crew with an impassive face and hatred blazing in his heart. Hatred for the radio operator who picked up the beacons so effortlessly. Hatred for the navigator who laid in a course on the chart table with such consummate ease. Hatred for the captain as he gave orders to the engines, to the planes, to the ballast reservoirs, that sent the ship soaring up into the evening sky. The sunset off the starboard quarter shone through the gondola's large windows and cast an orange glow that added to the air of unreality.

It was a two-quarter flight. Outside it grew dark

and cold. Dhon Do had not brought his cloak but he declined the offer of a fur-lined Skymight officer's jacket. Doubtless, further aft, the Domon'el had the wardroom's electric fire turned up and was nicely toasting himself, tucking into the ship's meagre fare with a glad heart and clear conscience, perhaps discussing forthcoming social events with his aides. Dhon Do let someone press a warm mug into his hand but he barely sipped at it as the ship flew on into the darkness. The compass still worked, the beacons still beeped quietly. The attack wing flew straight as a die towards its target.

'Go to battle stations,' the captain said. Bells rang up and down the ship. The illumination in the cabin snapped off, replaced a moment later by a red glow from the battle lights.

'Drop flares,' the captain said into the speaking tube. A moment later a bright white light shone through the windows from below. The captain gazed out and grunted in satisfaction. 'Excellent. Target in sight. Care to take a look, sir? Sir?'

Dhon Do snapped out of his reverie. 'No,' he said. 'But inform our Lord. He will want to see this.'

'Yes, sir.' Someone was sent aft. A moment later he returned to announce that Dhon Do's presence was commanded on the observation deck. So Dhon Do stood and walked out on to the mesh gallery that extended aft of the gondola, suspended beneath the hull of the ship. The bitter cold dug into him like sharp talons but he ignored it. The Domon'el was snugly wrapped in a nenokh-hair cloak and hat, and he glanced up from the rail.

'We do not plan to leave survivors, Dhon Do,' he said. 'We will need other witnesses. Observe.'

He pointed, and Dhon Do duly looked. He could see the shape of a town below, wrapped around a river. The spire of a church. A market place. At this time of night everyone would be in their homes. Sitting targets.

The engines changed suddenly, falling from their high cruising pitch to a more measured rumble as the ship dropped to attack speed. Astern, lit from below by the dying light of the flares, the prow of the second ship in the wing loomed like a fat man's belly. The double doors of the drop hatch swung open behind the gallery with a whirr, letting the cold rush of air and noise into the ship's red-lit interior. Inside, the crew would be hauling the bomb racks over the gap with practised ease. Dhon Do could hear the metallic clicks and clunks as they were locked into place. The ship was over the heart of the town.

Another bell rang, and death fell from the stomach of the ship on to the defenceless town below.

Twenty-Four

Air and Darkness

Once again Daniel had a hood over his head and his hands were tied. Buffeted by darkness and the chill evening air, he sat in the back of the cart and let it take him where it would. He had no idea where they were going, only that it was something to do with Cromwell's idea of 'due process'. He didn't even know who else was with him; no scents could make it through the hood's musty sackcloth. Someone must have been driving the cart, but when he had tried to say something he had got a foot in the ribs. Not hard, but enough to convince him he should stay quiet.

Over the creak of the wheels and the horse's measured pacing he heard night noises: wind in leaves, the staggered hooting of an owl, the short and angry bark of a fox. Suddenly, and to his surprise, his eyes filled with tears and he bit his lip. They were *innocent* noises. The noises of his home. The owl and the fox hunted and preyed, but they did it without malice, without religion or politics. Yet he, Daniel, was quite possibly being taken to his death by people for whom religion and politics were everything. They had taken upon themselves the right to deprive him of his life. To deny him these sounds of freedom. So *unfair.*

Eventually they were out of the trees, and a short while later, they were in a town. Daniel could scent it even through the hood. It was late in the night but the memories of people and livestock were fresh in the air. The sounds were different too: sharper, more defined, echoing off straight and solid walls. And the horse's hooves still plodded on dirt but the dirt was now compact and hard.

The cart stopped in an enclosed space that smelled like a stable. He heard the sound of a large, wooden door closing behind them, and then Cromwell spoke in his ear.

'Wait here. We will come for you shortly. Do not try to escape; you are guarded.'

Daniel could hear the sound of his guard's feet shuffling in the hay. So he stayed and waited while Cromwell and a third person walked off through another door. A while later, Cromwell came back and took him by the arm.

'Come this way.' Cromwell's tugging hand guided him as he inched along the floor of the cart. His feet found the edge and he slithered over it to stand on solid ground. Cromwell steered him out of the stable and into an adjoining building. His steps sounded hollow on a wooden floor and a light glimmered through the hood. Then he was pushed down into a seat, his hands were set free and the hood pulled from his head.

It was a plain room, thick curtains drawn over the

one window and candles on the wall to light it. Three dark-clad men sat at a table, looking bored and annoyed. His own chair faced them across the room. Cromwell and Khonol Le stood beside him and his guard from the stable had followed them in to stand against the closed door, cocked pistol in his hand.

Cromwell addressed the three at the table. 'Gentlemen, I thank you for your attention at such short notice. I have a dilemma.'

'Make it a good one, Oliver,' said the middle man. 'Some of us have families to attend to.'

Cromwell bowed. 'For reasons that are of no relevance to the proceedings, the son of Dhon Do has fallen into my hands.'

That immediately caught their interest and Daniel flushed under their triple stare. He sent back a sullen look from under his brows.

'Then what is the dilemma?' said the one on the right. 'Hang him!'

'For reasons that will become apparent, the case of Master Matthews is more ambiguous than that, gentlemen. Further, it is especially important now that justice be seen to be done. Today saw a lamentable decline in the integrity of God's Army. An entire cell was compromised due to the indiscipline of a trusted member. We will put things right.'

He hadn't looked at Khonol Le, but her face turned slowly red. He continued: 'Master Matthews, God's Army believes that any man is allowed a fair trial. You should know where you are. Master Ireton here –' he indicated the man in the middle – 'was once a lawyer of the Middle Temple and is a veteran of my Ironsides. These other gentlemen were magistrates under Parliament, and all three today are loyal soldiers of God's Army. They shall be the panel to determine whether or not you should be hanged.'

''Course he should,' the hang-thirsty man muttered, but Ireton shushed him.

'Now, I shall be prosecuting the accused; Mistress Connolly shall defend him.'

'What?' Daniel shouted. 'I don't want her!' Mistress Connolly herself burst out laughing.

Cromwell scowled. 'She will do as she is ordered, and I do so order. It amuses you, madam?'

Khonol Le smothered another laugh. 'Your sense of humour amuses me, General. But yes, I'll gladly defend the boy.'

'Is this agreeable to you, gentlemen?' Cromwell said to the panel.

Ireton looked tired. 'Oliver, there are already procedures for determining the truth of witchcraft charges.'

'Flawed procedures,' Cromwell said, 'which I do not believe will work in this instance. Gentlemen, the truth shall set you free. We need to establish the truth. Will you undertake this task?'

They sighed and said they would.

'But you lead the army!' Daniel said. 'Why have a trial? Why not just make up your own mind?'

'My inclination is indeed to play safe and hang you, Master Matthews, so I advise you to pay more respect to these proceedings. But to answer your question more fully, no man is above the law. The previous king fancied that he was, and the Rebellion was the result. Yes, I lead God's Army, but I do not decide its law. That right belongs to duly constituted officers of its court. Now, we shall begin.'

And they did.

Cromwell first asked Daniel a series of questions. Daniel, still convinced that the whole affair was designed to obtain a fairly-passed sentence of death, mumbled his answers in a monotone. Are you the son of Dhon Do? Yes. What faith do you espouse? The Christian faith. Do you follow the Pope? I do not. Describe for the court how you first met your father . . .

Only once did Daniel's temper flare up from beneath his cloud of despond. He finally decided he had heard the word 'witch' once too often.

'It's not witchcraft!' he shouted. Khonol Le, who was taking her job seriously, tried to shush him. Daniel ignored her.

'Look,' he said. He gazed round the room for an example and his eyes settled on the guard's pistol. He pointed. 'If that man pulls the trigger, it will release a spring. The hammer will fall forward. It will hit a flint and make a spark. The spark will fire the powder and the gun will discharge. Is that witchcraft?'

Cromwell smiled faintly. 'It is not.'

'Of course it's not,' Daniel said. 'Anyone could do it. It's . . . it's the way the world is made. The land-power is like that. It's the way the world is made too. Wise don't consort with demons, they don't—'

Cromwell held up a hand. 'If it pleases the panel, I am familiar with this argument. I have heard it from Mistress Connolly too, prior to her baptism, and it is a tempting falsehood. The argument goes that the power of the Holekhor witches is a mechanical process. It is not supernatural, simply an aspect of the Lord's creation that anyone can use. Well, Master Matthews. Can you use this power?'

Daniel flushed. 'No.'

'Can Mistress Connolly? Can just any Holekhor?'

'No,' Daniel admitted again.

'So, it is *not* a mechanical process. Only Holekhor with particular aptitudes can use it. Only the select few, who are known as the Order of the Wise, and I understand they require years of training. It is a craft.'

'I don't know how to build an airship,' Daniel said. 'That takes years of training too, but they are simply machines. You've flown in one. Was that witchcraft? Did *you* consort with demons?'

'I have flown in an airship,' Cromwell agreed. 'The first time I saw it, I was terrified. It flew over our heads – you were there, Mistress Connolly – and for a moment, just for a moment, I honestly thought that the Day of Judgement was upon us and the sky was falling. But even then I could see that it was an artefact, made by the hand of man. When I rode in one, I saw that it was made of metal and wood and canvas. The power that made lights shine in the darkness . . . that seemed more like witchcraft at the time, but since then I have learned more about it and I know that that, too, is a mechanical process. I have had the principles of batteries and the generation of power explained to me. It is a function of natural chemicals and magnets. It is confusing, but it *is* mechanical. It is something that anyone can do. I maintain that the witchcraft of the Holekhor remains witchcraft, and I refer the panel to Master Milton's essay *Of Man's first disobedience and the witchcraft of the Holekhor*. Sirs, I must ask for a ruling on this issue for my case to proceed.'

The panel deliberated for some minutes, and finally Ireton pronounced their ruling. The power of the Wise was supernatural and had no scriptural precedent. Those who wielded it professed no Christian faith, so it must not be derived from God, and hence was *ipso facto* demonic in its origin.

Satisfied, Cromwell asked a few more questions, mostly about Daniel's life after he had met his father and why he had chosen to remain at Povse'okh, and then Khonol Le took over.

As Daniel had hoped she would, she went straight to Brighthelmstone. Daniel described everything that had happened from the moment he saw the crosses on the hill. He described how he had preached to the men from the Bible. He told them his choice of subject matter and one of the panel nodded approvingly. Ireton kept his face neutral and the advocate of hanging continued to scowl.

Cromwell interrupted. 'Your father has given the Congregation licence in this country.'

'I didn't know that!' Daniel snapped. 'But . . .' His ears pricked up.

'Go on?' said Khonol Le.

'I . . .' Daniel said, but suddenly his mind was elsewhere. It sounded like . . . yes, it was an airship . . . no, air*ships* . . . And he could see Khonol Le was with him. After a moment even those in the room who were not gifted with Holekhor ears could hear it.

'Proceed, Master Matthews,' said Ireton. 'Ignore the airships. They are not here to rescue you.'

'Wait,' Daniel said. There were . . . *three* airships. He had seen a manoeuvre once, a practice on a deserted village on Salisbury Plain that involved three airships. It was the usual number for . . . He jumped to his feet. 'Sir, we should leave immediately.'

'Sit down!' Cromwell roared. 'Master Matthews, perhaps you have not fully understood but I am trying to give you a Christian chance—'

Bright light blazed through the curtains. Khonol Le pulled the curtain back from the window and the light flooded in, bleaching the little room in shades of white. At the same time, Daniel heard the engines change note. Yes, he had seen this manoeuvre before and he knew what was to happen.

'We must leave now!' he shouted.

'The boy is right,' said Khonol Le. She turned and headed for the door.

'Master Matthews, I warn you—' raged Cromwell.

A shrill, banshee whistle split the air.

'Too late!' Khonol Le shouted, and she dived beneath the table. Daniel, his Christian charity exhausted, joined her. The whistle grew louder and closer, sliding down the scale as it went, and then the world erupted around them.

The roar of high explosive rang in his ears. The glass of the window blew in, lacerating the guard who had stood by the door. There were screams and shouts from the others in the room and from outside the building, and then with a crash the entire house fell on top of them.

A wave of choking dust billowed around Daniel. He coughed and waved his hand in front of his face. He tried to stand but the bottom of the table stopped him. He strained but could get no further than a half crouch. A spluttering Khonol Le rose to her hands and knees beside him and put her back against the table. Together they stretched their Holekhor muscles and the table rose with them, then fell to one side.

The outside wall of the room had blown in and they looked out at a street lit by blazing buildings, dark frames of timber silhouetted against the bright orange flames. The three men of the panel were dead, caught between the table and the blast, and the remains of the wall were on top of them. They lay against the table with trickles of blood from their ears and noses. The ringing in Daniel's ears gradually turned into an agonized shrieking, not his own. Daniel shifted a beam that had fallen behind him, and beneath it lay the guard, his hands clutched to his shredded face. Khonol Le pushed Daniel gently to one side, then crouched and just as gently took the guard's hands from his face. The man's nose was missing, his upper lip hung by a flap, and specks of glass glistened in his face and eye sockets. Khonol Le quietly picked up the gun that had fallen beside him, put the barrel to the man's forehead and pulled the trigger. The screams mercifully vanished in the roar of the shot.

They both turned at the sound of a groan. Daniel pulled aside another pile of rubble, and Khonol Le helped him. A minute later they had unearthed the still living Oliver Cromwell. A beam had come down on top of him, but had fallen on a chair and so had not squashed him. It had even given some protection. Like them, he was dusted a ghostly white with fallen plaster.

'Master Matthews,' he gasped, 'your father does your case no favours.'

Daniel cocked his head. 'There's a second ship coming in,' he said. 'I told you we should leave.'

He and Khonol Le took Cromwell and they staggered out through the hole in the wall, just in time to hear the second shrill whistle slicing the air above them. There was no time to take shelter. They dropped to the ground, curled up and prayed. The stick of bombs marched in a line like the footsteps of giants through the centre of the town, and fire and death shook the world about them.

The heat of a hot summer's day burned against Daniel's hands and light glowed through his eyelids. He uncurled slowly. The town was ablaze, the tinder buildings crackling and sending sparks and flames fifty feet up into the air. Dazed, shattered men and women and children milled in the streets, screaming and crying up into the heavens. Cromwell had vanished.

Daniel heard the third ship approach.

'Run!' he shouted at the crowd. 'Don't just stand there! *Run!*'

'Take your own advice, boy.' Khonol Le pulled him away. His legs would barely carry him. He felt a sudden burst of pride and shame. Pride in his English blood, shame at the part of him that was Holekhor. He would *not* run. He belonged here, with his people; he would share their fate, he would . . .

'Mistress Connolly!' They both turned and to Daniel's amazement they saw Cromwell astride a horse. Perhaps it was the horse that had brought them here. He held the reins in one hand and favoured the other, letting it rest on his lap. 'Both of you. Get up.'

Five minutes later they had dismounted and were looking back at the blazing inferno that was, Daniel had now learned, Maidstone. The third ship had dropped its load and the flames were feeding themselves. Their heat funnelled the air up above the town and caused new, fresh air to sweep in below, to fuel the blaze and heat the flames still further. A storm of fire.

Daniel was weeping. He could not take his eyes from the holocaust.

He felt a hand on his shoulder and he looked up into Cromwell's desolate face. 'You must find your own path, Master Matthews. I see your tears and I know you had no part in this. But,' he waved a hand at the town, and spat. '*That* is what England can expect under your father. Make your own choice, young man. If you wish to recant of your Holekhor heritage and join us, there are plenty of folk around who will show you how. Mistress Connolly, come with me.'

He swung himself back on to the horse and Khonol Le joined him. Daniel suddenly felt very small and alone.

'You've got to help me!' he blurted suddenly. Cromwell glared down at him.

'I believe I have done everything that can be done for you, Master Matthews. Good day.' He kicked the horse's sides.

'No,' Daniel cried. 'You've got to help me stop them. I know how.' He shuddered. 'I can do it, but not on my own.'

Cromwell stopped the horse, looked back thoughtfully.

'You believe you can?'

Daniel nodded. 'Yes. Oh yes. Yes, I can.'

Cromwell held his gaze a moment longer, then steered the horse a few paces back to Daniel. He patted the horse's flank. 'Climb up behind us.'

Twenty-Five

Treason and Plot

'The *bastard*!' Charles howled. Every eye in the throne room turned to him. All the myriad background conversations among those who had come to Watch the King Eat Breakfast fell silent so that his scream could echo from wall to wall. The king swept his breakfast off the table and kicked the leg as hard as he could. He picked up the tray and smashed it against the tabletop. 'The lying, conniving, treacherous . . . *bastard*!'

Monk drew a breath. 'Sire—'

'No!' Charles shouted. He wheeled on his adviser and waved a finger under his nose. 'No, Monk. I know what you will say.' He screwed his face up in disgust and mimicked a high-pitched whine. ' "The Holekhor are too powerful, sire. We must be cautious, sire. We can work with Dhon Do, sire." ' His voice dropped back to its usual tone and he waved a screwed-up piece of paper at Monk. 'Well, d'you see this, Monk? D'you see this? All that clever, cunning talk of a daylight raid and the scum was lying to me. They took Maidstone last night – the town is flattened, burned to a crisp, its people lying dead in the streets. *This is war,* Monk! Do you hear me? Do you hear your king? *This is war!*'

The silence was shocked. The king had finally said out loud the word that everyone had tiptoed around for the last six years. The Holekhor were the enemy; they were at war.

'Please do not believe that I am under any illusions as to the humanity of the Holekhor, sire,' Monk said quietly. He had returned in *Ariel* from Lewes the previous evening and had already briefed Charles on what he had seen there. He took the paper between thumb and forefinger and gently plucked the signal from his king's hand. 'But I must also remind you that this is a very public place. I beg you not to commit us to any decisions made in the heat of the moment, simply because they have been spoken out loud and the king cannot be seen to lose face.'

Charles looked at him with hatred. He drew a breath, but when he finally answered it was in the same low tone. 'We are at war, Monk,' he said simply. 'I don't care what the appearance is. I don't care how nicely we must bow and scrape to Dhon Do and his people. We are at war, and our every action from here on in will be informed by that fact. Do you understand?'

'As your Majesty commands, sire.'

'Good. Good.' Charles took another breath, let it out. 'Dhon Do is meant to be looking for Lizzie and Harry but I doubt that he has our best interests at heart. He might get the boy-troll back, but my sister? My brother? No. I want the area around that ambush crawling with soldiers, Monk. Hunt down those God's Army creatures and exterminate them. If we can't fight the Holekhor, we can at least give them a decent show of strength. They will know we can't just be pushed around. See to it. And remember: for God's Army, no mercy.'

Charles's orders were carried out faithfully. Troops converged on the ambush site from London and from Dover. They spread out into the woods to the east and the west. Skilled huntsmen soon picked up the trail of Lilburne's men and followed it back to the hideout. They surrounded it silently, then burst in with guns blazing.

It was empty. Lilburne's cell had vanished, ordered on their way by Cromwell. Cromwell himself, Khonol Le and Daniel were already on travels of their own. Cromwell and Khonol Le had heard Daniel's plan out, vague and unpolished though it was. They had added the finer details that could make it work, and even Cromwell had admitted the need to call upon further resources. He had a contact whom they were on their way to visit.

'Oh, Charlie,' Miss Dolly sighed. Charles sat slumped in a chair in the drawing room of his private apartments, with the barely touched remains of his supper in a tray beside him. Unlike the king's breakfast, which had the dual purpose of breaking the king's fast and showing the world that he had emerged from another night alive and well, the king's evening meal was generally a private affair. The king's mistress stood behind him and slipped her arms around his neck. 'I can't bear to see you like this.'

Charles absently caressed her hands. 'I hate Hampton,' he muttered.

It had never been his favourite palace. When his father had fled London at the start of the Rebellion, the entire family had come here and slept in one bed, afraid for their lives. Charles had been twelve. Hampton was full of unhappy memories, and that was why he had decided to host the Domon'el there. He wouldn't have the ruler of the Holekhor spoiling his far fonder memories of, say, Windsor.

And that was why he had chosen to remain there, rather than head up the river to Windsor, or down it to Richmond or Whitehall. If he was to hear the news, sooner or later, that Lizzie and Harry were dead, it would be in this place already so full of gloomy recollections. His outburst that morning aside, nothing much had happened since. Monk had vanished, doubtless doing the Monkish things he did so well. Outside it was evening and the lowering sun cast the room in red. It was a cheerless colour, not enough blue in it.

Miss Dolly kissed the top of his head. 'Shall I light the fire, my love?' Charles shrugged, and she slipped the tips of her fingers inside his shirt. 'Or there are other ways I could warm my dear King.'

Charles raised his voice slightly. 'Lizzie and Harry might be dead, and Dhon Do's bastards have exterminated a town of Christian English,' he said.

'I knows that, my dearest, my sweetest thing, and I sees the mighty weight you carry.' She began to knead his shoulders. 'It's so unfair that one man should bear such a burden. I don't know how you does it.'

'Well, it is difficult,' he admitted. He shut his eyes and enjoyed the massage.

'If I was . . . oh, like, Sir George . . .'

'Which thank Christ you're not.'

'. . . then I might know how to lighten your load . . .'

'I wouldn't wager on it.'

'. . . but I am just a poor woman.' She sighed, as she had sighed in the part of Ophelia on the London stage where Charles had first seen her. She lowered her head and her red curls fell over his face. 'Oh, whatever can I, cursed with the frailty of womanhood, possibly do for my Lord and love to relieve his intolerable burden?'

This was blatant even by the king's standards. He opened one eye and looked up. 'Did Monk put you up to this?'

'If anything is to be *put up* . . .'

Charles chuckled reluctantly, and craned up and kissed her. Then he leapt to his feet.

'By God, you've persuaded me. Life goes on.' Miss Dolly whooped with laughter as he scooped her up in his arms, then staggered slightly and set her quickly down again. 'Blazes. You know the way to the bedroom.'

'It's engraved upon me heart.' Laughing, delighted that her beloved had perked up again, Miss Dolly led him away by the hand.

Five minutes later, Monk chose the worst moment possible to knock.

'Go away!' Charles's voice was muffled through the wood. 'State business!'

'Exactly, sire.' Monk stood in the small passage that connected bedroom and drawing room and pressed his face to the panelling of the door. 'We must talk.'

Inside, Charles muttered something that sounded like, '"Must" is not a word to use to princes.' Monk knocked again.

'The Devil take you, Monk!' Charles gasped.

'That would be the only way I will be removed without you, sire. And I have news of your royal siblings.'

A sudden, frantic scrabbling, feet on wooden flooring, and the door was tugged open. Charles had at least put a robe on.

'News? What news? Are they alive?'

'They are, sire.'

'Hah!' Charles stepped into the passage, fiddling with his sash to close his robe. Monk leaned in to close the door and caught a brief glimpse of Miss Dolly, propping herself up on one elbow in bed with no care for her modesty. She smiled winningly at him.

'Aw'right, Sir George?'

'Your servant . . . madam. Excuse me. This way, sire.'

Charles followed Monk into the drawing room, babbling happily. 'I knew it had to be important, Monk. The king can't be dead 'cos I'm the king, so I knew there had to be a better reason for you to pluck me from my cradle of fornication at *oh sweet Jesus Christ*!'

Charles took a frantic step backwards as he entered the room but Monk had already shut the door and placed himself in front of it. Charles stared at him in horror and betrayal, then swung back to face the man emerging from the shadows of the king's drawing room.

'"Cradle of fornication"?' Oliver Cromwell said coldly.

Charles drew a deep breath and opened his mouth to bellow, '*Guar*—'

Monk clamped his hand over the king's mouth. 'I'm sorry for this liberty, sire, but this is important. This is not treason, I swear it.'

'If we wished you dead, sir, you would be so by now,' Cromwell added. 'In your cradle.' Charles shuddered.

'Sire, you have always taken my counsel. I beg you to hear us out in this matter,' Monk said urgently into Charles's ear. Charles thought for a moment, then nodded. Monk took away his hand. The moment the king was free he jumped into a corner of the room to face them both. He snatched a sword from the wall and held it *en garde* in front of him.

'God's wounds, Monk, if your explanation don't satisfy then I swear you will be on the first boat back to the Tower!'

'You are safe, King,' Cromwell said. 'Monk is not so foolish as to let armed men into your presence. He checked us himself.'

Charles grunted. 'Us? Who else is here?' Another door opened and he swung his sword round as two more figures entered. His eyes goggled still further. '*Boy-troll?* What are you doing here?'

Daniel looked at Charles out of hollow eyes and said nothing. Khonol Le patted him on the shoulder. 'Our friend has a plan to save your kingdom,' she said. 'Show him some respect.'

'Eh? Who are you?' Charles frowned. 'And damn it, Monk, where's Lizzie? Where's Harry? You said they were alive!'

'They are alive and safe,' Cromwell said. 'We cannot return them to you, because if word reached Dhon Do that they had come back, he would ask about his son. We need to keep Dhon Do in ignorance, until it is too late.'

Charles bellowed an angry, wordless shout and slashed at a pillar. 'Jesus Christ, Monk, *tell me what is going on*! How did this man get in here?'

'I received a message from the gate with a certain phrase in it, sire. I directed the guards to bring its bearer to me by the back passages.'

Charles sagged weakly into a chair. '*What?*'

Monk and Cromwell glanced at each other, then at Charles. 'The general and I have been exchanging messages for years,' Monk admitted.

'You . . . and . . . *him?*'

'Monk is your faithful servant,' Cromwell growled. 'You were never compromized. On matters relating to you and your activities, he was always silent.'

'Likewise, the general was always less than

382

forthcoming on matters relating to God's Army of Albion,' said Monk. 'But on more important matters—'

'Such as the destruction of the Holekhor power in this land—' Cromwell added.

'We have always been in complete accord. And that is why we are here now, sire. Myself, Master Cromwell, Master Matthews, this Holekhor lady . . . and you.'

Charles waved his sword weakly to indicate the group and gave an interrogative whimper.

'We are here to bring down the Holekhor,' Monk said. 'You declared war this morning, sire. Let battle commence.'

The brief Puritan reign had been an aberration. With the collapse of Parliament, England's Cavalier past had erupted again like a boil under the reign of England's resolutely Cavalier king. And nowhere was it more evident than in the profusion of inns, brothels and bawdy houses that were attracted to Charles's various residences like fleas to a dog.

The King's Arms, hastily renamed after the defeat of Parliament six years before, was a five-minute walk from the gates of Hampton Court. Its proximity gave it a semblance of respectability; it was on the border-line between palace and town, and Holekhor soldiers and aircrew would drink there as well as courtiers and English tradesmen. There was a small knot of Holekhor there now, in one corner, keeping themselves to themselves but paying good money for the privilege. They wore the mustard yellow uniforms of the military, with the blue epaulets that denoted the Skymight.

Miss Dolly Witherspoon was not unknown to the English clientele. She threw open the door and marched straight to the bar, her head held high and her steps only slightly wobbly, to calls of 'Now then, Dolly!' and 'How's it going?'

'That'll be a pint then, Dolly?' said Bill, the man at the bar.

'A half pint is more ladylike, William.' Miss Dolly swayed slightly in her seat. It was obvious to all that she had already put herself outside at least one other lady-like half pint.

'I keeps forgetting you'se a lady now, Dolly,' said Bill with a wink at the others, but he poured out her drink for her. She took the flagon and her teeth clattered slightly against the rim.

'I might not be for much longer, William.' She downed a couple of gulps and her breath shuddered.

Bill was suddenly concerned. 'Not an argument, Dolly?'

'Just say that His Majesty and I have come to a parting of the ways. I can take certain of his *appetites*...' Raucous laughter from the assembled. 'But he can sometimes ask *too much* of a lady, if you gets my drift.'

'I think I do, Dolly,' said Bill, not getting it at all but determined to rectify this. He poured out another half pint.

'You're a gent, William.' Dolly drew another sobbing breath and briefly rubbed her eye. 'Men! He thinks he's so grand because he's king. Well I tell you, William, I could have any man in here . . .' She gestured expansively at the gathering crowd who were trying so hard not to seem to be listening. 'Any man at all, and I would gain on the deal, so I would.'

Time passed, Miss Dolly grew more drunk, the conversation even more suggestive as the patrons of the King's Arms tried to weasel the details out of her. Observers, like a Holekhor woman and a stocky, younger man in another corner of the room, saw her growing ever more flushed and annoyed.

Eventually she slapped one of her suitors and stood up.

'I despair of you all,' she announced. 'I shall find myself some gentlemen.' She staggered, and her gaze fell on the airmen in the corner. She beamed. '*Military* men! What knows how to treat a lady.'

She wended her way over and pulled up a chair. 'Aw'right, my dears? Don't mind if a lady joins you?'

The men smirked; one of them called for more drink. They knew enough English and body language to have followed her conversation and her progress over the course of the evening. Dolly leaned against the youngest and breathed fumes in his face. She ran a finger down his cheek, which was smooth due more to his youth than to close shaving. He blushed.

'So young! And so handsome in his uniform.' She draped her left arm about his shoulders and the fingers of her right hand played over the buttons of his tunic. The young airman's face flared while the sniggers of his colleagues grew more lascivious. 'I bet your mum's so proud of her handsome young son.'

('Not him!' muttered the young man in the corner.

'He's your size,' said the woman.

'He's my age!'

'This is war.')

Another airman, an NCO, reckoned his chances were better than the youth's and tried to lay hands on Miss Dolly. She shook him off.

'*If* you don't mind, General, I am engaged in conversation with my handsome young friend.' Miss Dolly fed him a sip of her ale with her free hand. She put the drink down and returned to playing with his buttons. She slowly, casually undid the top one, and he looked at her with eyes like saucers and perhaps the first daring glimmer of hope.

'It *is* hot in here, isn't it? Perhaps my young gentleman friend would like to escort a lady to somewhere a touch more cool?'

She gave him another sip, and her hand slipped down out of sight. The youth convulsed in his chair and sprayed ale. Miss Dolly was apparently satisfied.

'Don't worry about the bill, my dears; this is a service for our fine Hollykor allies. God save the king and all that.' Miss Dolly rose to her feet and gently tugged the youth by the hand. 'Come along, my darling . . .'

To whoops and catcalls from Holekhor and English alike she led the youth from the bar, and he managed a last, amazed grin back at his cheering friends before he was dragged out of sight. The two in the corner waited for the shouts to die down, then followed.

'Poor darling,' Miss Dolly said thoughtfully. She tossed the small purse she had taken off the airman up and down in her hand. 'Left robbed and naked in a back alley by a pair of scoundrels.' She frowned at Khonol Le, who looked innocently back. 'Such a young darling, too.'

They were back in the king's quarters. Daniel wore the airman's uniform and stood on a stool with his arms held out while Charles's personal tailor moved around him. The uniform fitted well, but not quite well enough. The conspirators stood or sat at different points around the room, Cromwell and Charles having chosen the furthest points from each other that they could manage.

Charles slipped his arms around Dolly and kissed her. 'I told them England's finest actress would put on her finest performance. Our funless friend here expressed doubts as to your ability to pull it off, my sweet.'

'Oh, I can *pull off* anything, Charlie, you know that.'

Cromwell leaned against the windowsill, his arms folded and his face black as thunder. 'Disgraceful. The attraction between man and woman is celebrated and ordained within the Scriptures, and you do the Lord's work by preying on a boy's natural weaknesses.'

'*We* are doing the Lord's work,' Charles corrected him. 'And perhaps you was never a boy, but when I was, I knew exactly what my weaknesses were and I was more than ready to be preyed upon. And it's not as if any fornication actually took place.' He looked at Miss Dolly from under his dark brows. 'Assure me that no fornication took place, my love?'

'Oh, Charlie.' She chucked him under the chin. 'How could I have a *boy* when I've had a *king*?'

Charles beamed, fond and foolish, and Cromwell growled beneath his breath.

'There you are, boy-troll,' said the tailor. He stepped back and admired his work. 'Fits you like a glove.'

Charles rounded on him. 'Master Matthews has a perfectly good Christian name, sir! Kindly use it!' He looked back at Daniel and his voice shook. 'By George, boy-troll, I can never repay you for this. *England* can never repay you. We will all be forever in your debt. Stay alive, and whatever you want shall be yours.'

Daniel stepped down from the stool. 'Thank you,' he muttered. He had been promised a knighthood once before, and all that had materialized had been a shot in the back. 'I'll get changed.' He headed back to the bedroom to change back into his travelling clothes. The uniform would be needed later.

Cromwell looked at Monk. 'You will need to get us out of this place unseen.'

'I can do that.'

'Wait, wait, wait!' Charles was suddenly pacing agitatedly. 'Damn it, Monk, this just will not do! This . . . this –' he waved a hand at Cromwell – '*outlaw* breezes into my palace as if the last nine years had never happened, suddenly we are all friends once more and now we just let him go again?'

'I ask no favours from you, sir,' Cromwell said. 'The Lord is and always has been my judge.'

'And bully for him, say I. Monk, he's the *enemy*!'

'He is our enemy's enemy too, sire.'

'But don't you realize how hard it will be, cutting off his head – as I one day will, sir,' he added, with a glare at Cromwell, 'knowing that he helped us?'

'That is easily remedied,' said Khonol Le with a wry smile. 'Don't cut off his head. You will need him when the remnant of Dhon Do's army sting you like a nest of hornets. You must have a good general on your side.'

'But, *him*?' Charles howled.

Cromwell gently waved Khonol Le down. 'It is more easily remedied than that,' he said. 'Pardon and recall Fairfax.'

'Sir Thomas Fairfax? The traitor who was knighted by my father and who led the rabble against him?' Charles sneered.

'Sir Thomas Fairfax, the finest general of his generation in England or Europe. He deserves better than to rot in exile. He is an honourable man. Bring him back and he will serve you loyally.'

'But ... but ...' Charles threw up his hands. 'Damn it all. Master Cromwell, sir, we thank you for your service to England this day and we will consider your suggestion. We will even consider a pardon for the traitors of the so-called God's Army who still wage war against us. But *you*, sir – you we do not and cannot pardon for your crimes against the crown. But we can give you amnesty for thirty days. If by the end of that time you and yours are not en route to the Americas, or the North Pole for all I care, we shall not be held responsible for your eventual fate.'

'You will not, sir, because only the Lord has that responsibility,' Cromwell said with a bow. 'But I take your notice in the spirit in which it is intended.'

Charles subsided, still muttering under his breath. Then he said, 'Well, there is still my part to play in this business. Bring it to me, Monk.' He sat at his desk and snapped his fingers.

Monk had been working on the document while Khonol Le and Daniel were out on their mission. He laid it out in front of Charles and handed the king a pen. Charles flicked his gaze over it.

'Dear God,' he said. 'I haven't felt this way since I was a boy. I was terrified at Edgehill and I'm terrified now. Well, if I can't lead my men into battle like my royal father, I can at least do this.' And with a flourish, he signed his name.

The Holekhor garrison commander had stopped smiling when he saw that Monk was accompanied by an armed guard of twenty men. He had led Monk into his office and sat down while Monk read from the pre-pared statement, and his eyes grew rounder and rounder.

'. . . and whereas the Realm of Golekh has most blatantly reneged upon its obligations towards the

Kingdoms of England, Scotland and Ireland as laid down in the Treaty of Oxford made upon the thirteenth of June in the Year of Our Lord 1645; and whereas the Realm of Golekh did upon the third of March in the Year of Our Lord 1651 launch a most cruel, heinous and unprovoked attack upon our loyal Christian subjects in the town of Maidstone; be it hereby known that from midnight on the fourth of March in the Year of Our Lord 1651 a state of war shall exist between our Kingdoms of England, Scotland and Ireland and the Realm of Golekh. By order of Charles, second of that name, by grace of God King . . .'

The list of the king's titles took almost as long to read as the declaration of war. The Holekhor commander leapt to his feet the moment it was over.

'You are *mad*?'

Monk didn't blink. 'It is nine of the clock. All citizens of Golekh have two hours in which to withdraw from this town and, indeed, this country.'

The commander's English collapsed under the strain.

'You . . . declare war while Domon'el . . . while still Domon'el . . . *Nekh! Om'veo!' Mad! He'll kill you!*

Monk handed the declaration to the commander. 'This has been transmitted to Povse'okh; here is your copy. God save the king.' He saluted, turned and exited.

'Remind me . . .' he said as they marched back to the palace. 'There's still a Holekhor ship at the airfield?'

'There is, sir,' said his second in command.

'Send a detachment to commandeer it.'

'Yes, sir.'

Monk smiled grimly and kept marching. Around him, the rising commotion and shouts suggested that the rumours he had planted were already spreading through the streets.

'Are you not glad you didn't hang him?'

Khonol Le stood with Cromwell and Daniel in a dark doorway, watching the panic build up.

Cromwell scowled at her, but slowly it turned into a smile. '"And he said, Lay not thine hand upon the lad, neither do thou any thing unto him". The Lord sent Abraham an angel to tell him he should not kill the boy. He sent me a fleet of airships. The effect was the same. The Lord has raised in you a mighty Christian warrior, Master Matthews. He has brought you to this time and this place.'

The mighty Christian warrior looked unconvinced.

'Sir, I'm no warrior. I can't even handle a sword. Compared to the Wise—'

'The Wise use trickery,' Cromwell said dismissively. 'It is not the same thing.'

'Trickery!'

'Oh, their powers are real, but it is nonetheless trickery. That is the way of the heathen, Master Matthews. Their false gods might give them power: power to strike down, power to hurt, power to curse, power to gain the whole world . . . but what then? Our God fights in a different way. He has joined you, and me, and Mistress Connolly, and even the fornicating papist who sits upon this country's throne, and he has united us. Out of our many differences and weaknesses he has wrought strength. That is our God's way. He might not give the power of the moment to his followers, but he prevails while the unrighteous tumble.' He looked out at the milling crowds. 'Go now. You must take your places.'

Khonol Le swung her bag up to her shoulder. 'Thank you, General. Come on, Daniel.'

Daniel waited a moment longer. 'Sir, will you take the king's amnesty? Will you go to America?'

Cromwell smiled. 'Perhaps. I almost went when I was a young man. That may still be where the Lord intends my real destiny to be revealed. Or perhaps I shall stay. England's troubles will not vanish with the Holekhor. The Lord be with you, Master Matthews.'

They shook hands, and then Daniel turned to follow Khonol Le. When he looked back, the dark figure in the doorway had gone.

The Holekhor sentry at the station was pushed back against the barrier, overwhelmed by the crowd. 'I tell you,' he shouted over the babble, 'I've had no orders.'

Behind him he heard the click of the gate unlocking. The commander stood there.

'Let 'em in,' he said. 'The Enkhlonki have declared war on us. They're panicking.'

'*War*, sir? But they wouldn't take it out on civilians, would they?'

'No, but the Domon'el will take it out on this

town. Let 'em in. Povse'okh's the safest place for them, and for us. We're clearing out too.'

'Right you are, sir,' the sentry said reluctantly. He stepped aside and let the mob throng through.

'About time,' snapped a woman, who had been one of the first to arrive. She carried a large, battered carpetbag that presumably held all the worldly goods she had been able to bring at such short notice. 'My boy's scared out of his wits. Come on, son.'

The boy, who had a cap pulled down hard over his head and who looked much too old to be following his mother around meekly, followed after her. They boarded the train and ten minutes later, packed with fleeing Holekhor, it pulled out of Hampton Court station. Daniel and Khonol Le were on their way to Povse'okh.

Twenty-Six

The Lady's Society Weekly

The Domon'el read the transcription of the message with his eyebrows raised above his round glasses. He looked around the Operations Room.

'The natives have declared war,' he said. No one spoke or moved. Finally he burst out laughing and immediately the Operations Room laughed with him.

'Dhon Do,' said the Domon'el, 'you will of course crush this insurrection at once. Brave Golekhi laid down their lives under you during the Toskhes Campaign, but that was for a good cause. To have Golekhi lay down their lives fighting these primitives would be utterly unacceptable.'

'Of course, Lord,' Dhon Do said.

'The boy king. He is clearly unfit for his position, to lead his people into a war they cannot hope to win. Have him brought here. His execution will be recorded and broadcast in all corners of Enkhlon.'

'I'll send ships to collect him immediately, Lord,' said Dhon Do, confident that Charles would have left Hampton Court the moment war was declared.

The Domon'el crossed to the map and mused over

it. 'Doubtless native military forces are marching against us. They will probably do nothing until daybreak.' Dhon Do had made that assessment within half a second of hearing the news, but he let the Domon'el continue as if there were only one military expert present. 'These are the nearest native garrison towns?' His finger tapped the map.

'Yes, Lord. Oxford and Reading.'

'Dispatch ships to flatten them. By daylight, have our forces deployed ready to meet their advance and destroy them utterly. Give your orders.'

The Domon'el stood back to let Khre Deb and his staff cluster around the map, and ordered Dhon Do over to a corner of the room with a jerk of his head.

'I feel very let down, Dhon Do,' he said. The light glinted on his glasses and his humourless grin had never appeared more savage. His tone was still entirely neutral. 'Had you acted decisively six years ago, none of this would be happening now.'

'I made my assessment as to their potential to be allies, Lord.'

'Of course you did. Sadly your assessment was flawed. Your talent is the military, Dhon Do. You should leave the politics to your leaders.' The Domon'el sighed, sucked in his cheeks. He shook his head. 'This is a difficult decision, but your men are more than capable of managing this campaign. I am recalling you. On the next out-tide I will send for your replacement.' He patted Dhon Do on the shoulder. 'You have served Golekh well during a long and illustrious career. Everyone has their peak. You deserve a retirement to a friendly, unchallenging position. Somewhere you can put up your feet and write your memoirs. Let General Khre Deb handle this; as of now, Enkhlon is no longer your concern.'

He turned to go and Dhon Do blurted, 'Lord!'

The Domon'el turned back and bared his teeth again. 'Please do not beg, Dhon Do.'

'I am my Lord's servant,' Dhon Do said quietly. 'I ask only that my recall be deferred until my son has been found.'

'Ah!' The Domon'el snapped his fingers. 'I was forgetting. You do seem to have been on edge recently, and that is a thoroughly reasonable request. Yes, find your boy. How could I ask a father to do different? Just don't let your search interfere with Khre Deb's work.' He yawned, stretched. 'It has been a long day and there will be no action on the ground until daylight. Escort me to my quarters, Dhon Do; I need my sleep.'

Conscious that the entire Operations Room had just heard him being sacked, Dhon Do led the Domon'el away.

The attack wings lifted off within minutes, rising from Povse'okh airfield and floating up into the dark night. The ground fell away, the lights of the airfield fell behind and for a moment they were surrounded by impenetrable dark. But then they were above the rounded silvery mass of the clouds and the light of a full moon shone down on them.

The radio beacons were working perfectly. The ships turned their noses towards their targets.

Half a quarter later, the three ships heading for Hampton Court sighted two coming in the other direction. One was a small, two-engine civilian model, Charles's *Ariel.* The gaudy royal colours of its covering were just shades of grey under the moon. The other was a Holekhor troop transport, whose capture Monk had thoughtfully ordered. Neither responded to signals.

Bells rang and gun crews ran to their positions – the machine gun nests in the noses and tails of the ships and along their spines, and the single-gun emplacements in the gondola and along the hulls. There was no mistaking the hostile intent from the two approaching ships. They fell into a line-astern formation and matched heights with the attackers. Night glasses showed the captured transport's own gun positions being manned, and a pair of machine guns had been mounted in *Ariel*'s gondola. Men were crouched over them, sighting down the barrels, and as the ships drew closer they opened fire.

Whoever was in charge of the enemy ships had a vastly inflated idea of the range of his guns – they opened up far too early – and, from the line-astern formation, had presumably learnt his tactics at sea rather than in the air. Meanwhile the attackers fell into keel formation, a vertical clip of airships that bore down on the natives. They waited until they were within range to open fire, and a gale of bullets ripped through *Ariel* from above, alongside and below. *Ariel*'s gondola shredded and collapsed in a burst of shattered glass and woodwork. The little ship began to buck and twist, still under power yet without control to its rudder and flaps, and with a tearing noise that could be heard across the gulf of air its hull split in two. The nose turned up towards the stars, spilling out crew and debris and coal dust from its open end. The stern continued onwards, still powered by its engines, and broke up still further under the twisting forces. The pieces glittered and flashed in the moonlight as they fell down to be swallowed by the clouds, and the broken-off nose section drifted away into the night, still with some crew clinging on to it for dear life. The attackers turned their attention to the other ship.

The captured Holekhor ship was of more sturdy design. It absorbed its shots and circled round the formation. Now it no longer had to worry about leaving *Ariel* behind, it throttled up and climbed to match the altitude of the topmost attacker. The English captain raked the top ship with all the guns down his starboard flank. The three attackers split up to mark the points of a vast airborne triangle, which swung about and bore down on the Englishman, surrounding it on all sides. Their guns opened fire.

A flash of blue flame just forward of the Englishman's starboard plane showed the lifting gas catching fire. Within seconds the clear blue fire played all along the hull. It would only be moments before it had burnt through the membranes of the gas bags and the captured ship would be finished.

Its captain knew it too, because he put his wheel hard to port, set the planes for down and pushed the engines to full power. The ship heeled over and swooped down upon the attacking ship at the bottom left of the triangle. The players in this aerial ballet converged with deceptive slowness. The prow of the English ship tore into the attacker's hull and ripped it open. One of its gas bags split down the middle and the ship erupted in a colossal blazing ball. The English ship kept on coming, and another explosion burst out of the first as the flames reached the coal dust reservoirs. Locked together in a cloud of heaving fire, the two ships tumbled slowly down to the clouds and out of sight.

The remaining attackers carried on their way, and bombed the palace and town of Hampton Court into a rubble. They signalled their success back to Povse'okh, where similar reports had already reported the same fate befalling Reading and Oxford.

'All out! All out!'

The train pulled into Povse'okh station and hissed to a halt, spewing clouds of oily steam into the night air. Its crowd of civilian passengers dropped out on to the platform and milled, not knowing what to do next. Daniel and Khonol Le tried to edge their way to the side of the platform.

'Attention! Your attention, please!' Reluctantly they copied everyone else and turned to the speaker. Daniel recognized Por De and shuffled slowly behind Khonol Le. The Centurion stood on a box, fortunately the other side of the platform and with a lot of people in between, flanked by armed guards.

'You're in Povse'okh,' Por De said. 'You're all safe

here, so you can stop worrying. Now, we've prepared an area for you to stay in. It's a warehouse just next to the loading platform. I'm sorry it's not a hotel, but we weren't expecting guests!'

There were a few laughs. The crowd did seem to be calming down. Por De had been wise to stress their safety. They all had confidence in their military.

'It's warehouse seven, just down this road,' Por De said, pointing. 'My men will escort you. There's bedding laid out, and we will be serving food in just a moment. Now, follow us, please.'

The crowd shuffled slowly off the platform. Por De had thoughtfully lined the way with rifle-bearing guards, just in case anyone fancied their chances at getting into somewhere they were not meant to, or was just too stupid to follow instructions. But Khonol Le and Daniel had slipped away from the platform while everyone was looking at him, into the night that lay beyond the platform lights.

Daniel had told Khonol Le about the layout of Povse'okh. On its southern edge were the living quarters and the offices. To the north lay the import and export area, a maze of warehouses and storage facilities into which the railway inserted itself like a needle, with the Povse'okh terminal at the end. And finally, poised at the edge of the Ridgeway, the great gate itself, two hundred feet high, surrounded by the flattened plain of the loading area.

They hurried down the road between warehouses, keeping to the side and out of the lights. 'This will do,' Khonol Le said. It was a small alleyway between buildings, off the lighted street and pitch black at one end. Daniel put the carpetbag down and Khonol Le opened it while he began to unbutton his coat.

The logic had been simple, and so far it seemed to be working. Daniel could never just return to Povse'okh: he would never get the chance to be on his own. He couldn't slip in as a soldier, because he would immediately fall under military orders and be exposed as a fraud. But he could enter in a crowd of panicking Holekhor whom no one would ever check on until it was too late, and *then* become a soldier.

But there would still be places he couldn't go in anonymity, on his own. He would still need Khonol Le.

'Who goes there?'

Light from a marshal's hand torch impaled them where they stood and they stared rabbit-like into the beam. Daniel had on the shirt of his stolen Skymight uniform but not the leggings. The torchbeam played over his bare legs, then over his face, then over Khonol Le.

'You're joking!' said the gruff voice. 'She's old enough to be your mother! Don't you know we're at war?'

The marshal came forward and waved his baton first at Khonol Le, then at Daniel. 'You, lady, can get to the civilian holding area. And you, lover boy, are on a charge.' He held out a hand. 'Identification, name and unit?'

Khonol Le moved too fast for Daniel to be sure what happened. He just heard a gurgle, and the beam spun suddenly as the torch fell from the marshal's fingers. There was the thud of a body hitting the ground, then Khonol Le scooped the torch up and switched it off.

Daniel blinked into the darkness. The beam had got him full in the eyes and now he could see nothing.

'Still there?' Khonol Le said.

'Yes,' he said nervously. She switched the torch on again, aiming at the ground. Daniel gasped as his eyes met the dead gaze of the marshal.

'Know him?'

Daniel swallowed. 'N-No. But . . .'

'But nothing,' Khonol Le said harshly. 'He was Golekhi; he was my enemy. And as you've chosen to be English at last, he was yours too. Now, keep changing.'

Daniel forced his mind back on to what they were doing. Somehow, the death of one of his father's men seemed a worse betrayal of Dhon Do than what he was planning to do anyway. Khonol Le pulled the body to the far end of the alleyway, as far from the streetlights as possible, and Daniel did up his last button, took out his beret and pulled it firmly down on his head. A minute later they were walking openly down the street, a young Golekhi Skymight soldier and a High Lady with a silver bracelet to prove it. The bracelet was genuine, and while it had Daniel's name on it, no one would look that closely. Daniel had a genuine Povse'okh pass, stolen along with his uniform but still *bona fide*, that showed him to be a youthful airman named Kher Men. Now there was no need for skulking or keeping to dark alleyways. Nothing could be more natural than a High Lady with a soldier as an escort, carrying her bag for her. Provided they did not enter any restricted areas, they could come and go as they pleased.

They came to the edge of the buildings and without a pause walked out on to the flat plain in front of the gate of Povse'okh. The ground hummed with the stored energies of the hole between worlds. Daniel had lived in Povse'okh long enough to ignore the effect the hole had on you; the feeling that the ground was sloping towards it, the pull on you as you walked. He had to keep Khonol Le walking in a straight line.

The great circle was on the in-tide; light spilled in over the vast concrete apron from the Old World, but the activity they could see on the other side was perfectly normal. There had been no way of communicating the fact of the outbreak of war against the tide. Hopefully there never would be.

Six years earlier, Khonol Le had had the right idea, but with only a stolen airship and some gunpowder her resources had been woefully inadequate. Now she was back to do the job properly. Tonight they would blow up the gate, and everything they needed was already here.

'It's hardly fitting for a woman of my station to walk,' Khonol Le said. 'Flag us a ride, soldier.'

There was no mistaking the way. A steady stream of steam wagons was coming and going, reminding Daniel of vast, clanking, gushing ants. The Might was at war; all the ammunition deposited so carefully in the subterranean tunnels had to be brought back up into the open. Those wagons that were coming towed trailers loaded with arms and ordnance; those going had delivered their loads and were bringing their empty trailers back for more. One of these was trundling down the road towards them now. Daniel squared his shoulders, stepped into its path and held up a hand. It drew to a halt with a shudder of brakes and a hiss of escaping steam, and the driver peered round the flywheel at them. The wagons coming up behind it steered around the obstacle and carried on their way.

'What do you think you're—' Then the driver caught sight of Khonol Le standing to one side, and the bracelet. 'I mean, can I help you, ma'am?'

Khonol Le drew herself up but said nothing, as befitted a High Lady. Daniel answered for her.

'The High Lady wishes to visit the magazine.'

This was the test. He could still remember Dhon Do's words of advice the first time he had put the bracelet on. His father had said it entitled him to anything and everything. *You can only be overruled by another noble from a longer pedigree . . . Use it wisely.*

But again, Daniel wearing the bracelet would be recognized. An anonymous young soldier escorting a High Lady should not be.

The driver had been well brought up and he didn't have the backing to refuse a High Lady. He simply said, 'Hop up. I mean, um, please climb aboard, ma'am.' He and Daniel helped Khonol Le up; Daniel swung the bag up behind her and climbed up himself. The driver let in the throttle, released the brakes and the wagon lurched forward again, reclaiming its place in the line.

A moment later they came to the edge of the Ridgeway, the sharp line where the country suddenly dropped down two hundred feet. A road had been cut into it, leading down and across the almost sheer slope. It was lined with lights and halfway down it curved out of sight, vanishing into the ridge itself. Daniel held on as the wagon's front wheels hit the ramp and they started to descend, down to the entrance to the network of tunnels that Dhon Do had had driven into the hill. All of Povse'okh's explosives were kept here.

The road twisted round to the left and they were at the gates into the hill. It was a stark, semi-circular lobby lined with white concrete, set into the hillside and lit brightly by electric lights. At the other end was a simple road barrier, there more to provide an official point of entry rather than any resistance to something with the weight and mass of the wagon. But this was where they had to stop. Even a wearer of a silver bracelet could not just breeze into a munitions store.

She did not try. They jumped off the wagon and thanked the driver as he showed his pass, let off the brakes and trundled into the hill. Two minutes later, Khonol Le was talking breezily to the sergeant in charge.

Yes, she had had a letter of introduction but she had left it on the wrong side of the gate. No, she hadn't checked in with anyone else – why should she?

She was a High Lady and just as much at home in Golekh this side of the gate as on the other. She had come through and jumped straight on to the wagon that brought her here. Well, not *straight* on; she had walked into the camp and found a native guide in the form of this charming young airman Kher Men. Yes, she had checked he had no other duties: Kher Men was on leave. Why was she here? Of course, she should have said: *The Lady's Society Weekly*, whose editor was the wife of General Khre Deb as the sergeant doubtless knew (he did not), had commissioned her to write a series of pieces on the army of occupation of Enkhlon. The editor expected her to focus on the officers, naturally, but she had found it was the enlisted men, the sergeants and the corporals, who actually made the army work. On this point she received no argument from the sergeant. Her imagination had been caught by the thought of those brave souls who toiled down here in the store, below ground, guarding the army's most precious resource and never seeing the sun.

The sergeant tactfully explained the notion of shift work but still, five minutes after that, she had been issued with a temporary pass, had signed into the book, and was being escorted by the sergeant himself into the depths of the magazine, with Daniel trailing behind.

They were led down a narrow passage lit by bare bulbs in the ceiling.

'I really can't show you the lower levels, ma'am,' the sergeant said. 'You have to understand it's no place for a civilian. The wrong move could have terrible results.'

'Oh, I should think so,' Khonol Le said with an over-acted shudder. Behind them, Daniel rolled his eyes.

The sergeant beamed proudly. 'But you're in luck you chose this day of all days, because it so happens we're on a war alert.'

Khonol Le stopped suddenly. 'War!' she exclaimed. 'Is it safe? Should you be spending time with us when you surely have more important things to do?'

'It's a privilege to serve, ma'am, and you're as safe here as if you were back in the capital. The natives tried, once, to attack Povse'okh and they failed totally. And that was before we were properly entrenched. But as I was saying, ma'am, it's lucky you chose today because . . . look!'

And they were out of the passage and into the loading area.

It was a vast cavern cut into the hillside and it echoed with activity. The wagons came and went through a larger entrance along the cavern's wall. Normally the area was empty, with the hoists poised over three large pits in the floor that led to the lower levels where the munitions were stored. But today the hoists were constantly in motion, hauling up ammunition for rifles and machine guns, bombs for the airships, shells for the artillery. And though the steady ant stream of wagons did its best, there was a backlog of materiel piled up. It was the racks and rows of shells and bombs that really drew the eye. Even on their own they would make a mightily loud bang. And the flash doors over the hoisting pits were open; the explosion would reach the supplies down there . . .

It would blast a hole a mile wide in the hillside, and if that didn't divert the flow of the landpower then nothing would. And the gate of Povse'okh, deprived of its energy, would close – snap shut.

'How fascinating. What's this over here?' Khonol Le strode forward and the sergeant, who had plainly been hoping to keep to the perimeter of the chamber out of everyone's way, had to follow.

He accepted the inevitable. 'Well, these are shells, ma'am. They're used for medium range artillery . . .'

Khonol Le marched on until she had found the place. Racks of incendiary bombs, airships, for the use of, made a small lane through the stores and for just a moment there was no one else present. She caught Daniel's eye briefly, wiggled an eyebrow at the racks, and began to ply the sergeant with questions about his family. She kept his attention and stood so that he had to face her with his back to Daniel.

Daniel quietly unbuttoned the carpetbag and felt inside it with his free hand for something solid. His fingers closed around something the size of a brick, and almost as heavy, and he slowly withdrew it.

It was a simple tin box, English-made, packed with gunpowder. The alarm clock strapped to it was of Holekhor design. It was a simple time fuse devised by Khonol Le, with its mechanism subtly altered. When the clock went off it would trigger the flint taken from a conventional English pistol. The flint would spark, the spark would hit the powder.

While Khonol Le asked the sergeant about the Gifting dates of his three children, a sweating Daniel gently slid the blocky package between two bombs at the level of his waist. He reached into the gap and his fingers found the flint, which he drew back gently until he felt it click. Then all he had to do was press the switch on the clock and . . .

'Message, sergeant— Oi, what are you doing?'

Daniel and the sergeant spun around together. Both had been so engrossed in their tasks that they hadn't heard the corporal come up behind. He was clutching a bit of paper, no doubt some annoyingly trivial bit of bureaucracy that needed dealing with.

'What *are* you doing, son?' said the sergeant. He cocked his head and his face clouded with suspicion. Daniel snatched his hand away from the bomb. 'I'll just take a look . . .'

And Khonol Le reached around him, grabbed his chin and pulled his head back. The knife in her other hand cut into his throat and he dropped to the floor. For a just a bare second, the corporal was frozen to the spot even while Khonol Le ran at him. Then he had turned tail. Khonol Le shot past Daniel and was haring after the corporal as fast as she could go. Her receding voice cried, 'Get out, boy!'

Daniel peeked round the corner of the bombs. Khonol Le was gaining on the corporal but he was shouting, 'Alarm! Alarm!' at the top of his voice. A squad of soldiers with rifles ran into view and Khonol

Le skidded to a halt. They faced each other for just a moment, and then Khonol Le had turned and was running back at him.

'Set it now!' she shouted, in English. 'Daniel! Set it—'

A volley of shots echoed around the chamber and she crumpled, falling flat on her face and skidding on the concrete floor, her arms flung out. Daniel's eyes met the soldiers', briefly, and then he ducked out of sight as he heard the echoing tramp of their boots hurrying near. He stumbled over the body of the sergeant and looked down through a blur of tears.

'Oh God, I'm sorry, I'm sorry,' he whispered. He found the bomb, heard the boots draw closer, pulled it out again . . . and paused. Part of him screamed to get it over with. The rest shouted that he wasn't a soldier. Why should he die? Hadn't he always been taught *Thou shalt not kill*? But this is different, he hissed at his conscience; this *needs* to be done, things will be worse if it isn't . . .

With a sob, he twisted the second hand of the clock towards the alarm hand . . . and stopped again. The boots sounded closer still. He could just do it now. Set it off, and vanish forever in the explosion that would destroy the hillside. His father, if he survived, would never know that it was his own traitor son who had done it. He would die. He would face the Almighty on the last day, and the accusing souls of everyone he had killed. Would he go to Hell? Would he be judged a murderer? Would . . .

The boots were just round the corner, and he

knew he couldn't do it. He would still die, but he would not know exactly when. For some reason, this was better. He twisted the clock to set it randomly, shoved it back out of sight between the bombs and ran.

'Halt!' The shout was behind him. He heard the clicking of rifles being cocked. 'Halt, or we fire!'

Not amongst the bombs, you don't, he thought merrily. Too merrily. He never heard that foolish, reckless shot that could have sent Povse'okh sky-high. He just felt the blow that hurled him to the ground.

Twenty-Seven

Death and the Domon'el

'A saboteur?' Dhon Do exclaimed. He and Khre Deb were in Dhon Do's sitting room, the place so painfully full of memories of Daniel. Dhon Do sat at a table surrounded by maps and lists. He had been given leave to look for his son and that was what he would do. For the hundredth time, he had been re-reading the report of the ambush investigation team. It offered no further insights and he was strangely glad of the diversion that Khre Deb has just provided.

'Two,' Khre Deb said miserably. 'A woman and a man. The woman was killed, the man shot in the leg. I'm having him brought back to camp for interrogation.'

'Enkhlonki?'

'Definitely Holekhor, they say.' Khre Deb spoke as if there were already a gun at his head. 'And that probably means Toskheshi. They had planted a bomb, sir. They were caught doing it, it was found, but only just. And, sir, the woman wore this.'

From a pocket he produced a silver bracelet.

Dhon Do's breath caught as he reached out to take it in his hands. He turned it slowly around. The device was the same as on his own bracelet, and Daniel's Holekhor name and the date of the Domon'el's Ruling were engraved on the rim.

He rose slowly to his feet and his eyes blazed. 'I want to know where they got this.'

'If you want to question the prisoner, sir, you're welcome. Just leave some for our own interrogators.'

'Thank you, Khre Deb. I am truly grateful,' Dhon Do said with all sincerity.

'This . . .' Khre Deb's voice dropped to a shamed whisper. 'This has been a serious, serious lapse.'

Dhon Do felt only sympathy, and nodded as he pulled on his jacket. He knew exactly what was going through Khre Deb's mind. For anyone to get as far as the saboteurs had done . . . it was an impressive achievement. One could almost say it suggested inside information. Even though no damage had been done, the Domon'el would hear of this and would want a scapegoat. And Khre Deb had only just been given his command.

'Blame it on me,' he said.

'General?' Khre Deb exclaimed.

'Blame it on me,' Dhon Do repeated. 'I'm in bad odour with our Lord anyway.' He reached down to buckle on his sidearm.

Khre Deb was horrified. All his career, he had looked up to Dhon Do. Dhon Do had taught him everything, got him where he was now. This was unthinkable.

414

'Sir! You . . . I . . . I can't, sir!'

'You can,' Dhon Do said. He smiled. 'And if you don't, I will. But if I may make a suggestion . . . ?'

Khre Deb was all ears as they walked out into the hall.

'They planted a bomb. They may have planted another. They may have planted several. Pull everyone out of there. In fact, clear the entire area for . . . oh, half a mile in all directions.'

'Except for the bomb disposal team.' Khre Deb seemed childishly ready to please. Dhon Do had thrown him a lifeline he had no right to expect; he wasn't going to argue, just make improving suggestions.

Dhon Do paused just a beat. 'Except for the bomb disposal team,' he said. 'Do it now. It could go off any second.'

Khre Deb turned to go, then stopped. 'If there is another bomb, if the magazine goes off . . .'

'We could be stranded here in the New World,' Dhon Do said. 'I know, and it terrifies me. But as there is nothing we can do except find the bomb, I suggest not telling anyone.'

'No, sir. And I'll have the area cleared immediately.'

They left the residence together, in different directions.

The prison block was a five-minute walk from the residence. He paced down the dark streets, acknowledging the salutes from the soldiers that he passed.

He came up to the block and a scream echoed out of its concrete walls.

'What was that?' he snapped to the guard at the front desk. The man looked surprised.

'They're questioning the prisoner, sir.'

Another shriek split the air. It must have torn the prisoner's throat raw. Every thought of what he had personally been prepared to do to the man vanished from Dhon Do's mind.

'They are not!' Guards saluted as he strode past them and threw open the cell door.

A young man in a Skymight uniform lay on the wooden bench, and a soldier – no one Dhon Do knew, just some enthusiastic marshal – stood over him with his baton raised. The prisoner's right leg was soaked with blood, tied up with a rough bandage, and the baton was poised over the wound. Dhon Do heard the prisoner whimper. For some reason he spoke English.

'Please . . . please . . .'

'Who was your accomplice? Tell me, and we'll make this easy.'

'No, please . . .'

The baton came down; the prisoner convulsed and his scream filled the cell.

'Stop that!' Dhon Do grabbed the marshal and flung him across the cell. The man hit the wall and raised his baton to fend Dhon Do off, before realizing with horror who it was.

'What do you think you're doing?' Dhon Do shouted.

'Sir, I was—'

'I can see! How could you? How *dare* you? Put yourself on a charge!'

'Sir,' the man pleaded, 'I was just—'

Dhon Do was flooded with fury of an intensity he had never known before. 'I am not interested in your excuses, you coward! *Get out!*'

The man got out, and Dhon Do turned to the prisoner. And then he shook his head to clear his eyes. He had Daniel on the brain, soon everyone would be looking like him.

Two tortured eyes in a deathly pale face met his. 'P . . . Pa . . .' the prisoner breathed.

Suddenly it was if Dhon Do was outside the cell, looking in. There were two people in there, a man in late middle age and a young, bloodsoaked soldier lying on the bench. The man standing took one hesitant step, another, then knelt down and scooped the prisoner up in his arms.

'Daniel! Oh, Daniel, Daniel!'

He pressed the boy to him tightly. He nuzzled Daniel's neck, smelled his hair matted with cold sweat. 'Oh, Daniel, those idiots said you were a spy, said you tried to blow up the gate.'

'Did,' Daniel whispered. Held firm in his father's arms, he began to shake with silent sobs. 'I did. I tried.'

Dhon Do frowned and shook his head. 'No, you don't understand, they said—'

'I tried to blow up the gate,' Daniel said bitterly. 'I was at Maidstone, Pa. They took me there, they were going to hang me and then the ships came . . .'

'Shh.' Dhon Do kissed him. 'Shh. Tell me about it later. We'll get your leg looked at—'

The door behind him opened. 'I said get out!' he shouted.

'I heard a saboteur had been caught,' said a familiar monotone. 'I can come back later if it's more convenient. You have an unusual interrogation technique, General Dhon Do.'

Dhon Do slowly laid Daniel down again. He stood, turned and bowed.

'I apologize, Lord. I just had occasion to discipline one of the men.'

'If it was the same man who has just reported to me that you physically threw him out of this cell, he was acting under my direct orders.' The Domon'el stepped into the cell and the door swung shut behind him. The light on his glasses made his eyes into blank, white discs and his jaw jutted beneath his beard. 'Perhaps it has not occurred to you that the presence of Toskheshi saboteurs inside Povse'okh – inside Povse'okh's most secure area, indeed – is somewhat of a disappointment? Such an operation could hardly have been achieved with just two operatives. For all I know, Povse'okh under your command is riddled with spies. There is important information in this prisoner's head, and as for you, clearly your replacement is long overdue.'

He stepped forward, peered down and frowned. 'Isn't that . . . ?'

'It is a strange resemblance, Lord,' Dhon Do agreed. 'I was surprised myself.' He snatched up the bolster, and Daniel's head fell back to the plank with a *thunk*. The Domon'el frowned.

'What are you doing?'

'If we're to interrogate him, Lord, we can't have him too comfortable. Why not ask him a question?'

The Domon'el looked warily at him, unused to quite so flippant a tone in his presence. But he turned to Daniel and leaned over him.

'So, spy,' he said, 'tell me— *What are you doing, man?*'

Behind the bolster, Dhon Do had drawn his gun. He pressed the barrel into it, pushed the bolster against the Domon'el's chest and pulled the trigger.

The crash of the shot was muffled by the down, and the Domon'el's knees folded. He dropped straight to the ground with a look of comic surprise on his face.

Daniel stared down, pop-eyed, as Dhon Do grabbed the Domon'el's body and tugged it behind the door. If anyone looked in, they would not be able to see it. Then Dhon Do checked his watch. 'I should have let him torture you a bit more to pass the time,' he said. 'Still two minutes to midnight.' Then he sat back down on the bench and took Daniel into his arms again.

I must stop this, he thought with a kind of drunken joy. *Must stop losing him to rebels, getting him back damaged . . .*

'What . . . ?' Daniel murmured.

Dhon Do shushed him again, held him, rocked him slightly. Eventually he said, 'Will you live?'

Daniel managed a very faint smile. 'I think so.'

'You have been very brave, boy. And very foolish. But I love you for it.'

A slightly wider smile. Suddenly Dhon Do rapped him on the forehead with his knuckles.

'Ow!'

'And *that*, boy, is for being young, and arrogant, and for never letting it occur to you that your elders and betters might have had the matter in hand.'

'What—'

'Shh. Now, I need to pick you up. Brace yourself. Put your arms round my neck.'

He slipped his hands under Daniel and Daniel drew in a harsh, shuddering breath as he was lifted up. Dhon Do gently laid him down on the floor beneath the bench. Then he lay down beside his son, partly covering him with his own body.

'Midnight,' he said, and a low rumble shook the ground, rising and rising to an overwhelming roar.

The lights of the Old World shone down through the gate upon the smooth concrete plateau that was Povse'okh's loading area. Then the ground rose up to meet them. First it was a dome that blurred into a hundred thousand pieces, a cloud of concrete and chalk, as the hillside simply lifted off into space. It rose with a deceptive ease and grace, almost at a leisurely pace, until you realized that within seconds it was twice the height of the gate, which had vanished in the dust. And then the rubble of the expanding dome vanished, absorbed by the scorching white light that burst from the ground, the flames of the Hell that had so worried Daniel. The blast tore across the concrete, vaporizing all that stood in its way. It reached the outer edges of Povse'okh and the buildings there vanished, and the remains of the hill tumbled down upon Povse'okh proper. Those caught outside cowered as solid rain fell from the skies, a torrent of debris that never seemed to end, and the ground bucked and heaved beneath them.

Finally, the cloud subsided. The flame passed away, the roar died down to a rumble again, and then faded altogether, though no one who was there that night realized it through the ringing in their ears. But now another sight caught the eyes.

It was the gate, suspended in mid-air over the crater blown by the blast. It was no longer a circle, sitting passively between the two worlds. It was a living, writhing thing. Fed no more by the lines of landpower, it blazed with every colour in the rainbow, twisting and shimmering as its residual energies dissipated, as it lost its coherence and its form. The conflicting forces vibrated the air, giving vent to harmonics that groaned and grinded like all the demons of hell mourning. And then it did *something*, somehow simultaneously imploding and exploding, collapsing back into the dimensions from which it had been created. With a howl and with a final burst of white light, it vanished.

The gate was closed and there was a crater half a mile wide.

* * *

Outside the cell there was pandemonium. The building still stood, but a layer of dust had shaken off the ceiling and it coated the two figures lying on the floor. Dhon Do propped himself up on one arm.

'Can you walk?'

Daniel looked blankly at him, struck dumb by the sequence of events.

'Can you walk?' Dhon Do said again.

'Um . . . yes, yes, I think so.'

'Let me help you. Your leg still needs attention.'

Daniel still looked blank. Dhon Do sighed and clicked his tongue. 'You little idiot. You forgot England is my country too, didn't you? Now, come on.'

With their arms around each other's shoulders, they hobbled out into the corridor. Out into an England where suddenly everything had changed.

Twenty-Eight

Diplomatic Relations

The sun rose over a subdued Povse'okh, which looked as if it had been on the wrong side of an exploding volcano. Most of the buildings were still intact, though windows had been blown in and shattered glass hung in the frames like jagged teeth. Fragments had crashed down on the roofs, knocking black, empty holes in the shattered tiles. Mighty fissures had opened in the ground, pulling walls apart. A layer of dust and debris covered everything and the air smelled burnt.

The panic had died down; people had gone back to the remains of their homes. But there was an added tension in the air, and it was not just the discovery of the Domon'el's corpse in the cellblock, the victim of an assassin who had obviously got away in the chaos after the explosion. War had been declared the night before, and it had seemed a joke. What could the natives do to the mighty Golekh? But suddenly Golekh was an entire world away, and the army from Oxford, which had been marching through the night, had been sighted by an airship.

The ship could have just bombed them. Povse'okh was a fortified island of Holekhor that could still repel anything the natives could throw at it . . . for the time being. But sooner or later they would run out of weapons, and the Enkhlonki – the English, as they would have to get used to calling them – would just keep coming.

Dhon Do, Khre Deb and their staff stood on the edge of the crater. It was a raw wound, a smouldering, gaping sore in the scorched English turf.

'Thank you for your advice, sir,' Khre Deb said quietly. 'Many more would have died otherwise.'

'How many did?' Dhon Do said.

'There were ten in the disposal team. Others were hit by debris. I don't know how many yet. Hospital's full of head injuries. Some still won't make it.'

To this list, Dhon Do added the sergeant Khonol Le had killed, and the marshal, discovered in the small hours, who had probably died the same way – he hadn't yet had the full story from Daniel. But even if there had been no other casualties, even if Daniel and Khonol Le had got to the magazine unopposed, ten of his own men had died at his own hands. The Domon'el had remarked that he had seemed on edge; that had been why. He had known this day would come for six years, though he had always assumed the Domon'el would be on the other side of the gate, and he had planted the bomb himself long ago . . . but when the time had come, he could think of no excuse to clear the area. He had set its fuse expecting that hundreds of his own men would die. Daniel and

Khonol Le had inadvertently provided an excuse to cut the number right down.

So, ten deaths, compared to an estimate of hundreds. As campaigns went it was thoroughly acceptable. But men went to war with the reasonable expectation that they might die at the hands of the enemy. They could have no such expectation about their own general, the man into whose care they had been entrusted, turning on them.

Dhon Do was glad that he had adopted a religion of forgiveness, of the cleansing of sins. He would do penance for those ten every day for the rest of his life.

'I heard Daniel is in the hospital?' Khre Deb said. Dhon Do couldn't help a wide smile that cut right through his depression.

'Yes, he is.' It had been a flesh wound, easily dealt with. Once his son had made up for lost blood and rested his leg for a good, long while, he would be fine.

Khre Deb frowned. 'The last I heard, he had been captured by the natives . . . I still haven't gathered how he came to be here.'

'Neither have I,' Dhon Do said truthfully. And Daniel was under strict orders to talk to *no one*, absolutely no one, until he had the full story himself.

Then Khre Deb sighed and he finally said the thing that was on both their minds. 'Do we fight, sir, or do we surrender?'

'Our Lord put you in charge,' Dhon Do reminded him.

'And I appoint you my chief adviser. Do we fight, or do we surrender?'

'I know the king; I know Monk. I believe I can get us decent terms. I expect they'll allow safe passage out of the country for anyone who wants to go home through Okh'Shenev. Our only other choice is to set out on a war of conquest now, *right now*, Khre Deb, this minute, that will annihilate the natives before they have the chance to regroup against us.'

Khre Deb shook his head. 'We're in no state for a war like that.'

'Surrender it is, then.'

'But . . .' Khre Deb said. 'Well, you might get terms for us, but . . . for you, sir?'

'For me?' Dhon Do said innocently.

'You ordered the bombing of Mhed-ston. You gave protection to the Congregation. You . . . you occupied Enkhlon! You are hardly going to be the king's favourite man. If he can find the remotest way of exacting revenge, he will.'

Ten men, Dhon Do thought. 'Then we will see what happens,' he said.

Lewes is east of Povse'okh; the sun rose there a minute later. The Hierarch Re Nokh paced about the downstairs room of the inn he had requisitioned and tried to shut his ears to the clamour. Tried to *think*.

But the room was full of wailing and sobbing, from the Speaker and voices he had never heard before. The voices of the other Wise in the cell. It had started hours earlier, at midnight. He had felt the shift; he had felt something vanish from his world. Seconds later the terrified howls of the cell had confirmed what he knew. Something had happened to the network. The landpower had vanished from Lewes.

He had tried everything. 'It might be a temporary effect.' 'Surely this has happened before?' But to no avail. The landpower was as fixed as the land itself. Only something terrible could shift the lines.

The chief armsman stood in the doorway and saluted.

'We've assembled the townsfolk, Excellency.' He shot a glance at the Wise. 'Do you still want to address them?'

Re Nokh groaned. *Oh dear gods, help me.* Right now, he *should* have been preparing his final notes for his sermon that day: 'On the proven superiority of the Pantheon over the native God'. He really thought he might be getting through to the natives, at long last. It had been a struggle. They had run out of empty crosses; those who had already been nailed up had had to be taken down and executed for their intransigence, to make room for more heretics.

But, he did seem to be making converts. The natives weren't stupid. And neither was Re Nokh; he knew full well that they were conversions out of fear. But it was a start. Win their souls first, and their hearts and minds would follow.

He nodded abruptly. 'Yes. However, the Order will not be joining us. See that the men are all fully armed. I'll be out in a moment.'

'Yes, Excellency.'

The armsman withdrew. Re Nokh crossed to the

Speaker, put his hands on her shoulders, gazed into her red eyes.

'I don't know why this is happening, my sister,' he said. 'Perhaps it is unprecedented, but even in the *Sacred Tellings*, everything had to happen for the first time, once. We know the Blessed Ones will not withdraw their favour from our holy cause. Have courage, my sister.'

She nodded, drew a breath to speak.

'*Murderers! Heathen murderers!*'

Re Nokh jumped. A native stood in the doorway, a cleaver in one hand. The man's eyes were streaming. Re Nokh didn't understand what the man was saying but the emotion was clear enough. Another distraught native who had somehow got past the armsmen.

'*My daughter! My only daughter, and you murderers put her on a cross!*' With an incoherent scream, the man ran at them, cleaver raised. The Speaker instinctively raised a hand and gestured, as if flicking away a fly. And then he was upon her, and with a howl he brought the cleaver down into her collarbone, almost severing her head.

The man looked down at the blood-drenched body, then slowly lifted his eyes – and the cleaver – to the frozen Re Nokh.

Dhon Do stood in front of the mirror, epaulets heavy on his shoulders and his gold-plated helmet with its silver hawk emblem tucked under one arm. His tunic and leggings were a gleaming snow white; his knee-length boots a deep, rich black; his nenokh-hair cloak a rich scarlet. His ceremonial hand axe hung at his waist.

He fingered the medals on his chest, moved them the barest fraction of an inch to make them just a bit more horizontal. Likewise the silver bracelet on his arm, which announced him the patriarch of a new High dynasty. He doubted it still applied. But it looked grand, so he left it.

Unexpectedly, he smiled at the reflection. He remembered another reflection, a long time ago.

It had been soon after the end of the Rebellion. He and Daniel had been eating their evening meal. Conversation between them was cordial, but still strained. They had yet to become real friends. Daniel had asked politely if he had any grandparents or other relatives he should know about; Dhon Do had explained that sadly, no, Daniel did not. His sisters and both his parents had all died during Daniel's lifetime. Daniel had said he had no family left on his English side either. And this had led Daniel finally to ask about his mother.

So Dhon Do had stood him in front of this very mirror – itself still a novel experience – and shown the wondering boy his own smile, his cheekbones, his eyes, even the shape of his face: all the legacy of Anne Matthews. Then he had shared every memory he had of Anne, going on at Daniel's request even when Daniel's eyes began to water. By the end he was holding Daniel in his arms and comforting him while the boy sobbed away twelve years of bereavement.

And that, Dhon Do thought, would be the

memory he would take with him, whatever was to happen next – all the way to the gallows, if that was what God had in store for him. He had loved Anne, but she was dead. He loved Daniel, and Daniel – his heart wanted to sing it – was alive. Dhon Do turned abruptly from the mirror and marched out to surrender his troops to the garrison of Oxford.

The Holekhor garrison were drawn up in front of the royal apartments at Windsor. Princess Elizabeth stood at the window and watched the ranks manoeuvre. The sergeant shouted orders. They wheeled. They stopped. They shouldered their guns, unshouldered them, grounded them, picked them up, fired a volley into the sky.

Elizabeth wondered whose idea this had been. They were not normally so obvious. She had no doubt they were making their point. The gate at Povse'okh was closed, and from what she understood of Holekhor politics, no reinforcements would be allowed by the Wise through Okh'Shenev ... but these soldiers were here, right now, and there was no one anywhere near Windsor who could oppose them.

She sighed, and a lady-in-waiting was immediately at her side.

'Your Highness?'

'Never mind.' Elizabeth managed a brave smile and waved her away. 'It is nothing.'

Nothing, but the knowledge that England was poised on a knife-edge between war and peace, and she could be the one to bring it down on one side or the other. Nothing, but the realization that this was her time. She was more than just the sister of the king, the daughter of her parents. She had been bred for a purpose.

'I will see my brother,' she said, and left the room.

'You have two options, sire,' Monk was saying as she let herself in. He stopped as the door opened, and bowed. Charles turned in his chair to glare at her, and she moved quickly to a chair at the back of the room and sat before he could ask her to leave. She smiled sweetly, and Charles turned back to Monk.

'Two options,' Monk repeated. He walked slowly around the withdrawing room of the king's apartments at Windsor. Charles sat at his desk and studied him morosely. 'Try Dhon Do, and execute him, as justice demands. Or pardon him.'

Charles and Elizabeth watched him pace.

'Dhon Do is the only man that his army will obey. They are cut off from their world, but they are a very real presence in ours. If he is arrested, they will be beyond our control, and the conflict resulting from your royal father's dispute with Parliament will be as nothing to what will come. Perhaps we will win – eventually. But they came as a conquering power. Dhon Do holds them in check, and without him they will revert to being conquerors.'

Charles scowled but said nothing. The man they were discussing was not present. He was under secure guard in the Tower – not officially a prisoner, but it was a pretence that fooled no one.

'Pardon Dhon Do, sire, and he will become your loyal servant. More important, his *army* will become your loyal servants. They will not gladly give up the Leased Territory and much negotiation lies ahead of us, but in time you will have the greatest force in all Europe. No one will be able to stand against you.'

'Pardon him?' Charles said. '*Pardon him?* After . . .' He waved a hand weakly. 'After everything? And . . . and won't it seem I'm just doing it because I'm afraid of him? I mean . . .' He laughed bitterly. 'I *am* afraid of him. Of course I am. But damn it all, I mustn't be *seen* to be afraid. I'm the king!'

Elizabeth spoke. 'There is an obvious answer, brother.' Charles twisted round in his seat.

'Please, Lizzie, this is—'

'Marriage,' Elizabeth said.

Charles gaped. Monk pursed his lips thoughtfully.

'I am your best asset,' she said.

'A *troll*?' Charles exclaimed. 'Marry my sister to a *troll*?' He flung back his chair and now he paced about the room himself. 'Never!'

Monk thought it through out loud. 'A union with your family will strengthen Dhon Do's ties to the crown,' he said. 'And as you so rightly say, sire, if you simply pardon him and leave it at that, it will be seen that you are afraid of him and of his army.'

Charles gestured weakly. 'But . . . marriage?' he moaned.

Elizabeth was resolute. 'It will legitimize the entire affair.'

'Marriage!' Charles said tragically. 'Oh, Lizzie! You

could have had any of the princes of Europe, and to save our throne and our face, you are forced into bed with a troll!'

'Dhon Do is a general among his own people and he is a member of what counts as their aristocracy,' said Elizabeth.

'Of course,' Monk added, 'with respect to Her Highness's thinking, if your Majesty were to grant Dhon Do a dukedom, say, that is recognized here in England, that would narrow the gap still further.'

'A dukedom!' Charles muttered. 'Lord Troll of Poxy Ox.'

'It—'

'I know, I know.' Charles waved a hand. 'But . . .' He looked up at them with a fresh horror. 'Lizzie, if I don't have any children, and Harry doesn't, and you do and then you come to the throne . . . one day, there might be a troll on the throne of England!'

'Then perhaps you should marry and begin breeding yourself, brother,' Elizabeth said equably.

'By God, you push your luck, madam.' Charles sat down again and slumped his chin into his hand.

'Of course,' Monk mused, 'a dukedom for Dhon Do will also raise Master Matthews to the peerage.'

'Dhon Do's old man was a farmer and boy-troll's from the wrong side of the sheets,' Charles said savagely. 'Ain't neither of them something unless I say so.' He sighed. 'Very well, the union has my permission, and may Christ have mercy on my soul.'

* * *

The wedding was held as soon as decency and the banns of marriage would allow, one sunny day in the chapel at Windsor. All things considered, it was a happy occasion and despite the king's well-publicised reservations the guests all wished the couple well. It was of course a Christian ceremony, and if anyone noticed the simple wooden arch raised over the porch – a matrimonial arch in the Holekhor style, giving the ceremony validity to English and Golekhi alike – no one commented on it. Even Charles finally gave his blessing to the groom at the wedding breakfast in the Great Hall, and though it wasn't quite the usual benediction – 'Give my sister some vile troll-pox and I'll see you on Tower Green' – it served its purpose and there was no doubting its sincerity.

Finally the bride withdrew. The groom waited a decent interval for her ladies to prepare her, then downed a glass of wine in one gulp and followed after her.

He entered the bedroom and turned to shut the door behind him. He paused for a moment and bowed his head to rest it against the cool wood. Then he took a breath, straightened up, and faced his wife with a smile.

Elizabeth was sitting in bed, propped up by pillows. She wore a nightgown but had the bedclothes modestly tugged up to her neck. They looked at each other across the room, taking each other in. The candles and the flames from the fireplace gave her skin a flickering glow.

'My husband,' she said, as if she could not quite believe it.

'My wife,' Daniel said. He felt much the same way. He waited a moment longer, then limped forward and sat on the edge of the bed. They looked at each other, both waiting for the other to say or do something.

'I always . . .' she began. She tried again. 'I always knew my marriage would be arranged like this. I am a princess and we don't marry for love. I had often wondered who my husband would be . . . and I am glad it's you. Is this how you imagined your wedding would be?'

Daniel took a moment to think. 'Not entirely,' he admitted. If his original plans for his life had worked out, he would have been in Virginia by now. On the whole, he preferred it this way.

No, he had not expected his marriage to be used as a political ploy, but he would work at it and do what was expected. Together they would make it special.

'We were married just a few yards from where we first met,' Elizabeth said.

'I suppose we were.'

'I will be a good wife,' she said, as if trying to reassure him. 'I barely know you, but I will love you. I . . .'

Daniel found the courage to take one of her hands in his own. It had the advantage of loosening her grip on the bedclothes.

'I will love you,' he said. They continued to look at each other across a gulf of a couple of feet. Two people, two friends, neither of them quite feeling ready to be one with the other yet.

Daniel wondered if he should take some kind of lead. He gently kissed her hand. She didn't make any move to take it away.

'After we have no further secrets . . .' she said, '. . . I would dearly love to know exactly what happened after Cromwell took you away.'

Daniel paused. Both he and Dhon Do were traitors to Golekh. So far, only Monk and the king knew this. If word ever got out – if word ever reached a loyal Golekhi . . .

'Shall we leave that the other side of the door for tonight?' he suggested. She considered it thoughtfully.

'Yes,' she agreed. 'For tonight.'

Author's Postscript

The New World Order is a work of fiction. Here are some of the things that really happened.

- Cromwell and Fairfax did indeed stay in Newbury on 2nd May, 1645. Fairfax then marched west to relieve the siege of Taunton and Cromwell marched north to pursue the king. This was part of the train of events that ended with the Battle of Naseby on 14th June, when the king's army was routed and the New Model Army emerged as the only serious military force in England.

- Donnington Castle withstood siege by Parliament for two years, surrendering in 1646. Like most of England's castles, it was destroyed by Cromwell with gunpowder to make sure that it could never again be used against him. Only the gatehouse remains. It can be seen from the A34 Newbury bypass.

- King Charles I (1600–1649) surrendered to the Scots in 1646. They promptly handed him over to the English. Every subsequent attempt at negotiation and settlement foundered due to the king's duplicity and double-dealing, which culminated in the outbreak of the Second Civil War. Cromwell saw that no resolution could ever be reached while the king still lived, and Charles was executed on 30th January, 1649.

- Oliver Cromwell (1599–1658) rose to become England's supreme head of state and government. He declined the crown when it was offered to him but took the title of Lord Protector, ruling until his death.

- George Monk (1608–1669), a loyal monarchist and one of history's born survivors, was incarcerated in the Tower of London for two years after his capture at Nantwich. In 1646 rebellion broke out in Ireland and Parliament had need of experienced soldiers to fight the rebels. They offered the job to Monk. It got him out of the Tower and he would be fighting the king's enemies, so Monk accepted the offer and remained in the army even after the king's death. He became one of Parliament's most senior generals and a close friend of Cromwell. When the Commonwealth imploded following Cromwell's death he marched on London and took power. After a brief period as the effective military dictator of England and Scotland, he appointed a Royalist Parliament which invited Charles II back from European exile to reclaim his throne. It later emerged that Monk and Charles had been in correspondence for some time, discussing the possibility of the king's eventual Restoration. Monk was rewarded with riches, titles and an early retirement – Charles only felt the need for one power in the land.

- The New Model Army was disbanded. All that is left of it today in the British army is Monk's old regiment, the Coldstream Guards.

- Charles II (1630–1685) landed at Dover on 26th May, 1660, to be met by Monk, whom he greeted as 'Father'. He entered London three days later, on his thirtieth birthday, and was crowned a much sadder and wiser man than the arrogant youth depicted here. He reigned until his death. Having no legitimate heirs – though at least fourteen illegitimate ones that he was prepared to acknowledge – he was succeeded by his openly Catholic brother James II, who was expelled from the country in 1688. James was succeeded in turn by his daughter Mary and her husband William of Orange (the son of Charles I's daughter, also called Mary, who had also married a William), then by his other daughter Anne. It was in her reign that England and Scotland were finally united. She left no surviving children, and the Act of Settlement had barred any Catholic from holding, or marrying the holder of, the English throne. There were no more Protestant heirs to the House of Stuart and the throne passed to a distant cousin: George, Elector of Hanover, who ruled as George I and is the direct ancestor of every monarch since.

- Princess Elizabeth and her brother Henry were kept in Parliament's custody after their father's death. The Third Civil War broke out in 1650, with their brother the uncrowned Charles II leading the Royalists, and for their own safety the children were moved to Carisbrooke Castle on the Isle of Wight. Elizabeth received a wetting on the crossing. She fell ill almost immediately upon her arrival and died of a fever on 8th September 1650, aged fifteen.

- Matthew Hopkins had a short but notorious career as Witchfinder General in the east of England, from 1645 until his death in 1647, still in his twenties. Some say he died of consumption; others say he fell foul of one of his own investigative procedures – he floated when he should have sunk – and was executed as a witch. Sadly for poetic justice, the former is the more likely.

- Around 35,000 BC, shamans of the proto-Holekhor tribes living in Eastern Europe discovered the gateway between worlds that in this novel is called Okh'Shenev. Within a generation, most of the Holekhor ancestors had migrated to the new world. Only a fraction of their population stayed behind, and when the gate unexpectedly closed they were stranded. Their numbers soon dwindled to extinction, replaced by the more numerous, agile and aggressive race that would one day be called *Homo sapiens sapiens*. Their existence was forgotten entirely, save perhaps in legends and myths, until in 1856 workers excavating a quarry in Germany discovered Holekhor bones in a cave in the Neander valley (in German, *Neander Thal*) near Düsseldorf.

- Because Okh'Shenev was never rediscovered, it never had the destabilizing effect on Holekhor politics that has been described here. Golekh never invaded Toskhes and Dhon Do never rose to military prominence. Apart from a few years as a conscripted infantrymen, he spent his entire life within fifty miles of his family's farm and was thought of as quite well travelled. Aged seventy-three, in the year that our world would call 1672, he took a nasty fall and succumbed to pneumonia. He died peacefully in bed, surrounded by his family. Anne Matthews lived and died a respectable widow; Daniel Matthews was never born.

Acknowledgements

Thanks to Chris Amies, Tina Anghelatos, Janet Barron, David Fickling, Liz Holliday, Jenny Jeapes, Tony Jeapes, Andy Lane, Gus Smith, John Toon, Jonathan Tweed and, um, anyone else.